WATCHERS

Far from the clash of man and sword, the hidden sanctuary of the Order of Magicians and Wizards lay nestled in the majestic Great Mountains. There, they watched from a distance the tumultuous course of battle in the shimmering valleys below.

WARLORDS

Since the fall of the Great Empire mercenary Anarchs waged endless war—using catapults to launch molten fireballs against their besieged enemies. Yet the Order remained neutral, content to preserve civilization and cultivate the Five Arts from the safety of their mountain stronghold.

WIZARDS

Then a grave peril arose. Vladur, former teacher of Crispan, expelled from the Order for necromancy—magic that tampers with the dead—summoned with his power a terrifying legion. And Crispan Magicker, the Order's most talented adept, journeyed forth into the world of men, where a pure heart is no substitute for a sword of might and a will of iron. But how can a wizard who has never taken life defend an entire civilization against his former Master—and an army of invincible soldiers?

MARK M. LOWENTHAL

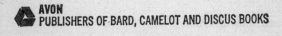

AVON
PUBLISHERS OF BARD, CAMELOT AND DISCUS BOOKS

CRISPAN MAGICKER is an original publication of Avon Books. This work has never before appeared in book form.

Cover Illustration by Carl Lundgren.

AVON BOOKS
A division of
The Hearst Corporation
959 Eighth Avenue
New York, New York 10019

First Avon Printing, February, 1979

. . . for Cynthia

Contents

I

The Fall of Aishar

The besieged city of Aishar rose above the plain like a wounded beast rearing up in anger and pain. Red scars of flame seared across its hide of battlements, while all around the siege machines hovered like jackals awaiting the great beast's fall. For over three weeks the city had withstood the assault, standing firm as each new dawn rose over the encampment of the besiegers off to the east. There, on the north bank of the river that nurtured the city itself, lay the myriad tents of Lord Syman's army of mercenaries.

He was a great warlord, already legendary, commanding one of the largest mercenary forces in the Middle Empire. Only Syman and one or two others could muster ten thousand men with no effort at all, and twice that number within two weeks. Only Syman and one or two others had lasted so long in such a tumultuous profession without having been broken themselves by other armies or by their ungrateful or distrustful employers. And only Syman and very few others could drive so hard a bargain and still be hired by warring dukes, courtiers and usurpers.

On this night Lord Syman was on his horse on a hillock just south of the city of Aishar, awaiting what he knew to be the final assault. After three weeks of incessant pounding the great walls had cracked, exposing their inner timbers. Then, instead of massive stone, huge barrels and sacks of boiling oil had been catapulted against the walls, firing the supporting timbers and eating away at the insides of the walls themselves until they buckled and collapsed under their own weight. Syman was an expert in sieges, having been notably successful since his first wars in the long gone army of a now forgotten commander in

1

the farther west. He had an innate sense for picking out the vulnerable section of a wall, and for knowing when to rain stones and when fire, and when to combine the two.

Secure in his talents, Syman watched with comfortable interest. He removed his helmet, a barbut with a black plume, and shook his head of stiff gray hair, leaning over to the wispy man mounted next to him, Jizar Korm, pretender to the dukedom of Aishar.

"My lord," said the mercenary, "tonight you shall truly be Duke of Aishar, and your brother will be either dead or a prisoner."

Jizar's tight little face slipped into a smile as he thought of his dead older brother, and his now doomed younger one within the falling city. Alizar had died almost half a year before and entrusted his lands to Kalzar rather than his hated middle brother. And now Jizar had bought himself a great mercenary army to supposedly defend the principle of the eldest son against his brother's quite legal will. That was the part Jizar Korm liked best, that he, the great outcast, was now defending the old legal precepts. Yet it was not easy, and it was not cheaply done. Jizar despised this mercenary sitting next to him, with his damned precise contract and expensive army. This venture had eaten up most of the fortune Jizar Korm had built in his years of smuggling, dealing in slaves, usury and other less savory pastimes. But now it all seemed worthwhile, for he, Jizar Korm, despised second son, would soon be Duke and Lord of Aishar, and with new taxes he could soon replenish his investment.

Jizar was roused from his musings by a sudden roar and flash that lit up all the plain. He looked at the city and squinted in the bright glare. He turned to Syman who now poked a nearby aide in the side.

"The game is up," Syman exulted. "The inner beams are gone and the walls begin to fall." His eyes danced as brightly as the flaming walls. He turned in his saddle to a group of messengers below him. "Boy," he bellowed. "A message to the catapults. Change back to stones until

2

the walls collapse and then the sacks of water at a signal from the front. Begone."

This was the moment Syman enjoyed the most, when the walls gave way and the defenders scrambled behind the burning heaps to prepare their last defense. Now Syman showed his true genius by dousing the flames himself and hurtling in his troops before the defenders were ready. His right fist, tightly clutching the reins, absentmindedly pounded his saddle pommel as he waited for the walls to buckle under their own unsupported weight. And then came the hideous groan as mortar parted and stones fell, and the city of Aishar lay exposed before the mercenary army.

An aide came riding up the hillock and leaned close to Syman, whispering a message to him. The commander stroked his thick beard, still black with gray flecks, and mumbled an apology to Jizar Korm before he rode down behind the hillock. He knew who awaited him at the base of the hillock, and what he wanted this night. Syman saw him easily in the light of the burning walls, a large figure totally swathed in black, with a voluminous cowl obscuring his features. The man in black spoke abruptly and pointedly, without ceremony. "The siege is over, Lord Syman. My Master's request is due."

The mercenary was annoyed. "The siege is not ended yet. We have still to enter the city itself."

"And where is the prize?" The man in black had an edge of icy sarcasm in his voice.

"I think he is at the front tonight. Do not worry, he will be safe."

"I trust so, my Lord Syman. My Master would be greatly displeased should some stray arrow or falling timber deprive him of his prize."

Now Syman answered in kind, not caring about the power of the master of the man in black, and not hiding his own displeasure. "You may tell your Master that I will be fully responsible."

"As you shall be, my lord."

"And just as you shall be responsible for incurring my anger. When the siege ends he is yours."

The hooded figure bowed slightly in mock deference and withdrew into the darkness, beyond the glow of Aishar's agony. It enveloped him just as his own hood enveloped and hid his features.

Syman rode back up the hillock and watched the walls, his chest heaving within his hauberk as its anger barely subsided. "Who commands before the breach?" he asked. An aide replied, "My lords Mikal and Zoltan, sir."

"Any signal from them yet?"

"No, m'lord."

"And who commands before the posterns?"

"M'lord Gordo."

"Good, good. . . . Send a messenger to Mikal and Zoltan, and to Gordo with the appropriate orders. And remember to tell Gordo that I want prisoners, not a slaughter."

Jizar Korm perked up at this last remark. "Surely, my Lord Syman, these men will be treated as proper traitors for having supported my brother. Surely—"

The veiled threats of the man in black and the weariness after a long siege now exploded in Syman. He wheeled around and bared his teeth. "I would remind you, Jizar Korm, of our contract. I have first right over all prisoners; those who would join my army are free to do so. Your precious dukedom has cost me many good men. Your brother is yours; the others are mine—and given the choice, most will join me."

Jizar sank back in his saddle, silently cursing this mercenary and his damned clever contract. First right among prisoners, no recruiting by Jizar in Syman's army, the damned high price. He silently cursed again, taking solace in the fact that tonight he would be Duke of Aishar.

The young messenger, barely twenty, jolted down the side of the hillock heading straight for the still-burning breach. His horse gingerly picked its way between broken wreckage that was once siege machines, stark reminders of a long and costly struggle. He threw a glance over his shoulder to see how far he was from the hillock. For a brief moment he espied Syman's broad figure and mused over the popular rumor that all the young aides and messengers were his bastards. The messenger wondered again, and then let it vanish, for if it were so, none of them had ever been shown any special favor by their commander.

The soft crunch of his horse's hooves over a dead body brought his mind back to his mission. The heat from the city was already growing as he passed newly fallen soldiers and entered the ranks of Lord Mikal's company. Everyone around him intensely watched the wall where more and more stones fell in burning hulks as bastions, bartizans and other fortifications crumbled. Finally he caught sight of Lord Mikal, sitting coolly on his fabulous cream-colored steed, under his own personal banner.

"My Lord Mikal, a message from my Lord Syman."

Mikal turned towards the messenger, his helmet obscuring all his features save for a border of straight black hair and bright green eyes. "Aye, what says he?"

"You are to signal for water whenever ready and then carry the final assault."

"Is that all?"

"Yes, my lord. I'm off for Gordo." The messenger wheeled his horse to his left and took off for the northwest gate of Aishar to warn Gordo that prisoners would soon be coming out. As he receded in the darkness Mikal turned and sought out his fellow commander, Lord Zoltan. For some moments Zoltan's bulky figure eluded him.

Then Mikal saw him silhouetted against the fiery breach. "Zoltan, word from Syman."

Zoltan brushed fresh wine from his red beard and snorted. "What's he say?"

"We're to begin when ready. I'll order the blue arrow. And let's hope they've learned colors since Sippian," said Mikal ruefully.

Zoltan snorted again and remembered the siege of Sippian, some four months past. Syman's commanders at the front used arrows dipped in different mixtures to send signals by flame to the catapults. Red signified fire and oil, white meant stones, blue meant water, and green told the catapulters to cease. At Sippian the troops had signaled blue and the catapulter mistakenly shot sacks of oil instead of water. The sudden conflagration killed several men waiting for the final assault and gained time for the defenders. As punishment the man who made the mistake was later strapped to a sack of oil and catapulted against the walls himself. As he watched the punishment Syman had said quietly, "A costly error, but he's left his mark on Sippian."

Several blue arrows arched over the battle and this time the catapulters responded correctly. The hiss of white smoke rose over the dying rumble of flames as sewn hides of water broke over the breach. Mikal and Zoltan eyed the spot eagerly as both flame and smoke parted and fully exposed the city.

"Green arrows, quickly," shouted Mikal, while Zoltan bolted toward the breach, sword swinging and screaming, "Forward! On! On!"

Mikal spurred on his horse while Zoltan had already gained the top of the still quite warm heap of masonry. The gruff warrior laughed loudly and shouted over his shoulder to his comrade, "A sack of gold and I'm first to the duke's palace!" Mikal waved his sword in response and then rose in his stirrups and shouted his war cry. Mikal's war horse was well trained, and as the cream-colored steed clambered over the debris it lashed a front hoof at an enemy's shield, unbalancing the soldier while his master's sword swung down hard and crushed his skull.

Blood rushed to Mikal's head; he felt his temples throb within his iron casque. The exhilaration of combat rushed over him as he swung his blade up and down, left and right, slashing out mechanically but skillfully at the foe, not thinking but moving as one with his steed, who was just as excited beneath him. Moaning men, clanging blades and roaring flames rushed at the warrior's impervious ears; his vision narrowed to that foe before him and yet remained alert to dangers on either side—the special talent of the veteran.

Mikal gained the top of the rubble, gazed for a moment at the broken walls and then checked behind him to see that his men were advancing apace. Beyond them on the

littered plain Mikal could see the men of Grygor and
Azjhan coming up fast to the breach. All was clear atop
the broken battlements as the defenders of falling Aishar
recoiled before Syman's attack, leaving bleeding men on
broken stone. Mikal shook his head to clear it of the craze
of battle and then plunged down the slope into the city itself.

Those houses lying close by the walls were largely intact, sheltered by the walls themselves. Those buildings
lying further inside the city had been struck hard by the
three weeks of flame and stone. Fires burned freely toward the center of the city and the roar of flames and
crumbling masonry continued there unabated.

Through the inferno and growing mounds of wreckage
Mikal spurred on his charger. The fighting had passed before him now, and he stood fast for a moment to survey
the battle. After so many turns down the narrow, winding
streets Mikal realized that he was lost. The closely packed
buildings and dense smoke made it impossible to see any
landmarks, especially the ducal palace. Jizar Korm had
briefed the generals on the city's plan, carefully explaining
that a broad avenue ran north from the main gate to the
center of the city. There it stopped and was crossed by
another wide street which ran east to west and bisected
the city. Just north of where these two met was a large
square, forming the courtyard of the palace. The rest of
the city was made of tightly packed concentric rings, laced
and crossed by small and winding streets. However, Syman had breached the wall west of the main gate, and
Mikal's men were caught in the labyrinthine passages of
the western quarter.

The shops and houses were so close together that
Syman's soldiers were losing cohesion as units, and were
easy prey to lingering bowmen. Mikal searched for a way
out of the maze, and stopped before a blackened building.
There, sitting propped against the wall, was an Aisharian
soldier, his hands clutching a gaping wound in his thigh.
Mikal signaled some of his own troops to him and had the
wounded man dragged to his feet.

7

Mikal leaned over in his saddle. "A rough night, brother."

The wounded man's eyes narrowed. "For some."

"How do we get to the palace, man?"

The Aisharian spat on the ground. One of Mikal's soldiers slapped at the soldier's wounds. His body jerked and then stiffened.

"Talk and you'll be well treated. Otherwise I'll have you left here. There are better ways to die."

"What matter how we die?" But then he reflected for a moment. "All right; bear right down any of these streets and you'll come to a broader way. To the right is the main gate, to the left the palace."

Mikal nodded and ordered the man taken away to be bandaged and then recruited. To those now gathering around him he gave his orders to proceed to the palace. "And Pabul," he added, "tell Grygor to proceed north along the wall until he reaches a broad avenue and then follow it. We'll converge at the palace!"

Now the mercenary and his company hacked their way towards the road leading to their final prize and the end of the siege. An occasional arrow dropped one of them as they made their way through the twisting side streets, and others would then enter the houses and shops and seek out the assailant. New flames rose to the sky as the invaders set the offenders' houses to the torch. Screams competed with the din of battle as women fled before the attackers. Many invaders withdrew from the battle in search of this prey, but Mikal's troops were well disciplined to pursue the fighting first.

Finally Mikal broke out of the western quarter and onto the broad avenue. His way was blocked by a vanguard from Zoltan's troops.

"What's wrong? Press on!"

"Look, sir, we're in between them," one replied.

Mikal could see that to his left was the ducal palace. But across the avenue barricades had been thrown up, manned by the last of Aishar's garrison. Turning to his right, Mikal could barely discern the main gate through the smoke and darkness, but he could make out a large knot of Aisharians there as well, preventing the invaders now within the city from opening the portals to the rest of Syman's horde. They had indeed broken into the middle of Aishar's last defenders.

"What do we do, sir?"

More men wound their way onto the main thoroughfare while Mikal mulled over a suitable plan. "All of Zoltan's command will assault the gate. Open it quickly. The rest come with me. Cavalry first! Let's be at them before they can fall back again!"

Zoltan's men rushed off to their right and flung themselves at the defenders of the gate. A cloud of spears thinned out the remnants of the garrison. The attackers hacked mercilessly at the men before the portcullis, and many of their own were killed by mistake in the thickening smoke and confusion of close quarters. The fighting became chaotic as each man struck out blindly on all sides in the blinding gloom, until one of the attackers struck wood with his battle-ax. "The gate!" he yelled, and although he was felled by an errant spear as he reached for the wheel to lift the portcullis, others gained the mechanism, and then the gates of Aishar opened with a great sigh. Bodies were quickly dragged away to allow the portals to swing fully open, and in poured Syman's massed cavalry, overrunning some of their comrades still standing amidst the carnage.

The masses of horsemen surged up the wide boulevard, unopposed by any defenders. By the time they had reached the first barricade beyond the gate, only the dead and dying remained in the gloom. Lord Mikal's assault had already carried towards the palace and he was regrouping when Tytir, the cavalry commander, galloped up. Mikal pointed to the two remaining barricades and Tytir divided his troops into two groups, the first to carry the next obstacle and the second to press on before the Aisharians could prepare for a final defense at the further barricade.

The thunder of their massed hooves lost in the roars of the dying city, the cavalry hurled itself at the barricade. Men and horses hurtled over stone and pikes, defenders fell under swords and steeds, riders pitched to the ground as their horses failed to clear the barrier. The second wave broke over this turmoil before the issue was settled, and attackers and defenders alike were swept up in the rapidity of the onslaughts.

A now wearied Mikal rejoined the battle at the last barrier, scrambling over the mound of stones and housewares and scattering the few remaining defenders. As his and Tytir's troops re-formed, Mikal looked back up the wide street. Bodies were strewn along its entire length and in large piles over and along the broken barricades. Smoke clung to the ground further down the street, obscuring the hordes of soldiers now streaming into the city.

Tytir, Mikal and the other commanders cantered forward and came to the intersection of the two major boulevards. The palace was quite visible now. It was somewhat squat, resting on a pedestal of encircling steps which were wide rather than high, of the sort that are difficult to climb at an even pace. Two of the three stories were masked by a thick white colonnade, leaving a terrace before the upper story. On the very top steps a line of soldiers stood resolutely awaiting the mercenaries' charge.

The cavalry commander was eager to begin and end the final assault, but Mikal stayed him. "They know they are done. Perhaps they will surrender now." Tytir left off waving his mace to signal his men as Mikal gingerly entered the courtyard, sheathing his sword and raising his right hand. As a precaution Tytir drew up his men across the mouth of the yard.

"Men of Aishar! I call on you to surrender honorably. Your walls are breached, your gates opened. Your city has fallen. Lord Syman is a merciful warrior."

A tall man standing squarely between two pillars called back, "And what about the dog Jizar Korm, you lackey? What does he know of mercy?" One of the soldiers on the steps raised up his spear and prepared to throw, but the mercenary backed off before the threat was made good.

"So much for talk," grunted a satisfied Tytir as Mikal returned to their lines. Mikal nodded and looked toward the man who had answered him. He was sure that this was Kalzar Korm. Tytir was again standing in his stirrups, now surveying his lines. He sat back in his saddle and then surged forward with a violent flick of his spurs.

A burst of spears and arrows met the mercenaries as they passed across the courtyard, but there was no time for a second volley as the mercenaries mounted the steps. Mikal's arm ached as he swung it up and down at the pitifully few defenders. With a quick thrust he pinned a man to a column and then looked around to see that his whole line had carried to the palace. The green-eyed warrior moved his horse forward across the vestibule and into the main hall of the ducal palace. At the far end was a white stairway which divided left and right as it rose out of the hall. On the landing stood one last group of Aisharians. By their armor Mikal could see they were nobles and officers, including the man he assumed to be Kalzar Korm. The mercenary general addressed himself to that man.

"My Lord Kalzar Korm, it is over. Spare your city and your people and surrender."

The tall man in the sky-blue brigandine stepped forward and removed his white-plumed helmet. He threw his sword down at the horse's hooves. "Who takes my sword?"

Mikal now held his helm and shook loose his sweat-matted hair. "Lord Mikal of Lord Syman's army." Others filtered into the hall behind him as he raised a victory paean. "The city of Aishar is fallen! Bring suitable horses to convey these lords to Lord Syman." Weary from a long and grim night and an even longer siege, he again donned his casque and left the great hall, guiding his horse out of the courtyard and down the avenue leading to the main gate now teeming with celebrating soldiers.

Wounded men sat on the edges of the street leaning against buildings or each other, while their comrades roamed amidst the corpses, looting still-warm bodies. Few looked up as the warlord rode slowly by, although some held up their booty for his inspection. The green-eyed warrior stopped at one group busy binding each other's

11

small wounds with strips from the clothing of the dead.

"Have any of you seen Lord Zoltan?" he asked. They all shook their heads and Mikal went on, crossing the avenue to the eastern quarter, where little fighting had occurred.

For this very reason Syman's men went there first for their looting. More shops and buildings were still intact, and the streets were crowded with refugees from other quarters and with Aisharians trying to shed their telltale armor. A scream from overhead attracted Mikal's attention, and he saw a young woman clutching at the window frame above him. Suddenly a hand appeared around her waist and she was gone, her continuing screams drowned by hearty, bellowing laughter.

A passing soldier recognized the general and tossed him a skin of wine. Mikal removed his helmet and drained the wineskin, letting the rich liquid flow over his cheeks and chin and down his shirt. He tossed the empty skin away and rode on, picking his way among scurrying townspeople and reveling soldiers. A woman running down an alley with her bodice in shreds, a soldier heaving gold plates out a window, a ransacked bakery put to the torch. Mikal moved on through the district amidst the recognized privileges of a victorious army. Finally he saw a familiar broad figure riding towards him.

Zoltan was drinking from a brimming wineskin while two more dangled from his shoulder. More importantly, a well-shaped woman was slung over his saddle, making only the merest pretense of a struggle. As he lowered his head after taking a large draught and saw his companion approach, Zoltan broke into a wide grin.

"Mikal! Ha! Ha! Good hunting, eh?" Zoltan passed the wineskin and slapped the girl's bottom.

"You owe me a sack of gold. Where were you?" Mikal discarded the already empty skin.

The burly warrior stroked his red beard. "I got lost in those cursed streets near the breach. We ran into some Aisharians by a fountain, and by the time that was done and I reached the main avenue you were already on your way to the palace. No sense fighting in another

12

man's wake, so I crossed into this quarter to clean up. They're all surrendering."

Mikal eyed the girl across his friend's saddle. "Yes, so I see."

"What? Oh! She's my share of the booty. Syman won't mind my protecting her from the terrors of a falling city." They both laughed heartily and broke open another wine-skin.

"Come, Zoltan, we must make formal presentation of Aishar to Syman." They picked their way through the chaos and revelry in the streets and out to the main gate. As they neared it a soldier rode up.

"My lord, the prisoners are coming out now. Will you escort them?" Kalzar Korm and his nobles were already visible through the persistent smoke, and Mikal signaled that he would.

Kalzar Korm eyed him coldly. "My Lord Mikal, are you proud of this night's work?"

"A fallen city must give itself over to the victors. You could have avoided this." Lord Mikal was tired and in no mood to be preached to. "Why did you fight to the finish?" he countered.

Kalzar sighed. "My brother Jizar is a demon. I would still fight if possible. Tell me this, Lord Mikal, how could you fight on his side? You seem to be a much better man."

"I am contracted to Lord Syman and he was hired by your brother."

"Is it all that simple? Is there no question of causes, of right and wrong?"

Mikal swallowed hard. "No." They had already passed out of the city and now rode in silence to the hillock where Syman and Jizar waited.

The sun had already begun its ascent when Syman finally returned to his tent, the smoldering city of Aishar still belching smoke into the graying sky. As the warlord dismounted, a figure swathed in black, the cowl of his cape obscuring his features, stepped from the shadows of the tent's awning.

MARK M. LOWENTHAL

"My Lord Syman, it is over and done. When will you deliver him to me?"

Syman made no effort to hide his annoyance from his visitor. "Not now. I am tired. The siege has been long—and costly. Your prize will be handed over tonight, after the banquet. I will let him celebrate one more time; he has been a good commander."

"My Master will not understand this procrastination. He would be greatly angered should this man escape," hissed the figure in black.

"Tell the Em-" Syman began to shout, and then caught himself. He shoved his face into the other man's and lowered his voice, virtually spitting the words through clenched teeth. "Tell your Master that he shall have his prize, he shall not escape. You shall have him tonight. Now begone! I have promised your Master this and he shall have it." Syman wheeled around and entered his tent, leaving the hooded man standing outside in the breaking day.

"Yes, m'Lord Syman," he said with a cold dignity. Then he rode unnoticed out of the camp.

II

Away Across the Plain

It was past midday when Mikal awoke, still feeling weary from the fighting the night before. He absentmindedly picked up a piece of fruit and bit into it as his eyes wandered around the tent. "Much must be left behind," he thought. "He travels swiftest who travels light." He moved about the tent, picking up items and putting them down, a goblet from Larc, a sword he took from a dead soldier in Kyryl, his best shield. He dressed quickly and quietly, putting on a full suit of armor, not one that he wore for show but his most comfortable and protective, and his best weapons as well. Then, as he exited to the outer room of the tent he stopped, remembering something else that had to be taken. Kneeling before the wooden trunk at the foot of his cot, he took out some small items hidden in the corner and shoved them deep into his saddle bag.

Mikal's eyes squinted tightly as he stepped into the harsh afternoon sunlight from the murky dark of the tent. The camp was quiet now, only a few soldiers stirring about, mostly men wounded earlier in the siege who had not fought last night. Only a few wispy plumes arose out of Aishar. Mikal went to his horse and loaded his weapons, sword, dirks, two short lances, moving as naturally as possible despite the pounding in his heart. Suddenly, his servant Willom came up behind him.

"My lord, I did not expect you to arise so soon. I thought you'd sleep until the banquet tonight."

"No, no. I couldn't sleep," he stammered. "I've decided to go hunting." He hoped the story was plausible.

"I shall be ready in a moment," offered Willom.

"No, that won't be necessary. I'll go with Zoltan. Rest

15

today, but be sure to have my gown ready when I return."

Willom agreed, and Mikal led his horse away towards Zoltan's tent, breathing easier having passed the first hurdle. He walked across the still-sleeping camp, waving to some of his company, praising some for their actions, until he reached Zoltan's. He sighed, as if crossing the camp this day were akin to being the first man over the battlements of an enemy city.

Zoltan's servant, like Willom, was quartered in the outer tent, and looked surprised to see Lord Mikal. "My lord is still asleep," he protested.

"Then wake him," Mikal ordered with as much bravado as he could muster. "This is no day to sleep. There are boar to be hunted before the feast tonight." And then he brushed past the servant and into Zoltan's chamber.

The heavy warrior was snoring contentedly through his deep red moustaches, his arm flung around the buxom girl he had carried from Aishar across his saddle. Mikal tiptoed to Zoltan's sword and brought it flat side down hard on Zoltan's rump.

"By the Spirits!" he bellowed. The girl screamed when she saw the fully armored warrior standing over her.

"Out, my young lovely," Mikal shouted as he pulled back the blankets. The girl screamed again and grabbed her dress around her as she flew out of the tent.

"Mikal," Zoltan protested, rubbing his backside, "she was a mere innocent. What's going on?" He reached for some wine as he sat up.

"Yes, as innocent as your ever-littering hunting dog. But come on, we're going out for a hunt ourselves."

"Hunting? Today? I want to sleep until the feast tonight." Zoltan let his wide body fall back onto the bed.

His friend leaned over him and looked deeply into his closing eyes. "Zoltan, I'm in trouble and I must leave. I want you to come with me." His voice had fallen off to a whisper.

"What sort of trouble?"

"I can't say. Trust me for now, as the man who saved your life in Kyryl, and come with me."

Zoltan sat up again and nodded a few times. Then he silently got up and gathered some possessions together. "I'll get the rest later."

"We're not coming back, Zoltan. Take what you need, and your finest weapons. We go at once and for good."

"Wait a moment. Is it Syman? Maybe I can intercede."

"No. Please trust me and follow my lead."

Zoltan moved about his chamber as quickly as his girth would allow, reassessing what he would take along. He muttered as he moved about, grumpy still over his rude awakening, but was soon ready.

As they mounted their steeds outside the tent, Mikal leaned over to his companion. "Act naturally or I am lost." Soon Zoltan was laughing and joking as he breakfasted from a wine flask.

They rode through the camp with its many tents of different hues, many flying pennants of ornate design, towards the south gate. More soldiers were awake and moving about now, but few noticed the two riders or would have dared to question the movements of two of Syman's best generals. Presently they reached the gate, where a lone sentry stood, kicking stones to relieve the boredom. As he saw the riders he raised his left hand to beckon them to halt. "Good day, my lords. You know the orders; where to, my lords?"

Mikal spoke up. "We're going hunting, after some boar. If we're asked after, we'll be back before the feast."

The sentry accepted this without question and stepped aside. Again Mikal breathed easier, and then poked Zoltan. "Race you to the far hill," he challenged, already spurring on his horse. Zoltan flicked his spurs quickly into his own steed's flanks and galloped after Mikal. They pounded over the dry grass of very late winter, grass grown yellow between the last run-off and the first spring rains. Mikal managed to hold on to his lead while Zoltan dogged his heels. They were almost even when they reached the crest of the hill, after which they would be out of sight of the camp and the army of Lord Syman. Mikal reined in at the crest, as did his companion.

"What was the meaning of that?"

"I'm sorry, Zoltan, but it was the quickest way I could think of to get away from the camp without arousing that sentry. Let's ride slowly over the crest, and once we're hidden by the hill we ride as fast as we can."

"Which way are we going, may I ask?" Zoltan passed his flask to his green-eyed companion.

"South until the sun lowers a bit, and then east, due east. It will be expected that I will go south, so we mustn't head that way too long. And now, no more questions; let's be off." And so they cantered over the hill, and once they reached its further base they took off again at a full gallop.

Syman's gift to his victorious troops, his traditional feast, had been going on for some time now in the large tent that had been raised in the middle of the camp. While lesser-ranking soldiers and the vast number of camp followers celebrated in small groups outside, Syman's leading commanders and the heroes of the siege of Aishar drank and caroused inside the huge red pavilion.

Torches and cressets lined both sides of the billowing structure. Two seemingly endless tables ran the length of the tent on either side, each able to seat over seventy men. Down the middle ran a third, similar table, and at the head of all three was the shorter table for Lord Syman himself. Servants bustled about continuously, bringing more wines and regional brews and huge platters of freshly killed and roasted game. Abundant bowls of fruit added a touch of color and gaiety. Over a huge open cooking pit at one end of the tent several pigs roasted slowly on spits. Women from the fallen city were pressed into service as barmaids, and confusion soon reigned among the revelers as to what the women were supposed to be offering. The din from the many loud conversations and raucous songs rose into the night sky, carrying almost to the sullen ruins of Aishar itself.

Many less hardy warriors had already passed out from the successive toasts and were sprawled across or under their tables, or slept huddled in their chairs. The new Lord of Aishar and Lord Syman had been toasted many times over, as had many of the leading commanders and soldiers. One knot of warriors were busily toasting their mounts, and the pledges moved quickly from horses to bed mates.

Lord Syman stood on his chair waving his tankard over his head as he acknowledged the toasts, splashing the rich red liquid on those about him. His eyes were turning as red as his drink, and his blearing vision did not notice one of his servants slip up beside him. The servant leaned up and whispered a message to him. The warlord climbed down, bracing himself against the table, and then headed for one of the closed chambers in the rear of the tent, stepping over a stupored warrior and chasing an amorous couple out of the chamber as he stepped in. Waiting in the shadows was the man in the black cowl.

"Will you have some wine?" Syman offered, suddenly sober but gracious.

The man in black was frostier than ever in tone and manner. "My lord, my Master expects his captive now. I would greatly fear his wrath, especially should this man escape."

Syman again was angry. "I told you he would be yours tonight. By the Spirits! I shall inform your Master of my displeasure with you."

"As you wish, my lord. But my Master wants that man, and I will have him tonight."

Syman was surprised how disagreeable the task suddenly seemed, especially for a rootless mercenary, but he could stall no longer. He looked around for some sentries and sent them into the feast tent, following behind them with the man in black in his wake. He clambered back up onto his chair while his visitor stood behind him. The smoke, the noise, and his own wine made it difficult to concentrate. He could not see all the revelers clearly.

"Where is my Lord Mikal?" he demanded, but his voice was lost in the celebration. He turned to the huge, intricately decorated bronze gong behind him and flung his heavy tankard against it. He pounded it again with the hilt of his sword, and again until the voices died away.

"Where is my Lord Mikal?" There was no answer. "Is .

19

he here? Has anyone seen him?" No one spoke up. Syman was raging now. "Fetch his servant! Look under the tables; perhaps he's drunk."

A low murmur arose as all wondered why Mikal was sought, and why he was missing from the feast. Finally, Willom was brought in, trembling.

"Where's your master?"

"I don't know, my lord." Willom was shaking most fitfully.

"Have you seen him today?" Syman moved towards the servant, who now fell to his knees.

"Yes, my lord, yes. He went hunting with Lord Zoltan, with Lord Zoltan, my lord." Syman looked around and realized that the burly red beard also was missing.

An enraged Syman jumped on the middle table. "Captain Frimir! Find all who were on guard today and bring them here!" Again the murmur rose as the guards were sought out and brought before their warlord. Over a dozen men were soon ranged before him as he paced wildly along the tabletop, occasionally kicking a stray tankard in his anger and frustration. A few of the guards were already quite drunk and had to be held up by their fellows.

"Did any of you see Lords Mikal and Zoltan leave the camp?"

Recognizing the names, the guard of the south gate tottered forward. "I did, my lord."

"When and where?"

"This midday or shortly after. They headed out of the south gate, hunting for boar, they said."

Syman pulled at his stiff beard, still glistening crimson from the wine. "The south! Of course! Goltho, wake up!" But Goltho was sprawled across a table, way past awakening. "Damn you! Mazjhar! Viktor! Mount your best men at once and ride south. I want those two back here —alive! A thousand pieces of gold for Mikal. Anyone may ride in the search." Several soldiers lurched up from their seats and stormed out of the tent. Some, however, did not quite make it, as their drunkenness betrayed and undid their greed.

Syman stormed back up the length of the table and jumped off. The man in the black cowl hovered near him, his voice heavy with sarcasm. "And so, my lord, he has escaped. My Master will not be pleased."

"Tell your Master that I will have Mikal in custody by tomorrow's nightfall. We'll catch him before he reaches the Southern border."

"I hope so, my lord. And I hope you carry out his capture better than you did his arrest. Good night, my lord." He exited silently through the rear chamber as Syman slumped into his chair. He grabbed for a flask of wine as hooves thundered and shook the ground outside the tent.

It was morning; the sun had been visible for some time. Syman sat uneasily now in his tent, listening anxiously for the sound of his returning horsemen. Instead he heard one of his servants enter. The servant approached and whispered, his message refocusing Syman's attention. "What? Bring him in."

Kalzar Korm, deprived now of his blue armor, his hands tied behind him, was brought before his conqueror. Two guards remained discreetly at the entrance.

Syman toyed distractedly with a dagger, and a sudden ironic smile crossed his face. "I have had you brought here to tell you that your brother Jizar Korm was killed while he slept last night, apparently by one of your—er, one of *his* nobles." The deposed duke's eyes opened wide, but he was unable to speak or even think of what he might say. Instead, his captor went on. "Frankly, this puts me in a quandary, but in the interests of securing my rear when I leave this place, and as the laws of inheritance demand, you are now the rightful Duke of Aishar."

Kalzar could not believe his ears, but again the mercenary went on. "My obligations under contract with your brother ended the night I took Aishar, so his death is his own affair. Of course, his obligations to me remain unfulfilled to some extent. As you have inherited his title, so you also inherit his debts. Those who have chosen to

21

join my ranks are now bound to me, and your city still owes me much in the way of victuals and supplies."

Finally Kalzar found his tongue. "I—I don't believe this. And I'm sure that your mercenaries have left little of value in my city, no matter what your cursed contract says."

"Hmm. Yes. But," said Syman, rising now and beginning to pace, "no matter. We'll take what we need. Of course, in the interests of my own security you will remain a guest, shall we say, until I am ready to break camp."

"This is incredible. You have fought an entire campaign, wasted men's lives, destroyed a city—all for nothing!" Kalzar's voice quaked with indignation.

Syman turned on him harshly. "For nothing? Nothing? Hardly, my lord *duke*. What do I care who rules where, who gains or loses what, so long as I have booty to keep my men happy and battles to keep them active and well-honed? Every battle is just a prelude to the next campaign, a means to holding my army together and keeping them sharp. What do I care if you or your brother rules in Aishar? Do you know what it cost him to depose you, and how much more it would have cost him had the siege continued? No, it was not for nothing, Kalzar Korm. It was worthwhile the moment your brother hired me." Syman turned again and motioned to the guards to remove his prisoner before the restored Duke of Aishar could reply. When the room was cleared he returned to his chair and resumed waiting for those in pursuit of the black cowl's prize.

Day became night became day as the two mercenaries rode away from Aishar. They stopped only to refresh their horses and then continued on, first south until sunset as Mikal had planned, and then due east. No pursuers were in sight as they turned eastward, and Mikal felt more secure as darkness and the long wind-blown grass obscured their movements.

It was only when they stopped for a longer rest on their second evening away from Aishar that Zoltan again asked why Mikal had left. "Surely you and Syman have only had a falling out, and it can be mended. Was it booty, or the new contract?"

Mikal started at this. "The new contract? I hadn't seen it. I didn't know that Syman had drawn and offered it already. What were the terms?"

"Nothing unusual. I signed for the usual sum plus my share of booty and promised to bring in two hundred men with my usual bonus for additional recruits. I tell you, Syman is getting stingy. He fought like mad against my fee, mind you. And he wanted to raise my quota to three hundred. He knows I can bring in at least four hundred or more, and where else can we make our money without a bonus for the additional recruits?"

The news of Syman's uncustomary greed was noteworthy to Mikal, but it did not tell him what he really wanted to know. "How long was the contract for? What was the objective?"

"Oh," said the red beard as he toyed with a blade of grass, "that was the worst part. He demanded that I sign on for as long as the next campaign lasts and refused to specify our foe. That's why I haven't signed yet. I would have, of course; I intended to do so after Aishar. But I didn't want to appear too eager."

It all fit together into the picture Mikal had expected. He lapsed again into the silence he had maintained since they had set out. Zoltan felt he now understood why Mikal had left. "Was it the contract? The fact that you had not seen it? Surely it was an oversight."

"No, it was no oversight. Does that sound like Syman?" Zoltan agreed that it did not. Mikal continued, "No. That is not why I had to go." Again he let the matter drop, leaving Zoltan no opening to press the matter further.

"Where shall we go then, Mikal? Surely we have come far enough east to elude Syman. There is nothing left for us in the east. Why not turn about and head west. There are plenty of armies there that we could join. Xavir, the Hegemon of Braza, is always looking for men. We could go there."

Mikal's voice was lower as he curled up in his bedroll.

"No. We're not looking for another army. We must continue east for a while, as there is something there I must do." He did not elaborate on this tantalizing morsel, but went to sleep instead.

"There was no way we could find them in the dark. What tracks there were led south, but we lost them after a while. Shall we refit and ride out again?"

Syman heard the words as if from some far-off voice. He took in deep breaths. "No, no," he said, waving his hand. His voice trailed away. "Give orders to break camp. Organize patrols to keep watch along the Southern border. Have them take enough gold for spies and informers. I want anything—news, rumors—anything. The patrols can join us in the north later."

Within a day the vast canvas city beside the still smoldering ruin of Aishar was dismantled and moving north. With the army went many of those who had lived in Aishar, the men under pain of death from the night of the city's fall, some of the women as captives and some as willing followers. Syman rode with the vanguard, feeling something he had not experienced since his very first battle. He was actually afraid. The Master of the man in the black cowl would be more than displeased over Syman's carelessness, and it was to this man that Syman now rode with his army, already under contract to him for yet another war.

III

The Incident at the Inn

It was late on the third afternoon since they had left Aishar. All about them the long waving grass, broken occasionally by knots of trees, stretched unimpeded to the horizon. It seemed more like water than vegetation as each breeze or wind sent rippling waves across its surface. Their horses, like ships, left momentary wakes which soon sank from sight amidst the bounding green. The undisturbed nature of the land imparted its tranquility to them. They slowed their horses to a more comfortable pace, feeling safer now from Syman's pursuit.

Zoltan spent most of the time talking, reminiscing about battles and women. Mikal had heard many of the stories before, but accepted the position of the polite listener. He always enjoyed Zoltan's lusty braggadocio, and now preferred it to more painful queries as to their destination. He listened easily as the burly warrior held forth, his heroics in the field as always surpassed only by his heroics in bed. Mikal lost himself in laughter, and it was only as his eyes stopped blurring that he saw the cluster of white sitting on the easily undulating plain. He nudged Zoltan and pointed. Both men brought their horses to a halt and leaned forward in their saddles. Mikal arched his brows and asked Zoltan what he made of it.

They sat a moment longer. "There's no smoke or other sign of habitation," Mikal said.

"There hasn't been any for some time. Do you suppose it's a village?"

Mikal shrugged and removed his casque to shake out his straight black hair in the gentle breeze. They sat a while longer. "Shall we?" Now Zoltan shrugged, and then agreed.

25

Cautiously they moved forward, taking care to move slightly off a direct path, going closer while still keeping themselves at a safe distance. The unvaried sameness of the plain made distances difficult to judge, and they went for quite some time before the cluster began to take any definite shape.

It was Zoltan who first discerned its identity. "Why, it's a great house, Mikal, or rather the ruin of one."

They edged closer, and closer still. "There are still no signs of any inhabitants," Mikal observed. Zoltan agreed but took steps to make sure. Standing in his stirrups, he cupped his wide hands and let loose a great bellowing salute. The horses and his companion jumped at the red beard's deep rumble, but beyond this there was no response from anywhere on the plain. Sitting down with evident satisfaction, Zoltan extended his arm towards the house, as if inviting his companion to enter.

Their horses went on at a deliberate pace, closing on the house until Mikal's horse stumbled on an object hidden in the long grass. Mikal came down out of his saddle and pushed the thick growth aside. A row of heavy white stones ran straight across their path. "It was a wall," he said. "This was the estate of a very great man, judging by the size of the house and the bounds this wall sets." Zoltan nodded in agreement, for the remnant of the wall was still a good distance from the house itself. "But long abandoned," the burly man added. "That grass has been given many years to grow freely."

The house itself gleamed in the late afternoon sun. The bleached effect of its white walls combined with the irregularity of the ruins reminded Mikal of the skeleton of a long-forgotten corpse left on a battlefield. Without any roof to impede them while still mounted, they rode through the entrance hall and into the room beyond. The floor was a curious mixture of graceful inlaid stone designs competing unsuccessfully with the rapacious carpeting of grass. The walls were remarkably untouched by weather or decay. Only their jagged edges told of their past suffering.

They dismounted, leaving their steeds to graze within

the walls, and both men drew their swords, fearful of some surprise. But as they passed from room to empty room only a playful wind tapped at their shoulders or sprang upon their backs. They passed a room purposely left open to the sky, with a central pool and fountain now overrun with weeds. The room beside it was obviously made for dining, and the next held clear evidence of having been the kitchen. They went on through what they took to be various bedchambers, large and small, all with those extraordinary gleaming walls and all stripped completely bare of furnishings after years of looters and wayfarers.

"What do you make of it?" Zoltan's voice came as a surprise in the stillness.

"No more than before. The house of some great man long since gone."

They passed on to another great hall centrally located at the rear of the house. As in most of the rear chambers, its roof was intact, giving a clearer picture of the room's use. Like the others, it had been picked clean. But the two-stepped platform at the far end remained visible.

"He was a man who held receptions and had others pay court to him," said Mikal as he observed the long walls and mounted the platform. There was a sudden and unfamiliar stiffness in his tone that made Zoltan turn towards him with renewed curiosity. His friend seemed elsewhere as he paced the platform, oblivious to the red beard's presence. There was something in that room that held special meaning for Mikal. Unable to grasp it, Zoltan moved about the room aimlessly. It was he who found the remnants of the inscription on one of the side walls, between two large windows. He broke into his friend's mental wanderings and beckoned him to the carving.

"I cannot read it; the script is unfamiliar."

Mikal ran his fingers over the wall. "This inscription was once inlaid with something precious, probably gold. That is why it has been disturbed so." He peered for some clue to the remaining letters. "This is in the court language of the nobles of the Middle Empire. That is why

27

you could not read it. So little of it is left it is hard to make out." Leaning forward, he stared intently at the words, removing his mailed glove to run his fingers over their outline.

"Wait. I can make out some of it. This word here is fragmented. It may have been some name ending in *'mir.'* " His eyes grew wide. "It would have been Palamir! The words before it say *'. . . in token of which . . . ,'* and then the name, *'. . . gives proof to all of his eternal friendship and beneficence to his loyal servant Balmir.'* "

He turned to his rather untouched companion. "Zoltan, do you know what this is? Palamir is probably Palamir VI, last Emperor of the Middle Realm, and this is the house of one of his great generals and statesmen, the Lord Balmir. It was probably a summer home presented by the Emperor as a sign of his appreciation and friendship."

All of which left Zoltan unmoved. He knew and cared little for the ceremonies of kings and lords, especially long-dead ones. What interested him was Mikal's ability to read the almost forgotten writing. But when he asked how Mikal came to know it he was met again with silence. Zoltan ignored it as Mikal had ignored the question. "Shall we spend the night here, then?" Zoltan asked.

Mikal was lost again, as he had been on the platform. His fingers continued to move over the inscription, almost caressing the letters. Zoltan repeated the question.

"What?" said Mikal, seemingly awakened from a dream. "No, no," he said, before Zoltan could ask again, "I don't want to stay here."

"But it will be dark soon enough. It would be better than sleeping again in the open," argued Zoltan.

Mikal's disposition had abruptly changed again. He was adamant now, almost frightened it seemed. "No! We can still cover some ground. Come, let's go. This place reeks of dead rulers and fallen empires. Let us be off." He headed purposefully for the door.

Zoltan, sensing his companion's sudden dread, followed him through the silent rooms to their horses. He let it all pass, and they left the white broken shell and continued

east to spend another night on the windy plain. Not once
did Mikal look back as they rode. Zoltan noticed this too.

True to his word, Mikal led them eastward. Traveling
by day and through the evening, they made swift progress
across the great plain. In a land devoid of laws and states
it was best to avoid those few campfires which beckoned
in the night. They also shunned towns and villages that
might be centers for mercenaries passing to and fro across
the carcass of the Middle Empire. They went on in this
way for days, until neither could bear the thought of another cold bed of thick grass. From a convenient rise they
found a seemingly quiet village and decided to spend one
night there.

The village was small, its few streets dusty, and the
deepening dusk enhanced its murky appearance. Mikal
and Zoltan rode slowly up the main road from the south,
their own grimy figures merging with the landscape. They
came upon some boys playing with a small bird captive
on a leather leash and asked if there was someplace they
might stay. They were directed to the only inn the village
had.

The narrow railed balcony that ran outside the second
floor of the building told them that the inn had once been
a rich man's villa. The inn was grandiosely called the
Crossed Swords. The first floor was the tavern itself,
and rather warm as provincial taverns go, but the gloom
of the village made its presence felt too. Tables were
ranged along the walls, with a few in the middle of the
room. Across from the door ran the bar, an aged affair of
very dark wood, now deeply stained, and behind this
hung green curtains leading to the kitchen and the owner's quarters. To the left of the bar were the stairs leading
to the inn's rooms and to an inner balcony that clung to
all four walls.

Local farmers were already gathering in the tavern
when the travelers entered, and they eyed the soldiers
coldly, for mercenaries were unwelcome in these parts, or
any other that had felt their sword and torch repeatedly
over the years. The two soldiers threw their packs on a
table in the far left corner, along the wall where the

door was, and Mikal sat down while Zoltan negotiated for a room and some supper. The red-bearded warrior returned with two tankards of ale and a big smile. "I've got us two single rooms." His eyes were wide and expectant.

"Fine," said his comrade. "Now get us one room with two beds. We're safer that way, and there'll be no time for you to search out some barmaid tonight." Zoltan slunk off to the bar.

It was then that Mikal noticed the group of men at the long table across the room. He immediately sized them up as mercenaries as well, and for a worried moment wondered whose army they served. But all was forgotten as Zoltan returned, with supper not far behind him. They downed the pork and potatoes avidly, and with bread and beer washed it down and sat back to linger a bit downstairs. Immediately after their plates had been cleared, Mikal and Zoltan noticed the eight men at the long table holding a short but meaningful huddle, and soon one of the soldiers began to head towards them. Both instinctively checked for their weapons. The man who approached was broad and of medium height, his graying hair cropped unevenly at neck length, his dark beard cut close to the skin. He carried his tankard in his left hand, while his right absentmindedly fingered the edge of his dirty byrnie. He extended his hand and gave a big smile as he came to their table.

"G'evening. M'name's Korl. Mind if I join you for a bit?"

The two answered noncommittally and motioned Korl to a seat, resolved to let him do most of the talking.

"My men . . . er—friends and I marked you when you came in. You have the look and weapons of soldiers."

Mikal answered affirmatively, rather than deny an obvious truth.

"Those are fine weapons," said Korl. "Where are they bound for now?"

Mikal answered again. "Home. We're heading home."

Korl showed some frustration at being forced into this interrogation. He persevered in his attempt at conversation. "Where've y'been?"

30

"South," burbled Zoltan through a mouthful of foamy beer.

"South? Where in the south? I've not heard of any fighting there."

"We've been way past the borders of the Southern Empire, down where even the great sea changes its name."

Korl seemed less than convinced with this response, but went on anyway. "How would you like to join a great army, perhaps the greatest ever assembled?"

"Whose?"

"The army of Lord Syman. That's where we're bound. Surely his name has carried to where you were." Both men's eyes narrowed at the mention of the name, but they denied knowing it. "What?" harrumphed Korl, as he waved for another tankard. "Why, Syman's the greatest general in the Three Realms. The man who sacked Sippian, the conqueror of Larc for the Emperor Zhyjman, and victor at Kend'har. I hear he's now engaged against Aishar. Surely you've heard of him and his generals—Mikal, Gordo, Zoltan, Grygor."

Zoltan put on his most innocent expression. "No, never heard of any of them." Mikal drowned his smile in his tankard.

Korl was incredulous at their ignorance. "Well, no matter. But listen—Syman's armies will soon be on the march again, this time for greater prizes than Aishar or even Larc. We hear he moves against the Southern Empire!" His voice had fallen off to a suspenseful whisper.

"I don't know who he is, or how great he may be, but no mere mercenary can challenge one of the Empires." There was an angry edge now to Mikal's voice.

"Of course. But he's contracted out to a great lord," said Korl cryptically. "There'll never be a war like this again in our lifetimes—a whole empire at your feet! And you, by your looks, have experience. You could even come in as officers, perhaps rise to be captains, like me."

Now it was Zoltan's turn to be angered. "No. As my friend said, we're on our way home. Enough wars and enough booty to live off." Captains indeed, he thought.

31

"But surely one more campaign. A little more coin in your pockets. Maybe an estate if you're lucky."

"Or dead if we're not," said the red beard.

Seeing that he was getting nowhere, Korl changed his tack, now trying one of camaraderie. He signaled the bar and had three tankards brought this time. "Well, it's your loss. At least share a drink with me, as soldier to soldiers."

"Thanks, but no," said Mikal coldly. "We pay our own way." He threw some coins on the table, blunting an ancient recruiting trick. After a short while Mikal got up, saying he wanted to check on the horses. When he returned he found Zoltan in the midst of some fabulous battle in the far-off south, about to crush an enemy beneath his sword.

"I was telling him about the siege of Tilena," Zoltan said, borrowing the name from the girl he had taken at Aishar. Mikal sat down quietly while Zoltan brought his battle to its glorious climax. When he was done, Korl pushed back his chair and rose.

"Well, I'll be off. I'm sorry you won't join us, it's too bad. But still, good luck." He picked up his drink and returned to his comrades across the room.

"Are the horses all right?"

Mikal nodded.

"Then what say we go off ourselves?" Zoltan let out a mammoth yawn.

"Not yet." Mikal stayed him. "I don't trust our friend over there. Let's stay put for a bit." And so they took their time and finished their drinks. Then they gathered their belongings and weapons and went to the bar, where Mikal ordered a full pitcher of ale to take up to their room.

After they had gone and evidently were not coming down again, Korl came up to the bar. He beckoned the tavern keeper. "Those two that were in that corner. I told them I'd see them later, but I've forgotten which room is theirs." The innocent host indicated the second from the right on the long street side, just off the stairs.

Inside their room Zoltan sat down on the bed further

from the door. "Nice of you to think of the pitcher, Mikal." But his friend prowled at the door, not noticing his remark for a moment. Then he said, "It's not for us to drink," just as Zoltan was raising it to his lips.

"What? Why not?"

"I bought it for effect. I want our friend down there to think we've drunk well."

Again Zoltan asked why.

"I want Korl to be overconfident when he comes to get us."

Zoltan was bewildered. "But we told him we were on our way home, that we didn't want to join him."

"Oh, Zoltan, don't be so naive. You know as well as I how many soldiers are recruited. And that trick of drinking the captain's drink is as old as the rivers. He'll be back, with his friends."

"What do we do then?"

"Well," said Mikal, "we sit here very quietly with the candles lit so as to seem to be draining that pitcher. Then we douse them and wait. Our horses are ready—that's why I went off to the stable before."

They sat silently for a while, and then Mikal motioned to his friend. The door opened to the right, so they would stand against the right wall, with a table between them, thus staying in the shadows when the door opened. Opposite were two beds. Mikal mocked up the covers on the beds so they appeared to be asleep. "When they open the door it will throw light on the beds and draw them away from us here."

"Is it wise to leave the door bolted?" asked Zoltan.

"Yes. Otherwise they might be suspicious. The sleeping traveler bolts his door. Ready?" Zoltan nodded and they assumed their positions against the right wall, Mikal nearer the door, Zoltan nearer the windows and the balcony. Mikal extinguished the candles.

They waited for some time in the dark, until their hands ached from sword and shield. It had grown quiet down below in the tavern. Mikal felt himself nodding off when he heard soft footsteps and saw shadows beneath the door. Zoltan heard them too and both were immediately alert.

An unseen hand lightly tried the door, but found that the bolt was thrown. The shadows moved back from the doorway. Then two figures came crashing through the door and sprang at the beds, their weapons drawn.

Mikal and Zoltan remained still for an instant to catch their would-be abductors off guard. Then the burly red beard gave a short shout. The mercenary standing between the two beds spun around in surprise. Too late did he lift his shield as Zoltan's huge claymore swung into him. He clutched his middle and spun around again, falling between the two beds. The other would-be captor saw the glint of Mikal's blade now and sprang at him, and they grappled with one another in the darkness behind the open door.

Yet another mercenary entered and Zoltan turned on him. It was Korl. "Dog!" shouted Zoltan, as his anger and battle lust rose. They went at each other and Zoltan managed to catch Korl's sword arm. As Korl reeled back, Zoltan grabbed the table against the wall and shoved it across the room. It caught Korl below the waist and sent him reeling out the door.

Meanwhile, Mikal and his foe fought closely in the darkness. Their shields locked in the confined space, and Mikal threw all his weight into his. The move caught his man off balance and rammed him hard against the wall, stunning the mercenary for a moment and giving Mikal time to pass his sword through him. As this assailant sank, Mikal saw his friend on the floor, having wedged the table into the doorway to form a barricade. Mikal looked beyond Zoltan and yelled, "Look out! The window!"

A mercenary came in off the balcony. Zoltan reached out for his sword, but his hand touched the pitcher of ale first. He seized it and flung it at the new threat, catching him full in the face. While the man struggled in his temporary blindness, Mikal ran up to him and with a strong boot sent him reeling and screaming through the window and out over the balcony. Mikal then glimpsed another man beating a hasty retreat off the balcony.

"How many's that?" asked Zoltan.

"Two here dead, one out the window . . ."

". . . and Korl wounded," added Zoltan proudly.

"I counted eight at their table tonight; that leaves four. Come on, this way." Mikal grabbed his pack and headed out onto the balcony.

They made their way to their right along the balcony, towards the stable and their horses. Once or twice Zoltan checked the street, but there were no assailants below. They were coming to the end of the building, where the balcony turned the corner. Against the glass of a darkened window Zoltan saw the glint of the blade first, and pushed Mikal down headlong. The descending blade cleft into Mikal's pack, but could not be extricated before Zoltan thrusted forward with his own. The victim jerked backwards and fell over the railing. Zoltan helped Mikal to his feet and they turned the corner and continued on until they were over a large stack of hay. Over the railing they went and down, and in the unguarded moment of their landing another mercenary fell upon them. Mikal rolled off the stack, but Zoltan's bulk carried him deeper into the hay and he lay helplessly on his back. Mikal grabbed at a harness close at hand on the wall as the mercenary scrambled up the stack; the harness whipped out and caught him behind the knees, tripping him and leaving him stunned on the stable floor. Both men ran to their mounts, which were saddled and waiting for them. They flung their packs over their saddles and spurred for the street. As they cleared the stable they saw one more of Korl's men running towards them, with Korl not far behind, holding his wounded arm.

"Let them go," he cried, disgusted at his dismal failure.

Mikal and Zoltan spurred off to the east, pounding out of the village. As they went, Zoltan joked, "If that's what Syman's got now it's a good thing we left." And the night gathered round them as they rode.

IV

Towards the Great Mountains

They rode on silently until well clear of the village or any other habitations. The horses were skittish at being deprived of rest, and their riders were equally weary. Finally Mikal turned in his saddle and said, "I fear we're back to our riding all day and sleeping in the open at night. I doubt any place in the Middle Realm is safe these days."

A quarter moon crept out past fleeting clouds, and enabled the travelers to espy a stand of trees. They made for it in order to pass the remainder of the night there and perhaps catch up on lost sleep. It was a small stand, some ten or twelve elms, and the ground around was thickly carpeted in moss and clover. They led their horses to the center of the little grove and bedded them down, and then collapsed quickly into their own bedrolls. Zoltan thought of asking where they were going once again, but sleep overpowered him and carried him off.

The sun, pale pink and new, had barely cleared the eastern horizon. Some blackbirds called out across the morning mist to announce the new day. But the mist, slumbering in hollows or nestling in leafy branches, ignored the harbingers of the sun. It clung tenaciously to the earth, blurring the distinction between damp earth and gray sky.

Mikal turned in his sleep and his hand struck a tree root which arced out of the ground. The jolt startled him and his eyes opened. He glanced over his left shoulder but Zoltan was not in his bedroll. Mikal sat up at once, but relaxed as he saw his companion coming towards him with wood for a fire. He greeted the hefty warrior, but received no reply. Mikal shrugged and proceeded to rise.

Zoltan made himself very busy getting the fire started, thinking about his unanswered questions. Finally, he turned to face his companion. "We have ridden and fought together over many miles and battles. We have fought back to back, trusting one another with our lives. And yet now you will not tell me why you flee."

Mikal looked at him and felt properly admonished. "I was in danger at Syman's camp, with Syman himself," he said, telling a half-truth. "I have always been honest with you, but ask that you trust me a bit longer. Until we are closer to my destination we are in danger, and I would spare you the burden of my secret should we be taken. Trust me," he implored, calling on that same comradeship that Zoltan had invoked.

Zoltan grinned. "Fair enough. Come, I've snared a rabbit." Mikal's grim expression eased.

They ate the rabbit and drank cool water from a stream. Then they carefully doused the fire, resaddled their mounts, and were on their way east again. They rode at a steady pace, less than a full gallop, trying to get the most out of their steeds. At Mikal's insistence they avoided main roads, especially the remnants of the Royal Ways of the Great Empire. Instead they stuck to vaguely marked lanes and farmers' paths, never lingering in fully open country, always going along the edge of woods when possible for the sake of a convenient refuge.

Some three days after the incident at the inn, they were just clearing a rise when Zoltan pointed to a gray-white line running across their path in the valley below. "Do you know where that runs?" he asked as he took some water. Mikal shook his head. "It's the Emperor's Way. Runs due north to Anrehenkar, the High City of the Emperor, and south to Gar."

Now Mikal showed an interest in the ancient road. "How far would you say we are from Anrehenkar?"

Zoltan perked up at the question. "Judging by the way we've been heading, some four days, maybe a little more or less."

Mikal nodded and was then lost in silent thought. Zol-

tan's curiosity got the best of him. "How far have we to
go? By the Spirits, where, Mikal, where?"

"Please, Zoltan. I'll tell you when I am able. Four days
you say."

The red beard let through a smile. "Then we're going to
Anrehenkar."

Mikal shook his head again and led his horse down to
the gray stone road. Grass was growing freely between the
large flagstones, and the stones were breaking up along
the road's edges. But as one stood in the middle and
looked north and south, one could only marvel at the
accuracy of the road as it plunged away in a perfect line.
But they resumed their journey east, putting much distance
between themselves and the still much traversed highway.

Their course altered now, heading slightly more northeast than due east. The question grew steadily in Zoltan's
mind: Where were they going? Each of his own ideas had
died as they rode on. Ernyr, Gar and Perrigar all faded
away to the west and south. They had crossed away from
the direct route to Anrehenkar and by Zoltan's calcula-
tions were passing the eastern edge of the Southern Realm.
On they went every day, east by north, now using the huddled peaks of the Falchion Mountains as a guide on their
right side. He ruled out Pyrin, the country of hermit magicians. Kyryl? Nor? Surely this was the long way about
from Aishar, and what business would Mikal have there,
especially after having fought against them in the past?
What business had he anywhere? Each day more and
more of Zoltan's thoughts were occupied by these musings,
and he grew resentful of his friend's reticence.

Finally, as they rounded the far northeastern tip of the
Falchions, Zoltan's restraint fell away, and he asked again.
"Mikal, you've dragged me across the entire Middle
Realm. We're at the edge of the Gates. Where are we
going?" His voice was at once both plaintive and demand-
ing.

Mikal's words were barely a response. "That's right, the
Gates. We'll rest here tonight, and enter the Westgate in
the morning."

"The Westgate?" Zoltan's eyes brightened. "Then we

are headed south." No one, he reasoned, would enter the Westgate and circle the Sentinel to head north. They must be going south.

But his words went unheeded. Mikal dismounted and began to unsaddle his steed.

The next morning they rode into a brilliant red sunrise and through the Westgate, formed by the pillars of the Falchions to the south and the Sentinel to the north. The Gates was an area formed by a broad flat valley running between the Falchions and the impenetrable Great Mountains to the east, and bisected at the valley's northern end by the lonely Sentinel. This peak was lower than its neighboring mountains, but topped by an abandoned fortress built early in the history of the Middle Realm. It had served as a watchtower over all movements in the three passages below, hence its name. Nothing could move beneath the Sentinel out the Westgate or Northgate, or away through the Southgate without being seen from above. But the fortress stood empty now, and only the silent stones of that barren region watched as Mikal and Zoltan rode past.

Zoltan's mood was brighter this morning, now that he felt seemingly sure at last of where they were headed. He talked freely, reminiscing again about battles on the field and in the confines of his tent. Mikal responded eagerly, hoping that Zoltan's inquiries were again at rest. But Zoltan fell quickly silent as they passed the last outspread fingers of the Falchions and did not wheel their horses south. Instead they continued eastward, and at midday began to veer a little to the north, just skirting the lower entrance of the Northgate.

By evening of the third day in the Gates, they were almost at the extreme southeastern edge of the Northgate, hard against the Great Mountains. The sun again hung red between the Sentinel and the Falchions, only now in the west instead of the east. The famed winds which inhabited the Gates at night had sprung up again and were careening freely off the mountainsides. For this reason Mikal chose a campsite surrounded on three sides by the edges of the Great Mountains. He busied himself unloading the wood they had thoughtfully brought with them for kindling and a small fire, as the area around the Gates was devoid of such vegetation. Zoltan sulked and huddled in his heavy red cloak, seeking shelter against the rocks.

Mikal eventually came over to him and offered him a bowl of broth brewed from their dried beef. The heavy warrior took it gruffly and drank it in silence. Mikal understood his friend's mood and saw that it was up to him to break the silence.

"Strange country around here. I have never been here before. Have you?"

Zoltan barely grumbled a reply, and so Mikal took another, more honest tack.

"I'm sorry, Zoltan, I know I haven't been fair to you. But you must have faith in my judgment just a little longer; my secret's not safe until we have arrived at our destination, especially in these lawless lands. We are within four or five days of our goal."

Zoltan jumped at this opening. "Where? There's nothing within that distance north or south of here. The closest place I can think of is Zifkar, and even that forsaken fortress is further away than that. Where are we going?"

"East, Zoltan, east. We are heading east."

"East? East! By the Spirits, Mikal! There's nothing east but impenetrable mountains that run to the end of all land until they reach the encircling sea. They're impassable, and with good reason—there's nothing there."

Mikal broke into a small grin. "Well, that's where we must go. Somewhere along this rim of mountains is a passage. Tomorrow we go through it. That's why I chose to camp here tonight. It'll be colder once we enter the mountains. Enjoy this while you can." And so saying he moved closer to the fire, as if to signify the end of the conversation. Zoltan wrapped his cloak tighter and harrumphed through his beard. "East? Bah!" His mood was still grim, but at least Mikal had told him a bit more.

They slept later than usual the next morning, the overhanging cliffs shielding them from the newly risen sun. It was the stirring of their horses that woke them, and the sun was already climbing through a cloud-laden sky as they made ready to go.

The horses fidgeted as they were saddled, picking hungrily at what little grass there was. Mikal looked anxiously at his red-bearded friend, looking for some sign of his mood. But Zoltan swung silently into his saddle and rode on, and it was only the discovery of the passage into the Great Mountains that moved him to speak.

"Mikal!" he called. "Is this it?" He pointed to the left, to a narrow cleft in the rocks, sealed at the top by long-fallen debris. Mikal dismounted to inspect the opening in the mountain's hide, for they had passed many passages since breakfast and he had rejected every one. He stood on the left side of the portal and, removing his glove, ran his fingers along the weathered stone. He slowly made his way down, stopping at every crack until he found what he was looking for. He blew and dusted the stone to make sure of the carving and, turning to Zoltan, said, "Good work, you've found it. This is the Eastgate." Zoltan peered at the rock and squinted hard but saw nothing.

"Here, Zoltan, look here." Mikal pointed out the carving. It was old, very old, and undoubtedly a representation of an eye, but oddly carved. It was a perfect five-sided iris set within a normal socket.

Zoltan shook his head. "What's it mean?"

"It is the signpost for the Eastgate. We might have missed it but for you." It was a newly happy Mikal that slapped Zoltan on the back. Zoltan was still baffled, but he was glad to have finally taken some hand in their journey.

The passage was exceedingly narrow, and too low for horse and rider to file through together. So Mikal led his horse in first and waited while Zoltan squeezed his bulk through. For a moment he was caught as his sword's scabbard snagged in a crevice. He sweated and groaned sideways, almost dropping his horse's reins. Finally he was free enough to move, but his sudden plunge forward only got him a knock on the head from the overhang. By the time he reached the other side, Mikal's bright-green eyes were alive with laughter. Zoltan tried to look angry, but broke into a grin as well. "This had better be worth it," he growled, and then laughed with his comrade.

They remounted and began their journey into the heart of the Great Mountains. The passage they followed was worn with age and not frequently traveled. Here, at the foot of the mountains, it was just wide enough for two riders abreast, as it wound vaguely to the northeast through the ever rising heights. It climbed steadily with the mountains, but the peaks on either side always rose faster than the path and left the riders with nothing to view but the rocks about them or the leaden sky above. The few patches of dried grass became more and more infrequent as they rode into the mountains, and those that were left were dull brown and added little color to their passage.

At irregular intervals other passageways wound off to the left or right, but Mikal passed each one by, staying unerringly on the path first indicated by the eye with the five-sided orb. There was a terrible quiet around them, broken only by the clatter of hooves on cold stone and the whoosh of wind down narrow byways. It had already grown noticeably colder. Both men were wearing their cloaks, and Zoltan had thrown his hood up over his helmet.

The wind became a third companion, but an unwelcome one that dried the lips and forced the eyes to squint and go watery. The horses slung their heads down as if to pass under the gusts, and their pace slowed as the upward slope gave no promise of an easy ride downhill on the other side.

Soon Mikal had his hood up as well, pulling it low over his eyes. Always the wind was in their faces, seeming to rush down to the Eastgate like a river over a falls. The wind hurled itself down from the jagged surrounding peaks, ambushed them from each intervening passage, kicked up dust at them from off the ground. And the great proud stones stood haughtily straight, throwing back their shoulders in a mockery of the huddled men and beasts struggling below.

Up and up they went, always winding past huge cliffs and towering stones. The path curved away to the right and then to the left, but always in an angle of ascent and always vaguely northeast.

By late afternoon the sun was throwing faint light devoid of warmth and murky irregular shadows down past the proud peaks. The cold and wind had taken their toll, and Mikal suggested a halt for the night, having covered less distance than he had hoped. He looked for another cove surrounded on three sides by boulders, but Zoltan pointed out that the first one he had chosen would not fit both them and the horses. So they trudged along, on foot now, until they found a larger niche in the mountains. Zoltan led the horses to a corner and unsaddled them while Mikal tried to build a fire among the sheltering rocks. The wind grew colder with the coming night, and the fire did little to counter its chilling effects.

Zoltan, who was not one to complain at discomfort, grumbled at the cold and wind. Mikal saw through the complaints and wished he felt safe enough to do the one thing that would ease his friend's edginess. But the time was not right, and he sighed softly and moved closer to the fire.

For the second straight day the sun shied away behind heavy clouds. The path still wound up and northeast, and unbroken mountains now stood in every direction. The sole comfort this day was that the wind abated somewhat and settled into a softer but still constant breeze. The chill of dying winter still hung in the air, and both men kept their cloaks about them with their fur-lined hoods thrown up. Another cold night was spent in another sheltered stone cove, only slightly more comfortable than the last, with the fleeting sight of familiar stars overhead in a briefly cleared sky.

By the third day the air held that wondrous clearness that only mountain air can have. Mikal noticed that his companion's mood was growing blacker with each passing day as the cold, the wind and the forced ignorance bore down on him. Mikal was worrying over this when the wind carried the sound to him. He sat bolt upright as he heard it.

Zoltan was roused by Mikal's sudden move. "What is it?" he asked, but Mikal only motioned him to be quiet. Zoltan looked about, and then thought he heard it too. He removed his helmet and strained forward in his saddle. For a moment he heard what seemed to be a distant gong, but then it was gone. He looked at Mikal but found no answer there, and his depression only deepened.

In camp that night Zoltan's feelings burst out. He sat towards the pitifully small fire, and spoke in a low, even voice. "I'm leaving tomorrow, Mikal. It's enough—you've dragged me across the entire Middle Realm, past all signs of life and men. You say I should trust you? But do you trust me? Who could I tell your precious secret to here— the frigid stones? Your secret will be safer when you're alone."

"Where will you go?"

"I'll take the next passage we see going south. Maybe it will lead out near Zifkar. I'll join a band there and head west. There are great stirrings there—the rumors that Syman was joining against the South. Maybe I'll get back in time."

"You'll never get out without knowing the way." There was neither anger nor vindictiveness in Mikal's voice; he was merely stating a fact.

"Perhaps. But I've had enough. At least I'll have a sense of what I'm doing, rather than freeze to death in ignorance." And with that he turned on his side and went to sleep.

Mikal did the same, and felt well rebuked. He hoped that Zoltan's outburst had done the man some good, per- haps relieving enough tension so that he could go on. Only a few days more, Mikal thought, remembering the gong he had heard, only a few days more.

But the next morning Mikal saw that Zoltan had been in earnest, for he had already breakfasted and was saddling his shivering mount when Mikal awoke. He said nothing as he heaved his great form into the saddle.

"Zoltan, where are you going?" Now it was Zoltan's turn to be silent.

"Zoltan, you'll never make it back." Zoltan was already

passing him and heading towards the mouth of the cove.
Mikal ran after him and grabbed at the reins. Zoltan
looked away, his eyes pained. "All right Zoltan, I'll tell
you." He took a deep breath. "My full name is Prince
Mikal, and I am the Heir of the Empire of the South."

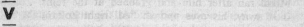

V

Mikal's Story

The words stunned Zoltan. He stared down in utter disbelief.

"It's true," Mikal said reassuringly. "I am the Prince and Heir of the Southern Empire. It is because of this that I left Syman's camp and also why we have come here. As you have said, there is a great war brewing against the Southern Empire. Only it's not just Syman and mercenaries, but the Empire of the North and its allies as well."

Zoltan dismounted and allowed himself to be led back to the fire. Mikal stoked it up a bit and told Zoltan more.

"Many years ago my father and I had a grave falling out, and as a consequence of this I left his realm. Thus I sought out my fortune as a mercenary, hiding my true identity. It would have been unsafe to be known amidst mercenaries."

Zoltan nodded rapidly in agreement, quickly appreciating the demands for ransom that would have been possible.

"I had no contact with my father all those years, and he none with me. You see, I was not always Heir, for I had an elder brother, Ivor. Some two months ago my father sought me out. It was at the time that we had begun the campaign against Aishar when the first word came. A messenger, plainly dressed but appearing to be a warrior, came into my tent one night just as I returned.

"Willom came in and announced him, but the messenger would not state his business to my servant, which angered me.

"'My Lord Syman picks damned hours to send notes,'

47

I barked as Willom brought the messenger in to my chamber.

"I lit a fresh candle and studied the man brought before me. He seemed oddly dressed and quite tired to have just come from Syman. I dismissed Willom and turned to the messenger. 'Well, what is it? What does my Lord Syman send me in the middle of the night?'

"He thrust the note at me from under his begrimed byrnie. 'I'm not from Syman,' he said very quietly.

"I opened the note hastily and moved towards the candle, not bothering to even pull my cloak back around me. The letter was fairly written, a scribe's hand. I read 'My Dear Son,' and got no further. I looked closely at the messenger, who was just standing there watching me, waiting for my reaction.

"I was suspicious. 'Who gave you this?' I asked, not believing it could possibly be true, not after so many years.

"The man answered guardedly. 'The writer has signed his name. He also gave me this, should you fear a trap.' The messenger removed his gloves and took a ring from his right hand, saying, 'He said you would recognize this.' I took the ring, a gold boar's head on a blood-red stone. It was my father's without a doubt. I nodded and read the letter:

" 'My Dear Son—I know this comes to you without warning and as a surprise. The man bearing this can be trusted. In seven years we have not written and I offer neither reasons nor apologies as we both know why this has been so. But now this must change, as the Spirits will it. Your brother, Prince Ivor, has taken ill, and there seems to be no cure—neither herbs nor prayers seem to have helped. We are told to expect his death, and so I am resigned to this as it must be. Ivor's marriage is without issue and his death will leave you as Heir to the Empire.'

" 'It is not only for this that I write. We have heard many odd rumors of late concerning events to the north, and this much is now clear. Zhyjman plans to move south against Anrehenkar in the near future and then lay claim to the Middle Realm, and with Ivor's death will also move against me in an attempt to bring all three Empires under his sway. He has the North united behind him. Moreover, it is said that a renegade from the Order has joined him. In short, the Northern Emperor plans to make the move he has threatened for so long, and now has the means and opportunity to do so. It is this that makes your renewed allegiance more important.'

" 'For what has passed in these years I ask you to understand, as do I. This has changed for many reasons and I now ask your assistance—if not for me, then for your inheritance and your home.'

" 'When the time comes I shall tell you what must be done. Until then, maintain your vigilance. Your father—Thurka Re.'

"The signature differed from the letter. It was my father's hand, with the ancient form of his title. I read the letter again and then put it to the candle. I turned to the messenger. 'Do you know the contents of this?'

" 'I know what any member of the Household knows, and the purpose of my mission. That is all.'

" 'Does my fath— . . . Does he want a written reply?'

"The man shook his head. 'No. He asked me to return with a token he could recognize as yours, but only if you assent. If not, I am to return with the boar's head.'

"I looked about the room, thinking, and then opened my wooden chest. 'He will recognize this medallion, it was once his present to me.' It was a child's piece of jewelry, the protective Eye of the Spirits over a sacrificial tripod, with my name on the obverse.

"I asked him if he would need to spend the night, but he said he must return at once. I acquiesced, and then I realized that I hadn't even asked him any questions. 'How fares your master?'

" 'Well enough, sir. Less distraught than many would be at his burden.'

" 'Yes,' I replied, 'he was always that way. One other thing—your name and post.'

" 'Churnir, Captain in the Bodyguard.'

" 'Tell me this—how did you find me?'

" 'It was not difficult. Syman's forces leave their mark on the Middle Empire, and your name carries its own banners.'

"I stammered a reply that if it was so easy for him, I would now have to be on my guard lest Zhyjman also try and find me. His reply made me ashamed for the first time of being a mercenary.

" 'Return to your master,' I said, 'and tell him this: I return for the reason I left—not the Empire or my own stake in it, but only for his sake.'

"I heard no more from father for some time. Then, after initially defeating Kalzar's army and upon our march to Aishar itself, Captain Churnir came to me again. The note this time was entirely in my father's hand: 'Your brother Prince Ivor died this morning. I do not want it known as yet that you have been found, and so my brother Prince Belka has agreed to be Heir in your stead, as he knows the truth. The time is coming for you to take up your mission. My next message will tell you when you must go, for you are in danger where you are.'

"I asked Churnir to explain the meaning of this last sentence, and he told me that it was probable that Syman was already in league with Zhyjman in preparation for the next war. He also told me that I was to go to the Order of the Magicians and Wizards, and how I should find it, and that I was to meet someone there and convey him to my father. My father's last sentence was thus a ruse, should the letter be intercepted or should I be taken first.

"Finally, during the siege of Aishar, Churnir came to me one last time, telling me that it was time for me to depart. I told him that I could not, for the city had not yet fallen. He stressed my danger, but I assured him that I was safe as long as the battle continued and that I could not leave until the campaign ended. I suppose it was my training as a good mercenary, but this was foreign to Churnir. I felt myself still bound by the contract with Syman and also knew that it was my protection as he too would keep his word even if he was in league with my father's enemies. I told Churnir that I would leave as soon as Aishar fell."

Mikal paused after this long tale and looked down at the dying fire. "And now, Zoltan, you know everything, why we left, and where we are going. I'm sorry I did not tell you before, but I feared our being intercepted."

"What I don't understand is why Zhyjman has decided to move at this time."

"I don't know. Perhaps we will find out at the Order."

Zoltan was on his feet again. "There is one last thing I would know. Do I call you Prince or Your Highness?"

"Neither," said Mikal, smiling.

"Then let's saddle up, Mikal, and be off to the Order."

As they rode, Mikal explained what little he knew of the Order. They were, he said, within a day or two of the outer gate of the Order itself.

The path grew steeper and more narrow, and wound on in tight, close curves.

The air remained cold here, and sharp winds careened off the close stone walls, forcing the riders to travel all day in their cloaks and hoods. By nightfall they still had not reached the entry to the Order, but they did hear again the sound of a distant gong. It was louder than when Mikal had first detected it, and he explained it to his companion.

"The Order went off into the Great Mountains when the Middle Empire fell. They have remained there ever since, training new magicians and wizards. They live partially on food they grow and partially on food from the outside, and that gong is a beacon for their caravans and a signal to them that the gate is open. We must reach them soon, for they only open the gate for four days under each new moon. Should we miss that, we may be stranded in these mountains for some time. We must reach it soon."

Mikal explained in camp that night how he had learned what little he knew of the Order from the wizard who had served his father when Mikal was still a boy.

"Every lord, be he great or small, endeavors to have a member from the Order as an adviser," Mikal said.

They awoke early the next day, breakfasting on cold meat and stale bread in the dark, in order to travel in as much light as possible. All day the cold clung in the mountains and the wind rushed at them, and all day the sky remained a sullen, leaden gray. They were riding single file now, threading their way along the narrow path. Mikal was growing increasingly anxious, fearing he had taken a wrong turn somewhere among the labyrinthine passages. He feared that the path would lead on interminably until it ended against a mountain wall. He feared there would not even be room for them to turn their horses around.

The path grew so narrow that they could feel their boots scraping against the rock walls on either side. It went into a sharp turn to the right, so sharp that the horses hesitated and negotiated it only with the utmost difficulty. Then, beyond the turn, the path opened up, wide enough for seven or eight riders abreast. It continued to rise, and at the top of the slope they could see the goal of their journey.

The mountain wall on the right ran along the side of the path and then rose suddenly and cut athwart the pathway. There, in the sheer living rock of the mountain wall was carved the outer gate leading to the Order. The wall itself ran thirty or forty feet high, and the portals covered half that height. They were huge, massive pieces of stone with no visible means of support from the outside, nor any indication as to how they might be opened. Only their surrounding outline and the surmounting eye in a five-sided socket carved over the gates betrayed their location.

The wind was fiercer than ever, pushing against the two riders as they made for the entry. The horses leaned hard into the wind, and Mikal and Zoltan bent forward with them. The four of them, horses and riders, literally pushed themselves up the slope and were dead tired when they gained the sealed portals.

"They're sealed," shouted Mikal against the wind.

"What now?" Zoltan yelled back.

"If we missed it, we're lost." Mikal scanned the sheer walls on either side. "I don't think we can scale them."

Zoltan turned to the gates and pounded hard with his sword hilt. What little sound it produced was carried away on the wind. He turned to his companion and like him huddled into his cloak as close to the mountain as possible.

"We'll have to wait. If we don't hear the gong by dark, we'll know." Mikal moved closer to the wall. He dared not think of what they'd do should there be no sound.

All day the raging wind tore at them, vainly trying to pluck them from the mountainside. Its icy fingers savaged them until they were both numb with cold. By mid-afternoon Mikal and Zoltan had all but abandoned hope, each pondering whether it would be wiser to sit and wait on the chance that they were expected, or go down out of the mountains and wait until the next moon.

Mikal studied the sky intently now, judging how much light was left. Zoltan's eyes reflected his own growing pessimism. They sat still, waiting. The afternoon had begun to fade perceptibly from the sky. Long shadows grew across the ground. Just as he was about to ask Zoltan for his opinion, Mikal was cut short by the deep throbbing sound of the gong.

"Quick, Zoltan, to horse!" he shouted.

Their limbs aching with the cold, the two travelers pulled themselves onto their shivering steeds. They sat as erect as possible, throwing back their hoods.

With a great groan and a continuous rumbling creak the doors parted ever so slowly. At first only the outlines of the gates became more visible, as if huge cracks were being driven into the mountain's tough hide. The cracks widened to thick black bands until the central vertical band dissolved to reveal a long, sloping plateau with waiting horsemen.

The riders on either side of the entry edged forward tentatively. One of those from within the walls, a man in a heavy gray robe, broke the silence. After looking at the two men before him, both of them well-traveled and

53

grimy, he said to neither in particular, "Prince Mikal?"

The thin man with the bright-green eyes answered. "I am Mikal. This is Lord Zoltan."

The gray robe nodded. "I am Master Ulric of the Order. Forgive my hesitation, but we were told to expect only one. Were you long? We have been coming down every day for the last seven, but were delayed today at the Order. Fortunately, it is not a long ride. We can reach it this night."

"Then let us go," the Prince replied. "We can use a warm meal and bed after all these nights in these mountains."

As they rode through the gates, both men looked to see how these huge stones were moved, but they could find no clue, no trace of machinery. The heavy portals closed behind them, and the two former mercenaries rode off into the quickening night with the men from the Order.

VI

Newcomers and Visitors

The boys sat nervously in the hall, some fidgeting, some talking with similarly anxious neighbors. They eagerly exchanged names and former homes, basically all the information that the more than twoscore newcomers had to tell one another. As they did so a babble of young voices filled the hall. They had all only arrived over the last several days, and this was their first chance to meet as a group.

Now, after their morning meal, they waited amidst the round stone pillars and large tapestries filled with bright mystic symbols and scenes from legend. The murmur they sent up filled the hall and grew, but dropped off all at once upon the entrance of a young man wearing the gray robes they had seen on nearly everyone since their arrival. The young man was of middle height and slim build, with red-brown hair cropped to neck length, and with deep-green eyes. He wore a pale-green medallion, his rank thus stated but still meaningless to the newcomers. He mounted the podium and scanned his new charges, an audience of boys ranging from late childhood to middle teens, varied in costume from richest gowns to poorest jerkins.

He cleared his voice, more for effect than for anything else. "My name is Elthwyn, and I am to be your Adjustor during your first months here. Let me begin by telling you how we, and you, came to be here.

"This is the Order, home and school for all the magicians, wizards and sorcerers of the world. We train new members, and rule over all who pass through these halls. We provide the rulers of the realms beyond the mountains with counselors, advisers and magickers. In addition, we have the grave responsibility of being the sole guardians of lore and learning in a world rent by constant warfare. Thus, while our members partake in the World, the Order itself remains above the strife that lies beyond the Gates. This above all has become our mission and our safety, for through this removal we have survived the civil war in what was the Great Empire, and the border wars of the North and the South.

"Let me ask a question," he said, surveying the varied faces and costumes before him. "How many of you are from the Northern Empire?" Hands rose timidly. "From the South? And from the Middle Empire? Well, from this day you are no longer to think of yourselves as Northerners, Vaduli, or the subjects of any other realm. From now on you are apprentices, Novices of the Order, and as such *this* is your home. I stress this as it is of the utmost importance, for in coming here you dedicate your life to learning and knowledge, which recognizes no borders and serves all men."

Despite his charges' evident restlessness, he went on. "You have all been selected because our members out in the World have perceived in you some talent for the arts we teach here. You will learn many, many things here, some which you will grasp readily, others which will at first escape you. When it has been decided that you have completed your training, you will begin your service. Some will remain here in the Order, others will be sent out into the realms. Some may not complete the training, but those who fall out will also be taken care of. Some of the greatest Scribes in the kingdoms were less fortunate Novices of the Order. Now, are there any questions?" A silence bred of unfamiliarity and the need for group acceptance prevailed. "Fine. Then you shall go and get your robes. We recognize no distinctions by birth here, and all dress and live alike. Some of you are the sons of great lords, others of you are poor farmers' sons. The Order sees only one distinction—the power and art of knowledge properly used."

Elthwyn the Adjustor stepped off the podium and opened the large double doors. A servant, dressed in brown jerkin and britches, entered. "Take them down to be fitted for their robes." He motioned to the boys to follow the servant.

They filed out, mostly silent, some talking furtively with partners. One or two of the better-dressed ones anxiously fingered their garments, while many of those poorly clad looked forward eagerly to the new clothes. Elthwyn stood by the doors until the last boy left and then exited himself and headed up the hall in the opposite direction.

Like every Novice, he had dreamed of the day when he might be an Adjustor, a recognized magician among his fellows. Now that day had come, and with it the expected exhilaration. But this elation was momentary as he walked along the gray stone gallery, and up the winding stairs, taking them two at a time. The feeling seemingly melted in the bright arced patches of sunlight which filled the arcade along the outer hallway. Soon it was gone entirely as he mounted another flight of stairs and turned the corner to stand before the half-open door.

Crispan leaned far out his bedroom window. He loved this time of year, when the snowcaps receded up the steep mountain slopes, when young falcons and hawks joined the hardy winter eagles in the brightening skies. You could feel it in the very air. He breathed deep and let the gentle wind tousle his light-brown hair and sway his purple amulet back and forth on his gold neck chain.

He felt himself smile as he looked down on the courtyard. There too was the bustle of new life as Novices scampered about in their new robes. Crispan watched them as they played tag, or pushed and shoved one another in innocent tests of strength. He wondered how soon it would be before they attempted other tests of strength, before they surreptitiously began to play the Game. He found himself smirking as he remembered his first challenges at the Game, and he could not suppress the smirk although he knew that the Game was frowned upon, that he would have to stop the students and admonish them whenever he found them misusing their new powers in this way. Yet he also recognized the irresistibility of the Game, the eagerness of the students to test and display their powers. How many times had he challenged or been challenged? How many students older and more advanced than himself had he bested? The Game was forbidden, but he remembered his victories with pride and that special satisfaction of having never been caught.

Watching the new students, Crispan thought back over all the other groups of Novices he had seen enter, back to the day some twenty years ago when he first entered the Order and donned the yellow talisman of the Novice.

A sudden flurry of wings snapped at the Magician's attention. Crispan was surprised to see a shiny black raven flying free over the Order. It could only be Gorham's, and Gorham kept his familiar on a close tether. The bird seemed to be lost momentarily, heading for Crispan's window before it realized its error and disappeared around the corner of the building towards its home in Gorham's chambers.

Then a new distraction arose to interrupt his musings over the changing seasons as Drisham, his servant, stuck his head inside the door of the inner chamber. "Master Elthwyn is here, sir."

Crispan nodded and moved towards his study, brushing back the hair from his deep-gray eyes as he went. He sat down at his desk and absentmindedly threw open a book and assumed a more studious mien, abandoning his reverie of spring. He braced himself for Elthwyn, knowing full well the student's purpose. After another deep breath and the creation of reflective wrinkles on his normally smooth brow, he signaled Drisham to admit Elthwyn.

The thin form of Crispan's favorite student entered, his pale-green amulet bright against his robes. Crispan motioned him to the chair opposite and waited for the Adept to begin. The student hesitated, fidgeting with the talisman. Finally he cleared his throat and began. "I've come to talk to you about my—er, my future."

"Yes?" Crispan tried to help him along and make this easier.

"It's my appointment. I'm not happy with it." Elthwyn let out a rush of air, having finally said it.

"Why? What's wrong with it?"

Elthwyn's eyes betrayed his anguish. "Vardimor is so far away, away from everything. It's on the very edge of the realms, like an exile. And I'm not even to serve in the capital. I'm to go to a border lord—in the west!"

His student's pride annoyed Crispan a little. His eyes wandered up and down over the familiar crowded shelves of books. "Even margraves," he said drily, "need magicians. Even lesser margraves. Where would you rather start, Elthwyn? Perhaps as adviser to one of the Emperors?"

Elthwyn was in turn piqued by Crispan's sarcasm. "What about Azimhar? He's only two years ahead of me and he's the Wizard of Rhaan-va-Mor."

"You know as well as I that Azimhar was posted as an assistant to Sule. Shall we send everyone to cities where the Magician is old, so that they may step forward when he dies? Azimhar was merely lucky, as you well know."

Elthwyn looked down at his hands. He spoke softly. "Yes, I know. What I would really like is to stay here in the Order."

Crispan shook his head slowly. "That you cannot do. You know that is not possible. No Adept can stay here upon receiving his Mastery. You must be sent to serve in the World. What reason would we have to exist if we did not go out and serve the worldly rulers with our knowledge and powers? How could we have survived all these years if we had not served those outside? No one can stay here after donning the deep-blue amulet. A man must improve and practice his arts through service before he can be recalled to impart them here. That has always been our practice and custom."

"You didn't."

Elthwyn's quiet words struck home. Crispan had never left the Order since the day of his arrival. He had gone from Adept to Master and had been told to stay in the Order, so great were his abilities. And he had become one of the Masters of the Five Arts at an age without precedent, younger even than Vladur or the legendary Tehr. Elthwyn, able as he was, was less talented than these Masters. He had had his problems with Thaumaturgy, and besides, there was no room for him in the Order at this time.

"I'm afraid there is nothing I can do. You cannot stay and there is no other post vacant. Would you rather go to Kyryl of Nor? I would not send you there." Crispan rose from his desk so as to end the interview. His pleasant and regular features sought to reassure the Adept. "Don't worry, Elthwyn, I shan't let you be forgotten out in the west. If the need arises I will recall you."

There was nothing more Elthwyn could do or say, and with great resignation he left Crispan's chambers.

Crispan remained at the edge of his desk for a moment, torn between the still-beckoning spring and his own duties. He let out a deep sigh and cleared his mind, preparatory to resuming his study of a complicated conjury which had eluded him the night before. "Drisham," he called out, "my vapors and potions, and several large vessels. And light some small candles as well."

Pale gray vied with crimson hues to gain the open air above the rim of the conjuror's pot. For a moment all the colors seemed to come together and hold, but then they dissipated into a not unpleasant design, but one without significance or meaning. Crispan sat back dejectedly, the conjury having failed again. Neither the *Ancient Conjuries and Manifestations* nor the massive *Conjura Magicka* were of any help, and the *Sacridi Conjurae Thaumaturgica* was as difficult to translate as the conjury was to perform. Still, there had to be an answer.

Crispan went back to Tehr's own notes on how he had twice performed the conjury before abandoning it as being worth less than the effort. But to know that it could be done annoyed Crispan. He wanted to accomplish it this day, but Tehr's procedure did not seem to work, and his own gray eyes were heavy with the smoke and vapors. He pushed the books and papers aside and made a mental note to consult with Eldwig after dinner. Perhaps the Master of Thaumaturgy could help.

Crispan rose to take a nap before dinner. He had just

reached the door to his bedroom when Drisham stuck his head in to announce, "Master Gorham, sir."

Gorham entered the room and sniffed at the somewhat acrid air. His sharp nose wrinkled up towards his other angular features, and his narrow eyes grew closer. "Working hard I see—or smell." He moved to the desk and gave a pained look when he saw the *Sacridi Conjurae Thaumaturgica.* "Oh no, not that dry tome." His familiar, the ebony raven, was perched on his shoulder; it croaked as if in echo, his sharp beak reflecting Gorham's own facial angularity.

"Nothing serious, Gorham. Just an odd conjury I've been toying with. Oh! I'm pleased to see your black friend. I saw him flying free this morning and thought he might have gotten away."

"Ris free this morning? No, no." Gorham seemed put off by the comment. Then he seemed to recover himself. "No, wait. You're right. He did slip off after breakfast, but he soon returned." Without stopping to allow this point to be further examined, he went right on. "But what I came here for was to tell you that Omir has called a meeting in his Council for before dinner."

Crispan was surprised. "Do you know why?"

Gorham shook his head. "No. But I presume it has something to do with the rumored visitors."

"Visitors?" echoed the younger magician.

"Shhh, Ris," his own visitor said to the chattering bird. "Yes, one of my Adepts said that Ulric arrived late last night with one or more men, and it could not have been the caravan as that arrived two days ago. That is all I know. But we shall find out more later."

"Yes." Crispan was intrigued by the news of the meeting and these mysterious visitors who came by night. "Thank you for telling me."

Gorham nodded and made a quick exit. As he entered the hallway he grimaced when he thought of Crispan's observation of Ris. Walking back to his chambers, he stroked the bird's breast. "No news there, Ris. Too bad. But at least he knows as little as we do, or so he lets on." The dark creature croaked affirmatively.

"Drisham, do you know anything about this?"

"No, sir."

Crispan was disappointed. If even the servants did not know, then who did? "Wake me in time for the meeting, please. And don't bother with the books and papers. But I will need a clean set of vessels for later."

VII

News from the World

Crispan entered the High Master's book-lined Council and saw that he was the last of the Masters of the Five Arts to arrive. He murmured an apology for being late and seated himself between Eliborg and Nujhir. As a servant closed the heavy oaken doors, Omir rose to address his colleagues. He stroked his fabulous long gray beard and, as was his custom, came right to the point.

"I have called a Council as we have important news from the World. The rumors we have received about the increased anarchy within the Middle Realm are unfortunately true." He sighed heavily. "It is difficult to imagine that after fifteen generations of incessant warfare this could be so, and yet it is.

"There now comes news that one of the two remaining Empires is moving against the other Empire, this time in great force, perhaps great enough to conquer all of the other realms beyond the mountains. I refer to the Empire of the North. Zhyjman II has been consolidating his domains and has now fully digested Tharn and Larc. He will soon move against Anrehenkar and the South. Should he succeed, I fear we would be endangered and eventually attacked in order to be brought under his sway as well."

Eliborg leaned forward and brushed his bald pate. "Are we sure that Zhyjman will move against us, or even that he will succeed? Surely the Empire of the South will be a more formidable opponent than was Tharn or Larc."

"Aye," interjected Gorham, "and what care we?"

"Because Zhyjman threatens the world balance," said Omir. "Ever since the fall of the Great Empire we have thrived. The Order has been the main source of all knowledge and learning. Our scholars and students have helped govern, and maintain what was left of civilized thought. And all this is now threatened."

"Be careful," Eliborg intoned, "lest you seem to argue in favor of anarchy for our own benefit. We have only served as the times have demanded."

"And they now demand our intervention against Zhyjman." With this Omir sat down heavily.

"Why?" asked old Nujhir. "It has always been our way to serve as individuals where we were needed, but never to act as an Order in the World, or to take sides in disputes or part in conflicts. Our neutrality has been our safeguard. To take sides would forfeit our privileged position and reduce us to base counselors and plotters. No, Omir, the safety of the Order demands our passivity. Should we come down out of the mountains we would be subject to the outcome, whoever wins. We must remain aloof and survive." Nujhir's was the voice of age and wisdom, for the old white-hair was the eldest Master at the Order.

Omir nodded at the truth of these statements but would not concede the point. "I think you underestimate Zhyjman. He has already taken Tharn and deposed the Duke of Larc. He has behind him the armies of Kyryl and Nor. And he catches the South at a bad time. I have news that the Emperor's heir is dead. His sole remaining son has been absent for some years. Eldwig, you know Zhyjman. Would he stop with the South? Would he not look across the mountains and seek to bring us under his sway as well?"

"When I knew him he was but a young prince—although cruel and grasping even then. You could be right."

Gorham snorted. "Bah! So he's not an ideal ruler. Still, the issue remains that the Order does not belong in the World as a force."

There were supporting murmurs from about the table. Servants began to move about the room, lighting candles against the dark and then withdrawing. Crispan was inclined to agree as well, and could sense that Omir had not carried the other Masters with him. He watched as Omir left his place and paced before the window, obscuring the dying rays of sunlight. The High Master wheeled suddenly and held the back of his chair, his knuckles white with tension. "There is one other problem. It is reported that Vladur is with the North!"

The Masters went silent to a man. They looked expectantly at Omir.

"Aye, the Renegade has made himself adviser to Zhyjman. He has continued his dark works, and we can be assured that *he* will move Zhyjman against the Order if the thought has not occurred to the Emperor himself."

"Are you sure of this?" asked Nujhir, aghast and trembling at the thought.

"As sure as we can be. He has lain low these two years while regaining his art, fearful of our actions. But now he feels safe and protected. His presence changes the issue, for Vladur is our responsibility. The Order taught him his art and nurtured his powers, and the Order failed to take the correct measures when we learned of his corruption. As long as Vladur remains with Zhyjman we must act, and most logically in concert with the South."

Eliborg then spoke. "This news is indeed staggering, and does change everything. But should we act with the Empire of the South, or should we not seek out the Renegade ourselves and destroy him? Does not our continued safety demand our continued neutrality?"

Again Omir sank into his chair, his fingers moving slowly along the table's edge. "I fear not. It appears that Vladur will first aid Zhyjman against Anrehenkar and the South and then turn against us. We should move with the South and hope to overthrow him before his protector grows overly strong."

Crispan pressed his hands together before him, still feeling the tension which arose at the mention of Vladur's name. "What do you propose?"

"That we send one of our own to join the South and aid them against the North and Vladur. This is all we can do if we are not to be subjected to Vladur's baseness. To use our own powers against Zhyjman directly would be a contradiction of our rules, as you all have said, and would indeed make us like the Renegade. Also, in sending only one man we can perhaps remain above the storm should events go against us."

Omir's plan did seem the only solution, especially as it seemingly maintained the neutrality of the Order while allowing them to act against Vladur and his benefactor. There was no voice raised to protest the scheme as each man remembered Vladur's hideous fall from the Order. There was but one question left, and that was raised by Gorham. "Who shall we send?"

"This I have given much thought," said Omir. "As High Master I should go, but I fear that I am no longer vigorous enough for a hard campaign. For the same reason our choice is limited to Eliborg, Crispan and yourself."

"I am honored," said Eliborg, "but I too do not feel up to a campaign."

"Yes," sighed Omir, "perhaps not. Then which of you will go?"

Gorham spoke first, before the question had barely passed the High Master's lips. "I shall be honest, Omir. I would be proud to carry out this task against Vladur, and shall accept if chosen. But I must admit that Crispan is probably more talented than I. Who else ever entered the Council so young, and who is better equipped to combat this foe? Who, indeed, succeeded Vladur as Master of Wizardry? For the sake of our own success I will gladly yield to him."

Even as Crispan's lips formed to sound a protest the High Master cut him off. "Your thoughts echo my own, Gorham. Crispan, you are our logical choice should we undertake this action, and I believe we must. But I shall leave this up to the Council to decide, for I alone cannot commit the Order to this. Surely, few decisions since we first sought refuge in these mountains have been so weighty."

To a man, they agreed on the need and the choice. Crispan did so as well, though as he voted and saw his face in the candles' reflection in the window he realized that his expression betrayed his hesitancy. Only the presence of the Renegade made him willing. He swallowed his disappointment and apprehension.

"Good. And now," Omir said as he moved to the door leading to his study, "let me introduce the harbingers of these tidings." He opened the door and two men entered the Council, warriors by their appearance, one thin, tall and handsome, the other large and strong. "Allow me to present Prince Mikal, Heir of Emperor Thurka of the South, and his companion, Lord Zoltan."

Both men bowed, and the thinner man, the one with the look of a regal hunting bird, stepped forward. "My lords, on behalf of my father I thank you for your support. Together we will right the balance that is now threatened by our common enemies." His own words surprised Mikal as the stiff formalities of learned protocol came back to him over the years.

Omir now went through the formalities as well, introducing each Master and his discipline—Eldwig of Thaumaturgy, Nujhir of Alchemy, Gorham of Sorcery, Eliborg of Astrology and Divination and Crispan of Wizardry. The Prince greeted them all and then sat down at the table with Zoltan beside him. As servants began to bring in dinner, Mikal amplified on the High Master's outline of recent events, adding what little he knew and answering what questions he could. To many he could only reply that he had been away from the South for some time and had seen little beyond his own service. Finally, as he speared a piece of fruit with his knife, Gorham asked the only question that really mattered to the men of the Order. "Are you sure that Vladur is with Zhyjman?"

Mikal's voice lowered somewhat. "No, I'm not sure. But as the High Master said, I have been away. My father's information indicates that Vladur is with the North."

This less than definite answer raised murmurs around the table. "It does not matter," said Omir. "Should he be there, Crispan must go and fight him. And if it becomes apparent that he is not there, then Crispan will return." This answer too was less than perfect, but had to suffice under the circumstances.

"The hour grows late," Omir continued, "and there are

still plans to be made. My lords," he said to Mikal and Zoltan, "my servant will show you to your chambers." Everyone withdrew from the table, the Masters to their respective studies to ponder these grave tidings, the two travelers to confer further with the High Master before retiring to the first bed they had known in many days.

VIII

Unpleasant Memories

Crispan lay in his bed, staring up into the darkness. Every time he closed his eyes he thought of tomorrow. Tomorrow he would ride down the sloping plateau and through the Gate of the Five-Sided Eye; tomorrow he would ride out of the Order. He had not left the Order since he had first entered as a Novice, save for occasional rides to the Gate to help fetch provisions. For over twenty years he had lived within these firm gray walls as Novice, Student, Adept and Master. His mind's eye rushed over those years, past Bellapon, Omir and Vladur, seeking out the more pleasant memories as if to cling to them and avoid the morrow. For some reason he dwelt unwillingly on his elevation from a newly confirmed Master to one of the six highest Masters in all three realms. Wyndholm, Master of Wizardry, was dead, and Vladur was occupying that chair as well as his own of Thaumaturgy. Crispan had the most remarkable record of any recent student, some said the best since Vladur's own extraordinary one of thirty years before, and the elder masters said it was probably better. Thus, with the vacancy caused by Wyndholm's passing, had Crispan gone from Master to Master of the Five Arts without ever serving in the World.

He rolled on his side and again tried to find elusive sleep. Now Vladur's long, thin face filled his mind. Crispan began to think about how much of his own life had been tied to that of the Renegade—his teacher, his colleague, the man who had betrayed his art and who had been exposed by Crispan, and the man who was now forcing him down out of the Order as well.

The knock at the outer door roused him easily. He jumped out of bed and passed through his study to the antechamber to find Omir standing in the dimly lit hall. "Did I wake you?"

Crispan shook his head. "No."

"I thought not. Can't sleep?" Omir passed by Crispan and went on into the study. He sat in the large chair in the corner, the one with the legs delicately carved like those of a gryphon. Crispan went around behind his still-cluttered desk. Omir pressed his fingers together in front of his bearded chin and waited for Crispan to begin.

After some moments Crispan did. "I'm not sure of this, Omir. I'm not sure of this at all, not sure that I should go or that we should take part. It's not our role. The Order has survived the chaos of the World by remaining above the squabbles of princes. To undertake this would leave our survival at the whim of war."

Omir drew a deep breath. "Yes. We've been through all of this before. But as I said this evening, Vladur is *our* problem. We must redress our mistake. That he is in the World and practicing his foul art is our fault. You know this—you unmasked him." The High Master could see that his arguments did not suffice to calm his young protégé. "There is something more that is bothering you."

Crispan became aware of the very heavy frown he was wearing. He nodded. "Vladur himself. He was my teacher."

"So was Bellapon, and so was I. And he was my companion in the arts. Will you let him betray us? I never told you this, but Vladur opposed your elevation to your chair, vehemently." Omir watched surprise supplant the frown. "Aye, he did. He wanted to keep both chairs for himself. Oh, he was proud of you all right, but only to a point. You threatened his own achievements here; I would say you surpassed his. Bellapon was right, you know, you are a born Magician. No one had ever become a Master at so young an age, or passed all his exams in the first attempt. Vladur, even Tehr, both took two years to achieve Mastery. Then, when I nominated you for Wyndholm's chair, Vladur objected. There were good arguments against it—you were just a new Master, you were young, you had never served in the World. This especially stuck.

The Order has always been against inbreeding. But what galled Vladur was your challenge to his preeminence as the most talented. He wanted to keep those two positions, to prove his superiority. We should have recognized his willful ambition then, before it was too late. Vladur was a driven man. And remember, too, that it was you who unmasked him and brought him down. For that alone Vladur is your sworn enemy.

"There is one other thing I must say tonight." Omir sighed, his voice growing grave and heavy. "While we may be more gifted than other men, even *our* powers are limited. Indeed, they may be more so than even you suspect. While we have refined our Art we have also removed it to a certain extent, greater or lesser, from the World which surrounds us and in which we are called upon to serve. This was the essence of the schism which led to the formation of Pyrin, as you well know. What you may not know is just where these limits lie, for you have spent all your life here within these walls. Your talents, great as they are, are untried in the World. Be careful when you are called upon to use your talents, both for the power they hold and for the limits which they have. I fear, Crispan, that these limits may come as something of a surprise to you. I trust and pray that you will know when these limits have been reached, but be prepared for them lest they take you unawares and impair your inner balance. I am sorry to have to tell you this now as I do not want to shake your confidence either in our learning or in your own considerable abilities. You *are* the one most fit to go out and combat the Renegade. Of that I am certain. But be aware of the limits on what we can do as practitioners of the Five Arts."

Crispan let the words sink in. At first he had wanted to jump up and blurt out a thousand questions, but his training taught him patience. If Omir said he would know when these limits were reached, then he would know, he hoped. And yet it was unsettling. This was more than a complex spell that would not form. There might be no time for experiment and renewed trial. It all added to his already considerable feelings of unease and unworthiness.

Omir sensed the young Master's inner doubts. "Crispan, I know that you have never left the Order. Perhaps that was a mistake. But you must go. Who is as young, who is as talented to face the Renegade? Believe me, Crispan, the mission is proper, and you are the logical choice. This mission is clearly yours. It will all still be here when you are finished, and you will have served your worldly mission. In fact, your going is our safety. The Order will go on without seeming to commit itself to either side. We shall be above the storm."

Omir's optimism was lost on the younger man. "Unless I fail," Crispan intoned, the words hurting as he spoke them.

"Ah, but that you must not do. Vladur will win if you stay here, and destroy us if you fail to destroy him."

"But what defense is there against necromancy?" asked Crispan, voicing near-helplessness.

Omir shook his head slowly and gravely. "I don't know. We shall all think, and work, and perhaps we can find an answer.

"I honestly feel," he said as he rose and crossed the book-lined room, "that you have the best chance of breaking Vladur. You *can* do it, Crispan." The High Master was standing over him now, and he lay his hands on his former pupil's shoulders. "You can." And you must, he thought, inwardly worried over the inexperience of this talented Master.

Crispan looked up and forced a meager smile which he hoped would pass for a look of confidence.

"Now for some sleep. Good night, Crispan." Omir let himself out and shut the door. Crispan sat a bit longer in the dark study and then returned to his bed to seek elusive sleep. Instead his mind wandered through the corridors of the past.

Crispan had been in his study, just rising from his desk to retire for the night, when Nujhir came in looking sickly white. His hands shook violently, and Crispan grabbed the older man by the shoulders and forced him to sit down.

"By the Spirits, man, what's the matter?"

Nujhir shook his head in disbelief. "I've just seen Tehr, Tehr himself, walking through the halls."

"What? Tehr has been dead for over sixty years."

Nujhir nodded slightly, his gray eyes remaining wide open and blank, unable to comprehend what he knew he had seen. "I know, I know. He died some time after I first came to the Order as a Novice. But I saw him tonight."

Crispan was torn between his own natural disbelief and his colleague's evident state. "Where did you see him?"

Nujhir straightened his robes as he composed himself, carefully sipping some wine that Crispan hastily offered. "I was going from Eliborg's chambers to my own, passing towards the stairs in the north tower. As I began to climb I heard a hideous low moan, and I went out of the stairwell. There he was in the hallway, slowly moving down the passage away from me. He turned towards me, a blank and mournful face, and then I panicked and ran. I passed your room first and saw the light under the door."

"Where exactly did you see him?"

"Near Vladur's chambers."

"Then let's go there and see for ourselves."

They hurried out of the study and down the moonlit hall, quickening their pace as they turned towards the north tower. They were nearing Vladur's chambers when Nujhir put his hand on Crispan's arm to slow him down. "There. I saw Tehr there," he pointed.

As they were almost at the threshold of Vladur's room a terrible stench rose into their nostrils, the smell of long-rotting decay. It filled them both with nausea as they moved to open the door. The stench was worse inside, where Vladur lay sprawled in a stupor across his desk. Crispan went to throw open a window and turned to Nujhir. "Go get Omir, quickly!"

Nujhir scurried out, and Crispan moved back and stood over Vladur's shoulder. He read the title of the book resting beneath Vladur's hand, Artis Necrómanci, *an ancient Southern text.*

Cool night air filled the room, and Vladur began to stir as it dissipated the foulness that had hovered tenaciously. Crispan moved around to the other side of the desk, just *beyond the candles' glow. Vladur raised his head and vaguely recognized Crispan. "Where is he?" Vladur blurted out, and then recovered himself. "I mean, where am I, what are you . . ."*

"It's no good, Vladur. You can't hide it. Nujhir saw Tehr. And the smell, and the book. You've been practicing it, haven't you?" Crispan's head sank, his chin almost touching his chest, as he contemplated his teacher's willful descent into the lowest depths.

"What do you mean? Why the look of pity?" Vladur's voice rasped contemptuously.

"Necromancy, Vladur. You've been practicing necromancy."

"What do you know of it?" Vladur became indignant. "What do you know? Yes, I've done so. For some time." His words came short and fast as his breath rose with excitement. "I've penetrated its secrets. Tehr was not my first conjuring. But he was too much for me to handle. His own genius struggled against my will, and I weakened and lost control. I must have passed out from the strain. But we needn't tell Omir. Listen, Crispan, this is a great and valuable art, one we must develop." His words flooded out in a torrent, and he jumped up and reached for Crispan as if to shake him.

Crispan stepped back, his face merely filled with greater horror and repugnance. The corruption so near to him frightened him. "You're mad, Vladur. You can't be allowed to continue this. It can only destroy you and the Order as well."

Vladur was about to answer when Omir entered behind him. "What's going on here? What's amiss, and what is that awful smell?"

Crispan spoke first. "Look at this," he said, passing the forbidden volume to the High Master.

Omir looked at it and then at Vladur, his face growing dark with anger and disgust. "Where did you get this?" Vladur stood quietly, having assumed a haughty pose, his angular features even sharper in the candle light. "Have you practiced this?" Again there was no answer.

"He has, Omir," said Nujhir. "I myself saw the great Tehr in the hall beyond these chambers."

Crispan echoed him. "It's true. He has admitted as much and more to me."

Omir was momentarily speechless. "This is quite serious. Summon some Adepts and have them take Vladur to my study. Crispan, summon the other Masters to meet at first light in the Council. Vladur, you have betrayed us all with this," he said, shaking the leather-bound text under the Necromancer's thin nose. "I am sick to think of what you have done."

Vladur still had not broken his proud silence, allowing only a contemptuous smile to pass his lips. Omir turned sharply and went off to his chambers to prepare for the imminent indictment of his fellow Master. No other High Master had ever faced such a problem, or so heinous a crime.

The two remaining Masters were awakened by an Adept and told to attend the meeting. No reason was given, and they were left to spend the last hours of darkness pondering the mystery, yet knowing the wisdom of keeping each to his own counsel.

As the cocks in the rear yard welcomed the sun's first rays, each of the Masters came into the Council. Crispan and Nujhir were the first ones there, looking tired and worn after the night's hardships. Gorham entered next and sat across from Crispan, soon followed into the room by Eliborg. A servant entered and drew back the curtains and then methodically snuffed out the candles between his moistened fingers. Pale smoke diffused with the similarly hued daylight. The servant tapped at the door to Omir's study, and the High Master entered, walking heavily, and sank into his carved chair at the head of the long oaken table. He spread his hands out along the table's edge and looked at each of the others. "It is with the greatest sadness that I call you here, and I apologize for the hour."

"Where is Vladur?" interrupted Gorham, his usually even voice a bit agitated.

Omir sighed, the air gently ruffling his long mous-

taches. "It is about Vladur that I called you." Faces looked anxiously back into his own. "No, Vladur is not dead, nor is he ill. The matter is far graver than that. Tonight Nujhir and Crispan discovered Vladur practicing," and here he shuddered noticeably, "necromancy."

The other Masters looked at each other and at Omir in disbelief. Omir sank back in his chair and beckoned towards Nujhir. "Tell us what passed last night."

Nujhir first, and then Crispan, recited the night's events. As they spoke the others looked on incredulously, hardly believing that such a thing could occur. When they were done the room was blanketed with a pregnant silence. Gorham was the first to break it. "Should we not hear from Vladur, so that he may defend himself?" Omir nodded wearily, and Crispan went to the door and opened it. In came Vladur, flanked by two Adepts, one of them being Elthwyn.

The trio remained standing near the head of the table, on Omir's right. Eliborg, with his customary bluntness, put the question straight to Vladur. "Is this story true?"

Vladur was disingenuous. "What story? I have been detained elsewhere, as you can see."

Eliborg was annoyed by this. His tone expressed it. "Did you practice necromancy?"

Vladur looked around the long table, looking each man in the eyes, although he avoided Crispan and Nujhir. Then, throwing back his angular head and thrusting out his stiff, pointed beard, he spat out his answer. "Yes."

The remaining Masters were shocked. To be accused of such a crime and to blatantly confess—there was no precedent for such a thing. Eliborg recovered first, and said in a low, sad voice, "Then there is nothing for us to do. The consequences are clear." His colleagues nodded gravely, each struck silent by the revelation of this foulness.

Vladur stood completely still, unmoved by the condemnation of his peers. "Wait before you pass judgment. Hear me out and let me explain what I have done."

He shook his head to move strands of his long gray and black hair from his face, and then drew in a deep breath.

"I stand accused of practicing necromancy, and I confess to this. Yet why is this considered a crime? Why do we accept this limitation on our powers? It is not natural for us to do so, and I, working surreptitiously, have done much to bridge this gap in our knowledge."

Vladur's eyes began to glow now as they had when he had tried to gain Crispan's support the night before. Their sudden liveliness reflected the relish with which he explained himself. "With books secretly acquired from throughout the three realms and beyond I have learned this art. I feel we must all practice it and add it to our other arts. Imagine our power if we could call upon our predecessors and cull their knowledge. Our ease with an unlimited source of laborers. All of this and more is possible. What I have done is merely a beginning.

"If we do not pursue this we condemn ourselves to stagnation. This is the time to open new paths of knowledge. I am guilty of no crime save the pursuit of even greater knowledge for us all." His entire face was alive with energy and excitement as he finished.

Shock was the only reaction to this mad outburst. Almost to a man the Masters sat with jaws agape. The practice of necromancy, then the confession, but now an impassioned defense of the crime! Seething with indignation at this madness, Omir rose to silence the fallen magician and to pronounce the necessary sentence. The initial feeling of shock subsided in Omir's expression and was replaced by one of deepest disgust, as if he had been brought too near to something putrid and contagious.

"When the High Spirits created man they honored him above all other creatures—they gave him speech, the ability to build and better his life, and the power of thought and knowledge. But here they stopped, lest they give man too much and make him indolent in his everyday life and at the same time envious of the Spirits themselves. And yet they granted to some of man, through long years of study, the power to go beyond the Spirits' original gifts. These men, the magicians and wizards, were allowed to pierce the veil erected by the Spirits above. But there was one veil which the Spirits would not

77

let man rend—the veil of death. To remind man—all man—of his lesser position, he was made subject to death. To go beyond this, to invoke the dead in our arts, and most especially to raise them, is to court the wrath of the All Highest."

Then Omir turned and looked directly at Vladur. "And it is of this crime—the highest and worst that any man, but most especially a Master of the Five Arts, can commit—it is of this crime that you have been accused and to which you have willfully confessed. I honestly tremble over that which you have done and that which you must suffer." With a flick of his wrist he said, "Remove the prisoner."

Sunlight was pouring into the Council, adding to the warmth reflected by the deep-red drapes, but few noticed it. After Vladur was removed, Omir turned back to the others and continued.

"Our laws are clear. There can be no discussion on this. It is only a question of how we shall carry out the execution."

All the Masters had known from the moment of his confession that this would be Vladur's fate, and yet this sudden and blunt pronouncement still came almost as a surprise. "To have lived this long, only to see the Order debased like this," muttered Nujhir. "Never have I heard of such a thing befalling the Order. Never."

It was Eliborg who reminded them that there was a prescribed method of execution, and he went on to describe the terrible ceremony that must follow. Then he asked, "Who shall carry out the sentence?"

Omir sighed mightily. "I will take the responsibility. I am the High Master."

"Surely there is another way," said Gorham; "a punishment worse than death."

"What?" asked the High Master. "Our laws are firm on this above all else."

"Deprive him of his art and books, his notes. Everything. Then let us exile him to the World. Let every member of the Order be told that he is outcast, and is not to *receive any assistance. Who would possibly take him in? How could he practice his arts then? Let him eke out a miserable existence, cut off from all he has known since his youth, shunned by all—especially those of the Order. Surely this would be a far greater punishment than a quick death."*

The night's events had all been so sudden that the Masters had not had enough time to fully comprehend the depths of Vladur's degradation and depravity. Instead they still clung to their thoughts of him as their colleague and peer, and now were only too eager to avoid the final dread punishment. Everyone agreed to Gorham's plan with alacrity, everyone but Omir. The High Master continued to express some lingering hesitation. "Our laws are firm," he repeated. "There can be no deviation." Yet even his voice carried a note of uncertainty.

"Could we not do as Gorham suggests, perhaps in view of all Vladur contributed to our knowledge before he descended to his debasement?" Crispan also was eager to save his fallen teacher. Eliborg supported him.

"After all," added Nujhir, "as far as we know, the sentence has never been carried out before."

"Of course not," said Omir. "Neither has anyone been accused of so heinous an act."

"Then we will not be breaking any precedent." Gorham was still hopeful for his alternative. "Instead we shall establish this punishment, and I still contend it is a far greater one."

Omir sat down wearily. "I cannot decide this alone. Let us vote. Who supports Gorham's idea of exile?" Each of the remaining Masters voted for exile, their hands rising warily from the table. "Then it is done. But the sentence must be carried out tonight."

Gorham seemed to want to speak again, but then sat back as if thinking better of it.

Vladur was brought back into the Council, still glowering fiercely at his accusers. His eyes still burned in their sockets, his chin remained raised at a haughty angle, jutting his beard out towards the others.

The High Master now stood stiff and erect at the head

of the great oaken table. "I will be brief, Vladur. It has been decided that you deserve a greater punishment than a swift death. Tonight all your books, notes and vessels will be burned. You will be escorted to the Gate of the Eye and sent out from the Order. Every member of the Order in the World will be told to shun your company. You will be anathema to us all. None will give you any help or even basic comforts. You are banned forever from our companionship and our arts. You will live out your days exiled from all you have lived by. Such is our decision."

The fallen Master remained unmoved by the sentence. His stance did not vary, his face betrayed no emotion beyond his continuing haughtiness. Omir moved around the table and stood before Vladur. Tired after this long ordeal, he wearily reached out and removed the necromancer's purple amulet and brought it back to the table before his chair, placing it on a silver plate that a servant had brought in. From the ornately carved chest behind him he took up the ceremonial mace of his office, wondrously decorated in gold with mystic symbols. With a sudden swift stroke he brought the mace crashing down on the talisman. Everyone in the room, including Vladur, jumped at the sound and the shower of gold and broken stone. Omir stood staring at the shattered remains. Not altering his gaze, he waved his right hand towards the prisoner. "The sentence is pronounced. Remove him until his departure."

Again Vladur was taken to Omir's study. The High Master turned to Crispan. "Send some Adepts to Vladur's chambers. Have them remove all his books and notes and implements and all else. Pile them in the courtyard."

A stiff breeze blew across the yard that night. Omir and the remaining Masters stood before the mound that had been deposited there. Servants carrying long pikes for stoking and flasks of oil hovered nearby. The High Master, his long gray beard whipping in the wind, motioned to them. At this command they tossed the flasks onto the pile, shattering them and spilling the bright, slimy contents. Omir raised his head skyward and held out

Vladur's main text, the Artis Necromanci. *Eliborg passed him a small lit brand.*

"We have been defiled by the worst of all crimes that a member of the Order can commit. Let his fate be a lesson to all who would dare transgress the limits which even we of greater knowledge must admit to." *So saying, Omir passed the forbidden volume through the brand several times until it ignited. As it did he threw the burning tome onto the pile, and the torch after it.*

A great whoosh went up as Vladur's belongings were engulfed in the bursting conflagration. Everyone instinctively stepped back as heat issued from the pyre. With the flames as a signal, Elthwyn and three other Adepts brought Vladur out of the main building. His hands still bound, he was helped into his saddle, and three days' rations in a haversack were slung over the pommel. The sound of clattering hooves joined the whistling wind and roaring flames about the yard.

The exile, his gray-streaked hair blowing wildly, could see the Masters standing in a small line before the fire far across the yard. Like bronze statues they remained motionless. He could feel their gazes penetrating the growing column of sparks and boring into him.

The Masters watched the small procession across the yard. Still there was no sign of repentance or regret in Vladur. His figure remained proud and erect as he was escorted to the wall that bounded the Order's buildings. Moving with easy grace with his horse's motions, he looked straight ahead, never glancing back at the figures and fire to his left once he was in motion towards the gate. The procession was soon swallowed up in the darkness beyond the open gate which even the light from the roaring pyre could not penetrate.

No one moved from before the fire as the exile and the Adepts disappeared from view. All turned back to the fire before them. Crispan opened his cloak as the heat continued to issue forth. A column of smoke and sparks now rose high above all the buildings, fleeing skywards to be borne away on the racing wind. All the yard was bathed in a bright orange glow. Crispan glanced up at the suddenly bright facade of the main building and saw the faces of all the students and servants filling the windows, the flames reflected on the glass and in their eyes.

He turned back to the pyre and looked to Omir, who was now performing the ceremonies necessary to destroy the remnants of the crushed talisman and to seal Vladur's fall. The light betrayed the pain written deeply on the High Master's face, but his expression was resolute. He had aged perceptibly over the past day.

And so they all remained until the final embers flickered and died amidst the competing light of a new dawn.

IX

Through the Great Mountains

It all seemed a dream. Somewhere night had given way to earliest, palest dawn, and Crispan could not remember sleep ever having intervened. He could barely remember getting out of bed and moving softly about his chambers, choosing a few precious books out of the multitude lining the walls. So much to choose from, to touch at least once before departing. And now he was standing at the foot of the great hall, before the ancient doors. He was absolutely alone, listening to the comforting silence of the Order asleep. And then he was outside of the warm stones and in the cold morning air.

The surrounding bowl of mountains was gray and pink under a mantle of morning mist. Crispan sighed as he gazed about him. He shrugged and walked down the stairs to the waiting mount and the two warriors. Zoltan was sitting back in his saddle, yawning mightily. He shook out another yawn and said, "Good morning." Crispan nodded in reply and swung into his saddle.

"Ready?" asked Mikal. Crispan nodded again.

"No one to see us off? No good-byes?" Zoltan's questions went unanswered. Crispan led the way down the yard. Omir had thought it best that no one see Crispan leave. It would be easier for Crispan, and would support the idea that somehow the Order itself was still above the petty wars beyond. And yet the painful irony struck Crispan that Vladur had been seen off by the entire Order, while he was forced to ride off alone. As he rode he glanced around to where he knew the High Master's windows to be. As Crispan had hoped, Omir was standing there.

Down to the courtyard to the gate in the surrounding

wall, and out to the narrow mountain track leading to the outer gate cut into the living stone. The chill of early morning hung tenaciously that high in the mountains. The riders drew their cloaks tighter as they went. Twisting and turning past the cold stone hulks, they picked their way down out of the Great Mountains towards the sprawling plain to the west. With every cautious step of his horse Crispan felt himself being torn away from all that had filled his life.

He did not quite understand his feelings as he later passed under the Five-Sided Eye carved into the mountain. He, like all the other Novices, had been down to the Entry as one of his chores, to help the supply caravans up into the Order. But he had never crossed out from under the Eye. He had helped swing open the groaning stone doors and greet the welcome traders, but he had always stayed within the bounds of the Order. Now he knew that he was truly going into the World and leaving the sanctuary of the Order behind. The trancelike dream that he had moved in since first awakening dissolved as he saw the Eye for the first time in so many years. He was, he realized, unique in the annals of the Order. One of the youngest Masters ever, he was now the first to undertake his first appointment beyond the mountains as a Master of the Five Arts. He looked back, hoping to see the Eye once more, but the twisting path had already taken it from view.

They spent cold nights and chill days in the Great Mountains, edging down the widening path in the light and huddling in protective coves in the dark. The journey was made no easier by conversation, for there was little. Mikal and Zoltan felt constrained by the presence of a stranger. The Magician felt himself to be lost and alone. He had nothing in common with these men, and he felt oddly unprepared to meet the task before him. If Vladur was out there, would his own powers be enough? Worse yet, what if Vladur was not there? What would he do then? He would be even more helpless.

The feeling hung over the Magician all the next morning, as oppressive as a burden on his back. Once he even shook his shoulders involuntarily as if to ease the burden. His fingers slipped down again and again on his right side, gingerly fingering the hilt of the sword Omir had given him. He ran his thumb and forefinger round and round the large knob that would stick out below his palm should he ever actually wield the weapon, then down the actual hilt, letting his thumb catch in the ring carved there, and then past the crossbar of the hilt until he reached the scabbard, where his fingers instinctively withdrew. Again and again his fingers involuntarily made the journey as he rode, and each time the feeling that oppressed him grew heavier. Now it began to build inside him, pressing against his middle, climbing spasmodically up to his gullet, until it jammed uncomfortably at the top of his throat. The further down the mountain they rode, the greater the feeling grew. Time and again, more quickly now, his hand ran down the hilt. The spasm inside him came more quickly now. Then his hand clutched convulsively around the hilt and pulled.

The scraping sound of a sword being bared made both his companions jump. Zoltan, his hand now on his blade as well, drew his horse up short. "What is it, man?"

Crispan looked down at the blade that was somehow attached to his hand. He looked at it blankly, and then at Zoltan and Mikal in turn. "This sword," he said, "I don't know how to use it." The two warriors looked at each other, perhaps a bit surprised. Mikal broke the short, embarrassing silence.

"You don't? I thought every man . . ."

Zoltan intervened with his customary bluffness. "By the Spirits! If that's all, we can teach you. A little training in the morning and a little at night. We can fix that."

Crispan smiled weakly and resheathed his blade. The pressure inside him eased as their horses started on again. But soon the feeling on his shoulders returned, seemingly leaping up behind him and clambering over his horse's back onto his own. The fears from that last night in the Order returned. He suddenly felt as if he were entering a huge and unfamiliar room, some place where he did not

85

know where anything was or where anything belonged. In the Order everything made sense to him, he was in command of his life and its surroundings. But out here it was different. Surely he would not feel this way if he were going out as an adviser to some lord. At least then he would be practicing his Art. But here he was going more as a weapon for a great warlord, a weapon with one purpose only, perhaps for a purpose that was either unnecessary or entirely wrong. He had been asked to cut adrift from all that had ever made sense to him and work for something that seemed elusive at best and infinitely wrong at worst.

The path grew wider and the air warmer as they descended towards the plain to the west. The stones were rounder and threw less menacing profiles against the sky. The patches of snow were fewer, but even more had already melted down and run into hollows carved by thaws beyond count over the myriad years. Everything pointed to their emergence from the Great Mountains. Zoltan had even seen a bird overhead the day before, not a mountain eagle but a crow or raven circling from the east. By now the path was wide enough for them to ride abreast, and this plus the days together promoted some small conversation. Crispan did most of the listening, to Zoltan's tales of glorious conquests off and on the field, and to what little Mikal knew of the situation they were riding towards. It was this conversation which brought to a close what was to be their last night within the safety of the Great Mountains.

They reached the inward side of the Eastgate while there was still some daylight. "Best we camp here tonight, where we can't be seen," Mikal said, thinking of the looming Sentinel on the plain beyond. "We must rest early and ride early. After tonight there'll be little time for rest and too much risk for warming fires."

"Aye," Zoltan added, "or for sword practice either. So set to, Crispan!"

While Mikal lit a fire, his companion and the Magician went at each other with their blades.

"My eyes, Crispan! My eyes! You'll see my blade anyway, even in the murky night. But my eyes will tell you where I intend to put it." As they swung at each other, Zoltan shouted and repeated his instructions. "And you! Don't tell me where you're going with your blade. Note your opening without staring at it!"

Crispan swung back and forth, heaving his arm up and down, although with less effort than on previous days. He could not tell whether he was looking for his chance or merely fighting for his life. Then, for an instant, he felt that Zoltan was vulnerable on his side. His eyes narrowing, his arm aching, he lunged. The better reflexes of the big mercenary barely saved him from the swipe. "Enough, enough! By the Spirits, that was close!" Zoltan took a step back. "You know, a lesser man would be bleeding all over these rocks."

Mikal inquired after the student's progress. "Not bad," Zoltan said. Crispan was crestfallen. "Well, you're no great warrior yet, Crispan. But I'd be willing to have you defending my back!" It was a very high compliment from a soldier, and Crispan accepted it as such.

X

The Meaning of Magic

They ate well that night, making the most of the fire. Crispan huddled into its warmth and thought back to his last trip across the plain and the Great Mountains. His thoughts took him far to the west to a village he had left so many years ago. He thought now of his family and wondered how they had fared over the years, who was left, did any still live where they had when he had left them?

His father was a burly man named Otho who ran the inn at the small village some six days north of the Vadul border, in the midst of the wreckage of the Great Empire. Life was quiet there, the land having been sacked and plundered countless times since the Empire first came tumbling down. Now the people eked out a bare existence from a land too worn to be more responsive to their efforts.

Otho did better than some, making most of his money from neighbors who dropped by at night, plus an occasional soldier or two passing through to join some mercenary army or other.

Around Crispan's eleventh year a more interesting traveler stopped at the inn. Crispan first saw him from a room on the second floor that he had been cleaning. The traveler was a remarkably tall man, thin, with a shiny shaved head and a beautiful flowing gray beard. Crispan noted that he was well dressed, at least compared to the usual wayfarer, and the boy fixed his glance immediately on the awesome lavender medallion around the traveler's neck.

Crispan dropped his broom and scurried downstairs,

ostensibly to help the traveler unpack and enter the inn, but actually for a better look. His father and two younger brothers were already so engaged, and were taking in the last of many bundles when Crispan saw the small book that had fallen unnoticed and been left behind. He grabbed it up and looked to see if he had been observed. Secure, he glanced at the cover, where the gold letters said The Magicker's Elementaries. This was the first new book he had seen in over four years, the only new book that would ever be added to the family's present dozen, which had all been taken from the belongings of a passing scholar who had died at the inn before having paid his bill.

Crispan clutched it greedily and, again making sure he was not observed, made haste for the cellar. He read the book for the rest of the afternoon, seated comfortably amidst sacks of flour, tenderly turning the smooth pages within the worn leather cover. Only when he saw how much he had read did he realize that he was late in helping serve dinner. As he was about to go upstairs he realized that this new treasure would have to be hidden. Crispan thought first of putting it behind the sacks of flour, but then worried that some wayward mouse might nibble at it. Instead he clambered up on top of some barrels of ale and hid the book behind the already disturbed tankards stored on the shelf above. Before laying it away he reread the name. The Magicker's Elementaries. What a wondrous title!

Otho saw him as he sneaked back into the kitchen. "Yer late. Where've you been, out to the river with yer friends?"

"No. I've been down below. I was—er, cleaning up and I ended up napping on the flour and grain sacks."

"Ha! You'll never be a worker, that's fer sure. Never mind. Here, take this out to the new visitor." Otho's heavy arms thrust a wooden tray at the boy as he shoved him towards the door leading from the kitchen to the main room. Dinner consisted of some beef and thin soup, along with bread and a little lard to spread upon it.

Crispan crossed the room nervously and put the tray

on the well-stained table, turning quickly back towards the kitchen. But he was frozen in his steps by the traveler's summons. "Come here, boy."

Crispan turned hesitantly. "Sir?" His voice wavered.

The traveler shook his voluminous beard as he asked, "How was the book, boy?" His voice was inquisitive but friendly.

"Book, sir?"

"Yes. I dropped one coming in today. Did you enjoy it, or rather, can you read?"

"Why, why yes. I can read."

The man's eyes sparkled ever so slightly. "And how was the book?"

Crispan's young face grew serious, having been apprehensive. "Well, it was interesting. I mean, I could understand how it worked, but parts of it weren't easy to follow. But I did see how it all worked. I even—" He swallowed his last words.

The traveler leaned forward. "You even what? What did you do?"

"Nothing, sir, nothing. I could just see how it worked. I mean that if you can really believe in it all, it will work."

The traveler was surprised, but again he drove on. "Yes, yes. But what did you do?" He grabbed the boy's arm for a moment and then apologetically withdrew.

The motion shocked Crispan, and he blurted out, "The rat. I saw a rat." The traveler passed his tankard to the boy to calm him.

"Steady, lad. I shan't hurt you. Now, what about this rat?"

Crispan swallowed and wiped the ale's foam from his lips. "Well, I was reading in the store room below when I saw this rat. We've lots of 'em, I guess, especially with all the food down there. Well, I was reading about presti-, er, presti-" He struggled with the word.

"Prestidigitation."

"Yes, and levitation. And I tried it on the rat."

"You did? What happened?" The traveler's eyebrows were arched with anticipation.

"Well, I raised him up all right, but I couldn't get him down again. I'm sorry."

The traveler laughed, his eyes twinkling again. "By the Spirits! What did you do with him?"

"I couldn't leave him floating there, sir, so I trapped him in an empty tankard and hid him."

"Ha! Marvelous! Boy, er—what's your name?"

"Crispan."

"Boy, take me to this rat." His eyes were aglow with mirth.

But Crispan protested, saying he could not lead him through the kitchen and past his father. "If you'd go around outside I'll open the door to the back stairway and lead you down."

The traveler agreed and wheeled from the table, and was out the door in a moment.

Crispan went back through the kitchen and skulked past his father. Upon reaching the rear door he ventured his head out and nearly shoved his nose into the traveler's robes. Crispan motioned him to be silent and led him down the stairs, carrying a large candle. Once in the cellar he headed over to the barrels of ale and scrambled up to the shelf. "Here it is." The boy pointed to a row of tankards neatly stacked one upon another. "Lift the end one."

Crispan withdrew as the traveler leaned forward. He lifted the tankard, and a cellar rat floated up from beneath it.

"Ha ha! Fabulous! Unbelievable! No, it's a sign, boy, as sure as my name is Bellapon. Why, this is fantastic!"

"You're not mad?"

"Mad? Not at all. What's your name again?"

"Crispan."

"Yes, of course. I must talk to your parents. Ha ha! Marvelous!" Bellapon gingerly replaced the rat and the tankard. "Come, we must see your parents."

They came up through the kitchen now, and Otho saw them emerge and his dark eyes narrowed. "What's this? What've you been up to? Not enough food on yer tray?" He reached for a cleaver as he spoke.

92

Bellapon stepped forward a bit, shaking dust from the folds of his gown. "No, no, my good sir, you don't understand. I was . . ."

"Did the boy show you the way?" growled Otho. "I know how to handle thieves."

As his father stepped forward, Crispan stepped in front of the traveler. "No! We weren't stealing."

Crispan's mother entered at the sound and saw the three frozen figures. "What's going on here? Otho! Put down that cleaver."

"They were thieving in the cellar," he explained. "Your son led him down."

Bellapon raised his hand in protest. "My good sir, you don't understand. We were merely . . . merely, well, talking. You have a bright lad here, and I'd like to take him with me on the morrow."

"Oh! So you're a slaver then." Again Otho reached for the cleaver.

"No, no, no. You still do not understand. Let me explain. My name is Bellapon, and I am a member of the Order, a Master of the Five Arts." Otho's bearded face still showed no sign of recognition. "I, sir, am a Magician, a Wizard, and I would like to train your son to be one. I have reason to believe he has extraordinary talent for our Arts."

Otho's eyes betrayed his skepticism. "I've barely enough here for us all to live on. I can't pay for him to be apprenticed. He'll be an innkeeper, like his father."

"Please, sir. We will not charge you a fee to train him. I will merely take him with me."

Otho obviously began to warm to the idea, while his wife dwelt on Bellapon's last remark. "Take him with you? For how long?"

"For quite some time. Perhaps ten years, probably longer. It takes time to train a proper Magician."

"That long? Otho, we can't let Crispan go for that long."

"Why not?" Otho was thinking of the prospect of free schooling for his eldest son, and of one less mouth to

feed. "He'll never be a proper innkeeper. He's a dreamer. I say let him go."

Crispan's mother sat on the one stool in the kitchen. "Perhaps. But for so long?"

Bellapon interrupted. "The boy is bright, too bright to be an innkeeper—"

"What's wrong with that?" growled Otho.

"Nothing, sir, nothing. But as you yourself said, he'd never be good at it. Why, he'd probably ruin your inn. Let him come with me. I'll see that he keeps in touch with you as best as the times allow."

Crispan's mother looked at her husband doubtfully. Otho's face answered affirmatively. She turned to her son. "What about you, Crispan? Would you like to go?"

Through all of this Crispan had had little time to really think about it. He looked at Bellapon, and thought of the rat floating in the cellar. He then looked to the door and saw one of his brothers come in laden with dirty trays and exit with some full tankards. "Yes, yes. I'd like to go. Can I?"

Bellapon rubbed his hands together. "Well then, it's settled. We leave tomorrow, for I must meet my escort, a caravan, in four days near the Southern border." Bellapon beamed down at his new pupil.

As Bellapon had said, they departed that next morning. Crispan's father was already doing his chores and setting the remaining children about theirs. His mother collected what clothing he could call his own and stuffed some food into his haversack. And then it was time. Bellapon was already mounted, merely waiting to put the boy before him in the saddle. His mother called her husband and the children out into the yard. Before they came she offered what little advice she could. "Be good, Crispan." She kissed his forehead.

Otho emerged from the inn. "Are you ready? Well then, best be going. And remember, mind what he tells you." The innkeeper turned to Bellapon. "He'd never make an innkeeper. But he's a good boy. Look after *him."* Then he suddenly hugged his son and lifted him onto the horse.

Bellapon knew when it was best to go and that time was now, before it became worse for all. He jerked the reins and set out, offering the family a warm "Goodbye!"

They rode long and hard that day, Bellapon talking all the while, cramming Crispan's head with all sorts of knowledge. Spells, enchantments, conjurings; and basic things like arithmetic and spelling. But best of all were Bellapon's stories about places he had been and wizardry he had done. They rode long and hard that day, and Crispan did not realize how far he was going or had come.

In their encampment that night Crispan stared into the warming fire and then followed a column of smoke with his eyes as it rose to join the clouds in the swiftly driven night sky. The sky had never appeared so to Crispan, so alive, so deep, so mysterious, so beckoning. He was aware of every movement above him, and the personality of each of the actors—the giddy, wispy clouds, the beautiful, proud stars, the warm, protecting moon. There was a life above him he had never realized before. Through the wonder and contentment that filled him came the reason, and that was Magic.

"Is it true, Bellapon, that the stars are the shining beauty of Spirits and Heroes?"

The Wizard smiled. "Who told you that?"

"My mother. She sometimes takes us out and tells us stories and says that they are now written in the stars as proof that they happened, for all to see."

Bellapon's gray-bearded face radiated as much warmth as the fire. "And what stories did she tell you?"

"There!" Crispan said, pointing to one group of stars. "About the Hunter who died for the love of the Maid. Do you see them? They come up and circle the moon and fade away each year, and she is always just beyond him. Mother says they find each other when they slip away out of sight, but get separated again midst the other stars and have to find each other again each year. And there, Jivir the Warrior, and Rosinfar the Dragon. Do you see them all?"

The boy's wonder and excitement pleased Bellapon. "Yes, I know them well. But there are other ways to see the stars. They are guides to the traveler."

"Oh, I know that," Crispan said proudly. "I know how to walk with Rosinfar to my left and Bronas the Falcon to my right."

"Yes, but there are other ways to see them beyond even these. A trained eye can read messages about days to come from the stars. They're tricky, and have to be carefully plucked like ripe fruit on a cluttered tree, but the trained Magician can do it."

Crispan's eyes went wide. "Can you do it, Bellapon?"

The Wizard gave a small shrug. "Yes, but not as well as some others. It's always been one of my weaker Arts. But here, look. When were you born?"

"In the sign of the Open Eye."

"Of course. I should have known. You see, that tells me something already. Many Magicians are born under that sign. Do you know exactly when, Crispan?"

"Near the end, I think. Only a few days from the Sword."

Bellapon looked a bit perplexed. "That is most curious. Most are born nearer to the Torch. You see, each represents a life. The Open Eye means the greater sight of the Magician, the Torch the greater light of the Priests, the Sword the Warrior. Magicians and Priests were almost the same once, even down to the last days of the Middle Empire. But like so many things, that close relationship fell when the Empire died."

"What do the other signs mean, the Eagle, the Horse, all the others?"

"The Eagle represents Kings, the Horse the farmers and peasants, the Plume the scribes and scholars, the Closed Eye those the Spirits have missed during their rest in the winter, the Crow vagabonds, and the Orb the Spirits themselves."

"And each one tells what a man will be?"

"Oh no!" Bellapon laughed. "It's not all that easy, or

*exact. I knew of a man once who was born right in the
midst of the Sword who was killed in his first battle, and
a man of the Closed Eye who lived to be rich and happy.
No, Crispan, they are only guides, like those in the desert.
Do you know what a desert is?" The boy shook his head.
"Well, imagine that all of the land as far as you could
see or ride was like the sand along a river, only there
were no rivers, or any water at all, only sand. That is a
desert, and men sometimes put guideposts there only to
have them covered as the sands move before the winds.
The signs of birth are like that, sometimes buried and
hard to read. They are only there to point the way sometimes, when the sand has not obscured them."*

"What about me, and my sign?" asked the boy eagerly.

"Well, as I said, many Magicians are born in your
sign. But so close to the Sword?" Bellapon's eyebrows
rose as he lapsed into silent thought.

The boy's eyes were huge with excitement. "Will I
learn to do that? To read the stars and to see ahead?"

"Oh yes. We call it Astrology, or Divination. It is one
of the Five Arts you will be taught. But you must not
plunge ahead so. There are other things to understand
first. From what you did at the inn I would say you will
be strongest in Wizardry. But tell me, do you know why
it worked?"

"Not exactly. But the book—the book said that if there
was no real reason why something couldn't be, then it
could be. And if you wanted it to be, then you only had
to find where it was, for the possible is always there." His
words grew hesitant, for he really did not understand
what he had done or why it had worked, only that it
seemed possible.

"Yes, Crispan. But I don't think you have really
grasped it yet. And still, there are more important things
to learn first. Before you learn the Magic you must learn
why you learn. You must learn why the Order exists.

"We represent, we are what is left of the wreckage of
the peace that was once with the Great Empire. While it
existed there was both peace and order in the World, and
men found other uses for their minds and hands than

war and battle. Oh, there were wars, and always will be, but man was always able to remember the other, better way to live. And we Magicians protected, nurtured that way, and helped it grow. We were the men who saw the new ways first and helped guide the others to it. It was easy, so long as peace prevailed, for men to travel and exchange ideas. As long as the three Empires survived, the balance of the World survived and much was possible.

"But," Bellapon continued, "when Palamir VI died without a direct heir, and when the Empire tore asunder as the distant branch of his family, the Tourides, fought their cousins the Roda-Tourides, and neither side would yield, all was lost. Why should one distant cousin rule in place of another? And if neither branch would do, could not any newcomer, be he courtier or general or thief, seize the great prize? It was an awful time, when fine cities were laid waste, when trade strangled to death at the hands of rapacious armies, when the Spirits themselves shook as the World below seemed about to crumble.

"So little survived that fall intact. Oh, the two remaining Empires enlarged themselves, gorging their greed on the body of their fallen neighbor. But to what end? To build wider, stouter ramparts and stare out at each other across the stricken Middle Realm, ever watchful of the other's attempt to push further. And the fairest city of all, Anrehenkar, survived to be ruled by the remnants of the royal line, in a mockery of dead glories amidst a sea of mercenary marauders.

"And it was here that we received our mission. We, whom the Spirits had entrusted to guide our fellows on, were now charged to safeguard what we had already achieved, to protect it until one day when the wars and pillaging stopped and man was ready to resume his true course. We resolved to take our knowledge and hide it away in the vast mountains, to let it grow and improve and be ready for the time to come. And we pledged ourselves to still help all who asked it of us, but above all

never to take sides in the petty bickering and senseless killing.

"Nor is the Order alone in practicing these Arts. In Pyrin there are the hermit magicians, once our kin, then our bitter opponents, now our valued friends once again. And abroad in the World there are some few women who practice as well. They are called Witches."

Crispan's eyes lit up in terror at the word. "Witches?" he repeated.

"No," laughed Bellapon, "not the witches as in the tales your mother told you. Witch, Wizard, Magician— it is all the same. But it is customary to refer to a woman as a Witch and her male counterpart as a Wizard. Witch-craft and Wizardry are taught as one discipline. There are differences, of course, between the Sorcerer and the Wizard, the Witch and the Magician. But by and large, these mean little to those untrained in the Arts.

"Those then are our reasons, our purpose. You must understand all that, why we practice our Arts and why we must not delve too much in the World as it is now, before you can ever master the Arts themselves. Forget our purpose, defy our aloofness, and you threaten to bring us down into the chaos that surrounds us, to destroy all that we have built and preserved. Remember that above all things, and understand it before you attempt to understand the Magic itself."

Bellapon could see that Crispan had listened atten-tively, and wanted to reward him. "Let me show you some Divination," he said, and then his voice drifted away and his eyes stared deep into the white heart of the fire. Suddenly his head lifted and his eyes grew wider, seeming to gather in as much light as they could from the stars above. He began to speak, very softly, his voice still distant. "You are close to the Sword. You ride under the Open Eye, but Jivir rides near you. There are many cities—of stones, of crowns, of water. Great triumphs and great sorrows. The best of the best, the last of the best. Wanderings. A woman by an unknown sea." Bellapon's jaw dropped, and he was silent.

Crispan stared at him wide-eyed. He waited as the

Magician slowly roused himself. "What does it all mean?"

The Magician's beard wagged back and forth as he shook his head. "Ah! That is the mystery, my boy. Some of it may mean a great deal, some may not. If you were older we could tell much more. Now is too soon, for you are just beginning, just setting out. But I can tell you this, Crispan. You are close to the Sword for a reason, and a time may come in your life when you will cross over to the Sword from the Open Eye, and a time when your life may leave both. But that is all I can say now."

Bellapon stopped to catch his breath and take a sip of water. He drew his blanket towards the fire. "And that is enough for one night. To sleep, Crispan, for we must reach the Southern border in time to catch the caravan and our escort."

Crispan wrapped himself in his blanket and turned his back to the fire. His eyes were open for some time as his mind raced over so many things, the sky, the stars themselves, what he had done already, and how little he really knew at all. But mostly he tried to remember what Bellapon had told him, and he fell asleep with the vision of his Magician companion standing huge and pure white over a city drenched in flames.

XI

Visions in the Fire

They emerged from the Great Mountains before the sun broke over them. Mikal slipped through the Eastgate first, leading his horse. Crispan followed, and both waited with amusement as Zoltan again squeezed his bulk through. The three of them mounted and were soon on their way across the Gates, moving as fast as they could.

"We must be quickest here," Mikal said as they took off. "This is as far north as we'll be, hence the most danger. I wonder if anyone is sitting up there watching." All three looked up at the Sentinel. As the land grew light with the rising of the sun, the craggy lone mountain resumed its vigil.

"I thought the Sentinel was abandoned many years ago," Crispan observed.

"Yes, but in these times who can tell? If what we hear is true, would not our enemies seek to keep watch there?" Crispan nodded at the truth in Mikal's remark.

"Do we go as we came?" asked Zoltan between bites on a stale loaf of black bread. "Or shall we ride south of the Falchions?"

Mikal pointed to the southwest. "The shortest way to the Empire is best, and safer than the lands north of the Falchions."

Zoltan remembered the incident at the inn, and all the mercenaries prowling the Middle Realm, especially now that Zhyjman and Syman were actively recruiting. And he remembered Mikal's warning that these two predators wanted the Heir of the Empire captive.

All that day and the next they plunged southward with utmost haste. Only their horses's exhaustion caused them to stop for rest on the deserted plain. For safety's sake they allowed themselves the luxury of a fire only in the misty morning, when light and smoke were less visible from afar. At night they took a cold meal, stale bread and dried beef. They slept lightly, listening for the sound of threatening hooves or voices in the night.

Some days after they had passed through the Gates, after Zoltan and Crispan had indulged in a short period of swordplay just to keep the Magician fresh, they sat huddled in a cove afforded by outlying boulders of the Falchions. Zoltan sat with his weapon across his knees, absentmindedly cleaning his blade. "Tell me, Crispan, about your magic. After all, I teach you soldiering. Tell me of your craft. Tell me more about the Order."

Crispan looked at him across the gloom. "The Order? The Order is the center of all magic, of all our learning. Everyone who aspires to be a Magician must go there to learn his craft and arts, to reveal and enhance his powers. One comes to the Order rather young and remains there until he has learned how to handle each of the Arts."

"How many are there?" asked Mikal.

"Five: Astrology and Divination, Wizardry, Sorcery, Alchemy and Thaumaturgy. At the Order each branch is overseen by a Master who has, after many years, proven himself in each of the Five Arts."

"And are you such a Master?"

Crispan nodded.

"But," said Zoltan, "you are rather young."

Crispan was embarrassed. "Well . . . yes. Anyway, each Art is overseen by one of the five Masters of the Five Arts. Over them all is the High Master, or Master of the Order, who is chosen by and from the five Masters."

Zoltan interrupted again. "Which Art is yours?"

"Wizardry."

"A wizard! Ha! Do you hear, Mikal, we travel with a wizard. What can you do?"

"Many things. Conjuration, the raising of visions, magic potions and spells of enchantment. I can do things that are not magic and things that could be." The thought of his beloved Arts warmed the Magician against the night.

Mikal looked interested but skeptical. "The others that you mentioned. I recognized them all except Thauma-"

"Thaumaturgy," Crispan offered.

Mikal nodded. "Yes. What is it?"

"It's like Wizardry and Sorcery, but much more difficult. The priests and unknowing folk call it miracles. But really it is only a more rigorous study of the Arts for more difficult achievements and spells. Thaumaturgy is a most difficult Art, requiring much skill and power. It can be most dangerous." Crispan was silent for a moment. His head lowered a bit and he added softly, "Vladur was the Master of Thaumaturgy."

Jovial Zoltan broke the silence. "What about the others, can you do them as well?" Crispan nodded. "Can you do something now? What about telling my future?"

Crispan smiled, wondering why everyone always asked after that Art first. "Another time, Zoltan. I'm too weary, and besides, the stars are hidden by the clouds. Without the signposts the traveler wanders. Tomorrow morning, when we have a fire. Then I'll show you something."

Zoltan was like a child deprived of a sweet, but now it was Mikal who interrupted. "Wait. If you can see into the future, why cannot you see where Vladur is, and who will win this war?"

Crispan smiled slightly, his eyes showing amusement at the questions of the unknowing. "Because what we see in the future is never definite, but only shadowy indications of what may be, often told in phrases so cryptic as to be misunderstood. And more important, we may never use our Arts to benefit ourselves, and such would be the case, I fear, against Vladur."

Their interest now thoroughly piqued, the two warriors kept Crispan up, asking him more questions about the daily life of the Order. He explained how they lived on food they raised themselves in the valleys surrounding the Order, and how they were also dependent on caravans crossing the mountains from Pyrin during the warm months.

Zoltan's eyes went wide at the mention of the fabled land of hermit magicians. Crispan told of how Pyrin was founded by members of the Order after the great schism, when the Order was divided between those devoted to the purity of the Five Arts and those who wanted to apply their learning to more practical matters within the World. Eventually those more interested in the World came down out of the mountains and settled in Pyrin. There, Crispan explained, they lost many of their deeper Arts over the decades, but became a major source of supplies for the Order once a reconciliation was made.

Zoltan was ready to pursue his questions further, but Mikal raised his hand. "We are barely at the entry to the High Pass across the Falchions and still have far to go before we are truly safe. Border or no, we won't be secure until we are deep within my father's realm. To sleep," he ordered.

"Come on, we've got to be moving." Mikal was already saddling his horse, although his green eyes betrayed his need for more sleep.

"Now wait, Mikal. Crispan here promised to show us some wizardry."

Crispan read the impatience on Mikal's face. "It won't take long. Is there any green wood? I need some to make smoke."

Mikal passed the fresh twigs and the Wizard fed them into the flames. A satisfactory white smoke soon was climbing above the fire. Crispan added dry wood as well to keep the flames alive, and drew his two companions closer. They huddled very close to the flames while Crispan knelt before it on the other side. His hands rolling loosely on his wrists, he eased his constantly moving fingers into the smoke. The column began to waver and break. Wisps and plumes writhed and twisted above the fire. Crispan's eyes narrowed as he concentrated now, bearing down, drawing on his power, moving his hands faster and faster. The smoke began to coil and twist more rapidly, like a snake mad in anger. He seemed to draw it out of the flames and shape it before their eyes. Then, with a twist of his right hand, it was over.

Zoltan shook his head as the smoke dissipated. "What was it, Crispan?"

"A conjuring. Tell me what you saw."

"It was strange. It seemed to form a picture. I thought I saw a big man, a warrior, fighting a great winged creature. But as the man closed for the kill, the beast turned into a woman and he gathered her into his arms."

"Ha!" laughed Mikal. "You see what you want to see!"

"Not so," admonished Crispan. "He saw what I conjured, but I created something based on his own thoughts. What did you see?"

"I saw a man riding a horse, seemingly for a long time. But then he came to a man seated on an ornate chair, a throne, and paid him fealty."

"You can do that, conjure different images at the same time?" Zoltan was more than impressed.

"At something simple like this, many conjurings are easy to control." Crispan shuddered inside as he said the words. There had been a third conjuring, one that *he* had seen, but not one he could remember creating. He had seen a man unwillingly suited up in armor and told to await his foe. The foe took the form of a phantom who toyed with the armored man but never came to fight, dooming the man to remain trapped in the uncomfortable armor. The Magician understood the vision too well. What he could not understand was how it had arisen without being summoned. He found this even more disturbing.

The day promised to be the same as all the others. They rode as fast as their mounts could bear, always keeping the great spine of the Falchions on their right. They tried to keep a cautious distance between themselves and the mountains, far enough to afford them protection from brigands camping in its rocks, close enough to afford them shelter should they need a place to hide. Mikal continually cast a nervous eye towards the mountains, wondering how far a man on its lower slopes could see.

It was late in the afternoon when Mikal let out an audible sigh. "Look. The High Pass is there." He pointed to the visible breach in the otherwise solid wall of the Falchions. "We are within the Empire." More refreshing now than an icy stream or a fresh bed, the words spurred them on, far into the night.

There was little talk that night as exhaustion and excitement silenced the three riders. Each was soon lost in sleep on the cold ground.

Sometime in the night Mikal heard his name being called. He was not sure if he was still asleep. No, he could hear Zoltan whispering his name.

Mikal grumbled. "What is it?"

"We have company."

Mikal opened his eyes to see a sword inches from his face.

XII

The Soundless Wind

Crispan was awake as well. He understood now what Zoltan meant about being able to see a blade at night. The one hovering over his throat was uncomfortably clear. It was more difficult to discern how many men there were about them, but he could make out six or seven for sure.

Mikal eased himself up onto his elbows and gently pushed the sword that faced him to one side. "What do you want? We're merely travelers."

"That's for us to determine," said a voice from deeper in the dark. "Where are you bound?"

"South, hopefully to Rhaan-va-Mor," he lied.

"Why there?"

"It's as good a place as any."

"You're mercenaries, aren't you?" The voice was growing edgy. Before Mikal could deny the accusation, the voice ordered a flint struck. Someone behind Mikal obeyed and passed the burning branch towards the voice.

"My lord!" the voice cried as the light passed over Mikal.

"Churnir?" Mikal let go a deep breath. "By the Spirits!"

The Captain of the Emperor's Guard stepped forward. "It's good to see you again, m'lord."

"How did you—but wait." Mikal turned to his companions. "Zoltan, Crispan—this is Churnir, of my father's household. Zoltan, he's the one I told you about, who brought me the letter." Both men quickly got to their feet as Mikal turned back to Churnir.

"How did you find us? Were you sent?"

"Aye, m'lord. The Emperor thought you would come this way and was worried about it."

Mikal was confused. "Why? We're within our own territory. We have been ever since the High Pass."

"True enough, sir. But things are worse than you know. We haven't enough troops to secure all our borders. Most of the army is drawn up near the three border kingdoms, waiting for Zhyjman to move. We control the entry to the Low Pass here, but the High Pass is harder to patrol effectively. And there are few travelers hereabouts now. That's why I was suspicious when you said that."

Mikal was taken aback. "Are things that bad?"

Churnir nodded glumly. "Afraid so. We've been out for eight days waiting for you. We've dealt with over a dozen brigands and mercenaries since then."

The Prince had no need to ask how the interlopers had been dealt with. He was more concerned about reaching safety with his party intact. "How many are in your party?"

"Eleven in this group. There are other parties out, smaller ones. They will be sent for after we have gotten you safely back. Shall we start tonight?"

"At once." Mikal looked to his companions, knowing their weariness. But Zoltan and Crispan were already gathering up their gear. "Fine. Where do we ride to?"

"Your father is camped before Gurdikar."

"Then that's where we're headed." Mikal turned to his own equipment and proceeded to saddle his horse. Soon the party of three and their escort were thundering through the night towards the fortress city of Gurdikar.

All that night and far into the next day they drove their mounts, until they were forced to rest in the mid-afternoon. Mikal had become impatient and uneasy now, and so they did not rest long. By the middle of the night they had covered much ground before they were compelled to take an even longer rest. Fortunately they were able to choose a site along one of the small rivers running south out of the Falchions.

Mikal and his companions joined Churnir as he inspected the placing of the guard along the river bank.

"Isn't it late for the river to still be frozen?" asked Crispan.

Churnir shrugged. "A bit, but it has been a long winter and a poor spring. The winds come down off the mountains here as well and it remains cool." Crispan nodded at the answer and gazed at the dull gray mantle encasing the river. Satisfied with the placement of the guards, they returned to the camp, sited on a rise beyond the bank. Soon all were asleep around the small fire they now allowed themselves.

"Captain! Captain!" The voice was a cry as it rode towards the camp. A rider came pell-mell up the bank and dove into the camp. All were on their feet at once looking to their weapons.

"Brigands, more than a score of them. I was with Dallin beyond the far bank. They've seen our fire and are heading for us." The rider was gasping for breath, sending out small plumes of steam.

Churnir deferred to his Prince. "What do we do?"

"Mount the horses. We'll decide then."

Zoltan's horse pawed eagerly at the ground, sensing the sudden tension in its master's body. "Any chance they're one of our patrols?"

Mikal shook his head. "No. They could have come in peacefully when they encountered our pickets. Besides, there are too many of them."

Churnir was back now, having redeployed his men as best he could along the frozen bank. Slipping his left arm into its shield straps, he said, "We'll get no protection from that river. There must be at least twenty-five or more coming." Even now the dull sound of their hooves was heard as they broke the frost-encrusted ground.

Mikal toyed with the raised eagle on his helm. "We've only fourteen. We must see that Crispan gets safely to the Emperor."

"And you, m'lord," added Churnir. "I suggest that you and he go. We can hold them for a while and let you both slip away in the dark."

The idea appealed to Zoltan, by now feeling the long

deprivation of a good fray. "I like it, Mikal. But you should take perhaps two or three men as an escort."

The Prince shook his head vehemently. "Leaving you only nine here. Those brigands would sweep you aside and still be able to ride us down."

Churnir suggested that they all ride out together, but Zoltan warned against that, fearing they would separate too easily in the night and be caught singly. The immediacy of the argument grew as the dull thud became louder and more distinct from across the frozen river. Mikal brought his helmet down over his head. "Too late now," he said, edging his horse forward. "We'll have to stand. There's some chance."

"But, m'lord," protested Churnir, "I was charged by your father—"

Mikal cut off the Captain. "Bring your men closer together." As Churnir was about to protest again he was caught short by Crispan's sudden move forward down the bank. The three warriors instinctively moved to stop him, but the Magician turned in his saddle and held up his hand. He said, "Stay." His voice was firm but quiet, and there was undeniable authority in his gray eyes. Each of them obeyed without really knowing why.

Crispan rode down to the very edge of the benumbed river. All was still save for the distant sound of hooves over the frozen dew. In the far-off mist on the farther bank gray shapes now began to take form as they neared the ice-bound flow.

Behind the Wizard the three warriors watched intensely. Crispan returned his sword to its sheath and stood in his stirrups, raising up his left hand, the palm towards the sky. His fingers beckoned to things unseen, and then, seeming to have caught hold of something, he passed it to his right hand. He repeated these gestures five or six times, beckoning, gathering and passing it. Then he suddenly thrust his right hand out across the river's frozen face, seemingly hurling whatever he had collected. All of the soldiers on his side of the bank were now watching anxiously, for on the far bank twenty or thirty horsemen were now dimly visible through the gloom. Mikal instinctively tightened his grip on his sword, as did every other waiting warrior.

The sharp, cracking sound of the hooves increased, and Crispan continued his invisible gathering, but with an ever-increasing pace. Again and again he beckoned with his left hand and thrust out with his right, until his arms were a frenzy of motion. A strangely silent wind picked up across the river and blew towards the onrushing brigands, dissipating the mist on the far side. By now the leading horsemen were on the river ice, swiftly approaching midstream. Still Crispan gathered and thrust, until nearly all the foe were on the ice. Mikal, Zoltan and the rest of their thin line began to trot forward in order to be with the Magician when the brigands closed.

Then, with all save three or four of the riders on the ice, Crispan gave one last thrust with his right arm. The wind now blew even harder, and yet made no sound. The only noise was that of galloping hooves over crystal ice. The wind continued to blow ever fiercer without a sound, and then there was an awful groaning, moaning noise that grew and grew until huge cracks appeared in the ice.

The leading brigand was but five spear lengths from the near bank when the ice before him parted with a mournful, thunderous groan. Soldier and steed plunged on helplessly, only to be swallowed by the liberated flood.

All across the river it was the same, the gusty, silent wind charging against the galloping brigands, and huge chasms suddenly opening in the ice. More and more of them were swallowed up amidst the breaking ice, and hideous cries now mingled with the groaning sound of the parting ice. Those further back tried to wheel and retreat, but most did so to no avail. Only one or two regained the opposite bank to join those few who had managed to rein in their horses before riding onto the fatal ice.

As the last brigand sank from view, the wind died away. All was silent save for the free-rushing river, now carrying armored men and horses to the sea.

Crispan sank in his saddle and wiped the sweat off his brow as his companions surrounded him. Wonder was written on each of their faces. Mikal smiled admiringly. "I now appreciate my father's need of you."

"But some have escaped," complained Zoltan.

Crispan let loose a heavy breath. "Aye. Let some go and report this night's events. Let the Emperor's enemies know that he too has magic. It will give Zhyjman and Vladur pause, I hope."

"Sound thinking," answered Mikal. "Gather the men. I want to ride at once."

Amidst the bustle and sudden preparations Crispan sat by silently. The chill of early spring hung in the air, but it was not cold enough to make him shiver as he did now. The thought was inescapable, even as he huddled deeper in his cloak. He had used his powers to kill. Everything that he told himself, that it was done to save their own lives, that it was done to stop Vladur, every excuse shattered against the inescapable fact. Perhaps if there had been more time. Then he could have freed the river before the brigands crossed it. But that answer did not help either. There had not been time, and he had used his powers to kill. He thought back over the rules of the Order, the Advisory, given to Masters going out on their first missions, and tried to remember the advice it gave about which deeds were permissible in the service of a lord. But he could not remember, for he had not read the Advisory in years, having never left the Order before, and he had never thought of taking it during his hasty departure.

"The rules of the Order bind us to one another within our learning and our Arts." At least he could easily recall the opening sentence. Then he wondered, if indeed he had transgressed the rules, was he any better now than the Renegade he sought?

XIII

Gurdikar

Gurdikar was an ancient border citadel. Its time-darkened walls stood where the frontier of the Empire of the South had been before the chaos began. In those days Gurdikar secured the imperial domain where the eastern frontier of Perrigar ended and where the northern frontier had stood exposed. In the years since the chaos and the Empire's expansion into the vacuum, Gurdikar had lapsed into a somnolent and decaying fortress, its battlements and crenelated towers falling into disrepair and neglect.

The arrival of the armies of Thurka Re and his allies had rudely awakened the secure city. Since it could serve as a convenient supply center, the Emperor Thurka set up his forest of tents under the ancient eastern walls of the city. It was to this camp that Mikal and his company now made their way.

The Prince paced impatiently on a hill but a short ride from the camp, kicking up clods on the ground. Captain Churnir sought to explain the delay again. "The Emperor requested it, m'lord. He wished to be informed by heralds before we rode in."

Mikal joined Crispan and Zoltan on a large flat boulder which protruded through the new green grass. But his impatience was too much for him and he resumed his pacing. Zoltan looked at the Magician. "You've been silent for a long time."

Crispan offered no response.

Zoltan knew when to leave, but as he rose, Crispan said, "Were you ever unsure about something, about something you did?" It was obvious from the red beard's expression that the question missed its mark. "What I mean is, did you ever question the cause for which you fought?"

The question obviously amused the stocky warrior. He smiled. "Crispan, my friend, a mercenary only questions how much he's being paid and whether it will be there when the fighting's over. Why do you ask?"

"Because," Crispan said, his voice sounding oddly hollow, "I don't think I belong here. And I have committed an unpardonable act. I have killed with my magic."

Zoltan paused before answering. "Do you think your High Master would have sent you here without reason? He would expect you to act in order to fulfill your mission. And you have been sent as the adviser to a great lord, the Emperor of the South. While your role is that of a Wizard, you are a soldier in the Emperor's cause, one with weapons unlike our own."

Crispan looked up. Perhaps Zoltan was right. But still he wondered what else he might have to do in order to combat Vladur. Then he remembered his first nights with Bellapon, when the elder Magician had pondered the meaning of Crispan's being born so close to the sign of the Sword. He would fight being dragged from under the sign of the Open Eye, yes. He would aid the Emperor Thurka, but only as a Master of the Five Arts.

Mikal was still pacing when Churnir came up to him. "It's time to go, m'lord." The Prince nearly flew into his saddle and fell in behind Churnir and two officers on the road to Gurdikar, with Zoltan and Crispan flanking him.

"How do you feel, Mikal?"

Zoltan's question puzzled him. "Why?"

"I just wondered how you felt about seeing your father after so many years, and how you felt about becoming the Heir of the Empire."

Mikal shrugged, his shoulders brushing his black hair. "I haven't really given it any thought." As he said this he was suddenly surprised, for it was quite true.

The escort kept up a good pace, but as they rode on, the Prince unconsciously prodded his cream-colored steed even faster. He almost overran Churnir as the Captain pulled up short at the crest of a ridge. "Why have we stopped?" Mikal demanded, his nostrils flaring.

"Because we are there, m'lord. Gurdikar lies just beyond us on the plain."

Mikal scampered his mount to the crest. Below him stood the dark gray walls of Gurdikar and the black weathered towers thrown up at irregular intervals towards the sky. In vivid contrast to the dull stone were the myriad tents of Thurka's army, representing every color and pattern known in the Three Realms. Mikal could make out banners floating above the camp before the brooding walls. There were those of Ernyr, Gar and Perrigar, of the exiled Duke of Larc and emigré lords from Tharn. Over a great gold tent in the middle of the camp flew a golden boar on a blood-red field. This was the personal guidon of Thurka Re, flying beside the dark blue banner of the Empire of the South. The Prince's blood quickened as he took in the sight. He felt as he had so many times before going into battle, but now he was going home.

Zoltan asked if he wanted to ride down on the camp at full gallop. Mikal smiled, his green eyes bright and clear. "No, I fear it is time for the Prince to resume his dignity." He extended his right arm and clasped Zoltan's. He then did the same with Crispan and Churnir.

"You know, Zoltan," Mikal said as they rode, "the Duke of Larc will be there. He is my father's ally now."

"What's it to me?" the red beard replied brusquely. "As I told the Wizard, I have always been loyal as a mercenary." He paused and then added, "Before."

Mikal strained to keep his horse to a canter, fighting his own impulse, not the steed's. The road ran straight now, cutting a dusty swath through the green-covered plain. It slipped effortlessly beneath them, carrying them on to the camp. Soon the tents were more than a cluster of colors on the plain. Soon the riders were among the outlying tents. Guards were posted along the road now, their armor flashing in the sun. The road ran on straight to the dark portals of Gurdikar, but guards posted in front of the gate detoured the riders off to a large square on the right.

They slowed to a walk as they approached the great central tent. A knot of men, obviously High Lords, stood before the gold cloth structure. Mikal reined in at the far end of the square. His fists gripped the reins even tighter as he sat very still for what seemed a lifetime. Drawing in a deep breath, he dismounted, hesitating again as he touched the ground. A well-built man stepped forward. His hair and close-cropped beard were black with broad strips of silver and lesser flecks of gray. He was slightly shorter than Mikal, but his eyes were the same intense green color. Mikal walked to Thurka and extended his right arm. Thurka clasped it and drew his son to him.

"Welcome, Mikal."

Mikal smiled in response. "How are you?" was all he could say. It was lame and he knew it, but after so long there was too much else to say.

As the Emperor began to lead him to the waiting lords, Mikal broke away and ran to a man who resembled them both. He was far taller than either of them, and his long, flowing hair was prematurely white, as were his long and elegant moustaches, which drooped dramatically over his upper lip.

"Belka!" Mikal shouted, extending his hand. "Belka, how are you?" This time the question had more feeling.

His uncle greeted him warmly, welcoming him home.

Thurka drew up to his son and brother, somewhat subdued by the warmth with which they greeted one another. "Come, meet the others." Mikal renewed acquaintance with many he had known in his youth, either as older lords or companion heirs. Mikal recognized King Anthul of Perrigar and Borgas of Gar. He was introduced to Prince Noal of Ernyr, a very thin young man in the family's traditional black armor. The Duke of Larc was next, a man of medium build swathed in a brown fur cloak. The surprise on his face gave both Thurka and Mikal evident satisfaction.

The Duke stood with his mouth agape. When he recovered he turned to the Emperor, stammering, "My lord, this—this is the man I told you about, the mercenary—"

Thurka cut him short, smiling. "Yes, I know. Your mercenary general."

"It's good to see you again, m'lord." Mikal was grinning.

"But, sir," protested Larc, "it is *I* who should be calling *you* lord."

As Thurka led Mikal toward a second row of lords and generals, Mikal stopped. "Wait, Father, there are others for you to meet." He beckoned to his companions as he led his father back.

Zoltan was fidgeting with his armor. Mikal drew him and the Emperor together. "Father, this is Zoltan, a fine warrior and my trusted companion."

Thurka shook the burly man's hand. "Welcome, Lord Zoltan. Welcome to the Empire." The title sounded much better to Zoltan coming from an Emperor rather than a mercenary general.

"And this is Master Crispan," said Mikal, indicating the man with the finely defined features wearing a gray cloak and purple amulet.

The Emperor was genuinely pleased to see him. "I am glad you are with us, Crispan. Master Omir spoke very well of you."

The Wizard bowed deeply. "Thank you, my lord. The High Master sends you his greetings and good wishes. We both hope I may be of service to you." Crispan bowed again, as form and ritual demanded.

Thurka threw back his heavy cloak and turned to the Captain of his Guard. "You have done well, Baron Churnir," he said, blithely bestowing a title on his faithful servant.

Thurka returned to the matter of introductions between his allies and the newcomers. All went well until Zoltan reached the Duke of Larc. The Duke's eyes flashed sharply as he saw the warrior, envisioning at once a night some few years ago when that warrior had lunged at him across a field of battle. Larc's bristling anger was apparent to all, but it lay stillborn in view of Thurka's icy stare.

With the introductions completed, the parties separated

to rest and prepare for the welcoming feast. As Mikal and Thurka parted, the Emperor grasped his son's hand again, but said nothing. The other nobles and soldiers dispersed as well. Crispan went to his tent alone.

The feast tent was a huge affair made up of five or six or seven of the largest tents raised one beside the other. It was erected close to the walls of Gurdikar. To this great hall built of cloth Thurka invited his lords, commanders and allies and their chosen retinues to celebrate the safe return of his son and heir.

Crispan wore the best gown he had taken, of deepest green with black and gold trim. Fingering his amulet of the Eye, he was escorted to the feast tent by an officer of the Guard. He was surprised by the quiet of the sprawling camp as he moved across it. He had expected a constant martial bustling of men, horses and weapons. Instead, silence had descended on the armed camp with the coming of night.

All inside the tent was in sharp contrast to the camp without. Torches burned brightly in their stands all along the lavish tables. Crispan winced as his eyes adjusted to the light, which danced brightly off the engravings on the gold and silver dishes and goblets. The light swam easily on the deep-red wine standing in huge tuns. It gently caressed the meats and sauces and many fruits, adding to the richness of their colors. It threw shimmering shadows along the walls that expanded and wavered as breezes shifted the tents' walls.

Crispan was escorted to the largest of the elaborately set tables, the one squarely under the central tent. Amidst the bustle of servants and guests he espied Zoltan already firmly placed behind an ornately decorated tankard brimming with wine. The burly warrior was seated to the right of Mikal, who now looked like a Prince in his silver and blue robes and three bejeweled bracelets. Next to Mikal sat Thurka, unmistakably an Emperor regardless of his dress, and to his right towered Belka, now on his feet motioning Crispan to the empty seat on his other side. Huge trays of delicately arranged sweetmeats faced him

118

as he sat down, each platter surrounded by silver bowls, each containing a different sauce, representing a variety of tastes and hues. There were freshly baked breads twisted and shaped into intricate patterns, and heaping golden bowls of tangy and sweet fruits. Crispan sat down, somewhat overwhelmed by the spectacle. Never had he seen such a feast. Belka reached over and poured him some wine from a golden ewer. In response to Belka's raised goblet, Crispan raised his own and drained it, sitting back a bit staggered as the heavy red wine coursed through his body. Belka was about to refill the goblet when there was a flourish of trumpets. Crispan looked up.

"The toasts," Belka whispered, completing his pouring.

Lord Gremard, the Governor of Gurdikar, began it all with a toast to the safe return of the Heir, to which the Emperor gave the responsive toast before offering one of his own. So it went down the table as each of the allied lords congratulated the new arrivals. Servants scurried about frantically emptying costrels of wine into the constantly drained ewers. Many, many toasts later, Mikal rose to give his response, mercifully bringing the ordeal to an abrupt conclusion by accepting the other toasts and offering his own in the name of himself and his companions. Finally, the banquet resumed.

The raucous scene all around fascinated the Magician. He sat back in his chair peeling a ripe fruit imported from the farther south, taking in all that was going on around him. Yet at the same time he felt uncomfortable, one apart from the many loud conversations competing to be heard across the tents. To his left sat Prince Noal of Ernyr, to whom he had little to say beyond the pleasantries. The Prince was a warrior born and bred, obviously looking forward to the coming war. Happily, Belka leaned over to make the Wizard feel more at home. They also began with small talk, and soon exchanged stories of their chosen callings.

"Have you ever been to Rhaan-va-Mor?" As he asked, Belka tore off a shank of beef and passed the tray to Crispan, who shook his head to the query.

"You should go there. Quite a city. Once part of the Great Empire, you know. One of the Seven Jewels."

"Seven Jewels?" echoed Crispan.

"Aye," said Belka, refilling the Magician's goblet again. "Second only to Anrehenkar itself, they said. The Emperors of the Middle Realm gave the names of jewels to each of their major cities—Anrehenkar the diamond, Izikar the sapphire, Ker-en-kar the ruby, and so on. Rhaan-va-Mor was called turquoise, after the sea, I suppose. Anyway, it's a fascinating place. A free city-state since the fall of the Empire, with a fabulous port. Vessels come from all over, even areas untouched by our own ships. And women! Fine noble women of great trading houses, beautiful slave girls from exotic places. I brought some back once—the slaves, that is. I tell you, Crispan, if a man wanted to see the World, not just the Empires, he'd have no better place to start than Rhaan-va-Mor. To the north we are girded by the mountains, but from Rhaan-va-Mor the entire world opens up."

Crispan wanted to pursue this point, for he had heard precious little of lands beyond the Three Realms. He would have liked to know much more about this and other matters of the World. But he had little opportunity as Belka recounted his own connection with Rhaan-va-Mor, when he had defended it against a great mercenary invasion by lifting their siege with his volunteer force and then withstanding an even longer and more bitter siege that had already become a legend. The tale was an old one by now and Belka was well-practiced in its telling, but Crispan found it all fascinating and new. He remained so absorbed in the siege that he failed to notice the absence of the Emperor and his son.

XIV

Return of the Heir

Thurka and Mikal left the feast tent with the celebration well in progress, their departure unnoticed by anyone save for the ever faithful Churnir, who followed them as they strolled across the empty camp to the Emperor's tent. Even in the gloom of night the gold of the imperial tent stood out brilliantly. As soon as they entered and passed to the inner chamber they dismissed the servants. Churnir stationed himself at the tent's entrance and drew up a cordon of his guards.

Thurka poured the chilled wine from the ewer himself. He was weary from many long days and nights of councils, from drills for the armies, and the night's feasting. He settled heavily into his fur-covered chair, squirming a bit as his son watched him over the rim of his goblet.

After an uncomfortable silence Thurka Re made the first move. "A long time, Mikal. Over seven years. You look well." It was not easy to start a conversation after so many years.

Mikal now made the effort, but more directly. "Did Ivor know I was summoned?" He sipped some wine.

Thurka nodded.

"What did he say?"

"He never told me. I trust he understood. What was there between you? Why did you hate each other so?"

Mikal rested his goblet on the arm of his chair and ran his free hand over the design. He sighed. "Ivor hated me for my abilities. I was smarter, I soldiered better, and he knew it. And I hated him for being first, for the way he threw *you* up to me. He constantly reminded me that *he* was the Heir and your favorite, that he would one day be Ivor Re, while I would always be *Prince* Mikal. He made me hate my title."

Thurka looked pained. He stared into the deep-red wine and shrugged. "Do you think I favored Ivor?"

Now Mikal nodded.

"Yes, I suppose I did. But he was first, he was older. I had to train him to rule, and he was less able than you. Should you have two or more sons you will understand one day. One son insures the line, but two secures it more. But then they may vie with one another for the throne. It's a dilemma no king has ever solved. But tell me this, why did you leave and where did you go?"

Mikal closed his eyes wearily and drifted back over those seven years. He drained his wine without realizing it, and only opened his eyes again to pour himself more. "You were ill. There was talk you might die. Ivor and I had fought again—I had outraced him to a boar one afternoon and slayed it after he had first sighted it. When we returned that night and learned that you were worse, Ivor came to me. He threatened me, saying that the spear I had saved him might soon be used should you die. He was drunk. I went to see the Queen . . . how is Mother?"

"She remains at Kerdineskar. She is well." Thurka winced at the mention of his estranged Queen.

"Mother hated you then. It was after you had taken up with that Vaduli girl. I told Mother of Ivor's threat, and she offered to lead a coup for me. I knew we would fail even should you die. The army has always been loyal to you, and they would stand for Ivor. I bade her good night and determined to leave at once, that very night. I trusted neither your health nor my brother's intentions, and so I left."

Thurka paused for more wine, as if the sweet liquid could clear the bitterness of seven years.

Mikal felt better but drained. The weariness of the long journey from Aishar seemed to leave him as he recalled his long years of wandering. "I rode to Vadul. I first thought to hide in the Great Woods for a while, living off the game and then returning. But as I went on

I decided not to go back, so I crossed over into the Middle Empire and rode on."

He needed no further prodding now and continued his narrative without interruption, pausing occasionally for more wine. Mikal spoke of how, once in the Middle Empire and short of money, he took the one course open to a trained warrior amidst that chaos, the life of a mercenary. He described in detail the world of the mercenaries, their firm internal hierarchy from new recruits to tried veterans to commanders of their own companies or even armies and finally to the great Anarchs, each man bound to the man above him by a contract which both parties observed strictly. Mikal told how few of the great mercenary leaders ever lived to retire to some roughly carved-out duchy of their own, but rather were compelled by the needs of their armies to fight on interminably, caught in a seemingly endless cycle of wars for booty to attract new recruits in order to keep themselves strong, only to need more booty after the last war ended in order to keep the men loyal in the future.

And then he described his own progress in that strangely closed world, first joining a band composed more of brigands than mercenaries, slowly amassing booty and gold as he drifted across the Middle and Northern Realms, from Vardimor to Kyryl and Nor, back to Larc. His only firm principle, Mikal said, was his staunch refusal to attack the Southern Empire or its allies, a policy which cost him at least one company that he'd built up under his own banner.

"So I lived for seven years," Mikal said, emptying the ewer, thinking back over his journeys across the sea of chaos which the Middle Realm had become, seeing once again the ruined cities and wide swaths of desolation. He shook his head and turned to his father. "But tell me, how did you find me with Syman?"

Now it was the Emperor's turn to hold forth, describing how the exiled Duke of Larc fled south before Zhyjman's unprovoked onslaught, which even Larc's green-eyed mercenary commander could not stop. Thurka repeated in detail the marvelous accounts he had heard of this

mysterious Lord Mikal, his delaying action in the borderlands of Larc, his successful withdrawal to Izikar, Larc's
capital, and his inspired defense of that city.

Mikal's eyes had closed as he listened to this tale. He
could picture once again the terrible siege of Larc's capital. He remembered mostly how the war had turned
around night and day, the dark nights brightened by
towering flames and the days dulled by the ensuing smoke.
He tried to remember when it was he had slept in those
days, but all he could see was himself rushing from battle-
ment to tower, constantly shouting orders and encourag-
ing his own men and Larc's, until he persuaded the Duke
to abandon the falling city for the sake of his own life.

"I knew I could land on my feet and survive, for that is
the lot of a clever mercenary. Death is the foe, not defeat.
But I also knew Zhyjman would never tolerate Larc alive
should he be captured."

Thurka nodded. "So you sent him south to me, and
when I heard his story I hoped you were that mercenary
he described."

"But you never sent for me." Mikal sounded hurt.

"No. Would you have come while Ivor still lived and
was Heir?"

Now Mikal said, "No."

The Emperor spread his hands across his knees. "Much
has gone between us, and there has been hurt on both
sides. You have come back changed, and perhaps that is
for the best. Perhaps it is Lord Mikal the mercenary we
need now. What do you make of our chances?"

"To be honest, I think they're poor. Zhyjman has the
troops, the training, the choice of time and place. He, like
Syman, is a very cautious man. He would not attempt
anything so big as Anrehenkar and our overthrow without very good reasons to expect success. Nor would Syman
undertake such a contract without some certainty on his
part. All Zhyjman's forces are not enough to take our
realm in direct assault. But armies, I fear, are not our real
problem. Perhaps that is where the Magician fits in. Perhaps he can counteract those reasons and destroy Zhyjman's

hopes and balance. Somehow I feel he may be our only true defense and weapon against the North."

"What do you make of him?"

Mikal shrugged. "I take it this was worked out between you and the High Master. We must accept their judgment that he is best suited to help us, although I feel that his powers are in some way severely limited by their own laws. But I tell you this, it will take more than sudden winds and thawing ice to defeat Zhyjman."

Thurka nodded again, although more heavily now, finally feeling the full effects of seeing his son again and the long night filled with much talk and much wine. They walked to the outer chamber and stepped beyond the flap. The stars shone tenaciously in the waning gloom. Already the deepest red of early dawn was inching up in the east. The camp and city were both peacefully quiet, the feast having ended long before. Thurka turned to his son and smiled. "Come! It's time we got some sleep."

Mikal did not know how long he had slept or what the hour was. He had lit a taper only to put it out again, and lay on his cot watching the smoke writhe towards the ceiling. He was lost deep in thought, thinking about places he had been in the last seven years, when Belka entered his chamber, his mustachios bristling. He waved slightly to his nephew and seated himself in the chair at the foot of the cot, carefully arranging his cloak about his knees before he began.

"Your father sent me to prepare you for tomorrow."

Mikal's brows knitted in perplexity. "Tomorrow?" he echoed.

Belka was bored by the question. "Yes, the investiture as Heir must be done at once so there can be no trouble."

The word alarmed the Prince at once. "Trouble? From whom?"

Belka took out his hunting knife and began to peel a fruit he had taken from the bowl beside the cot. He threw the skin on the floor and then watched intently as the point of the blade barely penetrated the fruit itself, releasing a thin trickle of golden juice. He sank the blade deeper and cut off a section, flipping it to his nephew. "There will always be disaffected nobles in an empire. Perhaps some who have received secret subsidies or promises from Zhyjman. I doubt that it will amount to anything, but we cannot leave anything to chance. Should we fail, there will be those who will desert us rather than join the fall. And that's why you must be perfect in your oath and in the ceremony. It will be difficult enough with your having been gone for so long. Of course, the fact that I will back you will help. After all, I am now the recognized Heir. But come, to work!"

For a good part of the rest of that day Belka put Mikal through the ancient ceremony which he had never had to learn. Belka began at once, even while Mikal was in the midst of breakfast. The oath came from that quieter time now lost, when the Southern Empire had been fully aware of the greater power of Anrehenkar. So distracted was he by the mention of possible disloyalty, though, that it took much concentration to learn it. Mikal would swear to protect his dependent lords to the east, north and west; to maintain the seas to the south; to live harmoniously with his brother Emperors and their dependents. That world had died long ago. Most of the dependent lords had given up their remaining independence, and only one brother Emperor now remained. And he, indeed, was as much a part of this ceremony and its crucial significance as Mikal and Thurka.

The day between the feast and the investiture had been a welcome one for the Magician. He had slept late the following morning, something he had not done since his days as an Adept, and had spent the rest of the day practicing his martial skills with Zoltan. Both of them now felt slightly out of place, the one deprived of the familiar surroundings of the Order, the other deprived of his friend's company.

They stayed together on the day of the ceremony, a day of dazzling, glittering beauty such as Gurdikar had not known in many decades. Every lord and prince and general dressed himself in his brightest robes and finest armor,

and they shone like jewels in the morning sun as they
marched in the procession to the Governor's Hall in the
city itself. Crispan and Zoltan were already in the hall,
seated with other guests in the balcony which overhung
the hall on three sides, leaving the wall along the entry
free to soar the full height of the palace. They too were
dressed for the occasion, Zoltan in armor trimmed in gold
and small chips of blackest onyx, Crispan in robes that
were fine in texture and color but which were outshone by
the gleam of his purple amulet.

Between them sat Lorkar, a member of the Guard, in
his dress armor with the obligatory red and gold plumes,
who had been assigned by the Emperor to guide them
through the day's ceremony. He cradled his barbut in his
left arm and pointed out dignitaries with his right.

"That is the Prince of Vadul," he said, indicating a
gray-beard in a white fur cape. "And there is Mabiz, one
of the Elders of Rhaan-va-Mor; his presence is significant,
as a signal to the North." Next to the Elder, whose balding
pate and long beard reminded Crispan of Bellapon, the
Magician could pick out the Princes of Ernyr and Gar,
Noal and Dhelo. The parade of lords continued for some
time, each one looking like a magnificent peacock who
knew he was on display accompanied by greetings or whispered appraisals as he entered.

The procession finally ended with the entry of Gran, the
High Chamberlain of the Empire. His enormous bur-
gundy robes were gathered about his waist by an ornate
gold buckle, symbol of his office as was his silver staff.
Gran's eyes, heavily hooded by bushy brows, swept author-
itatively around the room, stilling the murmuring voices.
When he was satisfied he stepped before the three chairs
on the dais in the center of the room and rammed his staff
three times against the carpeted floor. "Our Lord and Protector Thurka Re calls us to assemble before him that he
may consult with us. Have all answered his summons?"

Margrave Undhym, Steward of the Rolls while Belka
remained Heir, gave the response. "All are gathered. We
await our Lord and Protector that we may assist him."

Gran nodded and imperceptibly flicked his wrist to-

wards the door. A Guard relayed it to the trumpeters
without, who brought the assembly to its feet with an exu-
berant flourish. Gran withdrew to one side as Thurka entered, with his son and brother on either arm. Crispan was
much taken by the entire ceremony, for he knew nothing
of the ways of a great court, or any court at all. The only
rite comparable to this had been his own induction as a
Master and then Master of the Five Arts, and that had
taken place in dark rooms filled with eerie half-lights of
changing hues, suffused by smoke and flickering torches.
Here all was bright.

The two Princes assumed their seats, on chairs slightly
lower than the Emperor's. Thurka stepped forward to the
edge of the dais, thrusting out his chest against his golden
cuirass trimmed in fur, a clenched fist planted in silver
mail gloves on either hip. Gran announced that all were
present and ready to serve. Thurka nodded.

"My lords, I bring you glad tidings in these dark times.
My younger son, Prince Mikal, has returned to us and is
ready to assume his rightful place in our Empire." The
news was hardly news at all, for it had been rumored for
some time and confirmed for all since Mikal's arrival at
Gurdikar. "He comes at a most propitious time, my lords,
for with the death of his dear brother, Prince Ivor, he is
my rightful Heir. I ask you now to invest him as such and
swear your allegiance to him as you have to me."

There was a moment's silence. A lord stood up. "Count
Franzis," whispered Lorkar in a low sneer. "My lord,"
said the Count, "we are most gratified at this news. But
may I speak a word of caution?" Thurka nodded his assent, having expected this. Even from the balcony above,
Zoltan could feel Mikal's anger as his sword hand
clenched and relaxed a number of times.

"Thank you, my lord." Franzis's wispily bearded face
bore a smile of thinly veiled contemptuous pleasure. "My
lord, my only concern is for our safety. We live in dangerous times and must be careful. Prince Mikal has been gone
for some years. Are we sure that this is certainly he returned to us? He left as a very young man, he returns
fully matured. There have been changes. We must not let

the succession pass to some impostor foisted upon us by your enemies so as to deny the throne to your true and only brother. Let him present himself to us, my lord."

Thurka smiled graciously and beckoned his son forward. Belka whispered something to him as he rose, touching him lightly on the wrist, as if to calm him. Silence followed again, but now another lord rose, the Count Arganes, related to the Imperial family through a bastard line. The Count fastidiously rearranged his cloak before he began, and then addressed himself to the rest of the assembly while purposely and contemptuously avoiding the Emperor. "My lords, this young man indeed seems to be the Emperor's son, at least in appearance. But seven years is a long time; appearance alters, as Count Franzis has said. Can we not at least have some account of where the Prince has been, and indeed, why he left us for so long?"

Belka, watching, was a bit taken aback by this. He had not expected them to press this hard. Did the Count know that Mikal had been a mercenary, and had ridden with Syman? This would surely undermine Mikal's claim. And why the questions about his absence? Would Arganes drop the hint of a plot to kill Ivor? Thurka, also caught off guard, remained silent a little too long. But Mikal himself retrieved the situation.

"My dear cousin," he said facetiously, "is correct. Some accounting should be made. I left at the request of my brother," which brought gasps from many mouths, for Mikal seemed to be confirming the worst, "so that I might see something of the world that he could not risk seeing, and thus be prepared to help him in his own reign as my uncle has aided my father. I cannot say where, for I have been to many places, cousin, and have learned much that will be especially helpful to my father and our Empire in these dark days. I am sure my cousin has no wish to compromise our safety." The white lie he had rehearsed with Belka came out smoothly.

Arganes' eyes narrowed at this. "No, of course not. But still, we must be sure."

Belka was now on his feet as well. "Does my dear

cousin," and his pain at their even distant relationship was clear, "think that I would relinquish my claims if I were not sure?" There were wry smiles made at this, for Belka was that rarity, a Prince happy with his position. Everyone who knew him knew how much he prized his freedom and how he had disliked the necessity of becoming Heir. "I trust that my own willingness to cede my title is proof enough that this man is truly my nephew, the Prince Mikal, rightful Heir of the Empire."

Arganes was beaten and he knew it. He bowed stiffly and sat down, his face dark and scowling.

Gran stepped forward again from behind the dais. "My lord, we have sat and considered and do now recognize this man before us as your true Heir, and we will swear our undying allegiance to him and thus we renew our allegiance to you."

Mikal now began to go through the long ceremony. He received the accouterments of the title from Belka, the diadem, ceremonial shield and sword, and his mandate from Thurka. After the oath and gifts were given, each of the lords in order of precedence swore their allegiance to the Prince, their devotion to the Emperor, and their willingness to give all they had in the defense of the Empire. Crispan thought how much meaning this all had especially at this moment, and then let his eyes wander about the hall, studying each of the shields and crossed weapons that hung in the panels between the long, thin windows and the huge tapestries floating above the entries. His attention returned to the ceremony as Franzis and Arganes gave their oaths, the first defiantly, the second sullenly.

The oaths droned on through the afternoon, the sun's rays shifting completely around from one side of the hall to the other, until finally the lowest-ranking nobles, recently created Barons of the Southeastern Marches, had made their oaths. Gran closed the ceremony swiftly and led the lords out to a banquet of celebration. The Emperor and the Princes remained on the dais, where they were joined by Churnir at the beckoning of Thurka. The Emperor pointed to the withdrawing figure of Arganes and his coterie of young lords. "Have him followed, at a distance.

I want to know whom he sees and where he goes. But remember, at a distance." Churnir was on his way at once. Thurka turned to his family. "There was more trouble than I had expected. Do you think—?"

"No, brother. Arganes is eager, but very cautious. He may consider it, deep within his heart, but he will never approach Zhyjman or allow himself to be approached—at least to the point of commitment. But we must have him watched."

XV

With the Army of the East

For the first time in years Crispan was nervous about an interview. As he waited in the Emperor's antechamber he fidgeted with the cuffs of his robe and clutched at his talisman. His eyes flitted from object to object in the cloth chamber, the decorative weapons, the gold and silver plates offering hospitable fruit and drink, the comfortable appointments, but it was not as though he took any of it in, so distracted was he. Thurka greeted him warmly as he led the Magician to the inner chamber.

The Emperor was a bit distracted as well. It had been three days since the investiture, and all he seemed to do was hold countless and endless meetings and interviews. The initiative lay with Zhyjman, and the waiting made the Emperor of the South nervous.

"Well," he began, tugging at his close-cropped beard, "we have not really had time to talk."

Crispan agreed with a soft "No."

"Omir told me very good things about you. He said you were the best of the Order. I trust his judgment, in this and many other things."

Crispan blushed slightly. "You speak as if you knew him."

Thurka poured a small cup of light white wine, suitable for that hour of the morning, and mixed it with some water. "Aye, I knew him some time ago, when I was Prince. Omir was assistant to my father's sorcerer at Kerdineskar. That is how we met."

The mention of the Emperor's capital reminded Crispan of something he should have asked when he first arrived. "How is . . ." He was embarrassed by his failure to ask sooner.

"Xirvan?" Thurka offered. Crispan nodded. "Xirvan still ails, and so he has remained at Kerdineskar. He is very old, and aware of his declining skills. You need not worry. He fully understands your mission and specifically told me to wish you well. He offered any help you might feel you need."

Thurka began toying with his now empty cup, running an index finger around and around the rim. Crispan could see that he was going to change to a more pressing matter than the health of his Wizard at the capital. The Emperor's usually steady gaze drifted away from the Magician and his voice lowered. "What can you tell me of Vladur?"

The question confused Crispan. "What do you mean? His training, his ability?"

"No, no. I mean," and his voice grew emphatic, "do you know where he is?"

Crispan was staggered. "I thought you would know that." His eyes went wide with horror, his worst fears seemingly confirmed.

Thurka pleaded ignorance as well. "Not I. We have heard from many sources, including Omir, that Vladur was with my enemies. But I was certain that the High Master would tell you where the Renegade, as he called him, was."

"But he doesn't know." Crispan's voice had grown plaintive.

"We only know where Zhyjman's forces are, some still in Larc and two strong columns moving on Anrehenkar and the Gates. But there is no news of Vladur himself."

The Wizard let out a short, painful laugh. "In other words, you have no real proof that Vladur is amongst your enemies. Don't you realize what that means? My very presence here compromises the Order's position in the World. We have forsaken our neutrality and our safety only because Vladur is supposedly against you, and now you say you don't know where he is." His voice had risen to a shrill, accusatory pitch as he thrust out a shaking arm and pointed beyond the tent's opening.

"You do not understand," pleaded Thurka, squirming under the weight of Crispan's recriminations. "We are certain that he is among our enemies. Where else could he be? But we do not know exactly where. However, neither do we know where Zhyjman or his leading general, Kirion, are. We must assume they are all together. In this you must trust me."

"I'm afraid I must. We have already committed ourselves to your cause. But what am I to do in the meantime? Shall I just wait for the Renegade to appear from out of the north?"

The Emperor had not found a response when his son entered the chamber followed by his burly companion. They were both begrimed from a long ride and hunt, but looked undeniably refreshed. "Aye, Father," said Mikal, grinning widely, "what shall we do with our Magician?"

It was Crispan who answered his own question, his gray eyes growing wide and expectant. "What about Pangal's army, going to oppose the force threatening Zifkar from the Gates?"

"No," barked the Emperor, aghast at the idea. "It's out of the question. Why would you want to go there?"

Crispan's pain had turned to anger by now. He leapt out of his chair and began to pace. "Because I should like to help as long as I am here. I am already committed to your cause, m'lord, so I may as well be helpful."

Thurka remained adamant. "Absolutely not." He waved his hand as he said it, sending his cup flying off the arm of his chair and across the room, shattering it. "You said you came here only to combat Vladur. *He* is not moving against Zifkar."

"His allies are," Crispan threw back.

"Why not, Father? It will give Crispan some practical experience and it should not be dangerous. Who knows, he may be helpful to Pangal."

"And what if Vladur should appear while you are gone?" But this raised little problem, as Crispan could return with an escort in haste. Thurka still felt guilty after the Magician's outburst and so he acquiesced.

As Crispan walked back to his tent to prepare for the campaign he paused mid-step. He still did not know why he was out in the World, and now he knew not why he

135

had volunteered to go to Zifkar. The uncomfortable feeling that the control of his life, which he had always prized so within the Order, was now slipping further away from him not only lingered but thrived and grew.

The sight was admittedly impressive. Drawn up on the plain north of Gurdikar's bleak walls were two armies and the core of a third. Armor gleamed in the morning sun, flags, pennants and standards snapped in the cool breeze. The deep-red symbol of the Southern Empire, the green of Vadul, the yellow and red of Larc, the banners of the border princes and some high nobles of the Empire formed an imposing backdrop for the Emperor himself and his retinue.

Thurka sat tall and straight on his gray war horse, his eyes taking in the array of soldiers massed on the plain, his mind wondering if they would be enough. He signaled the heralds, whose clear, sharp notes carried swiftly across the plain. Thurka stood in his stirrups and held out his sword before him.

"Soldiers of the Empire, of Vadul, Ernyr, Gar and Perrigar, Tharn and Larc! Today you go out from Gurdikar to protect us all from the advances of the Emperor of the North. It is he, in his lust for conquest, who has brought on this war; it is we who must defend the balance of the Empires and defeat him. This is the reason for which you march today, not for greedy gain, but for the safety of us all. May the Spirits protect you and guide you to victory!"

A great roar arose from the host arrayed before him. To his right there was a mixture of war chants from the allied army led by Prince Zascha of Perrigar. The lancers of Ernyr on their swift war stallions waved their lances tipped with golden pennants. The swordsmen of Gar and Perrigar beat their swords against their embossed shields and shouted their war cries with lusty vigor. The dreaded bowmen of Vadul in their brown and green leathern outfits stood grim and quiet, for quiet and stealth were among their valued weapons. A supporting contingent of cavalry and infantry from the Empire gave the ancient imperial war cry pledging themselves to victory. "Victory for Thurka Re. Victory or death!"

From the Emperor's left side the entire force repeated the Southern cry. The sound welled up around Crispan, who sat on his horse uncomfortably in the unfamiliar armor. He sat in a place of honor, between Pangal and his second, Lord Oslon, as their men raised and repeated their war cries and shook their weapons.

Thurka led his steed forward down the broad swath of grass separating the two forces. Crispan smiled at the confidence of these men, who redoubled their shouts at the Emperor's movement, and for a brief and happy moment his own doubts were lost in their confidence.

First Thurka rode up to Prince Zascha and the army bound for the relief of Anrehenkar. "Yours is a most difficult task, for you must defend the capital of the Middle Realm so that Zhyjman can make no claim to it. Remember that you represent all the states of the South, so that Zhyjman may not say that it is we who have usurped Anrehenkar." Zascha touched his mace to his helmet in salute, and then took the Emperor's extended hand.

Then, still accompanied by his son and brother, he turned and rode to the waiting army under Baron Pangal. "General, you have three missions. You are to secure our eastern borders and relieve the High City of Zifkar. You are to clear the eastern regions of the enemy, and you are to keep our Magician safe. He is to accompany you to Zifkar and no further." Pangal too made his salute and shook Thurka's hand.

Thurka leaned forward in his saddle to speak to Crispan. "I still have my doubts about this. Keep yourself safe. Omir will be loath to send us another Wizard." He smiled warmly and Crispan did so as well.

Pangal raised his left arm high and his army snapped to attention. He stood in his stirrups and looked both left and right, his light-blue eyes flashing in a well-tanned face. His arm came down sharply and a chorus of drums and trumpets filled the air. In parade order the Army of the East moved out of Gurdikar on the road to Zifkar. Now the third body of troops, the meager reserve ordered to

137

stay behind, raised their voices in chants and war songs to wish their comrades well. There was more than a hint of envy in their voices, and they sang long and loud.

As they wheeled around to the east in great precision, a fourth rider joined the commanders and the Magician. "Stova, commander of the cavalry," he said, offering his hand. Crispan shook it, and they rode on.

Gurdikar was long gone from sight, the sound of drums and trumpets and cheers were echoes on the wind. Marching with the confidence of their rousing departure, the army of Baron Pangal covered much ground that day and rode into the evening. Their campfires lit the plain that night, mirroring the stars above.

"You seemed restless at Gurdikar," opined Stova, seating himself next to Crispan.

"It must have been the armor. I'm not used to it."

"Oh," said the cavalry commander, laughing. "If that's all, you needn't worry. We won't be marching in full dress. It'll be light dress and traveling pack until we're nearer to Zifkar."

"When will that be?"

"Twenty days or more. I presume Pangal will swing us south of the city."

Crispan was a bit surprised. "Don't you know? You are third in command, are you not?"

Stova's pleasant face broke into a sardonic smile. He wore his brown hair close-cropped in an unfashionable style, and sported a short beard without a moustache. "Yes," he shrugged, "but Pangal keeps his plans to himself mostly. He's a good commander, mind. A little cold perhaps, but he leads well. He'll let us know when he thinks it necessary."

"Does that satisfy you?" Despite this soldier's gruff exterior, Crispan found him easy to talk to. Perhaps it was their similarity in age, or his bluntness, or his soldierly bearing and appearance. His dark eyes squinted constantly, the reflex of a man who spent long days in the sun. He looked the part of a leader of cavalry, tall, thin and muscular.

"A soldier," Stova replied, "learns to accept many things. We have few able commanders anyway. Pangal is one. So is Oslon, though he tends to be a bit overeager. And yet he may even be better."

"Then why is he not in command?"

"For many reasons. Pangal is older, more experienced. And besides, his family ranks higher than Oslon's."

There was more than a note of bitterness in Stova's voice, and this did not go undetected. "Why does that bother you?"

Stova's lips drew into a thin smile. He took out his dirk and began to poke it into the fire's embers. "Because my social position is even lower. I am a bastard, the son of the late Margrave Humbyrt. It is only through my dubious claim to his paternity that I have gone this far. He was good to me, and at a very young age took me to be his aide. I was lucky and saw much action against marauders on the western borders, where Humbyrt's march was, and so I was able to prove myself. Without that I should never have risen so high; I am not likely to go much higher." He sat back and looked reflectively into the flames. "In many ways," he said in a voice half joking, half painfully serious, "this war may be my only chance." He rose abruptly. Patting Crispan on the shoulder, he bade him good night.

For the next several days they marched across land still suspended in that frustrating time of year when winter clings tenaciously and the promise of spring is tantalizingly close. Brown winter grass still held sway over large patches of the land, but there were signs of hope in the few small woods they passed where small dots of green hung on the branches.

Stova had recovered from his gloom of the first night. He rode in company with Crispan, seeking to draw the Magician out of his own subdued demeanor.

"I heard it rumored, Crispan, that you had volunteered to accompany us."

Crispan admitted it, and explained in answer to Stova's

139

further queries that he had done so because he had felt useless at Gurdikar.

"I know the feeling," Stova sympathized. "That's how I've felt these past few years, rotting on the border near Vadul. It was apparent to many of us that this was coming. Surely by the time Zhyjman took Tharn, it should have been apparent to all. That would have given us at least some time to prepare. Instead, we sat. Everyone was told it was impossible that he would go further—the anarchy we have called peace seemed so inviolate. And the threat of Larc to Zhyjman's flank seemed so reassuring. Now Larc is gone and Zhyjman is moving faster than anyone had dared to imagine. And here you and I are, eager to do something, posted on this mission to oblivion." The tone of bitterness had again crept into his voice.

Crispan was taken aback by the word. "Oblivion? Why?"

"There is little to be expected from this expedition. The relief of Zifkar will be easily accomplished, and so will the securing of the area around it. Some few troops will be detached to hold the area, while Pangal, Oslon and the rest return to Gurdikar with the others to resume their waiting. Ah! But you're lucky. Pangal will keep you safe from harm, and you will return with him when this is over."

"And you?"

"Pangal has not said, but I expect to be posted at Zifkar. It will give me an opportunity to watch events now from the extreme other side of the Empire."

Both men lapsed into silence. Crispan thought about this odd man riding beside him. He was a pessimist, but there was something in his openness and blunt honesty that appealed to the Magician. Stova was obviously a man who sized things up quickly and had seemingly chosen Crispan as a suitable companion and confidant. The Magician found that he liked him.

On the next day's march Stova wheeled in beside Crispan after conferring with Pangal and Oslon. "There's been news, a messenger from Ker-en-kar to the south. The governor there, Ludivo, rides out to meet us. We'll meet today. He wants to discuss the situation in the east, and Pangal has messages from the Emperor."

They halted early that afternoon for the conference with the Governor of Ker-en-kar. To the troops it was an unexpected holiday on a pleasant warm day. To Stova and Crispan it was their first indication of Pangal's plans. They had arrived last at the conference and had been introduced to Ludivo in an offhand manner.

"Magician?" said Ludivo upon hearing Crispan's title, arching his slim gray brows. "Ah, yes. I heard tell we had a sorcerer to counter some spell of Zhyjman's." He turned again back to Pangal.

"As I was saying," continued Pangal, "the Emperor wishes you to maintain your strength here. His only order beyond that is that you push your patrols further east. I shall relieve Zifkar and secure the area north towards the Gates. When that is done, we will regroup our forces and prepare for Zhyjman." At this, Stova threw Crispan a knowing glance.

Ludivo scratched under his bearded chin, a mixture of gray and black. "And that's all. Ha! So very simple." He turned to Crispan. "I trust you will help out should things go awry?" Crispan forced a smile at the sarcastic remark. Ludivo then asked his opinion of the plan, but Crispan demurred, saying he was no warrior. Ludivo muttered something about meddlers as Pangal led him away to talk in private. Oslon prepared the column to move on while the two commanders conferred.

"Steady, Crispan," advised Stova as they swung into their saddles, sensing his seething anger. "It's just that some in the army feel Thurka has waited too long and that this talk of magicians and spells on both sides is ridiculous, a way to hide weaknesses and true intentions, especially our weaknesses. We do not want to raise false hopes so late. It would be better to have it all out at once."

The Wizard was about to reply, but thought better of it. The sunlight reflecting off his talisman reminded him of the old adage told to those leaving the Order for their first mission: "Do not expect those with Two Eyes to understand." He repeated it to himself a number of times.

XVI

Zifkar

The army's march shifted now from southeast to due east for some days and then veered gently to the northeast. The grass became more sparse as they neared the scrublands that dominated the east, but what there was was a reassuring green, as spring was now clearly triumphant over retreating winter.

"Well," said Stova, in a voice both flat and terribly matter-of-fact, "as far as we know, the Empire is now truly at war."

"What do you mean?" said Crispan, looking at him in surprise.

"That stele," replied Stova, pointing to a nondescript granite slab slowly receding behind them. "It marks the eastern border of the Empire, as proclaimed in the first border wars after the demise of the Middle Realm. The Emperor Durghan II himself raised it after the battle of Ksir. We have now crossed out of the Empire and are at war. I suppose that calls for a drink." His voice remained flat. He reached over to the far side of his saddle pommel and brought up a wineskin. Drinking down two long spurts, he passed it to the Magician, whose first effort misfired, the stream of wine splattering against his chin and cheek. "Ha!" Stova snorted. "It's not so easy to ride and drink, is it? When you can do that, then you will truly be an accomplished soldier."

They both laughed heartily as Crispan dried himself with the back of his sleeve. He tilted his head and lifted the wineskin, squeezing it again. This time he was successful.

The night following their change of direction, Pangal summoned his commanders for a council. Crispan was included as well, more out of courtesy than interest in his opinion. Pangal offered them wine as he briefly explained his plans, his voice low and gravelly. He hoped to reach Zifkar within eight days, and would approach it from the west. They would confer again when they were closer and better able to assess the situation. Looking around him as he furled his map, Pangal asked, "Are there any questions?"

As Stova and Crispan moved away from the commander's fire towards their own, Stova snorted contemptuously. "Any questions? Bah!"

Crispan thrust his hands under his cape as they walked. "I thought you said he was a good commander."

"Don't get me wrong, Crispan. He is. His soldiers always know what he expects of them and always try to do it. I tell you, I'd rather have Pangal than one of those damned generals who are so friendly and jovial that their soldiers feel there are few demands on them. It was such a general that killed Humbyrt. We were routing some brigands and expected this other general's troops to join us. They did—half a day late. No, I'll take Pangal for all his coolness."

In the days before they reached Zifkar, Crispan came to appreciate what Stova had said. The soldiers continued on without complaint or question. They believed in Pangal, trusted in his judgment and his competence, and asked no more of him than a few words of encouragement and some small inkling of what they were about. Pangal would allow himself to be seen frequently, moving up and down the marching column.

Stova came flying past the bewildered Magician. Crispan spurred his own horse after him. Near the head of the column he caught up with Stova. "What is it?" he asked breathlessly.

"We must change the columns now."

"Because we're heading north?"

Stova's eyebrows raised a bit. "You noticed. You're improving at this." It was a compliment Crispan barely appreciated. Undaunted, Stova went on, "We must change our formation. We are near to Zifkar."

Together they rode up to the head of the column where Pangal and Oslon sat viewing the redeployment. Squadrons of light cavalry armed with two small lances and bows and arrows rode swiftly by on their small mounts. Columns of heavy cavalry with long spears and shields and swords thundered in all directions, forming guards around the army at this vulnerable moment. Groups of infantry marched at double time, shortening the length of the column.

Pangal inspected the new formations. An air of expectancy hung over them. "At the double, Oslon. I want to reach Zifkar the day after tomorrow." With renewed energy and a sudden grimness the army again set out on the road east.

A warm wind at their backs now shoved them gently on their way, making rippling waves in the fresh green grass that appeared in scattered patches on the treeless eastern plain that ran right up into the Great Mountains. A harsh vista of tough knots of scrubs and ill-defined roads spread before them.

As Pangal had hoped, they crossed this unappealing land in two days, carefully screening their movements behind a shield of scouting light cavalry. Their reports of the situation before Zifkar opened Pangal's last council of war.

"The enemy is camped north of the city. Cavalry mostly, little or no siege equipment. I think their intention was to rush the city before help could arrive. They are a mixed group, from Nor, Kyryl, and some mercenaries."

Oslon broke in asking, "Are they right against the walls?"

"No. The main gate faces north, and they hover beyond it. The city is blockaded, but not besieged."

Everyone was silent now. Pangal rested his chin on his fingertips, his eyes narrowing and forcing lines to appear across his brow. "We will attack tomorrow, with all haste. The infantry shall attack from the west and drive a wedge between the enemy and Zifkar. This will serve to relieve the city. The cavalry will strike the enemy on their flank and trap them before they can withdraw to the north. Will this be satisfactory?" There was no dissent. "Inform the troops. We march northeasterly in order to be in the proper position."

Crispan noted that the activity in the camp that night was different from any other night of their march, different from the bustle he had noticed at Gurdikar. Men were sitting in small, silent groups, busily cleaning and sharpening their weapons. Fires were forbidden this night lest an enemy patrol spot them. By the light of a fleeting moon swords were drawn and honed, shafts on spears, lances and arrows were tested for any crack or infirmity. Quiet fell over the army as soldiers turned in for some needed rest before the business of the next day.

Moving according to plan, the army did not come upon Zifkar until past midday. Crispan, who had not seen any city until Gurdikar, noted how different Zifkar appeared. Its walls were gray-white, gleaming against the dull hues of the scrubland. Various towers peered over the walls at irregular intervals. His eyes were especially caught by the special hallmark of this former high city of the Middle Realm, the bright-colored towers rising from the palace of the Chamberlain and the city's three great temples. He noted too how welcome the city looked after a long march.

The host moved cautiously forward as one man, its approach obscured by a high thin ridge due west of the city. Luck was with them, for the slothful enemy had posted no patrols and expected no aid to come to faraway Zifkar. Pangal noted all this as he rode on the edge of the rise, his helmet tucked into the crook of his left arm. Assured that everything was ready, he turned suddenly to Crispan, addressing him for perhaps the fourth time since they had left Gurdikar. "And what shall we do with you, Magician?"

Crispan shrugged helplessly, perplexed at the question. Before he could ask to be assigned to Stova's command,

Pangal went on. "You will stay here with the reserves and the baggage."

"Baron Pangal!" he protested.

"The Emperor's orders were clear. I am to keep you safe, and that is what I shall do. Let me be honest with you, Lord Crispan. I have never quite understood what you were doing here and I do not like people accompanying me for the sake of adventure. So you will stay here either willingly or under force of arms."

Thoroughly deflated, Crispan led his horse to the crest.

Below him, on the westward slope, Oslon formed up the army. The enemy, as reported, had camped just above Zifkar. They had the city surrounded but had not pressed the siege. It would be easy to implement the Baron's plan.

Oslon joined Pangal to report their readiness. "Then begin. Lead in the infantry at the run. I will follow with the cavalry in support. Stova and the rest of the cavalry on their flank."

Oslon tipped his sword against his plumed helm and reined his horse over the ridge. Companies of infantry followed at a trot, each man's spear jogging up and down as he ran. They formed into a tight wedge on the plain between the ridge and the city. Their silent approach and the enemy's carelessness allowed them within range of their spears before the foe began to react. A great howl arose from the enemy encampment, like the sound of a suddenly angered beast. It was too late. The leading companies were too close. They heaved their spears into the scrambling foe, and then quickly drew their swords and closed. By the time the first blades clashed and clanged Pangal was on them as well with three squadrons of cavalry.

One of the soldiers sitting by Crispan pointed across the plain. "The wedge is working," he cried. Driving hard before the enemy, Oslon's soldiers were firmly between them and the gate of Zifkar. For one dread moment the defenders of Zifkar were too surprised to react. Crispan had trouble following the flow of the battle as swirling dust and smoke rose and the enemy turned for one desperate counterattack. Flailing, charging bodies were obscured in a dusky blur.

"The gates!" shouted Crispan as the huge oaken portals swung open and the defenders poured out.

"Now," said Crispan's guardian, "watch Stova. It is time for the kill." In two broad columns Stova led his cavalry against the enemy's flank. It was all over so quickly that Crispan could hardly believe it. Pressed hard in front, the invaders now tried to guard their flank as well. "They're breaking! They run!" Crispan exulted as the foe's ranks wavered and then broke. Panic gripped them in an instant. Those to the rear made straight away towards the north, while those up front struggled to disengage themselves from Pangal's host. Those still in their tents were caught and overrun in the crush of their own fleeing comrades and the onrushing victors.

Crispan was already dashing towards Zifkar with his escort and the eager reserves. It had all happened so fast that Crispan had not associated that rapid movement of men with killing and death. Only as he neared the open gates and saw dead men, men who had only moments before been hardy charging soldiers, did the realization come to him. He shuddered as his horse passed the still warm bodies.

Oslon and Stova were sitting on their well-lathered mounts before the open portals. Soldiers whom Crispan took to be from within Zifkar stood beside them.

"Crispan! It's over quicker than we dared hope." Stova's words only brought a curious look to the Magician's face.

"Where is Pangal?" he asked.

Oslon motioned to a knot of troops before the gate. "He is dead," he said quietly, pointing to the Baron's body, surrounded by an honor guard. "A stray arrow cut him down."

Crispan was offended by Oslon's matter-of-fact tone. He found this suddenness of death incomprehensible. "Dead? But it was hardly more than a skirmish. It was all so fast. How—"

Stova prodded his horse forward and grabbed Crispan's arm. "Calm yourself. It happens. In war each man is vulnerable. Pangal was a good warrior and a fine leader. It was his time."

There was no response Crispan could make to that, no way to protest the seeming senselessness of it all. Further conversation was impossible at any rate, amidst the joyous shouts of victory. Pangal's soldiers prowled through the tents so hastily abandoned, seeking out prisoners and booty. "Stova," snapped Oslon, "have the army drawn in, and send scouts and cavalry to follow the enemy and harass their retreat. We are not yet done."

Preceded by the body of their fallen commander, borne before them on several shields, Oslon, Stova and Crispan entered the High City of Zifkar. The streets beyond the gates were crowded with milling soldiers, slowing their progress. Only the approach of a squadron of riders, all wrapped in shining bronze armor that was more decorative than functional, parted the human sea before them. A short, fat man rode in the wake of this squadron, encased in ceremonial armor made of gold. Baldomir, the High Chamberlain of Zifkar, resembled a golden bowl rather than a fearsome border lord. His face was a fleshy sphere decorated with a wispy red-blond moustache and goatee, framed by a helmet designed to show his features to their best advantage, accenting his blue eyes and light hair. Upon reaching the saviors of his city he extended his hand, encased in a glove of delicate golden mail, and introduced himself.

"I am Oslon," came the reply, "commander of this Army of the East dispatched by my lord, the Emperor Thurka. He bids me give you his salutation and greeting. These are General Stova, commander of the cavalry, and Lord Crispan—er, an adviser to the Emperor."

"You are young, Lord Oslon, to command an army."

Oslon raised a hand in a self-effacing gesture. "My Lord Chamberlain, I am but the second in command. There is the body of our general, the Baron Pangal, cut down before your gates." Over the Baron's body lay his own black cape, over which a deep stain had spread.

"We join you in your grief. We may take solace in the

knowledge that he died in full glory. We would be honored to bury him here at Zifkar with all due honors." Crispan found the words hollow, but kept his silence.

Pangal was laid to rest that evening in a hastily constructed tomb just inside the gate of the city he had died to save. The bodies of that day's dead, mostly enemy, were burned in a huge pyre where their camp had been. "It is an old custom," Stova explained to Crispan as they watched the acrid smoke fill the northern horizon. "Nowadays we bury our dead if possible, but when a commander dies in battle we do him honor by reverting to the ancient custom. A pyre of his soldiers and his defeated enemies to see him on his way."

The light from the pyre was clearly visible in the Chamberlain's council, high in one of Zifkar's colorful towers. The glow of the flames danced on the intricate blue and gold mosaic which overlay the walls, depicting scenes of fabulous beasts amidst lush vegetation. The beauty of the room was lost on all the soldiers who gathered there, but not on Crispan, who felt there was something in that chamber to which his powers responded.

Oslon was all business as he explained to his officers and to Baldomir and his councillors his plan for the continuation of the campaign.

"I will take two-thirds of the army and pursue the enemy, commencing at first light on the morrow. I will pursue them as far as the Gates if possible, and secure this region. Stova will remain here with the reserves and as the garrison for Zifkar. You will make the necessary forays to the east. When I have completed our business in the north I will return straightaway to Gurdikar with as many troops as possible, for the east will then be safe."

Stova's shadow leapt across the wall as he rose to his feet before the light from without and the dancing candles. "Surely you are taking too many men that far north. You will be open to attack from all sides."

Oslon brushed the thought aside, gesturing with his hand. "This was Pangal's plan before it was mine. I shall merely be following the Emperor's orders and wishes."

"No," protested Stova. "He only said to secure the eastern borders. There was no mention of an advance as far as the Gates." Stova walked to the map etched into an animal skin which hung between two long tapers. "Look how wide the plain to the north is. An army could easily slip past you and threaten Zifkar or even the Empire. We need only secure the immediate region and the lands up to the High Pass."

"Nonsense," said Oslon contemptuously. "You worry needlessly. The enemy is broken by our victory here. If we pursue him vigorously there will be no further threat to Zifkar or the east at all. How can Zhyjman raise another army so quickly? And look at your map. Obviously the Gates are the bottleneck from which the east can be sealed." Without any further comment from his deputy, Oslon turned to the Chamberlain. "Will the forces I described be sufficient to safeguard your city?"

A man of little military knowledge, Baldomir answered politely, not daring to challenge Oslon's arrangements. "If, as you say, you can crush the remainder of the enemy's force, then it will suffice."

"Fine." Oslon pushed back his chair. "Issue the necessary orders. We march at dawn."

Crispan felt compelled to say something. Oslon's cavalier comment about Zhyjman's raising another army troubled him for reasons he could not fathom. Had he been alone, in his study in the Order, he might have been able to plumb this nagging feeling, but instead he felt intimidated in the presence of these soldiers and drowned his doubts in the round of toasts which followed.

XVII

Garrison Duty

In the smoky hours of earliest dawn all were assembled by the northern gate of Zifkar. The departing force was a shadowy mass waiting on the plain above the city. Figures moved in that not-quite-light awaiting their commander.

Oslon was all confidence. He knelt in silent salute before Pangal's guarded tomb and then shook hands all around. "Be vigilant, Stova. You will hear from me soon."

Stova managed a tight smile while Oslon drew down his helmet and rode out under the portal of the High City, mist swirling about him and his staff as they moved north. Soon only muffled voices and the soft shuffling movement and clatter of an army on the march were heard, but the sounds were strangely disembodied by the fog. Stova sat looking out from the city, staring at a blank gray wall of mist. After a while he let out a massive yawn and withdrew into Zifkar. "Close the gates," he ordered.

"What now?" asked Baldomir, betraying more than a touch of anxiety now that Oslon was actually on his way.

Stova looked terribly bored, and annoyed by the Chamberlain's tardy concern. "I intend to go back to sleep. I would suggest you do the same. There is nothing to be done in this fog. When it burns off in the sun there will be time to make plans." And true to his word, Stova returned to his quarters in the Chamberlain's palace.

The days which followed brought renewed activity as plans were made for forays into the plains and scrublands around Zifkar. But after the few days that it took to verify the emptiness of the plains to the east and south, a stultifying boredom settled down over Zifkar and all its troops. Each passing day made Crispan more and more restless. No word came from Oslon to the north, little news from the Emperor to the west. He would haunt the place before the Chamberlain's palace where the couriers arrived, but there was only disappointment as those few who came from Gurdikar brought no word of Vladur. Crispan tried to spend the rest of his time in Baldomir's fine library, studying and honing his Arts. He felt himself growing stale and longed to be back in his well-equipped study, reading and practicing rare conjuries and spells far into the night. But there had been no member of the Order at Zifkar for many years, and so the library held few of even the most basic works. The markets, too, disappointed Crispan, for all he could purchase there were the most simple ingredients and herbs. Limited as he was, and not wanting to try out his deeper powers within the confines of the garrisoned city, he reverted to minor tricks, simple potions, mere sleights of hand, mind and eye. These did not satisfy him in the least, and only served to increase his anxiety and growing frustration.

Disgusted, he would throw aside his primitive tools and turn back to the Chamberlain's library. But the many beautifully bound volumes of poetry and cycles of sagas did not distract him either. Instead he would wander aimlessly about the city. He became a familiar sight to all the citizenry; he got to know the city well himself, the narrow streets far away from the palace, the joyful noise of the many markets. Two feelings mixed incongruously in the air, the feeling of relief displayed by the Zifkari and the bustle of the garrison as Stova kept it busy improving the city's defenses.

Crispan took to roaming the battlements by day and night, staring out over the plains for some sign. He would lean on the massive crenellations on the northeastern tower and stand there for hours at a time, his expression as empty as the seemingly interminable plains. Wrapped in his gray cloak at night, hood up against the wind, or in a leathern jerkin by day, the Magician became a common sight along the walls. He was on the battlements one night watching the stars, trying to divine their messages, when Stova came upon him.

"What do they tell you?"

Crispan stared blankly at the question.

"The stars—what do they say? You can read them, can't you?"

The Magician shrugged. "Some and sometimes. Not tonight."

They lapsed into silence. Stova huddled against the wind, while Crispan remained still. After a long while Stova intruded again. "What bothers you, Crispan? I see you in the palace, barely eating. You have become a specter about the city, moving aimlessly about the streets, clinging to these walls. What is it?"

"Do you know what it is like to feel useless, to be out of one's proper time and place? I have gone through the Chamberlain's library. I've tried history, poetry, epics. I've dabbled in my Arts. I've practiced with your swordsmen. But none of it does any good. Don't you see, Stova? My very being here is pointless unless Vladur is out there somewhere. Imagine! I've become dependent on the necromancer for my reason for being here. I hated him for what he had done, and yet without him I can no longer justify what *I* have done or what I am doing."

Stova sympathized. "I know little of magic, Crispan. Is what Vladur has done so foul that you had to come seek him out?"

Crispan turned to face him, almost grinning thinly at his naiveté. "Do you know what a necromancer does? He is an abomination. He takes the dead and brings them back."

"To life?"

"No, not quite. To a state of being undead, but not alive either. When they are in this condition, he can to a large degree control them."

"Then how has Vladur used this power?"

Crispan shrugged. "I do not know. Perhaps he has raised past Magicians and Wizards and used them to increase his own powers. Perhaps he has used it in some other way. I do not know."

Stova felt he was beginning to understand the Magician's feeling of helplessness. He asked quietly, "If you do not know, then how can you combat him?"

"That is the heart of my worries, and remains to be seen. It matters little what he does with his evil, for there is little or nothing written on how to combat it. That which was banned never required a countermeasure." His voice rose in pitched anger. "Oh! He is a debaser of our Arts, a violator of our compact with the Spirits!" The tone of Crispan's voice subsided now. "There are some passages in very ancient tomes, but they are mostly descriptive and vague. What it will come down to, if he is indeed out there, will be my powers as a Master of the Five Arts against his, plus whatever others he has gained since his exile. I just wish I could be certain he was out there at all."

"It's late," said Stova softly, putting his arm around Crispan. The Magician nodded and they climbed down the battlements to their respective chambers in the palace for some sleep.

Having unburdened himself to Stova, Crispan slept better that night than any other since they had come to Zifkar. Wrapped deep within his blankets he truly rested, his fears and doubts not disturbing him that night.

Somewhere, far away from his sleeping self, he heard a voice calling his name. "Crispan, Crispan. Wake up." A hand gently rocked his shoulder. The voice became clearer. "Crispan, wake up." He opened his eyes to see Stova standing over his bed.

"What? What is it?" He blearily rubbed his eyes.

Stova's voice was very low and even. "There's news. There's been a messenger."

That served to bring Crispan fully awake. "What does he say?" he asked expectantly.

"It's from Oslon. There is trouble. He says he was advancing along the southern rim of the Falchions north of the High Pass when a large enemy force descended on him. He's been cut off and is trapped on the slopes of the mountains. The messenger says he was the fourth man sent to us. He says the enemy force is so massive that while part of it contains Oslon in the Falchions and grinds him into submission, the rest is already advancing south to take Zifkar. He says this second army is large, and that this time they have siege equipment aplenty."

Crispan just sat in bed listening to this, lost in his own thoughts. The easy victory won before Zifkar had suddenly come apart. The army he had marched with was threatened with extinction. Zifkar and the eastern borderlands seemed lost already.

Looking at the Magician's expressionless face, Stova poked him. "Crispan, did you hear me?"

"Yes, yes. What are we to do?"

"I have summoned a council in Baldomir's study. Get dressed." Stova departed for the Chamberlain's quarters. Crispan sat for a moment in his bed, pondering the sudden change in their fortune. As his feet touched the cold stone floor beyond the small fur rug and he pulled on his britches, he thought how unlike his life at the Order this all was. "Where," he asked himself, rolling down his sleeves, "is the progression of facts and circumstances? It is all so very unsettling," he decided, clasping his buckle into place and bringing his talisman out from under his jerkin.

Both in the palace and in the city there was a renewed and meaningful activity. Additional lookouts were posted on the walls, and foraging parties scoured the surrounding plains. All the wares of the markets were requisitioned for rationing before the news had spread very far. The siege had begun before the enemy had arrived.

All the now-familiar faces had assembled in Baldomir's study by the time Crispan arrived. He accepted a piece of fruit for his breakfast and joined the circle around the map spread across the large table.

"How long ago did this all happen?" Stova asked the pale and weary messenger.

"Ten days. But I was the fourth man sent, as I told you. Since then the enemy has separated. They were already on their way south in great force when I left Lord

Oslon. I managed to skirt their eastern flank to get here."
His voice had a nervous and unsettling edge to it, and he
constantly sipped from a cup of deep-red wine.

"That means your ride took even more time." Stova
stopped to calculate for a moment. "We have perhaps
five days at the most, maybe six depending on how fast
they can move with their siege machines." He gazed at the
map, dragging his dirk back and forth on the plain between Zifkar and the Falchions. "I do not see what we
can do. We cannot abandon the city." Baldomir bristled
visibly at this idea. "Do not worry," Stova reassured him,
"that we shall not do. Zifkar is their goal and we must
hold them here for as long as possible. Time will be on
our side if we can get word to the Emperor and he can
spare the forces to relieve us." His voice then dropped to
a worried whisper. "I wonder where Zhyjman got so
many men."

"It is too far to Gurdikar," observed the Chamberlain,
tugging nervously at his moustaches. "The Emperor
could never reach us in time."

"And this may only be a feint by Zhyjman to divert the
Emperor to the east and then threaten elsewhere." Stova
turned to Crispan, now standing beside him. "What would
you suggest?"

Crispan looked at the map. "How far is the nearest
sizable fortress-garrison?"

"Ker-en-kar. It is at least fifteen days or more from
here. Look at the map. This is where Ludivo is quartered."

Crispan's deep-gray eyes narrowed. "That is too long.
Surely it is not fifteen days' ride from here to there," he
said, indicating the straight line between the two cities.

"But you cannot ride straight. Across the Karsh?
Never! A rider would never make it. Better fifteen days
than never."

"Fifteen days there and a longer ride back with a relief
force? You cannot hold here that long, Stova."

"But my Lord Crispan," interjected the Chamberlain,
"General Stova is correct. The Karsh cannot be crossed,
especially at this time of year."

Crispan admitted to himself that for all his knowledge, even of geography, he knew little of conditions in the World. "Why not?" he was forced to ask.

"The Karsh is a huge bowl," Baldomir explained, "ringed on all sides by low mountains. Its floor is cracked and dry clay that crumbles to the touch. There is no water, not a plant or animal alive in it."

"Be that as it may, Chamberlain, it remains the shortest route."

"Of course. Perhaps ten days, perhaps even as little as eight. But no one has ever tried, or at least succeeded. We are told from generation to generation that the Karsh was a part of the World purposely left bare by the Spirits to remind man of their power to create or deny life. In summer it becomes an oven, intensifying the heat of the sun. In winter it is a bowl of winds that howl madly across it from down all the mountainsides."

"And now, in the spring?"

"And now," Stova answered, "it can become a sea of mud as the spring rains fall, becoming more impassable than at any other time if that can be imagined, the mud dragging down the feet of men or beasts until they collapse of exhaustion and die amidst its barren wastes. And even if it doesn't rain it isn't safe. A party crossing the Karsh when it's dry would raise a huge cloud of dust from the broken clay, easily visible from the surrounding mountains. Zhyjman may have scouts this far south already. A party would be spotted and intercepted. The southern route may be longer, but it is safest."

Crispan drummed his long, thin fingers on the table. "No, it is too long. No, Stova, we must cross the Karsh and hope that it does not rain. Order my horse and an escort mounted at once. We leave today. Have them pack sufficient food and water, and fodder for the horses."

Stova's eyes went wide with fright. "But certainly *you're* not going!" The purpose of Crispan's questions now hit him all at once. "You cannot go, you're too valuable. I will go."

"Stova, be practical. I am no warlord. Let me go to Ker-en-kar while you defend this place as is your job."

"But—but if you should die in the Karsh—I'd be held responsible by the Emperor."

"Would it be any better if I were captured here in Zifkar? I am the logical choice to ride to Ker-en-kar. If I ride across the Karsh I can send a relief force as quickly as possible and also send messengers from there to Thurka at Gurdikar." With that, Crispan left the council and headed for his room, while Stova made plans with Baldomir for the coming siege and the defense of the High City of Zifkar.

Crispan moved about his room quickly, throwing what few things he would need in his saddle bag. As he was buckling his sword about him, Stova came in to renew the debate.

"Do you know what you are doing?"

"Only what must be done," said the Magician, shaking his head. "I am the most expendable member of this garrison."

"But the Karsh—"

"How far is it to the Karsh from here?"

"Two or three days."

"I will be in Ker-en-kar within ten." Crispan put his hand on his friend's shoulder. "The Karsh or Zifkar. Maybe it will not matter either way." He gave a short laugh as he embraced Stova.

Crispan was the last member of the relief party to emerge in the courtyard, where his escort waited, already mounted. The High Lords of Zifkar and Stova and his officers stood by as the Magician prepared to mount his steed.

"I have given you the best riders. Good luck."

"Wipe that terrible frown off your face, Stova. We'll reach Ker-en-kar. I only hope we return in time to save *you*. Listen to no offers of peace; your choice is fortitude or torture and death." Crispan swung up into his saddle.

"May the Spirits guide you, my lord," shouted the Chamberlain, as Crispan and his party rode under the gate of Zifkar.

Out from under the same portal where Oslon had confidently ridden they rode west across the scrub and patchy grass. Crispan knew the commander of his escort, Captain Portar, a cavalier well respected by his men. A veteran of many border campaigns, he wore a number of scars on his face as medals, including one very jagged one that interrupted the right side of his deep black beard. As Stova had said, Portar was one of the best riders and lancers in the entire army.

"How much rations do we have?"

"Stova saw to it that we have enough for eleven days plus one extra, and the same amount of water, four jugs per man."

"Well, it will have to be enough. We must ride as hard as possible here on the plain. There is no telling how the going will be once we reach the Karsh."

They rode as fast as they could towards the Karsh, taking advantage of the few streams they crossed so as to save their own supplies. They rode hard until two suns had set over them and Zifkar. It was evening of the second day when they reached the edge of the Karsh. The dull light of day's end obscured the great maw in the earth that lay before them.

"It is too late to start down today," Portar advised.

Crispan agreed. "Let's rest here and start early in the morning. Have the men light fires. It will be safe and comforting."

The Magician moved among the men that night, talking with each small cluster of troops.

"You know," said one named Trofan. "I didn't believe you when you told us we were crossing the Karsh."

"Does it bother you?"

"No."

The answer was simple and direct, and Crispan took no little comfort from the confidence evident in all their faces.

XVIII

The Karsh

Before the sun had lit the far eastern sky behind them Crispan had aroused his party. In the chill of the early morning the men huddled close by the few fires and ate just enough bread and dried meat to take the edge off their hunger. Portar, clapping his hands to chase the cold, came up to Crispan. "We're ready to ride. Shall we mount?"

"Yes, but hold here. I want to wait until the light reaches the Karsh."

They killed the fires and mounted, waiting on the eastern rim for the first light of day. The sky behind them went from dark blue to light gray as the sun rose. They all sat in total silence, some watching the retreating edge of night as it was pushed further west, those in front watching the great bowl beneath them where morning mist still slept on the ground.

Pale pink had been summoned up to follow light gray in the east; the fingers of darkness were no longer overhead when Portar gently tapped Crispan's arm and pointed down into the Karsh. Crispan leaned forward in his saddle and peered down the slope. The mist had begun to disperse, and he could see the Karsh.

No man in that party had ever seen the Karsh before, its pale-red floor seeming solid enough from where they stood, stretching out interminably before them.

All about them was now suffused in that soft light of earliest morning as Crispan signaled the men to proceed down into the Karsh. They picked their way down the gentle slope, the noise of the hooves the only sound to disturb a silent world. Crispan reached the bottom first, with Portar close behind. At the very rim of the Karsh, just on the bottom of the slope, lay the bleached skeleton of a man. He had managed to get that far, that close to safety when the Karsh claimed him. Crispan shuddered at the sight, wondering what sort of omen Eliborg would make of it with his divination. Crispan halted and turned to his companions. "We ride at a moderate pace, so as to cover as much ground as possible without tiring the horses."

He then led his horse onto the Karsh. His horse's first steps came as a surprise, for the seemingly level plain was actually a huge blanket of dust over a broken floor of firmer clay. The horse sank in past his ankles, sending small plumes of dust up with each step. Crispan moved slowly at first, letting Portar catch up with him and giving the others time to reach the floor and gingerly try it. Then, when all had assembled in a rough column of twos and threes, he set off at an easy gallop.

Immediately on all sides columns of dust rose, obscuring much of their vision and choking off any effort at conversation. Worse still was the absolute silence they rode in, no noise to comfort them other than the small clatter of their own equipment and soft murmur of hooves in dust and crumbling clay. It was as if they had cut themselves off from the living world and entered into one where even healthy men were seemingly blind, deaf and dumb.

They had not gone far, the eastern hills still in sight, when Crispan and Portar heard voices behind them calling for them to halt. They did so and turned to see Artor, one of the last riders, coming towards them. He was covered in dust.

"M'lord, we can't go on in this way. Those in the rear are choking to death on all the dust."

Artor was covered in dust. He seemed to be more a part of the Karsh than a rider across it. "Very well," ordered Portar, "form into three small groups, one to include Crispan and me, one on either side of us. That way those in the rear will be little discomforted. Do not spread out too far, lest those on the ends stray from the troop."

164

As the column rearranged itself Crispan looked back over their path. The dust they had aroused had already settled, and there was little evidence that they had been there so recently. For a moment he felt as if he had been swallowed whole by the Karsh, and he shuddered.

With the men redeployed, Crispan again signaled them forward. As the horses made their first moves forward, new columns of choking dust arose, and the way they had come was lost behind a soft red curtain.

They rode in absolute silence, none daring to part his parched lips lest he let in the clouds of clay. All was timeless in the Karsh, twenty men suspended in a barren world. After some distance Portar dared speak to Crispan, suggesting that they halt for a short rest. Men and animals alike started at the sudden noise of his voice. Crispan agreed and reined in, surveying his company. They all seemed to be turning into small pieces of the land they rode over.

Crispan moved for his first jug, cautioning the men to take just enough to wet their lips and clear their throats. The troops eagerly opened their jugs, perhaps taking more than the Magician had suggested. They stretched in their saddles and cleared dust from face and beard as best they could.

It was Portar who noticed the horses' sudden restlessness. All were stirring and straining uncomfortably under their riders, some making sharp hissing sounds. Crispan looked alarmed. "What is it?"

"They're thirsty too," said Portar. "They sense the water."

It all came down on Crispan at once. In their haste to leave Zifkar they had taken enough provisions and fodder for the ride across the Karsh to Ker-en-kar, but had never thought of water for the horses.

Portar frowned, dust falling in cracks from his scar. "They'll never last without some water."

Crispan's eyes narrowed as he brushed some dust away. "We have four jugs each. Then two from each man will be used for his mount. Men! Give them just enough to calm them so that we can go on."

As one man dismounted he looked up at Crispan. "But what if we run out? We need water too."

"At least we can deny ourselves and continue. Our horses do not know self-denial, and we need them to reach Ker-en-kar. We'll have to hope it lasts."

Crispan too dismounted to water his steed. As he reached the ground he looked down. He had not walked on the Karsh yet, and he saw that the dust covered his boots way past his ankles. All around the party there was a low cloud of disturbed dust as men and horses stirred about.

As they prepared to remount, Crispan saw some of the men tearing their sleeves and wetting down the strips of cloth, then tying them about nose and mouth. Crispan followed suit and ordered the others to do the same, for it seemed a good way to perhaps avoid most of the choking dust. He also ordered that similar strips be wrapped around the horses' nostrils. And thus the dusty red band moved on again, deeper into the Karsh, which seemed to laugh and grow as they went on.

As the light passed over the far end of the Karsh, the stifling heat of day quickly disappeared, unable to cling to the barren surface. Cold now joined the omnipresent dust and wind. Men and horses rode closer together, huddling against the chill. On they pressed, with only the sense of touch active, responsive to the cold and dust.

Finally, his own horse swaying beneath him, Crispan called a halt and rest until early morning. He and Portar agreed that they might better ride during the cooler hours of predawn and thus avoid the chill of night and heat of day. Crispan looked around and saw men and horses collapse, too tired to eat or drink, or to care where they fell. Some horses went to their knees and were asleep before they had been unsaddled. And all around the wind and dust danced merrily . . . expectantly.

The sky was still pitch when Portar roused Crispan. "M'lord, we have some time before dawn." Crispan removed the cloth shielding his face and stretched his cold-numbed bones. Portar moved amongst the others until all were awake and tearing at cold beef and hard bread. A little water was spared for the horses, and they were off before the slightest hint of daybreak.

The second day of riding was a bleak continuation of the previous day's horror. The three groups trudged on westward, no one noticing the newly risen sun which did little but warm the Karsh and illuminate the all-encompassing walls of dust which had hung invisible in the dark. No noise but the muffled sound of the hooves and rattling kits, and of course the wind; no sight but the walls of dust and one's companions slowly fading into the Karsh's own color; and now, in the middle of this forsaken bowl, there was no sense of progress, little sense of motion.

Trofan, riding in Crispan's group, pointed out that they barely cast any shadows. "Look," he said to the Magician, "the dust even screens out the sun—we've no shadows. Every living thing, even every rock casts a shadow. We're worse now than corpses! We could be standing still with the sun just passing over us and never know."

Crispan's parched lips parted to form a reply, but there was nothing he could say and so he huddled deeper behind his mask of cloth and just rode on.

By the middle of the third day the men began to talk again, valuing their sanity over their dried throats. Stelba, another warrior in Crispan's group, wondered if Zifkar still held out, and Artor answered him by minutely describing every detail of the defenses. Another soldier, who had fought as a mercenary in the region, spoke of the tactics of siege, and again Stelba asked, "Will Zifkar hold?"

A soldier to the rear of the left group came back saying lightly, "Does Zifkar even exist?" But no one laughed, and all soon fell silent again.

At the end of that day, as the men checked their canteens and judged how far they had to go, they knew that their situation was serious. One or two of the horses were near madness with thirst and exhaustion, and it was obvious that some would not last another day.

"What do we do when they drop?" one soldier asked his companion.

"We walk. I'll die here anyway, but I'll die on my feet —the wind will have to knock me down before it buries me."

Crispan sat watching the men as they fell to the ground. He had never felt so helpless in all his life. How could he explain to them that his powers were not enough to transform this hell, to safeguard their journey? He himself had never realized until this moment how limited his powers really were. He could summon a wind, melt chunks of ice, conjure great imaginings—but most of his powers centered on things that were or could be, or on illusions that spoke of reality. But the Karsh was none of that; it was the very absence of life, of form, of existence. There was nothing onto which he could grab to make use of his powers. He could not even delude the men into imagining different surroundings. For the first time since he had joined the Order, he felt as weak as Those With Two Eyes, as the ancient Magicians called the untrained. The thought seemed to open his body to the night's cold, and he shuddered deeply.

Crispan was sleeping fitfully when he felt his arm being tugged. He looked up into Portar's face, his fingers over his mouth. "What is it?" Crispan whispered, but Portar only said, "Listen!"

Crispan sat up, but heard nothing save for the wind. Portar beckoned him to remain silent, so he listened again and still heard nothing. But no, there was something. It was far away, ever so faint, yet perceptible. He looked hard at the Captain and said, "Thunder?" Portar nodded as Crispan's eyes went wide at the realization.

Both men were on their feet now, trying to gauge how far away the storm was. Far, far off in the west it seemed they could see an occasional faint glow of lightning, but the noise was unmistakable. "How far do you make it?" Crispan asked.

Portar shrugged. "Who can tell here? It could be at the edge of the Karsh, but who knows where it is? I'd guess that it is at the edge, or just beyond. Do you think it will catch us?"

Now it was Crispan's turn to shrug. "I can't tell if it's

north or south of us. It may pass by us, or it may lose its power coming over the rim. If not . . ." His voice trailed away in the night. "It's almost time we started. Rouse the men, but don't say anything. I pray it passes us ˙ . . . If not . . ." And again his voice died away.

They moved slower now, on their fourth day in the Karsh. The horses moved more from memory than from will, and each rider went slowly so as to preserve his mount. Each rode anxiously, fearing his horse would drop away beneath him.

Around what they assumed to be mid-day, Stelba was riding beside Crispan. "How many days is it supposed to take, m'lord, five?" Crispan said maybe more, perhaps seven. "That's the trick of the place," the soldier continued. "Anywhere else, on any map it'd be six days at most—what with a road or at least water and fodder. But here the journey gets longer the further you've gone! That's the awful part of it."

Crispan, taking in this terrible truth, once again felt the impotence of all his learning and training. He did not notice at first that a few of the soldiers had drawn up simultaneously. Then the others did likewise, and as the curtain of dust receded, Artor, on the far right, stood in his stirrups and pointed dead ahead.

There, barreling down on them, was a huge storm cloud, hurling bolts of lightning as it boiled eastward, filling the sky. "I thought I heard thunder," Artor said, and then all looked to Crispan.

His first inclination was to apologize, not for the storm but for leading them beyond his own powers and to their probable deaths. But then he remembered that he was a warrior now as well as a Magician, and a commander. "We ride as fast as we can, cover as much ground as possible before the storm closes in on us. Any man whose horse goes down is to be picked up, do you understand?" He looked across the three groups and watched as the men began to fix their cloth masks and pat their steeds reassuringly. His words had heartened them, especially those with failing mounts. Yet Crispan himself felt odd, as the soldier supplanted the Magician, as he moved from the Open Eye to the Sword.

They set off at what was now a fast pace for them, but was really little more than a rapid canter. The sky darkened overhead and deepened the murkiness of the dust. Those in front could begin to perceive before them the line of the storm as it raced down on them. They staggered and plunged through the dust, half dreading the impending impact with the rain, half welcoming the relief it offered. It was barreling towards them now, barely eight lengths ahead and moving closer.

Like a moving gray wall the storm rose before them, and then suddenly they had crossed into it. It was strange at first, the refreshing coolness of the rain after so much dust and heat. And the ground became firm again as the rain tamped down the dust and soaked into the arid earth. Like dry sand brushed by a wave, the ground was firmer than the shifting dune or the sodden sea bank. The horses' heads plunged up and down with delight, and they stepped livelier as their footing improved.

But then, in a moment all too brief, as the rain continued running streaks down their dusty faces, the firm moist ground gave way to oozing thick mud. It was worse than the dust had been. It sucked at the horses' hooves and sent waves splattering up across the face of the Karsh. The horses grew wild as their legs failed to respond and remained immobile in the grasping mud.

Crispan called for a halt in order to steady the horses. The beasts panted and shook, but calmed down as they slaked their thirst in the rain. The men lifted their faces skyward and wiped away the grime, filling their helmets with the cool water, drinking it, pouring it over themselves. Portar, his beard now flecked with mud instead of dust, turned to Crispan. "We must move on quickly, m'lord. It's getting worse. It will be impossible if this rain continues for long."

The rain did go on, somehow falling more heavily, until it was as all-encompassing as the curtain of dust had been. They were slowed to a trot as the muck pulled at them, begging them not to move on. As the rain continued, the ooze deepened until it was well past the horses' fetlocks and well up their shanks. Then, as they plodded on through the steady drumming of the rain, the riders in front heard a voice behind them yell, "Help!"

Talmon, the soldier who had jested about Zifkar's even existing, was on the ground, his steed's left foreleg broken. Portar rode up to him and extended his hand. "Come on, mine's in fairly good shape." Talmon slung his kit and canteens over Portar's pommel, but as he was about to mount he turned and slogged back to his horse. He straddled the fallen beast and cooed at it to stop its whimpering. Then Talmon pulled his dirk and slit the horse's throat from behind. Red blood mixed with red-brown clay and deepening pools. Talmon climbed up behind Portar. "Better to do that to a faithful steed than let him suffer," he said as he let the rain cleanse his blade.

Again they set on their way, the rain as steady as ever, the ooze still sending out grasping fingers to slow them, suck them down, and give them their last caress. Where there had been heat and piercing, blinding dust there was now mud and chilling rain. The Karsh, in all its raw power, proved that it could destroy by water as well as fire. By evening three more horses had gone down, one dying of exhaustion, the others injured and dispatched as the first had been. The passing of the day merely emphasized the gloom of the storm, deepening the lead-gray skies to black, but never diminishing the steady downpour.

They slowed as darkness gathered, fearing to lose one another and eager for that night's rest. But Crispan ignored their exhaustion, and had them go on as best they could. Finally Artor came up beside him in the dark, saying, "M'lord, the men, they're dropping off in their saddles." Crispan was tired too, but was determined to push on.

"What would you do," he cried out through the rain. "Where shall we camp tonight, in the mud? Let's go on, it's our only chance. We'll rest here for a moment and then push on. With any luck we'll be near the western rim by tomorrow." Even as he spoke, Artor's horse went out from under him, dying as it collapsed into the deepening mud.

Artor peered up through the darkness. "It's no use, m'lord."

Crispan's eyes flamed. "By the Spirits, we go on! Get up here!" He extended his arm to Artor. This seemed to stir the men, and Crispan realized that his powers had been transformed. All his mind and effort were going towards keeping them on the move, keeping their faith burning amidst the deluge.

"Listen," he said as he rode up and down. "We must not get separated or some of us will surely die. Who's on the far right?"

"It's me, Efrim!"

"Fine," said the Magician. "Every man will call out his name, and the man to his left shall respond with his. If you fall behind, sing out. No one is to be left behind!"

After a chilling rest in their soaked clothes, the party started out again, but as they began, another horse fell to his knees and died. Some men shook their heads while waiting for the rider to join a man on another horse, and then they were off.

All through the night the litany of names rang out— Efrim, Trofan, Analdo, on through Portar and Talmon, Crispan and Artor, until they reached Stelba and then back to Efrim.

The rain was a series of thick sheets now, driven against them by the steady night wind. The floor of the Karsh gave more and more, deepening the muck, slowing them further. The horses sank ever deeper with each step, and by the middle of the night two more had to be killed as their riders abandoned them. An occasional bolt of lightning arced across the sky as if the Karsh wanted them to see what they had become. But they merely squinted in the glare and lowered their eyes to the churning mud.

In the morning dark, Trofan's horse died on its feet, and its body sank into the sea of mud, not even allowing him time to retrieve his kit and canteens. Crispan peered through the rain running off his helm as Trofan climbed up behind Analdo, and then nudged his own horse to go on.

The steed lifted its right foreleg and took a step, and then remained stock still, save for a swaying from side to side. Crispan prodded the beast in the flanks again, but the horse's rear left leg would not move. The swaying continued, and the horse began to whimper. Artor pushed himself off and landed thigh-deep in mud, but Crispan remained in his saddle. He tightened his knees against the horse's girth, but there was no response. The shaking continued, the moaning increased, and all at once Crispan felt him go down on his forelegs and lean to his right. The Magician freed his right foot from the stirrup, now deep in the mud, and vaulted over his saddle to his left, barely clearing the horse as it rolled over. It was dead before Crispan regained his balance.

Artor waded through the mud to help steady Crispan. Now they had but ten mounts among twenty men. Artor went over to a nearby soldier, and Crispan climbed up behind Stelba, motioning the others to go on.

They were moving even slower now, barely at a walk, each horse struggling against the ever-deepening mud to take one more step, every pair of riders fearful that their horse would be the next to break.

The rain began to ease as the morning drew closer, but each drop landed with a sparkling splash against the pools and mud, laughing at the riders' fitful progress. The men had become sodden lumps on horses of two colors at once, glistening wet atop, and thick brown mud on a line roughly across their saddle bottoms. The rain ran streaks across their muddied legs and flanks, and mingled underfoot to help further churn the Karsh.

Gradually the sky went from black to iron gray to light gray, without the rain ever pausing. As visibility improved, Crispan leaned out from behind Stelba's broad back and peered ahead, squinting against the rain. There was no sign of the western edge of the Karsh. He wondered if they could have turned in the night, if they were traveling about in the center of the Karsh without realizing it. All the land on all sides was the same, a restless sea of deep mud, its crown broken by the splash and ripples of the constant rain. He looked up, but the clouds were too thick to determine if the sun was truly behind them. It seemed to be, but he could not be sure. They could easily be moving northwest, or worse, southwest and deeper into the morass.

Crispan's ponderings were disturbed by a shout, and another horse went down, overcome by exhaustion. In its crazed state it lapped up the mud level with its sunken mouth, and in a moment choked on the liquid earth. The two thrown riders looked at the Magician, their faces asking what he would do now that there were only nine horses left.

He shut his eyes against the rain and thought. He heard Portar's voice beside him. "Shall we ride in relays, m'lord?"

Crispan was about to assent, but suddenly shouted, "No!" Portar was startled and perplexed, but Crispan went on. "Everyone dismount. Everyone! We go on on foot. Without the horses we can never reach Ker-en-kar once we make the western rim. Everyone shall travel in pairs and lead their horses. Without them to get us to Ker-en-kar this is all meaningless." So saying he sprang to the ground and stood in mud halfway up his thigh. Stelba, Trofan and Artor followed suit, as did the others. Soon all twenty men were ranged in pairs, Crispan having rejoined Portar.

Even through the gloom of the rain Crispan could read the doubts and questions in the men's faces. How could he explain to them the limits which he sensed, which he felt? There was nothing he could do, no power he could call on amidst all his Arts, which could work against the awful magnitude of the Karsh. He remembered, bitterly, Omir's warning about the limits of the Five Arts. But how could he convey this to the soldiers? How could he expect them to comprehend a power so refined that it could not always be applied? To soldiers power was force, force to be used. How could they be made to understand?

For a moment he thought of imposing a spell on their minds, casting an illusion to divert them from the dreadful reality facing them. But he realized that this would be unfair, for should they not escape the Karsh he would not be able to maintain the illusion as they each slipped away towards death. He could not allow them to suffer that sudden terror in their minds as illusion faded and reality returned, as he tried to prepare them for a death which they no longer expected. No, he must face them honestly. Having led them here, he owed them that.

He took off his helmet and let the rain run courses down his cheeks, the rivulets picking their ways amidst the accumulating brown stubble. "I feel I owe you some explanation as to why we suffer without respite. I can only say that even Magicians are limited in what they can do. We can make spells and potions, foster illusions. We can see increased realms of possibility, suggest courses and avenues, alternatives unseen by others. This is the true value of our advice. But a stated reality cannot be dispelled in its entirety by magic. Alterations are possible within limited circumstances. Our talent lies in sensing these circumstances and knowing when to apply our powers to them." He shrugged heavily with an air of defeat. "That is why I cannot change the Karsh."

Most of the men peered quizzically, trying to understand but not wishing to force the Wizard to explain further, as it evidently pained him. But Efrim, too confused, could not resist. "What about the river? We heard you melted an ice-bound river."

"Yes, I did. But that was such a circumstance as I mentioned, one limited in scope and one which offered a quick and even plausible alternative. This," Crispan said, sweeping out his arm across the unvarying horizon, "offers no such alternatives. In its size and scope it is the very absence of all life."

Crispan's voice trailed away amidst the continuing patter of the rain. All stood silently for a moment, listening as the rain continued to strike incessantly at their helmets.

"Enough," shouted Portar. "M'lord, you owe us no explanation. That our Emperor has chosen you is proof enough of your powers. And that you do not attempt to spare yourself our privations, or escape alone, is all that matters to us. You are more than a Magician to us—you are a loyal comrade. Am I right?" he bellowed to the others.

They agreed to a man. Crispan smiled. Before he could say anything else, Portar relieved him of the need. "We'd best push on m'lord, at once!"

Now came the true torture, making the days of dust, nights of chill and the ride through the rain and slime seem even pleasant by comparison. Each man ponderously lifted his leg against the swirling, sucking mud and dragged his body forward. Some men tried shifting their weight quickly from side to side, but tired after a brief effort. All were soon covered in the red-brown mud, as each eventually pitched forward when a leg stuck fast. Many of the men discarded their shields and helmets, and soon every remaining horse was carrying the deadly dragging cloaks.

They pushed on now as if entranced. Before them, they trusted, lay the refuge of the western rim. The thought of hard and steady rocks danced before them, beckoning. Behind them lay only mud; to stand still meant death. All about them the renewed heavy rain poured down.

They found that they could move more easily if one man moved one leg while his partner stood still. Then the other man would respond with the same leg, and so they alternated and went on like some awkward four-legged creature. Ever so slowly, they went on.

By what they assumed to be midday another horse died, and one soldier almost drowned in the ooze after falling forward. Portar, grunting as Crispan took a step, asked, "Will we get out of this?"

Crispan was breathing heavily. "I—I don't know. If we don't reach the rim soon, tonight—I fear we are lost." He shook his head and watched Portar's left leg slog forward. Then his left, and Portar's right, and on, and on through the terrible slime and steady rain.

They were reduced now to mere clods of mud themselves, rolling slowly over a sea of drenched dust. Shields and helmets had long been discarded, and soon all the saddles on the remaining horses were cut away to ease their march. Nothing they discarded showed where they had been, for all soon sank from view. The Karsh, ever faithful in its mischief, deprived them of any sense of progress. As afternoon wore on, Portar asked Crispan to stop, and did what he would never have thought possible. He unbuckled his outer belt and let his sword be dragged away from him as he moved forward. "A general gave me that," was all he said as he stepped ahead. Soon all the others did likewise, and in that band of soldiers none was armed now with more than a dirk or a dagger.

They must reach the rim very soon or not at all. They had not slept in almost two days, and Crispan dreaded that moment when one of them would be unable to go further. His determination that they all survive had kept them together and moving. When the first man was lost, that spell would be broken, and all would fear for their lives more than before. Crispan laughed to himself at the irony. Just as at the Order, he was struggling to preserve civilization from chaos, but by his own will now rather than his powers. He shook his bemused head from side to side and went on, echoing Portar's steps. He turned and looked behind him to where he supposed the east was, and the darkening skies afforded some small reassurance as to direction. His eyes were squinted against the rain in what had become a habit, when he realized that it was not really raining any more, but merely a fine and dying drizzle. He looked about him, but the men were too preoccupied with each leaden move to notice. He wanted to shout to them, but for some reason did not. Who could take joy in the ending rain if there was still eternal mud?

Analdo noticed it soon after, when he realized he was walking in sunlight. He shouted madly, pointing to the sky. For the first time in days they saw daylight above them, undisturbed by choking dust or falling rain. For a moment they all stood mesmerized by the streaks of blue through parting leaden clouds. There was sky, and sun and blue above them. They were still alive. But the reverie was broken as Portar growled for them to move on, and they suddenly remembered their very earthbound bodies.

As he plodded on, Crispan studied the patches of sky to gain some idea of the time of day. The color was past that brightest blue of mid-afternoon and was heading towards that whiter blue that presaged the pastels of evening. The day was dying all about them and still there was no western rim. Crispan lowered his head and watched as the muck churned about the top of his knee as he lowered his leg. The swirling mud fascinated him; he was engrossed by its currents and ripples. The top of his knee! The thought jarred Crispan in his tracks. The mud was up to the top of his knee. It had been well up to his thigh before. He had not noticed the change, but he could see it now. His upper leggings were spattered and filthy, but not thoroughly soaked in fresh mud. The Karsh could not be drying so soon after the rain. The ground had to be rising. He walked on in rhythm with Portar, watching carefully to see if it was true. He looked at his companion's long legs, and they seemed to confirm what he thought, Still he said nothing, not daring to raise the men's hopes without a more visible reason.

They kept walking, slogging, every step heavier and more difficult than the last as their exhaustion bore down on them. For yet another horse the agony ended, and now only seven were left. Above them the sky was already light blue and purple. Crispan swallowed hard with every glimpse of fading light. Yet he was sure they were closer, for the mud was even lower now against his knee. His eyes searched anxiously across the flat horizon, begging for a change as the light faded. Left to right and back his eyes ran, hoping for some bulge in the unending flatness. Then, for a moment, he thought he saw it. Just a little to the left of their march. But no, could it be only a mound of mud? He looked on all sides, but the mud was level. Crispan's step quickened, and Portar jolted at the faster pace. "What's this?" he growled.

"There, there! Do you see it?"

"See what?"

"Look." And even as Crispan pointed, sunlight broke

through the regathering clouds and struck the mound. It was black and gray, darker than the red-brown mud surrounding them. Portar was still unsure, but Crispan jumped and pointed, shouting, "The rim! The rim!"

The others were startled by his yelling and looked where he pointed. Some further back could barely make it out, but those up front got a glimpse and began to lunge forward. Up and down their legs pumped in the thick ooze. They careened forward, many losing their balance time after time as they tried to run towards the beckoning rock.

It hung just on the edge of their vision, just clearing the mud. But as they ran, there was still no sign of the rest of the rim. Was it just a huge stone placed there by the Karsh only to raise and then dash their hopes? Crispan was again assailed by doubts. Had he called too soon? It was Talmon, having passed the rest of the troop, who stood up and screamed, "Look! Look! It is the rim!"

There was no restraining them now as they pounded across the sea of mud. Columns of spray and ooze rose into the air as they scampered towards the haven of the rocks. Their excitement was even transmitted to their horses, and they too stepped livelier than they had in days. In the dying light they all raced, man and beast alike, for the firm harbor of the waiting rim.

They ran so hard that each pitched forward at one time or another, and a passing comrade would stoop and drag the fallen man to his feet. This was no time to wallow in the demon mud.

Talmon was still in the lead, shouting madly at the top of his voice. The others yelled as well, cheering. All across their front the rim was visible now, barely two hundred spear lengths away. Pell-mell they ran. Some stretched out their arms as if to embrace the safe ground. One hundred lengths, and their paces grew swifter. Fifty lengths, the mud now midway below their knees. Twenty lengths, ten —and Talmon flung himself on the cool black boulder, hugging and kissing it in relief and disbelief. Soon the others were upon the rocks also, screaming, laughing, weeping—yet none were willing to let go of the stones in their joy. Each man clung to the rim lest he somehow get dragged back into the Karsh.

For quite some time they gave vent to their joy, and let their exhaustion seep out of them. It was Portar who regained his composure first and climbed to a rock above them.

"Come!" he shouted. "We have only beaten the Karsh. Remember our mission. Remember Zifkar."

They looked at one another, smiling now and nodding eagerly. Remember Zifkar, on to Ker-en-kar. They began to scale the western rim, scampering like mountain goats up from the base of the rim over the steep stones. The Karsh, cheated of their bones, plucked one last victim from among them. One of the horses gave a loud neigh as it lost its footing just below the crest. Men scurried in all directions as it tumbled down the rocks and into the waiting mud. Its broken body groaned away its life as the men anxiously made for the top as fast as they could.

XIX

Grim Tidings

As each man rolled over the crest he flung himself head-long onto the cool long grass. Those still leading horses had to be careful lest their mounts overeat. Portar and Crispan lay on their backs like the others, watching the stars come slowly across the sky.

"What now?" sighed the Magician.

Portar was surprised. "Why, we're off to Ker-en-kar!"

"On six horses?"

"Then we must leave most of the men behind. They can find a village and join the others later."

"I thought of that," Crispan admitted. "But how do we choose who's to go and who's to be left? I can't just select randomly, not now."

Portar sat up and faced Crispan, his face caked in mud like the others, but his gray eyes piercing through all the grime. "You underestimate these men, m'lord. They are yours now, they would follow you anywhere. You have led them through the Karsh safely without losing a man. Why, they'd storm Mujdhur, Zhyjman's High City, itself for you if you only asked! Simply put the situation to them. These are soldiers and they will understand."

So saying, Portar got on his feet to address the others, but Crispan cleared his voice so as to stop him, and bore the duty himself.

"We must get on to Ker-en-kar, for that is still our mission. Only six can ride now, and so our problem is to choose who shall go."

"Aye," said Trofan, "and where."

Only then did Crispan realize that they had no idea as to where they had come out of the Karsh. The others realized this too, but Efrim raised his hand a bit tentatively to explain that he had been raised near Ker-en-kar. "I know this part of the Empire, and I would guess that we probably veered slightly north in crossing the Karsh, and that Ker-en-kar lies more south than west of us."

"Are you sure?" asked Portar.

"No, sir. But there should be a road if we went due west from this side of the Karsh. I am sure that the closest village could still be reached before sunrise."

Crispan nodded thoughtfully. "Then the riders shall head due west for the road and then south to Ker-en-kar. The others shall follow behind on foot."

"With our tired horses, they won't be far behind," said Artor laughingly.

The six riders were quickly chosen, Crispan and Portar, Efrim and Analdo because they knew the area, and two others. Stelba was put in command of the rest. This business done, they rested for a bit more. Then it was time to go.

"The first village we find," promised Crispan, "we'll send horses out for you. We shall see you in Ker-en-kar." Then he led the five other riders off into the night.

The horses behaved well, having fed and rested somewhat. They were eager under their riders after the long ordeal, and glad to feel the thick grass and solid earth beneath them. By the middle of the night they had carried their party to what seemed to be the road Efrim had described, a wide, beaten path little used since the end of the Great Empire.

Efrim, in the lead, leaned forward and pointed to the right. "There are lights there, a village. Shall we make for it, sir?"

Crispan and Portar answered the query by pointing their horses towards the distant glowing lanterns. Down the dark slope they pounded, their horses moving easily through the cool night's breeze. As they closed on the village they could see that the lanterns hung on small earthen watchtowers which formed part of a stockade, a common feature of villages in that borderland. Their coming had been announced before them by the sound of the hooves, and more lanterns became visible on the walls.

Then they could distinguish individual men, and soon they were below the stockade facing a closed gate.

"Who are ye?" growled a burly man standing over the gate. "What d'ye want at this time of night?"

Portar spoke first. "We are soldiers of the Emperor Thurka and are bound on his business for Ker-en-kar. We need fresh mounts. Open these gates!"

The burly man was unmoved and annoyed. "Who orders me to open these gates?"

"I am Captain Portar," he said, wisely leaving Crispan's identity a mystery.

Instead of the gates opening, a lantern hung on a spear was lowered over the wall. "Soldiers, ha! No armor, hardly any weapons, not even saddles! Ye're nothing but filthy vagabonds, probably the vanguard for a band of cutthroats come to kill us in our beds. Begone, and be thankful you go unmolested!" The lantern was drawn up over the stockade.

"By the Spirits! We've crossed the Karsh because there is danger at Zifkar. That accounts for our present state. Now open these gates or—"

"Crossed the Karsh?" The guardian was incredulous. "No one's ever crossed the Karsh. Now begone or we will sally out and deal with ye, or perhaps set the village dogs on ye." He withdrew from the wall.

Portar rode up until he was against the gate and pounded it heavily with his fist. "O-pen, o-pen!" Now the burly one reappeared, his spear raised. Portar continued to pound.

"Stop, or I let fly!"

But Portar continued to pound, his right eye warily watching the raised spear.

"Stop! My last warning!"

"What is this, Edvar? Who are those men?" It was a new voice, firmer, quieter.

"They say they're soldiers, from Zifkar. Say they've crossed the Karsh and must reach Ker-en-kar with news."

The body belonging to the new voice appeared. He was a slight man swathed in an officer's cloak, clearly the commandant. "Who are you?" he called.

Crispan spoke quickly, cutting off the now raging Portar. "It is as your man says. We must get to Ker-en-kar in order to bring relief to Zifkar."

The commandant was silent for a moment, torn between his possible duty and his natural caution. "How do I know you're not spies, out to penetrate Ker-en-kar, or worse?"

Crispan thought for a moment. "True, sir, true enough. But if we are spies, we could be revealed by your escorting us to Ker-en-kar. We have others with us as well, following on foot. We lost many horses in the Karsh. I would hope that you could also send horses out to them. There are fourteen."

This news disquieted the commandant. "Should we fail in our mission," interjected Portar, "you will be hanged from your own walls, I promise you."

The commandant shrugged. "Fair enough. Edvar, mount an escort of eight to accompany these men to Ker-en-kar, and another twenty to bring in the rest. How shall we find the others?" he called down.

"One of us can accompany you from whence we came. And we will need some food and water."

Still wary, the commandant had the required supplies and the fresh horses brought out to the dusky riders, rather than risk bringing them within the walls.

In the pastel light of the next evening the city of Ker-en-kar shimmered softly, seeming to beckon them onwards. The city and its fortress offered rest and comfort, and safety. It was the furthest outpost of the Empire of the South in this region and was still brimming with troops for service in the east against Zhyjman. As soon as word of the war came, Ludivo had raised all the local levies he could, without waiting for the authorization from the Emperor, which came later. The fortress bustled with activity at all hours, for Ludivo was a stern leader, keen on discipline and constant training.

Still looking like brigands, at best, the men from Zifkar were admitted within the city walls only because they were under escort. Portar gave Crispan a sly smile as he realized finally why the Magician had asked for the escort. It had been more for their own safety than to assuage the commandant.

The narrow streets of Ker-en-kar were just settling down for the night, shopkeepers closing their doors, people making for home. But closer to the citadel, the streets grew more and more crowded with milling and marching soldiers, with small units practicing quick marching to and fro, with wagons bringing in more supplies against a possible siege. Ker-en-kar served a twofold role, as a citadel for the eastern borders and as a base for the Southern armies stationed in the eastern reaches of the Three Realms.

At the entry to the citadel itself they were again confronted by hostile, wary guards. Crispan demanded to see their captain, and when he appeared Crispan finally used his name to full advantage, knowing it would be recognized and safe. "I am Crispan, Magician and adviser to the Emperor." He bared his talisman, still clean after having been carefully protected all across the Karsh. "Take us to General Ludivo at once. I have news from Zifkar."

The captain jumped at the name of Crispan and quickly opened the gates for them. Suddenly self-conscious of their bedraggled appearance, they tugged and pulled at their filthy raiments in a futile attempt to make themselves presentable. Guards all along the way, through the main hall and across the wide stairs, up the gallery and past the arcade, all cast them suspicious glances. Finally, after a winding flight of stairs, they stood outside Ludivo's quarters, weary but eager to tell their news.

The captain knocked gently at the door, and was a bit taken aback when the General himself appeared. The captain stammered for a moment while Ludivo eyed the seeming derelicts brought before him. "Well, are they spies? Ours or the enemies?"

"No, sir," said the captain as he stepped aside. Rather lamely he said, "M'Lord Crispan, sir."

Before Ludivo could even reply, Crispan stepped forward. "M'lord Ludivo, we have news from Zifkar," he said as he swept past him into the chamber, beckoning

Portar and the three others to follow. The ordeal of the Karsh and his memory of his last meeting with Ludivo had emboldened him.

Crispan poured himself some wine and passed the flask around while Ludivo closed the door, his mouth still agape. As soon as the General had reached the table, Crispan told of all that had happened, the words pouring out.

"By the Spirits, man! Slow down!" Ludivo protested.

Crispan began again, more slowly, using a map to explain all in detail. Ludivo sat stock still, obviously disturbed by the news. He stared at the map for a while, gauging distances and available forces. His lips drew tight across his gray-black-bearded face; he ran his fingers nervously through his stiff shock of gray hair.

"As you say, Zifkar must be relieved. It will take a few days to mount an expedition. How long can Zifkar hold?"

Crispan's temper soared. His gray eyes went afire. "You don't have a few days. We left Zifkar some nine days ago. The siege probably began at least three days ago. Stova is undermanned. Most of the army is trapped on the Falchions, if it still exists at all. I did not risk the lives of twenty men to give you a few more days!" Crispan's voice rose noticeably and his color blended with the red wine trembling in his glass.

Ludivo calmly smoothed the map before him. "I realize the imperative of time, but I cannot be ready at once. And we must not introduce our troops piecemeal, nor can I denude Ker-en-kar of men if the situation is as bleak as you suggest. Surprise is our main advantage. It will be considered impossible that news should have reached us so soon. Give me two days."

Crispan's fist came crashing down against the arm of his chair. Ludivo's coolness frustrated him to exasperation. "Two days! In two days Zhyjman can have scouts posted on the edges of the Karsh and be preparing to hurl himself against you here. You must move sooner—at least by the morning after this, not the day after as you suggest. And scouts must go out in force tonight to guard our way and watch for the enemy."

"Well, well," Ludivo smirked. "You've become quite the military man, haven't you? All right then, we'll try for the morning after this, and scouts will go out tonight. You must need sleep. We can talk further in the morning. I'll have you all posted in the officers' quarters."

With much prodding from the Magician, who hovered over every meeting and worried over every preparation, Ludivo was ready within the promised time. Messengers were dispatched to Gurdikar and other outposts, scouts were sent out both north and east. Selecting his fastest squadrons and hardiest troops, Ludivo had gathered a sizable force of cavalry. He planned to lead them to Zifkar by forced march, to be followed by whatever infantry could be spared.

Following the path Pangal had used so little time before, Ludivo led his force towards Zifkar. Portar and Crispan rode with Ludivo and his staff, anxiously counting each fading sun, trying to be as optimistic as possible against what they knew to be utmost gloom. Ten days, eleven days passed as they pressed eastward, Ludivo struggling to gain as much ground as possible without fatiguing and ruining his force. On the twelfth day out from Ker-en-kar scouts rode in to report they had come within sight of the beleaguered city three nights before. It still stood and resisted, they said, but had obviously been very hard-pressed. At once heartened and chilled by this news, Crispan and Portar urged Ludivo to even greater efforts. But the Governor of Ker-en-kar needed little urging now, knowing full well the value of Zifkar and the opportunities and perils it presented.

XX

A Night of Fire and Blood

Now, at last, they stood before the anguished city of Zifkar. Their approach had been covered by nightfall and by the besiegers' preoccupation with the city itself, whose fall seemed imminent. "These mercenaries," snorted Portar, riding with Crispan. "They are sloppy soldiers. Again they post no pickets."

As Pangal had done earlier, Ludivo masked his army behind the spiny ridge to the west of the city and awaited the reports of his scouts. Crispan was eager now for the assault. But Ludivo kept his own counsel, not moving until he knew more of the situation before Zifkar. "It will have to be at once," thought Crispan. "The city cannot stand much more." His fears were somewhat assuaged by the fact that Ludivo kept his men under arms that night, refusing them the luxury of a proper camp. Even more heartening was the arrival of some infantry commanded by Ludivo's lieutenant, Nedivir, who had scoured the garrisons and villages along the eastern border, stripping their manpower to the barest minimum. "Surely this presages an attack," Crispan hoped.

Unable to sit by while Ludivo waited, Crispan relieved his anxiety by pacing his horse across the ridge, just over the crest on the side facing Zifkar. He could see the fires burning fiercely and freely in the city and along the walls. Two forces were converging on the agonized city, night and the enemy. The living inferno defeated the gloom of the first and made it possible for Crispan to follow the progress of the second. The huge main gate on the northern wall was most clear to him. He could see defenders through the remnants of the flaming portals and enemy soldiers hovering all around. Broken assault ladders lay about the ground below the walls, and others hung limply abandoned against the ramparts. The Magician kept pounding his pommel as he watched the plain, and then looked back to the summit of the ridge where Ludivo sat with Nedivir and the commander of the cavalry, Droba. Almost in pain, he looked back again on Zifkar.

From over his shoulder Crispan heard a horseman hurrying up the slope. He reached Ludivo and was away before Crispan could regain the crest. When he did, only Ludivo was there.

"What did he say, General?"

"All the scouts are accounted for and waiting at the bottom of the ridge. Two had managed to slip through the enemy camp and have heard that Oslon is still fighting but remains trapped."

Crispan was impatient. "Fine, fine—but what about Zifkar?"

"They say it could fall, maybe tonight, easily by tomorrow night. The enemy has been on the walls already, probably twice. You were right, Crispan, we are just in time." Ludivo pulled his helmet down over his shock of gray hair.

"Then why do we sit here?" Crispan's voice approached a scream.

Ludivo remained icily calm. "I am told, Crispan, that your magic is a subtle art. So is warfare. We cannot just run down there. First we must gather our forces, and then we must wait. Let the enemy become engaged in his assault and we shall fall on him. They do not know yet that we are here, so let us not tell them until we are ready, lest we lose what little advantage we have. Remember, Crispan, that the ripe fruit falls without plucking."

The two men turned their horses to face the city as the enemy hurled himself against the weary walls. They struck hardest at the north wall where the main gate barely hung together. Other forces pressed towards the smaller entrances to the west and south. Crispan's breathing grew heavier as each assault ladder went up against the walls. He looked at Ludivo. The Governor of Ker-en-kar felt his glance and acknowledged it, but turned back towards Zifkar.

The defenders were no longer able to hurl back the myriad assault ladders, and enemy soldiers had gained a foothold on the western wall. Crispan began to edge his horse forward, thinking of Stova, the Chamberlain, and those with whom he had first ridden to Zifkar. Ludivo noticed Crispan's movement. "Steady, steady. Soon, not yet," he said, in a voice that was low but very firm.

At least part of the western wall was firmly held by the foe, and even more men were pressing forward below. Crispan's sword found its way into his hand as he watched the first surge towards the main gate. He could see the gates buckle for a moment before they held. His arm moved into its shield straps. His feet were swinging quickly in their stirrups. His thumb moved up and down across the hilt of his sword. He could feel his knees twitching. His lips and throat were very dry, and he felt he had to force himself to keep from screaming. And still Ludivo sat firmly in place.

More assault ladders were put up against the walls, the fires burned brighter and more freely, and Crispan's heart pounded even louder. His horse, sensing his anxiety, pawed at the ground. Crispan sucked in his lower lip and then ran his tongue across the salty sweat on his upper one. He was sure now that he was going to burst. Then he heard Ludivo order, "Droba, forward with all the heavy cavalry. Light to follow at once! Nedivir, follow with the rest at the run. Forward!!"

Crispan was off as quickly as the words were out of the General's mouth. He was unaware of his horse's speed as it plunged down the slope. He kept his eyes fixed on the northern gate. The line of scouts at the bottom of the ridge came up on him before he realized it. Crispan swept by them screaming, "Attack! Attack!" and waving his sword over his head. Their line swept along with him, and the reassuring sound of charging hooves followed.

His body moved easily with the rhythm of his charger. The ground beyond the ridge was level and seemed to sweep him on towards Zifkar. All he could think of were his comrades inside, and the very name Zifkar pounded in his skull as the battle madness seized him, pulling him on unthinkingly towards the melee. Then he saw before him two scouts who had outridden him on their swifter, lighter mounts. He saw them each bear down on the soldiers of the North, and each hacked away with his sword as he came upon the first of the enemy. The sight cleared Crispan's head and he began to slow his steed.

He then heard Ludivo behind him. "Crispan! By the Spirits! I thought we'd never catch you. Here, you soldiers. Form a squadron around the Magician."

Crispan shook his head at this command. "What is the meaning of this?" he asked with great indignation.

"The Emperor prizes your safety and I will see to it that you remain safe. He will little prize the relief of Zifkar should it cost him your services, whatever they may be. Captain, keep him safe." Ludivo was gone at once. Crispan, still stunned, sat for a moment, then shook his head again. He spurred his horse, and then his squadron plunged on as well.

Ludivo had swung his force around to the northwest of the city, so that when they struck they were athwart the enemy's rear. With this deft maneuver the besiegers were suddenly pressed between a fresh foe and a desperate but newly heartened city garrison. Ludivo's cavalry drove into the enemy's ranks, pushing them back against Zifkar's walls. The suddenly driven besiegers began to scream as they were forced further and further back, until they were hemmed into a tight and immobile knot. The very crush of their bodies began to bring down the narrow siege ladders. Hurtling bodies added to the growing panic in their ranks. Defenders began regaining their ramparts above and hurled weapons, armor and burning debris down on their antagonists. All the while Droba's cavalry closed in even more tightly, flaying at the defenders like a huge knife peeling a ready fruit. To the west and south Nedivir brought his infantry to bear, isolating the besiegers there, eliminating each ladder and siege machine. The siege turned to battle, the battle to slaughter.

Crispan and his escort were among the first to successfully cut through the horde and reach what remained of the smoking-hot gate. Bloodlust suddenly seized him, overcoming his training, drawing him from the Open Eye to the Sword that day. His protectors all around him, he joined in the kill, receiving a glancing blow from a desperate spear. He led his horse over the entangled bodies of defenders and attackers, and passed under the narrowly held portals of Zifkar just as they swung open, barely avoiding being swept along in the surge of defenders gone over to the attack.

"Crispan!" Stova's voice carried out over the battle. Crispan peered through the night and smoke and found his friend standing atop a barricade just inside the gate.

"Stova! When I saw the city I never thought to see you again." He stretched out his arm in greeting.

"Nor I you whenever I looked west towards the Karsh." Stova's eyes danced brightly against his begrimed face. As he took the Magician's arm he noticed the wound. "You've been cut!"

Crispan had not even noticed it during the fray. "No, I'm all right."

"Then come, there's killing to be done. And these dogs deserve it." He swept his sword over the vista of a sorely wounded city and then sprang off the barricade and out the gate.

Crispan lost track of time as he watched and listened to the sounds of battle just beyond him. The fires on the walls above caught his eye as they reflected on his drawn blade. He looked at his weapon and was at once fascinated and repelled by the sight of still-fresh blood. He could barely remember using his sword. He remembered his squadron pushing and cutting through the trapped besiegers. He remembered blindly lifting and dropping his arm, swinging it back and forth, occasionally feeling resistance at the other end. But he never associated it with killing. Only now did he realize what he had done, what he was a part of, what was still going on.

Ludivo was beside him now, sitting silently before Pangal's still-fresh tomb, wiping his blade against his leg. He sensed the Magician's mood and made no attempt to disturb him. They sat and watched as the triumphant soldiers from Ker-en-kar mingled with the defenders of Zifkar and streamed into the city. A few of the victors escorted prisoners, most came with fresh booty. Droba was swept in with this victorious flood and had to cross the rush of the torrent to reach his commander.

"Good work, Droba. But where is Nedivir?"

"That's what I came to tell you. The enemy soldiers trapped on the western wall refuse to surrender. All the ladders are down and Nedivir is below them. They are holding the garrison at bay along the wall."

Ludivo sprang forward against the flow, Crispan following in his wake. They emerged from the city and circled to the left towards the western wall. There they found Nedivir and his infantry standing amongst the remnants of the enemy. All were looking to the battlements, where a large body of enemy soldiers were clearly visible on the walls silhouetted against the continuing flames.

Ludivo growled at Nedivir's report. "Send some of your men up the walls on the inside," he ordered, "and clear away a space here below." Nedivir comprehended at once and dispatched the men.

"Surely you are not going to slaughter them." Crispan's face was masked with horror. "That is not war."

As always, Ludivo was icily calm. "The rules of warfare are clear. There is but one answer to a refusal to surrender a hopeless position."

"But—but what about Zifkar? They were in the same position this very night. They also refused to surrender."

"Yes, and they would have paid the same price had you not brought us here in time. And what is more, they knew it full well. You have much to learn, Magician."

Ludivo drew his horse back and Crispan followed. He could not believe what he saw as Nedivir's soldiers mounted the walls and pressed their last attack. The soldiers of the North fought as if they could carry all before them, but they were slowly worn and cut down. Nedivir's troops and eager members of the garrison of Zifkar kept advancing, hemming the foe into a smaller and smaller space. Single soldiers began to fall, mostly those who were

194

wounded. Then others, forced by the press, hurtled over the battlements, first single ones, then in groups. Crispan was both horrified and attracted by the scene. Everything within him said that this was wrong and useless, that it was beyond the needs of warfare or revenge. Yet he was compelled to watch by the Northerners' bravery, for barely a man among them uttered a sound as he plummeted to the ground.

Crispan slept well, and poorly, that night. His exhaustion from the last several weeks overcame him at first and he slumbered heavily, dreaming of the ridiculous sight of the corpulent High Chamberlain jammed into his ceremonial armor anxiously awaiting the fall of his city in his main hall, as Crispan had found him that night. But as his mind traveled down the corridors of sleep, the vision faded. His body began to toss feverishly as he watched soldiers falling from the ramparts. It seemed as if he were tied to the ground, and each body fell straight for him, each somehow missing at the last moment. He could see their anguished faces, their gaping, bleeding wounds. He awoke amidst crumpled, sweaty sheets, and waited for the comfort that only sunrise can bring after a lonely, sleepless night.

XXI

A Mission to the West

Crispan was already standing on the broad balcony known as the Chamberlain's Terrace when the sun revealed how much Zifkar had suffered in the siege. Columns of thick black smoke continued to writhe out of shattered buildings, limiting the damage visible from the palace above. But Crispan was familiar enough with the city to see through the pall that whole neighborhoods had been gutted, and that the marketplace he had found so alive had been cleared to serve as a place for the wounded, who had quickly overflowed into the surrounding streets. People were about on the streets again, but their movements lacked their former vitality. They walked slowly and cautiously, picking their way through the destruction, seeking out homes, possessions, family, friends among the ruins.

"Have you been down into the city yet?" Crispan turned at the sound of Stova's voice. They had not seen each other since the soldier had leapt into the fray the night before. He was all cleaned and spruced up now, wearing bright ceremonial armor. But although he had slept the night before, his eyes and face still bore the strain of the siege.

Crispan shook his head in answer to the question.

"You know," Stova said as he leaned against the balustrade made of carved gryphons, "you can fight a hundred battles and never get used to the sight of the field or city the next morning. The stench, the smoke, the already-rotting corpses. It never gets any easier. But come, we must join Baldomir."

As they turned from the balcony into the palace, Stova explained that the High Chamberlain planned to ride through Zifkar in order to give new heart to the citizens and to help celebrate their deliverance. "And he expects all the commanders to lead the parade." He nudged the Magician in the ribs.

Crispan went back to his chamber to select his wardrobe for the procession. His armor from the recent campaigns lay in a filthy heap in a corner near his bed where he had shed it the night before. Rejecting this, he went to the closet. The High Chamberlain had thoughtfully put there a full suit of gaudy ceremonial armor, its cuirass embossed with silver and ebony in a pattern repeated on the barbut and the greaves. He was about to don a byrnie before putting the armor on when he saw his gray robes hanging where he had left them. He peeled off the hauberk and slipped into the robe, bringing his amulet out from under his jerkin. He could not believe how good it felt to be dressed as a Master of the Five Arts again. He trusted that Baldomir would not be insulted.

In the courtyard where the procession assembled, Crispan noted that Droba was missing. "Gone north," Stova explained, "to relieve Oslon."

Stova spoke out of the side of his mouth as the procession began. "We must pursue the remnants north. Even if they are not caught we must continue the pressure, the terror. Nedivir follows later today."

"But they will be dropping in their saddles!"

Stova made no reply as they emerged into the city proper. The Chamberlain rode in the first line, flanked by his Captain of the Guard and General Ludivo. But as they rode through the streets, it quickly became evident that the people's attention was centered on the second rank, where Crispan rode between Stova and Nedivir. It began slowly at first, barely audible amidst the chants and cheers. But as they rode on, weaving between rubble and ruins, it grew louder and louder. Word passed among the crowd in advance of the procession, until the chant drowned out all other cheers. The Magician could not believe it at first, and his bewilderment grew with the sound. In their broad eastern accents the crowds were chanting his name. "Cris-span! Cris-span!"

Stova's smile knew no bounds. Crispan turned to him. "Why me? How do they know?"

"We had to tell them something to keep up their hopes. So we told them you had gone to bring an army, that you as a Master could succeed at this."

"What if I had failed?"

"Then who would be here to protest?"

"Cris-span! Cris-span!" It had become a roar, echoing off the buildings, bouncing off the walls of the city. Crispan smiled in meek acknowledgment.

"How does it feel to go from a raw recruit to a conquering hero?" Stova's hearty laugh muffled any response.

Round and round they rode, past whole sections that were nothing but blackened, smoking shells, up streets that had been miraculously spared. And always it was the same, the happy crowds chanting his name. As Baldomir said as he raised his goblet at the feast that night, "To our Lord Crispan we are eternally grateful, for he more than anyone else has saved the city of Zifkar."

The Emperor Thurka echoed Baldomir's sentiments when he welcomed Crispan back to Gurdikar. There was much news to catch up on. The scouts of Vadul had reluctantly posted themselves on the northern edge of the Forest of Swann; the city of Rhaan-va-Mor grudgingly looked to its defenses. "It's odd," mused Thurka. "For years we guaranteed the balance here in the South and they all gratefully accepted. And now that we require help from them they are reluctant." Less heartening was the news Belka reported. "Syman is said to be moving on Anrehenkar to commence his long-expected siege. He approaches from the west and north with an army of perhaps sixty thousand men."

All the members of the council were taken aback by this. "Sixty thousand!" exclaimed the Duke of Larc. "It is not possible. No one has ever raised so large a mercenary force in the Middle Realm."

Zoltan toyed with his dagger "Any mercenary would risk his life to get at the treasure vaults of Anrehenkar. There will be a division of booty there unlike any ever seen in any of the realms. No one has ever successfully despoiled those treasures. Syman could easily raise an even larger army with that goal to lure them."

But none of the others could comprehend so large a force being mustered. "Especially when we know that Kirion, Zhyjman's main general, is not with Syman," said the Emperor. "He undoubtedly has his own army in the field. Wherever he is, there lies Zhyjman's main strength. Yet how many more soldiers can we have, after losing two armies before Zifkar?"

"And where," asked Crispan, "is Vladur?"

The silence which followed was embarrassing. Finally Thurka admitted, "There is no news of him either."

"In other words," concluded Zoltan, barely masking his contempt, "only one of our enemies has surfaced. What do we do, wait for them to conveniently appear, perhaps on the borders of Gar and Perrigar? You don't fight a war by waiting for your foe." The voice of the former mercenary was bitter, and even the looks of his old comrade, Prince Mikal, would not still him.

"Perhaps," smirked Larc, "you would like to tell the Emperor and these princes how to run their Empire and the war? Have you learned so much invading free states?"

"No, but I know as well as you how to lose a state!" And with that, amidst Mikal's aghast look and Larc's daggerish glare, Zoltan reeled out of the tent.

The others left soon after, leaving only the Magician and the Emperor to face each other across the large map. Crispan's gray eyes remained fixed on the wide expanse between the two remaining Empires, thinking about the Renegade and the future of the Order.

Thurka could read the pain in the Wizard's eyes and guess his thoughts. "Vladur must be out there, just as we know Kirion to be, without knowing exactly where. Omir believes this as well, or you would not be here. Trust me."

A look of great pain swept over Crispan's fine features. "I have to. I have already gone too far."

Mikal realized how late it was when he saw how few breakfast fires still sent up white plumes of smoke amidst the tents. A gentle breeze blew the scattered wisps back towards Gurdikar, caressing the camp as it did so. The entire camp bustled under the warm spring sun. Soldiers honed their weapons, cavalry practiced formations on the plain. Tradesmen and peddlers came out from the city to offer their wares, fruits and fresh breads, bright cloths and odd trinkets. Despite Belka's orders, women from the inns came offering an evening's entertainment. The camp was alive with people, save for the burly warrior whom the green-eyed Prince sought.

He strode quickly down from the tents closest to the walls past the larger communal tents housing six to eight soldiers. As he neared the open ground that Belka had cleared for training, he espied his father and uncle, the Duke of Larc and Crispan, and some others in a small knot. He moved towards them briskly, but slowed as he felt the effects of the previous night's carousing.

"Have any of you seen Zoltan?"

Thurka's eyes turned quizzical. "Is he not in his tent?"

"No. I looked there. I thought he would be out here."

But no one had seen the hefty warrior. Mikal sent a soldier to fetch Zoltan's servant. While they waited they watched the charging cavalry, training under the direction of Stova, who had not been left at Zifkar after his heroic defense. Crispan was impressed by their precision and vigor as they wheeled and charged, but he could not help wonder what they could do against Vladur—if he was out there at all.

"Aye," said the servant when questioned by the Prince, "my Lord Zoltan arose very early this morning, before first light. He dressed in his armor and rode off."

"Which way, which way, man?" Mikal was ready to shake him violently.

"North, sir. He rode north."

The reply was crushing, and Mikal dimly echoed, "North."

Larc could barely hide his triumphant glee. "I suppose he succumbed to his own tales of the fabled treasure of Anrehenkar."

Mikal's hand began to move for his dagger, but Belka

stepped between them, facing the Duke. The towering Prince snarled, "Go back to your tent, Larc!" His nephew drew back now and stood silently. All the others withdrew from him, but he did not notice. He was lost in thought, remembering not so very long ago when two men had stealthily ridden south together in the early morning, south from Aishar.

The days which followed Zoltan's apparent desertion passed quietly. No news came of Vladur or Kirion, or of Zoltan either. While the army spent its time in drill and maneuver, Crispan spent most of his time in his tent. In the mornings he too would practice with his weapons, and his proficiency with them increased. But to be a good soldier was not his goal. He tried to spend the rest of his time in studies, practicing spells and incantations, but he was hampered by the lack of books and equipment. He did not dare write to Omir for what he needed, because he wished to maintain the fiction of his own independence and the continuing neutrality of the Order. So he did the best he could with the few familiar books he had brought with him and those he was able to borrow from old Xirvan at Kerdineskar. The ailing Master had already sent Crispan the rare *Incantatia et Contra* to help him prepare against the Renegade. "But what good," he brooded, "were preparations against a foe as phantom as his evil conjurings?" Crispan found that his mind could not or would not concentrate on the task. There was little in any book that dealt with the forbidden art of necromancy or its mastery.

Again and again his impotence flooded over him. In the Order he had been contented, happy, he felt he was in his proper sphere. He was one of the six great Masters, well-respected by all and doing the only thing he cared for. His every day had given him deep satisfaction. And now he had come down out of the mountains to serve a warring lord. His one guiding light, his magic and its art, seemed to be in constant jeopardy, either distorted or rendered totally useless in the affairs of the World.

Crispan began to realize how much he had sacrificed when he left the Order.

His practice with weaponry, which had been a source of pride as his skills improved, now became drudgery. Worse yet, it became a reminder for him of how far he was from the Order and his own preferred way of life.

He was practicing with Portar at swordplay one day when a sudden streak of prankishness came over him. Portar swung his heavy blade to the right, trying to feint Crispan into opening his own right. But Crispan parried the move easily, and yet even as he did so Portar dropped his sword, his eyes wide and his mouth gaping.

"Why, what is it, Portar?" Crispan tried to sound concerned while fighting down a smirk.

"My . . . my blade . . . it seemed to be on fire." Portar bent down, staring intently at his weapon.

"Surely it was but the glint of the sun." A giggle escaped and caught Portar's attention. He stood up, and as he did his weapon rose in the air. He grabbed at the proffered handle even as he stepped backwards.

"No! You did this, didn't you?"

Crispan shook his head in denial, but continued to smirk.

Portar, rather than being angry, was impressed. "How did you do it?"

"A simple illusion and levitation, Portar, nothing more. I'm sorry."

Portar raised his hand. "No, don't be. Can you do more?"

For a moment the Wizard felt his boredom leave him, as he looked about for a tempting target. Across the drill field he saw Mikal training a demi-squadron of cavalry to charge, hurl their spears, and then wheel. Time and again they rode down on the empty barrels meant to represent enemy infantry and loosed their javelins, wheeling sharply to avoid imaginary arrows and darts. Crispan watched closely to be sure of his timing.

On they came again at full tilt. They were in range and they hurled their weapons. As each struck a barrel it sprouted a cabbage at the end of the shaft. Portar stared in amazement. The soldiers hardly noticed, for they went into the wheeling maneuver. But as they did they found it impossible to guide their mounts straightaway; instead, the horses continued to wheel in place, round and round and round.

And then the horses stopped, not showing any effect or reason for their actions. Only their poor riders reeled dizzily in their saddles. Two or three slipped to the ground, their heads spinning. Many more slumped sickly over their pommels.

Portar and Crispan were now laughing uncontrollably and did not notice the presence of the Emperor behind them. "Tell me, Crispan," he intoned, "can you do this to an entire army?"

Crispan detected the slightest hint of sarcasm. "Perhaps."

"Then is this how we shall bring down Zhyjman, as you have my soldiers?"

"No, m'lord. It was but a prank." Even as he said it he tasted bitterness in his mouth. "Pranks," he thought. "I am reduced to pranks. Is this what has become of my Arts?"

One morning Thurka strode into Crispan's tent with a suggestion. "Rennar might know if Vladur is out there, if he waits with our enemy."

Crispan stared into the Emperor's hopeful eyes. "Rennar?" The name of the powerful witch who lived in the west came as a surprise to him. "Do you think she would know? She is both wise and powerful, but would she know?"

"I have been very kind to her in the past. And," Thurka revealed with some hesitation, "there is something else that I want to know. If Zhyjman has embarked on this war with the aid of the Renegade, I fear they would try to influence her to join their side. As you say, she is powerful, perhaps too powerful to be left alone. But I am not so crude as to ask her to join our side. I respect her integrity and independence. All I would ask is her neutrality and whatever news she could give."

"Is that then what I am to ask her?" Crispan's voice was heavy with resignation. He had not so much volunteered as accepted a request.

"Yes. Ask her for what news she has, and what she has heard. Ask her if she has been approached and if she will remain neutral." After a polite pause the Emperor added, "How soon can you leave?"

"As soon as my escort is formed and plans are made."

"You may have Portar and those who were with you in the Karsh as are available."

Crispan thanked him for that and once again set about his packing, his body moving slowly and heavily through the now familiar routine.

XXII

Familiar Terrain

There was little to be said of Crispan's journey westward. As Thurka had promised, Portar commanded his escort once again, and of the eight others in the party, five had been with them in the Karsh. Some of the others were back in Ker-en-kar, or with Oslon at Zifkar, and three or four had fallen during that night when they relieved the eastern city, including Stelba and Efrim.

Dressed plainly, without insignia or uniforms, they resembled any of the myriad bands of soldiers roaming across the Three Realms. Their journey was uneventful save for a brief run-in with some Vaduli scouts who shadowed them across the Forest of Swann thinking they were brigands. When Crispan established their true identities, the men of the forest melted away again amidst the trees.

Once out of the forest they moved swiftly across the great plain that had once been the Middle Realm. For days the land passed with little change as they made for that particular wood where Rennar made her home. In truth, Crispan did not know exactly where it was, but he relied on his instincts to lead him to it. All the land seemed the same to him, although he felt he knew where he was going just the same.

And yet, on one particular day the land suddenly became very familiar. It was not the pull of Rennar's cave he felt. Rather, he felt he was going home, and yet he could not be certain. The only man who could ever have told him exactly where he had come from had always refused to do so. Actually he felt that he asked Bellapon more out of curiosity than a real desire to know. But the elder Magician had declined to answer, reminding his protégé that at the Order one's past did not matter. The elder

Magician had added gravely, "At the Order we believe that where you have been before does not matter; all that matters is where you go from here." So Crispan had let the matter go.

But now, riding to see Rennar, he sensed that he was nearing his old home. For all the similarity between this terrain and that over which they had come, these hills and streams, the small hollows and wide plains exerted a special pull on him.

At dusk, a few nights later, Analdo scouted up ahead and reported that there was an inn not far up the road.

"Shall we stay the night?" Portar's face was bright and expectant.

Crispan hesitated. He removed his helmet and let the evening breeze loosen his light-brown hair. "No. I want to see it first."

"It is quite safe, m'lord," assured Analdo. "I checked."

But the Magician held firm and insisted on first seeing the inn. They reached a point on the road from which the inn was visible, but still at a great distance. He could not be sure at that distance or in that light. He peered and stared into the gloom and still could not tell.

Portar was becoming impatient, longing for the soft beds and warm food which seemed to beckon. "Well, sir?"

"No. We'll camp here tonight. But I want you to send two or three men to stay there. I want them to take careful note of everything they see."

Portar's face showed his puzzlement, his scar flushing bright red.

"You have your orders," Crispan said flatly.

The anxious Magician awoke early the next morning. He paced along the side of the road, ignoring the nearby comfort of the small campfire, waiting for the riders to return. After what seemed to be a very long time they came. With Portar hovering curiously behind him, Crispan interrogated the returned scouts.

"I tell you, sir, we saw nothing unusual there."

"Who ran the place?" Crispan asked eagerly.

"A man and wife. A tough bird he was, tight with a

meal. I almost had to beg for a piece of bread to go with my stew," said Trofan.

Portar growled perceptibly at the mention of fresh warm food. Crispan ignored him. "Were they the only ones there?"

"No. There were two young men."

Crispan smiled widely at the news. Portar looked at him and simply shrugged.

"Get the men ready to mount, Portar. We leave at once. I want to circle the village, to the west." As soon as the words were out of his mouth Crispan wondered why he had said that. "Too many years," he told himself. "What could we say to each other after all this time? Bellapon was correct, we are strangers." The thoughts hurt a bit, but he determined to ride on, although he led the men in such a way that the village remained in sight all the while that they circled it.

For a few days more they rode north and west from the village. The flat land gave way to rolling hills with thick woods nestled in between. Crispan inspected the woods one after another, scanning them from the hilltops, cautiously riding along their fringes. But each one proved to be unsatisfactory and so they rode on, always led by his vague notions.

Portar was disquieted by their lack of a map, but Crispan could not convey to him how he knew where they must go. He himself was not sure, but he felt a tugging that was so real as to be almost physical. At times it seemed to be in his body, seated in his heart. At times it seemed to be in his head, as though his powers were being attracted by a kindred force. "If that is true," he thought, "then I can never find Vladur on my own, for his powers and mine are now opposites, and we shall repel each other across time and space."

They had been following a road intermittently for some days, alternately riding it and then leaving it so that Crispan could scout from some hill or inspect some forest. Now, suddenly, he decided they were close enough. "That forest below," he said, pointing down from the hill.

"Are you sure this is the place?" asked Portar.

Crispan hesitated. "I'm not sure. I think this is close enough to her dwelling. I shall seek her out tomorrow, but tonight we must rest. There was a village back down the road. Were there any inns?"

Portar growled, "Yes," remembering the last time one had been available.

After explaining his plan Crispan divided the men into three discrete and separate groups and they rode to the inn, never acknowledging one another's presence beyond perfunctory greetings. So they passed their mealtime and a short while in front of the fireplace before retiring.

Crispan had not been in such an establishment since Bellapon had first taken him away. Far into the night he lay awake in his bed, breathing in familiar smells and remembering his long-gone boyhood. Somewhere his musings and memories passed into enveloping sleep, and dark night soon passed on to hazy morning.

Crispan and Trofan rose and breakfasted first and were ready to leave when Portar and three others came down. As Crispan had planned, he and Trofan would ride on towards Rennar alone. Portar and his group would join Trofan on the edge of the woods while the Wizard met with the Witch. The remaining four would keep guard at the best listening post in that or any other region, the inn.

XXIII

Rennar

Crispan smiled up into the warm sunlight as they rode. Spring was firmly upon the land, and he rode without his helmet so that his hair could blow free in the breeze. The forest was not very far from the village, and the sounds of its inhabitants carried on the wind. They rode north, moving faster than ambling travelers but not so fast as to raise the eyebrow of a passing stranger or unseen observer.

Like a loosely coiled brown rope, the road followed the ever-increasing undulations of the countryside. They were back among the hills where Rennar kept her home. Crispan slowed their pace to a walk as he tried to tell which of the many thick but separate woods was hers.

"Tell me, m'lord, who is this Rennar?"

"A powerful woman, perhaps the most accomplished Witch in all the Three Realms."

Her title puzzled Trofan. "Then she is a Witch, as in the stories one tells little children, and not a Magician like yourself."

Crispan chuckled into his hand, but went on to explain the differences just as Bellapon had once explained them to him. They rode on, in this way, with Crispan trying to make as clear as possible the differences in each title and its Arts. It all became so involved that Trofan never even got to ask why it was so important that they see the fabled Witch, Rennar.

For quite some time they rode along the southern edge of the wood that Crispan had chosen. It was one of the larger ones, completely filling its dell and spilling over onto the surrounding hills. Crispan slowed his mount to a walk, waiting, searching for the right spot in the wall of trees. He stopped repeatedly, hardly moving at all. Then he stopped completely, his gray eyes narrowing, listening. "This is where we enter." Trofan led his horse forward and was about to enter the woods when he was stayed by the Magician. "Wait," he said in an ominous whisper. "Check the roads to see that we have not been followed or seen." Up and down the road they looked, they scanned the hills, but they saw no one, no gleam of far-off weapons, no betraying plume of dust. Satisfied, Crispan led the way in among the trees.

They had gone but a little way among the sheltering trees when Crispan turned to his companion. "This is where we must part. Stay here and keep a careful watch on the road. Portar should be able to find you. Make sure you go no closer to the road than this, lest you be spotted. From here you will be able to see the others without being seen yourself. I hope to be back in a day or two."

Trofan assented and dismounted, tying up his horse and looking for a comfortable vantage point. He settled into a hollow between two protruding roots that was thickly covered in grass. Occasionally he would look into the woods and follow the vanishing figure of the Magician.

Crispan moved among the thick dark trees like a thread being woven into an intricate twisting pattern. He was happy to be alone in the placidity of the woods, watching the passing trunks with their leafy tops sprinkled with sunlight and their garbs of moss pointing the way. He was enjoying the ride, but expected it to end soon at the abode of Rennar.

Morning passed into afternoon and the woods stretched on with little change, transforming his easiness and expectation to anxiety and doubt. "Perhaps these are not the proper woods. Perhaps I entered in the wrong place," he thought. "But no, I could feel it, it was right. Perhaps a wrong turn somewhere amongst these trees." He looked for the sun, but it was shrouded in heavy clouds now. Only the moss imparted some small reassurance.

The doubts rode with him as he steered the horse up the increasingly sloped terrain. He was leaving the dell, and evening was upon him. Chill breezes leapt now among the branches. Dimming sunlight grew even dimmer under the leafy branches. "Too late to turn back now. I'll ride at least until dark, and then stop for the night. If I don't reach her tomorrow . . ." His thoughts trailed off into the darkness.

Despite the fact that it was spring the forest grew cold at night, the chill air clamped in among the trees and whipped up by the wind. Desperate for a guide in the increasing dark, Crispan's eyes fixed on an errant shaft of moonlight ahead. "But," he realized, "there hasn't been any moon tonight, too many clouds." With conflicting feelings of relief and wariness he approached the still-flickering beacon.

It shimmered and moved, but Crispan soon realized that this was only the effect of the leafy branches swaying in the wind. He cooed softly to his horse as he dismounted and took to leading it by the reins. He reached a broad and ancient elm that stood before the light yet hid him as he peered around it. Through the night he could see a small lantern hanging from the mouth of a small cave in the hillside.

Crispan moved into the clearing before the cave and secured the horse's reins to a bush. He climbed up the hill and stood before the cave, trying to see into it. The lantern lit what was a natural antechamber, beyond which a blanket hung to mask the interior of the cave. Plagued still by doubts and wariness, he drew a deep breath and pushed back the blanket.

Once beyond its mouth, Crispan could tell little but that the cave was not unlike a small hut tucked into the hillside. Several candles suspended from the ceiling provided light, but their smoke left the den murky.

He waited for his eyes to adjust to what little light there was. No sound came from the cave save for the crackling of the flames in a small pitfire further in. Finally he discerned the figure of a woman beyond the fire. Her hair was the gray of iron, flecked with a few stubborn strands of black, all falling haphazardly about her shoulders. It was difficult to see much else of her, for all but her thin, leather-skinned arms and wrinkled

213

face lay hidden in a dark red cloak and cowl. Her eyes, burning like coals, stood out above all else. Crispan doffed his hood and stepped into the ring of light cast by the fire.

"Greetings, Rennar. May the Spirits ever enhance your powers." It was a warm greeting to a fellow practitioner of the Arts.

Rennar replied noncommittally. "Welcome, Crispan. I have heard much of you, and am surprised at your youth. I expected you to be a little older. Please, please, be seated." She motioned to the aged cushion on the opposite side of the fire.

"You know who I am?"

"I foresaw your coming some time ago, and helped guide you to this place. Before I saw your coming I heard your name, and it was highly praised."

"Your reputation has always been of the highest at the Order," he responded.

She nodded, passing him an earthen mug. "Will you have some?"

Crispan hesitated but accepted, not knowing what sort of a brew it was, or whether she was to be trusted. He lifted the cracked mug to his lips and happily found the liquid to be an herb broth, which gave him welcome warmth, especially after the cold ride up the hillside.

"You were surprised, eh?" Before he could reply she went on, saying, "Let us drop this ceremonial. We both know why you have come, so out with it. Why should I aid Thurka?"

He was both relieved and caught off guard. Again Rennar cut him off. "Will he coerce me? I have always been left alone by the Empire of the South and I have never acted against them. But the same is also true of the North. So why take sides?"

"We do not ask that you take sides," he replied with some unease, wondering at this seeming lapse in her powers of foresight. "Our only fear is that Zhyjman would prove to be too powerful should you join him."

Her eyes filled with wonder and surprise and, above all, contempt. "What can he possibly offer me?"

214

"Protection, support. Aid to increase your powers."

"Bah! Is that all?"

Crispan had no answer to this. He put his empty mug down on the beaten dirt floor and gazed about at the innumerable nooks, niches and crannies filled with phials and small jars, at tiny crevices sprouting herbs which glowed faintly in the dark.

"And it's all your side has to offer as well." Her voice was sharp and dry. "These warriors do not understand the true practice of the Arts and what we really seek. And be careful, Crispan, lest you become one of them. I will side with no one, as ever. Like the Order, my safety lies in my neutrality."

Crispan felt relieved. "That is all I thought to ask for, just your neutrality. But what if Zhyjman is victorious? He may not take your neutrality so kindly. Thurka will always respect your position, but Zhyjman . . ."

"He wouldn't dare!" she croaked, her voice rising indignantly.

All was silent for a moment as Rennar stirred the broth on the fire and Crispan continued to take in his remarkably cozy surroundings. When the heat of the moment had died down he asked, "Has Vladur sought you out?"

"No."

"Not at all? What about Zhyjman, has he?" Crispan's voice rose noticeably.

"He sent me some trinkets recently. That is all, but I guess it is his beginning."

"Then tell me this, do you think Vladur is with the North? We, of course, heard that he was, but I really do not know for sure." Crispan was desperately fishing for answers now, and sounded it.

"One hears many things and little truth. I had even heard that you had renounced the Order to become a warrior!"

Crispan laughed at this, but Rennar shot back quickly, "Then why are you here in the World?"

"To counter Vladur if he is here."

"You sound like a man who lacks conviction. Take my warning seriously, Crispan. You may become one of them, they may drag you down. In the region where I lived as a girl they told a fable about a golden mountain eagle. He was a hunter of great prowess, and very proud of his golden plumage. But the day came when he was out hunting and could not find any prey on the mountain slopes and so he circled down and down into the forests. Here too he searched until he grew weary and came to rest on a low branch. While he sat there, a pack of wild dogs passed below him, carrying freshly killed game, rabbits and squirrels.

"The eagle greeted them warmly. 'Good morrow. I see you have been busy. May I ask where you found your prey?'

" 'The forest abounds, more so than your mountainsides,' the pack's leader replied. 'Come and join in our meal.'

"As he alighted onto the ground the eagle asked if he might not join them in their next hunt.

" 'We hunt again tomorrow. But you must be able to keep up with us. Tonight you are our guest, but we do not feed slackers.'

"The eagle, trusting to his powerful wings, said he could match their every step. The next morning they all set out together. There was the scent of rabbit in the air, and the dogs set a furious pace, tearing through the woods. The eagle flew above them, skimming under the branches. Their prey this day sped away as fast as they chased it, and as the eagle flew he began to scrape as he passed low branches and leaves. From his vantage he could see the rabbit better than the pack below and he flew even faster. The rabbit made for a stream, sending sheets of spray up at the closing eagle. Finally the eagle lunged, his talons wide and extended. He grabbed at the rabbit and caught it, but was dragged down by its weight and went tumbling through a brackish puddle.

"At the feast that night the eagle went to a pool to drink and saw himself for the first time that day. His feathers were dirty and badly ruffled, and he was covered with drying mire and bits of leaves and bark. He looked at his spoiled finery and he wept."

216

Having finished her story, Rennar sat back. She lowered her cowl and poured herself some spiced drink from a jug that sat up above in a niche. Crispan watched her. He poked at the fire and quickly changed the subject. "What is your answer to the Emperor?"

"Tell Thurka Re that while I will not aid his enemies, neither shall I aid him. I wish him well. And you may tell him that I have never conveyed that wish to Zhyjman."

Understanding her meaning, Crispan looked for his cloak as he prepared to leave.

"It is late, Master of the Order, and you may go astray in the woods. I cannot lead you out as I led you in. You may spend the night here, before a warm fire."

As he settled back onto his cushion he could not help asking her a question he would never have asked old Eliborg. "What can you see as the outcome of this war?" As soon as he said it he regretted it.

Rennar rocked slowly and shook her head back and forth, back and forth. "I do not know. There is much confusion in the World, for reasons I do not understand. Magic does not work today as it did or as it should. There is a heaviness in the air. Perhaps there is an omen in this, but I cannot say or tell."

Her answer disturbed him greatly, but he knew he could not have left without asking. Rennar plied the fire with some kindling and retired to a chamber further within the cave.

It was past midday when Crispan emerged from the dense forest and joined his waiting escort. Relieved that the Magician had returned and that they could now return to Gurdikar, Portar greeted him warmly. "I am glad to see you, m'lord. Have you accomplished your mission here?"

Crispan merely nodded.

"Shall we spend this night at the inn?"

"No," said Crispan, dashing Portar's hopes. "We will only stop to get the others and then we go straight to Gurdikar. There is news I must convey at once to the Emperor."

The emptiness of his words rattled in his mind. He had something to tell the Emperor, but it was only that once again there was no news of the Renegade. The hopes he had placed in his journey to Rennar had given way to the lurking doubts and uneasiness once again.

XXIV

News from the North

The days following his return to Gurdikar were a continuation of the frustration which had hounded Crispan before. Rennar's warning haunted him, and with new resolve he plunged back into his studies. Xirvan sent up some books from Kerdineskar, and he spent restless hours day and night searching for answers to questions that might never be asked, and which should never have been allowed to arise in the first place.

His greatest sense of accomplishment in these days was in achieving a certain sense of security in his surroundings. Soon there were books and scrolls and manuscripts joyously littering the inner chamber of his tent, and an impressive and growing collection of pots and vessels and vials for his potions and conjurings. And yet these were also a sign of frustration to him, for his work advanced little, and he spent most of his time repeating simple conjurings he had learned years before. Nothing brought him closer to solving the problems posed by Vladur. No spell or divination brought him any answer. There was nothing in any known and permissible tome. No honing of his powers improved his ability in combatting necromancy.

Mikal too spent seemingly endless days of routine. Training soldiers became mere ritual, and there was little else to occupy his time. He would spend hours in Crispan's jumbled tent, sitting in a dark corner while the Magician worked his Art. While Crispan struggled desperately against the ignorance imposed by the Order itself, Mikal coped with the gnawing feeling left by Zoltan's sudden and unexpected desertion.

At noon they crossed the small compound to where the lords' tents were pitched and went to Mikal's for some

219

lunch. Warmth exuded from the red-draped walls hung with small ornamental shields. Cheeses, fruits and dried meats filled the small round table centered in the inner chamber. Mikal reached across and poured another cup of wine for them both. The light from the surrounding candles danced in golden ripples on the carafe. Crispan looked into the Prince's melancholy face. "Have you thought about going to Kerdineskar for a rest?"

Mikal looked over the top of his raised cup. "Why? What's in Kerdineskar?"

"Your mother, for one."

"The Empress and the Emperor are not on the best of terms, and have not been for years. Now that I have returned and gone to my father, I fear I have crossed over. So why go to Kerdineskar?"

"There's the Countess Celine," suggested Crispan, tugging at a piece of dried meat.

"You've been talking to Belka, or rather he to you."

"She is not married, you know."

"That was a long time ago. We are not the same any longer, either of us. And I dare not risk being away from Gurdikar for as long as such a journey would take."

Crispan smiled as he cut into a ripe apple. "Mikal, I believe that the vaunted mercenary leader, the Heir to the Empire, is actually afraid."

Slightly embarrassed, the Prince took refuge behind his glass. A servant slipped into the chamber as Mikal took a long draught, draining his cup yet again. The servant moved unobtrusively behind Mikal and whispered in his ear. His eyes widened as he listened. "He's back, Crispan. Zoltan's back." Both men jumped up and rushed out of the tent, running fast for the tent of the Emperor.

Standing in the plaza before the tent was the portly red beard, defiantly under the guard of Larc's troops. The gleeful Duke was triumphant before the assembling crowd. "You see, my lord, my soldiers captured the deserter as he returned to spy on us."

"Not so quickly, Larc," said Mikal as he ran up, "let us hear Zoltan's story first."

"You would accept the word of a deserter, a mercenary?" asked the indignant Duke.

"I would remind you, my dear Larc, that I was once a mercenary as well, and that I fought for you."

Thurka stepped between them. "Please, let us take this discussion into the council chamber." He turned to the ever-present Churnir. "Summon Belka and the other Princes."

Zoltan was sequestered in another part of the Emperor's pavilion while the council gathered. Belka entered first and took a seat next to his nephew. "Is he really back? That is good news." Mikal shrugged noncommittally.

Churnir led in the remaining lords, and Thurka then took his seat, carefully spreading his black robes across his knees. He signaled Churnir to bring in the prisoner.

Zoltan, still silent, and grimy from much riding, was brought before the council. The Emperor looked up at the broad figure and sighed. After a moment's silence he began. "You were found at the edge of camp by scouts from Larc's troop. They say you were trying to avoid notice as you entered the camp. Is this true?"

The mercenary nodded. "Yes."

"This is rather damning evidence. Can you explain it?"

Before Zoltan could begin, his old friend cut him off. "Should we not let him tell his own story from the beginning? We can question him when he is finished." No one voiced an objection, and so Thurka motioned Zoltan to begin.

"I have been to Anrehenkar, my lords." Larc hissed triumphantly at these words, feeling his accusations were true. But Zoltan ignored this. "I went there because there was no other way we could get reliable information on our enemies. We have been sitting here making guesses in the dark, and so I took this mission upon myself.

"I rode hard across the Middle Realm and approached the enemy camp at night, for Lord Syman has a long memory and short temper, and I feared that my return would not be a welcome one.

"The mercenary camp is much larger than I expected,

the largest I have ever seen. It was twice as large as the army at Aishar." Mikal looked both surprised and worried, trying to conceive of so large a mercenary horde. "His army is in close siege, but the forces under Prince Zascha seem to be holding quite well." Zascha's brother, Prince Farnar, smiled widely at this.

"However," Zoltan cautioned, fidgeting noticeably now in his bonds, "there is reason to believe that this is not Zhyjman's main force. I think that force is to the east, but no one at Anrehenkar is certain."

"And who at Anrehenkar now provides us with information?" asked Larc maliciously.

"Some of the members of my former troop, and Mikal's. I was able to bribe those who were once most loyal to us and form them into a small band of spies. Our names are still honored in certain quarters of that army."

Here even Thurka Re was skeptical. "And you did all this without being noticed?"

"In a camp actively pressing a siege it was easy. I waited for a storm-ridden night and slipped into the camp. One soldier looks more or less like another under a cloak and cowl, and certainly no one expected to see me there. Ulham, Rober, and one or two others are still loyal to Mikal and me, especially after the rude treatment they got after we left. Syman refused to allow them freedom to negotiate a new contract, and arbitrarily placed them under Viktor. They feel he broke the mercenaries' rules and thus were free to treat with me. We have some spies in their army this very night and others roaming the Middle Realm for more news."

"And with this corps of loyal spies this is all the news you can give the Emperor?" Larc was relentless in his distrust.

Again Thurka had to agree with his disaffected ally. "Aye, Zoltan, have you no news of Kirion? And what about the army the enemy has placed at the Gates?"

"The Gates?" echoed the burly warrior.

"Yes, Zoltan," explained Belka. "Oslon's scouts at the Gates were forced back by a much larger force from the North. That is the third one they have raised there. We

222

have sent reinforcements from Ludivo at Ker-en-kar, and there is no immediate danger of a third siege for the enemy seems content this time just to occupy the Gates. Do you not know their purpose?"

Zoltan's red brows wrinkled. "I do not know. Perhaps just to keep us off balance. Perhaps Kirion is with that army, but I think not. And as long as he is hidden, Zhyjman has not committed his main force. I do not know how the North can commit so many men on so many fronts."

"Bah!" Larc spat contemptuously. "I tell you he has been sent here to blind us with lies."

Bound as he was, Zoltan began to move towards the Duke. Larc rose out of his chair. Mikal too was on his feet, seeing the hatred in both men's eyes. "Zoltan!" he cried, extending his strong sword arm. "This is the arm that saved you at Balluskar. Give me the arm that saved me at Sippian and swear that what you have said is the truth."

Churnir deftly slipped behind Zoltan and slit the bonds. The burly warrior extended his arm and swore. "His word is good enough for me, my lords. I will guarantee his word and pledge before you all that if he has sworn falsely I will use this arm to kill him for the traitor he would be."

To this no one could possibly object, much as it discomforted the Duke of Larc, who soon left the council in a fine rage. The others pressed around Zoltan and deluged him with questions.

Once again he went over what news and information he had. "Syman is deeply committed to his siege. To disengage now would demoralize his forces. And yet he cannot crack the city. Either way he is in an unfamiliar and uncomfortable position." But again he repeated that he had no news of Kirion or the purpose of the enemy at the Gates. Then, seeing Crispan's eyes on him expectantly, he admitted with much gravity, "There is no word at all of Vladur either." But one last item he did have. Turning to the Emperor, he said, "There is no confirmation of this, but many rumors say that Zhyjman is not at his capital and that he left Mujdhur recently."

It was only a rumor, but Thurka pondered long over it.

All of that night Mikal kept Zoltan awake with questions. Like a captured hawk suddenly freed, Mikal felt released from the tedium of camp life and the rigors of his title. News of the mercenary camp reminded him of happier days long gone, and he listened eagerly to all Zoltan said and asked about all that was left unsaid. They discussed Syman's abortive hunt for them, the fate of their soldiers and servants, but above all else, the siege of Anrehenkar.

"As I said, Mikal, never has Syman commanded such an army. His camp lies west of the city and is some six miles across. The siege machines stand like a forest about the walls, although they have not yet made a breach. And it has been costly, too. Pyotir is dead, and Azjhan, and Grygor will never fight again. But still Syman remains locked in his siege, refusing to budge. Ulham says Syman is deeply frustrated by it all, and that the men begin to grumble as well. But they are bound to him just as he is to Anrehenkar, until this war ends or Zhyjman so orders."

Mikal let out a short laugh, one of the few he had uttered in recent days. "It would seem that our Lord Syman may have finally been out-bargained in a contract." They laughed, and Mikal passed the wine flask to his friend. "It is good to have you back, Zoltan."

"Aye, and good to be here. But this is not the place to celebrate. Come, I know a little place in Gurdikar where there is wine aplenty—and women." Both laughed again as they sought out their horses and headed for the narrow, winding streets of Gurdikar in the waning hours of the night.

XXV

A Book from Xirvan

"**M**y dear Crispan," the note from Xirvan began, "I found this book at the bottom of one of my trunks. I do not remember where I got it, but it would seem to have come by way of Rhaan-va-Mor if the original inscription is any guide. Who knows where it came from before there? I have only glanced at it, but perhaps it will help. May the Spirits ever enhance your powers."

The young Magician thanked the messenger warmly and then set about unwrapping the carefully packed ancient tome. His dirk, a gift from Belka, moved slowly back and forth against the cords. The several strands parted under the blade's motion, and then the final one gave and the cord fell away. Gingerly, yet eagerly, Crispan unfolded the covering leather skin Xirvan had provided and meticulously spread it flat away from the tome.

In faded gold letters across the binding was the title, *Thaumaturgical Demonology and Goety.* Crispan ran his finger hesitantly over the cracked red leather which held the book together. "Surely Vladur has seen this," he thought as he pondered the title. "Is this the answer, or will it corrupt me as Vladur has been corrupted?" His fingers trailed up over the front cover, toying with the ingrained design. "Thaumaturgy—that was his Art." Like a blind man groping for the certain edge of a cliff, Crispan's fingers lingered before the right edge of the cover. There was a strap inserted in a lock keeping the cover shut. He tried the catch. It held fast. Again, and the same result. "What would Eliborg say with his Divination? Is this an omen?" For longer than a moment he sat pondering the possibility. With a seeming will of its own his right hand forced the issue by bringing the finely honed dirk against the stubborn strap.

The inside cover was inscribed to a name Crispan recognized, the name of a famed merchant family from Rhaan-va-Mor, presented by one of their trading captains. The author's name, Feinno of Uindarh, held no meaning for him. He turned to the next page. Fortunately the work was written in a variant of the common tongue, so Crispan was able to proceed through the Prefatori.

"In traveling down the unknown ways closed to most men, one encounters many twists and turns, doors of opportunity and doors of dread. I have gone down many of these pathways and opened many new doors. Some should never have been touched, others led to great new vistas. I record here my knowledge and experiments for others to follow my way and avoid my errors."

Crispan sat back. "A curious introduction," he thought. "This Feinno of Uindarh has seen much, and gives a note of warning. Yet he offers a hint of hope."

With sudden resolution he called out to his servant. "Clear my table of everything!" In came his servant, Lenid, who scampered about picking up dirtied vessels and blackened chambers.

"There is a proper shop in the city, isn't there—potions and so on?" Lenid nodded at Crispan's question. "Fine, then I want you to go and purchase the following items: I want new flints, some fine and coarse tinder, and—No! I'll go with you."

"Yes, m'lord," said Lenid, smiling at his master's activity.

In all the time he had spent in the camp before Gurdikar, Crispan had rarely entered the grimy fortress' walls. Squatting on the plain as a reminder of an older age of warriors, the city offered little to entice or invite him. Despite invitations from the Governor to join him for dinner and blandishments from Zoltan to enjoy a night there, Crispan had largely shunned Gurdikar.

"The shop where you bought my vessels and powders —is it the shop of a trained practitioner of the Arts?"

Lenid, who had been a servant to Xirvan, opined that the owner was not trained in the Arts but that he carried a good range of supplies.

Under the open portcullis and past the lounging guards Lenid led his master to the tight little alleyways of the eastern quarter. They rode in single file in the narrow streets, almost bumping their heads on overhanging second stories of low, squat buildings. The sights and smells held a fascination for Crispan, as if the hope promised in the new book had reawakened him to much of the World.

"Crispan! Crispan!"

Hearing his name shouted from an upper window surprised the Magician. He turned this way and that looking for a familiar face. Then he saw Zoltan's huge body filling an entire window. Barely visible beyond his shoulder was a blond wench tugging at his arm.

"Have you finally come to enjoy the city with me?" shouted the former mercenary. "Come up, she has many willing friends."

Crispan smiled. "No thank you, my friend, I have work to do." He chuckled as he waved good-bye, realizing that Zoltan could never quite understand that women and the Arts were largely incompatible.

"But Crispan," Zoltan yelled at the passing figure. Crispan waved and rode on.

The shop that Lenid led him to was on the tightest and darkest street in the city. Barely visible in its narrow building wedged between two others, the shop appeared to be a long-forgotten afterthought of some builder or merchant. Crispan's efforts to peer in were rendered futile by years of dirt and dust. Lenid beckoned him to the crooked entry and pushed down on the latch, but it held firm. He pushed again. Finally, together they both pushed and forced the door.

The room was quite dark, only one candle battling against the gloom. Its light was diffused and filtered through myriad cobwebs. Crispan and his servant stood in the center of the room, waiting for their eyes to adjust to the dark. An old man appeared suddenly, taking advantage of their momentary dislocation.

"Masters?" his squeaky voice said as he rolled one hand over the other.

Lenid stepped forward, sending up small puffs of dust across the floor. "This is my master, the Lord Crispan."

The proprietor bowed low, the stray gray hairs on his chin bending against his robes, which were old and tattered in some places. "How can I help you, my lord?"

"I need some powders and potions, and various vessels. Can you read?" The old man nodded. "Here is my list. Can you fill it?"

The proprietor's brows arched decisively as he scanned the paper. "Some of these are rather rare—and expensive. Hm . . . odyl stones, moly, darkling philters. I have most of them, and can give you substitutes for the others." He pulled back his cap and scratched his head. After another look at the list the old man began shuffling about the room, stretching for shelves and stooping under counters. Slowly he amassed a collection of jars and vials on one of the counters.

"Tell me," Crispan asked the bustling form, "were you ever a member of the Order?"

The old one cackled. "Ha! The Order? No. But you are. Your talisman told me that when you walked in. Your servant never told me who sent him for these things in the past, but I knew that no local dabbler or would-be sorcerer could use or even know of these potions. You are the Emperor's Magician, are you not?"

Crispan was taken aback by the question. He suddenly felt naked and exposed when he realized that his presence was such common knowledge among the most common folk, although there was no reason why it should not be so, especially after the oft-told tale of the saving of Zifkar. Crispan swallowed hard. "Yes, I am."

The old man continued moving about the dusky shop, cackling and talking to himself as he went through his inventory, most of which was hidden in the gloom or under layers of dust. Finally he had collected an impressive pile of flints and vessels, fine and coarse tinder, phials, powders and bottles.

"Is that all?" asked Crispan.

"All except the moly. I've not seen any in a long, long time. I could possibly get some, perhaps in several days. I had heard that up north much of the moly was being hoarded."

Crispan turned on this. "What's that? Who is hoarding the moly?" His eyes were alive and fiery, and fear tore suddenly at his stomach.

The old proprietor stepped back a bit, fearful without knowing why. "I do not know, my lord. Truly. I have only heard from traders whom I know. They say that much of the moly in the Middle Realm and north has disappeared, that scavengers have gathered it all up. One told me that the Emperor of the North was paying a huge bounty for the herb."

Crispan was about to ask why he had not reported this to anyone, but did not, knowing it would be futile. "Can you get me some?" he said instead. "I will take whatever is available. I will need it, now more than ever." He beckoned Lenid to pack up the goods on the counter and passed some gold coins to the old man.

Crispan was at the door when he turned back again to the shopkeeper. "One thing more. No one is to know that I have been here, and should they know, they are not to be told what I have purchased. Also, I want to know whatever else the traders can tell you. You will be well rewarded for all of this." He tossed a coin across the room. The old man caught it and touched it to his forehead in obeisance.

Goaded by the rumor he had heard, Crispan worked far into the night and beyond, poring over the book, reading, writing, rereading. From spells, incantations and their accompanying potions the table and floor were littered with dirty vessels and pots. Tufts of smoke clung about the oil lamp hanging in the center of the tent. The acrid smell and dust bore down on his eyes as heavily as the lack of sleep, until he finally had to seek the refreshing air of dawn.

Lenid lay curled on his cot in the outer chamber, huddled within his blanket. Crispan yawned deeply as he came out of the tent. The chill air cleared his head. He raised his eyebrows and rubbed at the sleep lurking just below them. Large clouds of dark blue and deep gray rolled across the lightening sky. Crispan looked up at them and thought of the smoke hovering in his own tent. Without even realizing it, he began to walk slowly about the sleeping camp.

"There's no answer anywhere," he thought. "None of it has worked. The casting of spells and conjuring of spirits cannot compete with necromancy. Is it Vladur who amasses all the moly? What power can I call on to vie with his?" His hands thrust deep into his robes, he walked absentmindedly around clustered tents and dying fires.

He hunched his shoulders against the chill which still prevailed in the spring morning. His mind restlessly grasped for some answer, some glimmer which would help him against the Renegade. As he meandered back towards his own tent he seemed to hear a passage from Feinno's tome, referring to an experiment he had undertaken in which the spell had overwhelmed him.

"I felt the vapors clutching at me," Feinno had written, "I felt my head swim. As I slipped under the effect I watched my conjuration grow before me. It writhed and coiled to a huge size until it filled the room before me. I could feel its growth deep within me even as I watched it before me, for it seemed to be feeding on my very powers which had first nurtured it. I was so weakened by the vapors that I was unable to dismiss the specter. Instead, it demanded more and more of me, draining my powers, struggling with me for them. I watched helplessly as it became a parasite, drawing on me, on my powers, draining me further. I know not how long the combat continued, for I lost all sense of time in the seemingly endless struggle. It was only when the vapors began to dissipate and my senses cleared that I was able, by extreme concentration of thought, to force back the phantom. It was turmoil—my mind struggling to overcome its own creation. That I succeeded was due to my concentration of thought, which slowly starved the specter of nourishment until it withered and strangled. I burned all the vessels and potions I had used that very night, and never did I repeat this conjuration."

Crispan turned the passage over and over in his mind as he lay down and prepared to give himself over to sleep. "The passage, the passage. . . ." There was something in it which called for his attention, and yet he could not tell exactly what. Something kept calling his mind back to it, but he was weary and could no longer grasp at such things. His thoughts went from the passage to the Game they had played at the Order and back. Why did he remember that now, he wondered. But he could not concentrate on one or the other. In complete exhaustion he let the passage slip away, falling into a deep sleep.

XXVI

A Grave Interruption

"**T**his war confuses me," Thurka admitted. "It is so unlike any that I know of. In the old days kings would gather their armies, march, fight a few battles, exchange some land and prisoners and go home. For all of its uncertainty there has been a strange sense of security in the Chaos, a lack of ultimate threat, a limitation. But now, now we have four and five armies marching across the face of three Empires. I fear it is beyond my grasp, and perhaps even Zhyjman's. I fear the Chaos spreading and overwhelming the two remaining Empires."

Mikal sought for words to comfort his father, but could not find them. Thurka saw this and asked, "You are worried too, are you not?"

"Yes."

Thurka was at once relieved that his own fears were not groundless and anxious over his son's concerns. "Why?"

"Because our enemies behave strangely, unlike their former selves. Zhyjman, Syman, Kirion—they all act as if they were different men. Zhyjman has never before moved so rapidly against his objective, or so soon after his last conquest. Why the haste? And where has he recruited so many soldiers? Where is Kirion? Why is the North's best general silent for so long? And Syman—for him to press an unsuccessful siege for so long is hard to believe. Every mercenary leader hates sieges, fearing what a long and unsuccessful one can do to his armies. They all behave like men entranced."

"Perhaps Vladur has done this to them."

"Hardly," said Crispan as he swung back the tent folds. "His absence remains the most perplexing thing of

all. And what if he is not with Zhyjman? What then?"
The now-familiar anxious note had crept into his voice
once again.

"And so," said the Emperor with apparent resignation,
"we sit here at Gurdikar not knowing who we face or
what we should do. The initiative remains with our enemies, and they mock us with their inactivity."

"Perhaps there will be some news today." Mikal stood
up. "Let us assemble the others in council and see."

Once again the High Princes, lords and generals took
their accustomed places around the long table covered
with maps for yet another attempt to decide on some
strategy beyond that of waiting for their enemies.

One of Zoltan's captains came in, followed by two
soldiers carrying a new map showing their latest information as to where Zhyjman had placed his seemingly endless forces. Thurka waved wearily for the captain to begin,
and he drew out a long dagger and stepped before the
map.

"M'lords, here are the latest reports from our scouts.
They report large forces here and here," he said, pointing
to the now-familiar wings of Syman's armies.

"But we still do not know what this force is doing, the
one that recently cleared the Gates of Lord Oslon's outposts. In addition, a large force has recently moved
south of the Kyryli border, half Kyryli and Nor, half
mercenary, but Kirion is not with them, which would
seem to mean that Zhyjman still has his reserves uncom-
mitted. The positions of these forces have effectively
screened the North from our scouts. Information becomes
harder and harder to get." The captain turned as he
talked and saw the Magician leaning far forward in his
seat. Glumly the captain added, "And there is no word
of Vladur, either."

Thurka's hands dropped into his lap. "Thank you, captain. That will be all. Lord Zoltan can tell us the rest."

After the three soldiers had left, Lord Gwyn of Perrigar
turned to the red beard. "Why does Zhyjman throw so
much of his weight to the east. What do you know of that
force at the Gates?"

"Very little. It is a large force, perhaps fifty thousand. After they swept Oslon's outposts to the south they stopped. We feared again for Zifkar, but they have not budged beyond the South Gate."

The Duke of Larc now took the floor and strode purposefully towards the map. "Look, look at Zhyjman's forces. Syman here at Anrehenkar, that force near Kyryl, the force at the Gates. As Lord Gwyn says, most of their strength lies to the east. If we move now we can force his hand."

His eyes narrowed now as he warmed to his new strategy. "To do this we must threaten something vital to Zhyjman. With the west entirely open, even if his own force with Kirion is still in the North, we can move swiftly against Mujdhur, bypassing Syman. Zhyjman will be forced to defend his capital and—"

"And," interrupted a peeved Zoltan, "you can reestablish yourself in your dukedom."

Venomous hatred crept over Larc's aquiline features. "Well, surely we could raise Larc to our cause and use it as a base. Whatever forces Zhyjman has there will not be enough to hold down my people and stop us. How can he stop us?"

Zoltan went now from anger to contempt. "Why, not at all!" he said facetiously. "But tell me this, how do we defend the South while we stealthily sneak across the Middle Realm to restore you? We cannot raise the armies he has, and if we could, how could we train them in time? And what if Syman breaks his siege and moves against our right flank on the march? And even if we should arrive there with our forces intact, what happens if Zhyjman and Kirion cut us off once we are in the North? A fine plan—at least you will get to die in Larc."

Larc's face was now a volcano of erupting emotion. "What," he screamed, "am I to take military advice from a mercenary?"

"At least I can see beyond my own needs. Go north, and let us get down to more serious matters."

"I don't have to take this from you, you nameless scum!"

235

"I should have killed you when I had the chance in your stinking dukedom." Zoltan's hand was on his dagger, and Larc was reaching for his sword, snarling. Mikal, Belka and the others were on their feet at once, hoping to separate them, for this time it seemed certain that blood would flow.

Belka wrapped his huge hands around Larc's arms and pinned them behind his back. As his sword clanked to the floor he screamed, "I demand an apology, and that this cur be dismissed from our presence."

"Cur?" spat back Zoltan as he jostled behind Mikal. "I'll kill—"

Mikal thrust his chest before his friend's dagger. "Zoltan! No!"

Now the Emperor was between the two men as well. "Larc, you have been warned in the past. Zoltan is a trusted member of my House now, and a reliable commander of our scouts. There will be no more such outbursts or I will pack you off to Kerdineskar. And you, Zoltan. You are never again to theaten any of my allies, lords or generals."

Both men now stood very still, and Thurka could see that they were still glaring at one another. "What have we become?" Thurka said. "Is Zhyjman to defeat us without even moving against us? Is this his strategy?"

But these words were of little effect. Still there was no movement, and everyone remained as if part of a hectic frieze. The spell was broken only by a young man hurtling himself into the tent. Crispan stepped back at the sight of him, crying out, "Elthwyn!"

Churnir rushed in behind him and grabbed at the young man clutching his teacher's robes. The Captain of the Guards turned apologetically to his Emperor. "I'm sorry, m'lord, he forced his way . . ."

"It is all right, m'lords," reassured Crispan, his face torn with perplexity. "He is a student of mine." The Magician looked down at his sobbing Adept. "Elthwyn, what is it? What brings you here?" His voice betrayed a deep foreboding.

Elthwyn, his eyes red and bleary, looked up pitiably at his teacher. Shaking violently with his sobs, he forced out the words. "Master . . . they've destroyed the Order!"

Crispan sank back into his chair.

XXVII

Elthwyn's Story

They brought in wine to calm down Elthwyn, and Crispan sent Lenid to his tent for herbs should these be necessary. Soon the weary and worn Adept stopped his sobbing and looked up again at his teacher. "How long ago was this?" asked Crispan, controlling his voice.

"As long as it takes to ride from the Gates to here, plus four days or so."

Mikal drew up another chair. "All right," said Crispan calmly, "now tell us what happened."

Elthwyn drained his cup, and while Mikal poured him another he began his tale. "After you left the Order, sir, all was quite normal. We had little news from you or of you, but life went on as before. In fact, I heard it said that at a meeting of the Masters it was generally held that all went rather well, that we had managed to aid the South without jeopardizing the Order's position of neutrality. That was after we had heard vague stories about some battles at Zifkar.

"I suppose I'm the one who discovered what was happening. I was in the forecourt, instructing some Novices in their daily tasks, when I heard wings fluttering above me. I looked up and saw Gorham's raven, his familiar, flying across to the south tower, making for his quarters. Of course, I did not give it any thought at the time, but it was only shortly after that I saw Gorham coming away from the storages heading for the Hall, and he had his raven with him. I didn't wonder about this until later, when I passed him near his chambers.

"It was then, as I passed him in the hall, that I realized I had seen his raven twice, and yet never saw Gorham enter the Order to fetch him. Still I was not sure, and so I stupidly delayed and doomed us all."

Here Elthwyn began to sob again, and Crispan patted his arm and urged him to continue.

"I was outside early the next morning. I had to ride down to the outer gate. That morning, as I rode out, I was sure that I saw the raven passing over me, also heading west, but that night when I returned, the raven was on Gorham's shoulder. All the next day I contrived to watch Gorham's window, but no raven returned from beyond the mountains, and yet Gorham was never without his familiar. This continued the next day, and the next. But two days later I was certain that I saw a raven come across the courtyard and enter Gorham's window, a raven who presumably had always been at the Order.

"That very night I watched again and saw the raven fly out and not come back. I kept my watch as best I could, fearful of accusing a Master unjustly, and early in the morning, three days after, I knew I saw it return again.

"Gorham was engaged that morning, I knew, giving a lecture to the middle students on spells and medicinal herbs. I checked in the classroom to be sure that he had his familiar with him, and he did. I made straight for his rooms. As an Adept, I had no trouble in getting a set of keys, and when the passageway was clear I stepped into his chambers.

"Gorham's outer room is bare and has a small window, not the one I had seen the raven enter and leave. The next room, his study, was cluttered with books, of course. I looked around once, but saw nothing there except a stand that the raven must occupy while Gorham works or studies.

"I then entered his private room, and there most assuredly was the raven's nesting place. But his cage was empty, and Gorham did have a raven with him in his class. I stuck my head out the window, and knew that this was the window I had seen the bird use. I went back to the study and checked behind the books for another cage. I don't know how long I was there, but I found nothing.

"I went back into the bedchamber and looked out the window again. As I leaned out, my hand slid along the left wall to give me support. The panel at the bottom swung away, and I heard the unmistakable 'Caw!' of a raven. I went to the front of the wall and pressed anxiously against the wood panels. I pushed in so many places that I do not know which one did it, but the panel slid open, and on an inner extension of the window sill there sat another raven, with a paper tied to his leg."

Elthwyn paused for a quick sip of wine to moisten his lips and tongue, and then went on. "I untied the thong and unrolled what was a message. All it said was 'I can see the Westgate. My last message until I see you. V.'" Crispan gasped at the initial.

"I began rerolling the paper and was so busy trying to tie it to that blasted bird that I didn't hear Gorham enter. Not until he said 'Was it interesting, Elthwyn?' did I freeze in place, turning only my head to face him. He moved towards me and settled his raven, the one on his shoulder, down on the table near his bed. 'So you've discovered me,' he said. 'It does not matter, of course, for he is on his way, but I should hate for the others to find out. Not just yet.' His hand went beneath his robe and came out with a dagger.

"I was scared, desperate. I felt my left hand still holding the raven's foot, and I tightened my grip and flung it at him. The bird screamed and squawked, and feathers flew as it flapped uncontrollably towards him. Gorham instinctively raised his hands and his dagger flashed across the raven's body. In that moment I dove at him and knocked him down. The other raven sprang at my back. I clutched at it and sent it across the room, out of control.

"Gorham was knocked out, or so it seemed, and I tore past the study and the outer room and went running into the hall. There was a student passing by. I screamed at him to get Omir, and then I went back into the chambers.

"The door to his bedroom was closed, and the bolt had been thrown. I pounded and then hurled myself futilely against it. Then I remembered the pass keys I still had. I fumbled madly for what seemed to be forever, but then the bolt gave at the next push. Gorham was hunched over the live raven, the one I had stunned, and was tying a message to its leg. I made for him as he lifted the bird towards the window. He was pushing the bird out with his right hand, urging it to fly, but I could see that it was still dazed. I lunged across the room and thrust for the bird as Gorham shoved it out the window. For a moment our hands met in mid-air, and one of us, I think it was me, grabbed the bird's talons. Our hands and arms grappled and forced each other down, and the bird, caught between, went careening against the outside wall and plummeted to the courtyard below.

"Even as it fell Gorham's free hand was around my throat. Just then Omir appeared at the door. 'Gorham!' he shouted, and Gorham's hand froze and then dropped away. Mine instinctively went to my throat as I gasped for breath. 'What is going on here?' Omir demanded.

"Gorham spoke first, taking advantage of my gasping. 'Omir, I came back from my morning lecture and found Elthwyn rummaging through my rooms. When I questioned him, he turned on me and attacked me. Look—he even killed my familiar as he tried to escape.' Gorham pointed to the dead bird he had stabbed himself.

"I cried out in my own defense, but Omir silenced me with a raised hand. He walked about the room, looked at the dead raven and then at me. 'Is this true, Elthwyn?' I admitted that I had entered the chamber, but before I could explain how it happened Gorham broke in, crying. 'There, he admits it. I demand that he be taken and held.' Even as he spoke Gorham tried to edge towards the window so as to hide the still-open panel.

"Omir walked slowly about the room again and then asked softly, 'What do you suppose he was after?' Again I tried to defend myself, but Omir said, 'Silence. It is quite serious when a student intrudes on a Master and attacks him. But you shall have your chance. Now, silence!' Two of the Adepts who had accompanied Omir came to me and held me on either side. 'Now then, Gorham, what was he after?'

"Gorham feigned ignorance. 'How should I know? All I know is that I came in, found him here, and then he attacked me. He knocked me down and then rushed out. Omir, I demand that he be held and punished.'

" 'Yes, yes, said Omir, but why was he here? And why was it *he* and not *you* who summoned me?'

"Gorham looked perplexed at this and tried to construct a plausible answer. He said I must have been seen coming out in a rush and tried to cover up, and anyway, he himself was at that moment stunned in his chamber. I then screamed out, 'Then why did I return?' and my two guards gripped me tighter.

"Gorham said to Omir, 'He came to finish whatever it was, of course, hoping he could leave before you came. Perhaps he hoped to murder me and leave no witness. Luckily I had partially recovered by then.' Gorham was groping for a story, and I was forced to stand silently by while he uttered these vile lies.

"But Omir did not look convinced at all. 'Still,' he said, 'I would have known that it was Elthwyn who had sent the summons. He could not hide that. Perhaps we had better hear him out now.'

"Gorham turned white, calling me a thief and a murderer, reminding them that I had already admitted the greater part of my guilt and that they had seen me fighting with him. 'I demand his arrest, Omir. We can expect no truth from this scum.'

" 'Then we shall trap him and discover the truth,' said Omir. 'Go on, Elthwyn. Tell us what you were doing.'

"I told them about the two ravens and the secret panel, and the message, and how Gorham and not I had killed the raven. Gorham was by the window. Omir motioned him aside, and there was the open panel. Then Omir went to the window and looked down. It had grown cloudy and dark outside and had begun to rain. Omir motioned to a third Adept and told him to retrieve the body of the other raven. By now the other Masters were present, and we all waited for Rollin to fetch the raven. Omir was in

243

the center of the room now, occasionally glancing at Gorham. I looked at him too and noticed that his expression had changed from self-righteous insult to cold and haughty anger.

"It seemed like hours before Rollin reappeared. Omir motioned the other Masters closer and had one of the Adepts bar the door to the study, for now others were collecting outside in the hallway. Omir took the raven from Rollin. Its broken body was shiny black from the rain. Omir untied the message on its leg. The words were smudged from the rain, but they were still legible. It read, 'Have been discovered. Come at once.' Omir passed the note around to the other Masters and turned to Gorham.

"He was standing quite still, but he let go a sharp laugh. 'It does not matter, Omir, it is too late. He'll be here soon, and nothing you can do now will stop him.'

"Omir looked terrible, not frightened but very much broken. He finally asked, 'How could you, Gorham, how could you?'

"Gorham's voice kept its cold, haughty edge. 'I knew about his work for a long time. But I kept silent. I thought he was right. We must seek new ways. And he made me promise that should he ever be caught and punished I would not jeopardize myself by defending him. That was when he gave me the twin ravens, should he ever be discovered, so we could communicate unnoticed. He even counted on your leniency should he be discovered. You are too late, all of you.' He swept his hand across the room.

"Omir just shook his head and ordered Gorham taken away, and asked Rollin to summon all the other Adepts and teachers to the Main Hall.

"That very day our expected shipment of provisions did not come." Elthwyn paused and downed a small piece of bread and another sip of wine. Crispan watched impatiently as his student regathered his energy to resume the tale. The Emperor, concerned over the young man's health, suggested that he rest for a few hours. Crispan was aghast at the idea, but happily Elthwyn insisted on going on.

"We met later in the Main Hall. Omir reviewed what had been discovered and then told everyone quite frankly what he expected. 'We can assume that the Renegade will be coming, undoubtedly backed by an armed force, seeking his revenge. The younger students and Novices are not to know; all is to go on as normally as possible. This will place an extra burden on you Adepts, as you are responsible for keeping the others in line. We cannot hope to defend ourselves against soldiers, we have no place to run to, and help probably will not reach us in time. I have taken the precaution of sending a messenger to the Emperor of the South. With some luck our plight will be known. Should Vladur arrive first we can only hope that he will act only against those who condemned him, and that the Order will survive. That is our main duty—the survival of the Order.'

"After that meeting broke up there was a separate meeting of just the Masters. I do not know what was said there, but I gather that someone said all this was Omir's fault, that none of this would have happened if the High Master had not consented to send you out of the Order and into the World, violating our neutrality. But they all agreed with Omir when he said that Vladur's crime, not your mission, was the cause of our peril, as Vladur's giving the ravens to Gorham so long ago showed he had been prepared should he be discovered. The Masters all agreed that now we could only wait.

"Our provisions did not come the next day, or the next. They had never been that late save in deepest winter. Two servants were sent down to the Outer Gate and should have returned by the next morning's light, but did not. Omir concluded that sending any more messengers to you was probably futile.

"For days we waited and nothing happened—no provisions, no reports, no sign of an approaching army. The strain had begun to tell on everyone as we tried to maintain our normal routine and yet remain on guard. I visited Gorham once during those days, and even his confidence in his imminent rescue had wavered.

"Very early in the morning, some seven or eight days

after I had discovered Gorham's treachery, they came. It was still dark outside when I heard the sound of clattering hooves in the forecourt. I ran across the hall to Juzher's room—he was already at his window. Soldiers were clambering into position on the walls, some had already swung the gates open and others were riding in. Instinctively we ran down to the main entry.

"Others were coming down from their chambers as well. Some were already there holding torches against the lingering dark. Omir stood in the middle, squarely before the open door, with Eliborg, Nujhir and Eldwig about him. We could hear the horses clattering up across the courtyard. Presently a party of riders approached. One of them rode a bit to the fore and first entered the light thrown by our torches. It was Vladur. As he swung out of his saddle he said, 'Good morning, Omir.' "

Crispan was now at the edge of his chair, his knuckles white as he gripped the seat. "You are sure it was Vladur?"

Elthwyn nodded. "I know him well enough, sir. I too studied with him before his exile." Crispan sank back and let Elthwyn go on.

"Soldiers continued filling the yard. Omir sent some of us to calm the youngsters, but I stayed behind. Vladur entered the hall. He was wearing a black cape, I remember, and a traveler's gown, and he wore an amulet, but not a regular one. It was different, a red orb with a white eye at the center. Anyway, he looked around and noticed Gorham to be missing. He asked after him but no one answered. Then he asked Omir directly, and the High Master told him that Gorham had been discovered and was under arrest. Soldiers were sent to release him.

"While we waited Vladur paced about, watching the soldiers take up positions in the halls. Then, as Gorham and his escort approached, Vladur ordered everyone back to their quarters, warning us against any resistance. 'These soldiers have orders to kill any troublemakers or rebels, and I should hate to punish the little ones later for your stupidity.' He positively smiled as he said it! As we withdrew he led the Masters to Omir's Council.

"I learned later from Eldwig what happened. He said that Vladur sat in, or at least stood by the chair of the High Master while he relegated Omir to another. Vladur said that Omir was responsible for what was happening this day to the Order, for having interfered in the World. Omir replied that he was indeed responsible, but only in that he had not pressed for the full and proper sentence, and that Vladur's aid to Zhyjman had made our intervention necessary. At this Vladur got up and ended the meeting—he walked out."

"What happened then?" Crispan was again on the edge of his seat.

"I really cannot say. We were all kept in our rooms for the rest of that day. Anyone even sticking his head out into the hall risked a jab from a spear. But that night some of the Tutors living along the north corridor managed to slip out and take some of the younger ones with them. They got away into the hills and were not chased down. Anyway, that next morning we were called to a meeting in the Great Hall. The Masters and all the Tutors and remaining Adepts were there. Vladur stood behind the lectern with his jackal Gorham at his side. As I entered I was pointed out and taken to one side under guard. When we were all there the doors were shut, and Vladur stepped forward to address us.

" 'I am accused,' he said, 'of great crimes against this Order. All I did was try to expand our limited powers—and for this I was sent into hideous exile, shunned by all my brethren. Now I have returned to rectify this.' His voice was strange, sir, still powerful but struggling to remain under control. Then he said that in his exile he had met the Emperor of the North, a ruler of vision who understood the need for new ways in the World, and that together they would create such ways, but that old ones needed to be removed first.

"At this Omir jumped up, yelling, 'You cannot mean this, Vladur. Yesterday you said I was responsible. If so, then punish me, but not the Order! Surely not the Order.'

"Vladur turned to him as the guards shoved the High Master back into his seat. 'Fool! Did you think I ever intended *not* to control this Order? From the moment I began my work I saw the need to have everyone working towards this new knowledge. I hoped you might listen, but even then I doubted it. I only hoped I would escape detection and be ready before I had to make my move. But *you,* you and your lackeys stepped in. In my exile I found the time and the patron I needed, and now I am ready. You shan't pay with your own skin, nor shall your young flunky who is out in the World. I shall finish with you here, and with your pup outside, and then I shall create another Order to go in directions that I want. I can insure Zhyjman's victory and he will give me *my* Order.' His voice kept rising as he spoke until it was almost a shriek. And then it suddenly dropped, and he ordered the main building evacuated that day."

Elthwyn began to struggle with his voice again, fighting down sobs and holding back tears. "We were all forced out. I was herded along with the Masters. It was awful to see Omir. He was crushed, broken. The others tried to console him, but it was no use. He just sat shaking his head and sighing while Vladur's soldiers cleared us all out and then set fires. Gorham helped by preparing mixtures which caved in the walls when warmed by the flames —as if a catapult were stoning the place. We just stood there, helpless, watching the Order burn—it even burned against a sudden rain. It rained all that night, and Omir became feverish. No one could help him. By the morning all was a smoking ruin, and when Omir saw it in the first light he gave out a low moan. Oh, sir, it was hideous." Crispan got up and put an arm around Elthwyn. "Omir died that morning, and we buried him—the remaining Masters and I—in the rain. We used the still-warm stones from the Order to cover the body. It was terrible—and there was nothing we could do."

Upon hearing the news that he had feared all along, Crispan felt his knees grow weak, and he returned to his seat and let his body fall into it.

"We were all herded together in the remains of the forecourt. Vladur rode out and told us he would have need of us later and did not trust us to remain in the mountains. We were to be marched out and taken to be held in the Empire of the North until the war was over.

"The march was brutal. It was cold and we were not fed properly. It was especially hard on the older Tutors and on the Masters. Those young ones who had not been spirited away did not comprehend what had happened, and some began to whimper and cry. We tried to carry those who were smallest and most afraid as long as possible. Anyone falling behind was prodded by a ready spear. We all had to walk and keep pace with their horses. Poor Nujhir could not take it, sir, and he died on the second day. They just pulled his body aside and left it there. We were not even allowed to bury him. We couldn't even—" Sobs overwhelmed him at last.

Crispan too was on the verge of tears, as were others in the silent tent, but the Magician blinked to hold them back as he tried to calm Elthwyn. "Easy, easy. I understand. Try to tell us how you escaped."

"We were past the Eastgate already. It was morning but still dark. Our guards were away, fetching what passed for our breakfasts. I just got up and went to one of the horses. They were all tied together. I chose one that looked swift and loosed his reins. When I thought all was clear I jumped on him and rode south as fast as I could. I never really stopped until I got here."

Mikal now broke in. "But weren't you chased?"

"I suppose so, but I must have really surprised them. And many of the other horses were freed when I took mine. I just outran them. There was no one following me when I passed the Southgate."

"The Southgate?" Prince Belka moved eagerly to the map. "But didn't you pass soldiers, and didn't they try to stop you? We had heard that Zhyjman had troops in that area."

"I saw campfires on the slopes of the Falchions, but I avoided those."

Thurka spoke. "We can talk again later. Churnir, take him to Lord Crispan's tent and have him put to bed."

As Churnir helped Elthwyn out, the others reassembled around their maps. The Emperor looked across at Crispan with concern. Crispan caught the look and waved his hand to show that he was all right. Belka spoke first. "His story explains one thing at least. Now we know why that force sat at the Southgate without moving on Zifkar again."

"Aye," said his nephew. "It was a cover for this move of Vladur's. And now we know for certain that Vladur is with Zhyjman. But now what? Elthwyn said Vladur was taking his prisoners north. What can that mean?"

"No." Crispan's voice was tightly under control. "Elthwyn only said that they were being conveyed north, not that Vladur was going north as well. No, I know Vladur. He would move only when ready, or when he had to. Elthwyn's escape was a lucky warning. They are ready now to make their final move against us or Vladur would not have come out into the open. Do not ask where they will strike, for this I do not know. They have all the options and choices. But we must now expect Zhyjman to move against us, and soon. I leave the strategy to you," and so saying he sprang from his seat and rushed out of the tent.

XXVIII

A Delayed Departure

Crispan lay very still in his tent. He had not moved all night and could not remember sleeping at all. He had been somewhere else, remembering the ghastly look on Elthwyn's face as he recounted Vladur's sacking of the Order. He saw Omir, Eldwig and the others scurrying down smoke-blackened hallways with bright sword points not far behind them.

No matter what he tried to think of, his thoughts always came back to the same point. By interfering in the World they had destroyed the Order. They—in his grief he blamed Bellapon, Omir and himself. Bellapon he blamed for having first brought him to the Order, and Omir for agreeing to have the Order aid the South. But most of all he blamed himself.

"What is left of the World we sought to preserve?" he asked aloud. "Nothing. I have become an Anarch!" he said in irony and bitterness.

Suddenly he sat bolt upright, feeling that fear which can only come in the lonely darkness of night. His heart pounded almost audibly as he moved in a trance about the tent. Elthwyn slept undisturbed, still overwhelmed by terror and exhaustion. There was so little to gather, just some clothes, some food, oh! and his sword. Zoltan would want him to take that along. There are many ways that Vladur can be stopped. Vladur, Vladur, Vladur! His thin angular face hung before Crispan like an evil beacon.

The day was further advanced than he had realized. How long had he lain there? No matter. Crispan moved from the tent to his horse and saddled it, hardly aware of what he was doing. He was about to climb into his saddle when Mikal came running breathlessly towards him.

"Crispan! Stop! Where are you going?" Mikal's words came between heavy gasping pants for breath. He had feared that the Magician might be doing just this.

"Where do you think?" Crispan's voice was flat and distant. "I am going to find Vladur. I know now that he's there. I owe him much."

"But you cannot find him, not you alone!"

"But I can, Mikal. His pride will allow me that, at least a final confrontation. It will give me a chance to stop him. Only I can do that. And," Crispan said as an afterthought, "it is what I was brought here for."

"Then let some of us come with you."

"No!" The Magician's eyes glared. "Alone, I must go alone. Your support will hardly matter when I am face to face with the Renegade. And should I lose, you will all be needed to defend yourselves against them. Belka would say I have already lost the first encounter—for I go to meet my enemy on his terms. But," he said, finally mounting up, "no matter. This was always destined and I cannot avoid it."

Crispan tugged the reins free and began to ride off at a steady, determined pace. Mikal's arms dropped hopelessly to his sides as he watched Crispan go. Then he remembered Zoltan's scouts and ran to find some to follow the Magician.

The Prince had barely begun running towards Zoltan's tent when he heard the frenzied clatter of a galloping steed and turned to see a scout racing through the camp. Mikal ran for his father's tent and reached it right after the messenger. Thurka was already on his feet, and Belka was there. As the Prince came in, Thurka turned to the breathless rider. "Repeat your message."

The scout wiped his brow and let out a huge gasp of air. "It has happened. All our scouts along the north report the same thing. Zhyjman is moving south, and Vladur and Kirion are with him." By now the Duke of Larc and a very sleepy Zoltan had joined them, with other lords and generals close behind.

Thurka's fingers drummed nervously on the table. "Are you quite sure of this?"

"Yes, my lord. All the signs point to it. The army on the slopes of the Falchions has pulled closer to the Southgate, and Syman has definitely broken off his siege at Anrehenkar, leaving only enough troops there to mask it and keep Prince Zascha there. A party of our scouts from Zifkar shadowed the enemy army retiring to the Southgate and was able to reach the High Pass across the Falchions. They crossed it and spied a huge army running the same way as the mountains some two days to the west of the pass, moving south. Our spies with Syman say he too is moving south, south by east, and scouts at the Low Pass have seen them all together, still moving south. They are all there, m'lord—Zhyjman, Syman, Kirion and Vladur."

Thurka paced before the table. "Then it is time." He looked around. "Where is Crispan?" Mikal made a nervous movement and was about to answer when the Magician stepped through the flap. "Here, my lord." Mikal looked around in great surprise. As Crispan moved towards the map he passed the Prince and whispered, "I stopped when I saw the messenger."

Belka drew a dagger and dragged it over the map. "Where were they last seen?" The messenger pointed to the west of the Falchions. Belka nodded. "It is simple then. We must move at once to meet them, and with luck before they reach any of our lands. We have anywhere from four to eight days, I would say. We are outnumbered, I am sure, but an advance by us will be least expected."

Lord Larim, commander of the forces of Ernyr, cleared his voice. "Is this wise, Lord Belka? As you say, we are outmanned. Is there no other way? Perhaps we could mass on the western slope of the Falchions and strike their flank. We certainly cannot overthrow them head on."

Before Belka could answer, Larc made a motion betraying his eagerness to speak. Zoltan glowered at him, but their clash was interrupted by the one man who could settle the issue. Thurka Re shrugged heavily. "I think not. Belka is probably correct, General Larim. We must strike for them before they are firmly set before us, and before they can spread destruction and discontent among our own lands."

The Emperor was about to go on but Crispan stepped forward, shaking his head. "Your armies do not matter now, my lords. Zhyjman has moved only when certain of success, and now he is relying on Vladur for that. I know Vladur's Art and his crime, and I think I know what he has promised or given your foes. March to meet them, by all means, but expect nothing unless I can overcome Vladur. Zhyjman will risk this battle only with grave and foul Magic." He spoke these words calmly and evenly, simply stating the truth for his beset friends. He knew he had to be honest with them before they set out.

After so many months of inactivity the army made ready cumbrously, moving like a rusty piece of armor. With a creaking slowness it pulled itself up out of its camp at Gurdikar and began the march north. Crispan's sobering words had cast a pall over the Princes as they rode. They showed little enthusiasm for the impending clash, a reluctance born out of realistic pessimism rather than cowardice. Even Belka and the usually ebullient Zoltan were grimly silent as the Army of the South and its allies moved north. But most silent of all was Crispan, riding apart among the Princes, lords and commanders. His face betrayed no emotion beyond grim determination. He spoke only when necessary.

Disturbed by the Wizard's black mood, the Emperor sought out the student Elthwyn, who rode with the army as Crispan's assistant. "No," the Adept said, "I've never seen him like this. But he is all right, I think. Now he is sure of his purpose and is determined to destroy Vladur. In this he is our only hope. We are no more than escorts delivering Crispan to battle."

The word struck Thurka's ear. "What sort of battle will that be?"

"I do not know. I doubt that even he knows yet. He was one of the best the Order ever produced, and yet even his Arts may not be enough."

The enthusiasm and eagerness with which the Southern troops had begun the war had long since turned into sullen determination, reflecting the difficult battles they had fought and the desperate one they still faced. The army of the Empire of the South and its allies headed north, making for the gap between the Falchions and the Inland Sea. They had been marching for days, and still the scouts who swept before them in a wide arc could find no trace of the enemy. Only the rich panoply of the army's varied armor and their many proud banners added life to the otherwise grim march.

Belka's arm fell hopelessly to his side. "I do not know what to make of it. Here, look," he said, pointing to the map spread before the campfire. "We are three days out of Perrigar and still no sign. Nothing. According to the report we had at Gurdikar, we should have made contact at least a day or so ago."

"Do you think they are trying to draw us north?" asked Mikal, his green eyes glowing against the flames.

"No. They have pulled back into the Gates. We control the Low Pass and the entry here into Perrigar and have as strong a force as we can spare at Ernyr." Belka turned to Zoltan.

Zoltan shrugged. "My scouts were sure. Syman, Kirion, Zhyjman and Vladur. All together. Perhaps they have had trouble disengaging before Anrehenkar. There is no news from there either."

Through all the discussion Crispan sat silently as usual, staring into the fire. Absorbed in the crackling wood succumbing to orange fingers of flame, he did not even notice as the members of the futile council dispersed into the night. Talk of armies and scouts held no meaning for him any longer. The crushing awareness of what had befallen and what might still await him isolated him from those who could see conflict only in terms of men and arms. All that had passed since he had come down out of the Order was meaningless now. Two members of the Order would decide the fate of the Three Realms after generations of Chaos.

Their pace slowed as they resumed their advance, lest

Zhyjman draw them too far north and slip behind them into their lands. Crispan chided his companions over this. "Do not worry, they are still before us. Vladur is their power now, and we shall find them when he is ready to confront us. He is still before us, waiting."

For the first time in days Crispan spoke to Zoltan. "What news from the scouts?"

"None," he said grimly.

Crispan shrugged off his friend's edginess. "No matter. We are getting close. I can feel it. Vladur is ready and is searching for me across the plain."

Zoltan looked a little skeptical, for there had been no reports of enemy scouts, but he had learned by now not to question the Magician.

"Have Belka change more to the north. It is a matter of days." With that, Crispan relapsed into silence.

Crispan barely noticed the passing days or changing landscape. He could feel Vladur seeking him out, tugging at him, confidently drawing him northward for their ultimate confrontation. Day and night became all the same to him and passed unnoticed. Crispan's senses narrowed to a point he could not see, but where he knew he must go. As if traveling down some long tunnel, he only saw the far-distant end and was oblivious to all on either side. Now he felt the need to move faster across the great plain, drawn by the Renegade's compelling power and his own eagerness to finally face his teacher turned tormentor. How many more days passed he could not say.

A leaden autumnal sky hovered above them as Zoltan, riding with Mikal, fidgeted in his saddle. "It's like traveling blind," he complained. "My scouts ride out before us and find nothing, report nothing. And yet we continue north. Damn! It's frustrating."

"But Crispan seems certain of our course."

"Aye," nodded Zoltan. "Only my faith in him makes a difference. With anyone else I would have grave doubts —and would voice them!"

Mikal's eyes twinkled momentarily. "I'm sure you would, my friend. I'm sure you would."

Zoltan paced the edges of the campfire wildly, like a caged animal on the verge of a desperate act.

"How much longer, Crispan?" The Emperor's voice betrayed his own edginess as well.

"Very few days more. I do not know exactly how many. But Vladur is out there, beckoning."

Conversation had grown impossible in the tense atmosphere. Then the silence was broken by commotion from beyond the light of their fires.

"What is it?" demanded Belka of one of the bodyguards.

"A scout, m'lord." Zoltan's eyes burned as fiercely as the flames at this news.

The man escorted into the warlords' presence was a pitiful sight. He was obviously bone tired, and bore signs of having been in a fierce melee. But the most striking thing about him was his look of overwhelming, uncomprehending fear. Thurka motioned for wine to be brought to the scout at once. He gulped at it spasmodically, breathing heavily.

As he spoke, his voice was a mixture of terror, awe and grief. "It was terrible, sire," he said, seemingly beginning in the middle of his tale. "We were in two groups, six men each, riding to the northeast. Ulnar's group was slightly ahead of ours. He left a message for us on a spear stuck in the ground, knowing we followed his track. He told us to veer eastward, to a village we might find there.

"We followed them to the village, but it had been abandoned, obviously in great haste. Furnishings had been overturned, cloaks even left on pegs—as if the people could not get out fast enough. We continued to follow Ulnar's tracks—until we got to the graveyard. All the graves—every one of them—were disturbed, thrown open. There were a lot of skeletons about, mostly small ones, none of grown men, it seemed. Maybe all women and children. And the stench, m'lord. It was terrible.

257

Even our horses shied away from it." The scout's eyes were wide and terrible now.

"We spurred at once to find Ulnar, and we did, or what was left of them. They were all dead. But they hadn't merely been killed, they were slaughtered, their bodies mutilated. I've never seen wounds like those in all my years of service—horrid, gaping, ferocious wounds." His voice rose now as he spoke. "And their eyes, those that we could make out, had a horrible look in them. I've never seen terror like that on any man's face. And not an enemy body in sight nor a stray weapon, and not a mark of blood on the weapons of any of our men. I knew Ulnar, and he would never have fallen without taking some of the enemy with him. But there weren't any there. And there was that awful stench again.

"We thought we heard hooves and clattering armor and we followed the sound. I swear to you, sire, we saw nothing, and I felt we had best report back at once lest we be ambushed as was Ulnar." He then turned towards the Wizard. "What happened to them out there?"

All eyes now turned to Crispan, who sat by strangely serene. "There is nothing to worry about. Are the rest of your party in camp?" The man nodded. "Join them."

The scout rose to go, and as he passed beyond the camplight Crispan turned to Churnir. "Find the rest of his party and have them all sequestered at once. They must not be allowed to terrify others in the camp, for that is what Vladur intends."

"That is all?" asked Thurka, nearly angry.

"Yes," said Crispan, his voice eerily calm. "It is a warning from Vladur, one that I understand. We will meet them soon."

The very next morning scouts rode in with the message he now expected. "A day distant," they reported, pointing northward. "They are encamped to the west of the Bow and Arrow."

Mikal's eyes narrowed. "I know the area. We should move swiftly to seize the southernmost ridge, the one called the Bow."

"There is no need for haste, my lord," the scout offered. "We could not get very close, but from what we saw they were encamped, not ready for marching. They seem to be simply waiting for us."

"And how many are there?" asked an anxious Belka.

"Fewer than we expected, much fewer. They still muster more than we do, but they are not so numerous as we had supposed."

Instead of bringing relief, this news seemed to unsettle the Southern commanders. Their minds raced over the possible explanations. Was it a ruse, a feint while they attacked elsewhere? Where? Anrehenkar? The Gates? Zifkar? Ernyr? Vadul? Rhaan-va-Mor?

Crispan, hovering again on the periphery like a specter, spoke in an almost laughing voice. "No, we have always overestimated Zhyjman's strength. It lies in Vladur. We must take the southern ridge by tomorrow nightfall." Thus advising them, he walked away, leaving the warlords with little to do but give orders to get the army to the designated place.

A new tension and determination settled over the advancing Southerners. The deadly archers of Vadul in their leathern outfits sang songs of their beloved forests. The contingent from Rhaan-va-Mor countered with lusty ballads of the sea; and above all else came the confident war songs offered by the men of the Imperial Army of Thurka Re. In his self-imposed oblivion Crispan rode along, concentrating on the day to come.

XXIX

The Eve of Battle

Behind the southern ridge that arced like a giant bow facing north the Army of the South huddled on the uncommonly cold summer night. Beyond the ridge the plain rolled on again, only to run into the companion height vaguely resembling a loosened arrow flying obliquely to the northwest. On the western slope of the Arrow and far beyond onto the plain twinkled the myriad lights and fires of Zhyjman's army. They filled the plain as if the stars had fallen from their places in the heavens.

Mikal, Zoltan and all the other lords and generals rode to the crest of the Bow and stared long and hard at their apparently quiescent enemy. "Never have I seen so large a force," mused Mikal as he leaned forward in his saddle, mailed gloves braced against the pommel. "Yet surely this is not much larger than what you said Syman had at Anrehenkar."

Zoltan removed his helmet and scratched his head. "Maybe half again as many fires as we counted there. I would have expected more, but we are still outnumbered. Their strength is probably twice that of ours."

"Where are their scouts and guards? You can hardly see any across their front. If I were Kirion I would have made some demonstration to contest this ridge. Better for them if we were forced out completely into the open plain." Belka's military sense nagged at him. His horse's pawing at the ground reminded him of the unseasonable chill. "Come, let us discuss this below, where the wind cannot get at us so freely."

The company clambered down to the base of the ridge and sat on their mounts and war horses in a suddenly embarrassing silence. Belka deferred now to his brother, and the Emperor turned to Crispan. "What do we do?"

"Have the tents raised and post what guards are needed. Have the men rest tonight. There will be no battle, no surprise attack. They should be fresh for tomorrow."

The terseness of his advice caught them all short, but the Emperor knew better than to ask if that was all. There was much more, he sensed, that he might never understand, regardless of the morrow's outcome. Instead he turned to the ever-ready Baron Churnir. "Give the necessary orders. Let us sup, and then we shall discuss our plans." But what plans, Thurka asked himself silently. Only Crispan had an inkling of what they might face, and he would not or could not tell them.

Mikal shared his tent that night with his old companion, as they had on the eve of countless earlier battles. They ate in silence, each man moodily picking at his food. Finally Zoltan pushed his plate away and went to sit on his cot. He drew his huge claymore from its sheath and held it at arm's length, turning it in the candlelight. Then, as so often before, he took out a stone and cloth to hone and clean his blade. The Prince watched the ritual that he had seen many times, and tried to cope with an uneasiness he had never felt before. As was the custom among warriors, they exchanged tokens should one or both not survive the next day. Mikal toyed with Zoltan's gift to him, a beautiful dagger, the blade plated in silver, the handle done in filigreed gold. The Prince knew it was no chance token, as it was engraved with his name. Zoltan had had it made for this battle. The burly warrior also expected the worst.

In most of the other tents it was much the same. Men looked to their weapons and tried to keep busy, tried not to think about the next day. Arrow shafts were inspected, bows restrung, blades sharpened, shields toughened. Every battle brings anew that terrible uncertainty, the fear that despite one's skill and bravery and caution one may be unlucky. This night the soldiers from the South felt it worse than before. Rumors ran back and forth across their camp. Zhyjman had raised an innumerable host; he had magical powers greater than any; only a fraction of his strength was before them. Each rumor was both true and false in its own peculiar way, as rumors so often are. The wiser soldiers kept themselves busier than most, or sought release and refuge in sleep.

The Emperor, too, this night felt the uneasiness which hovered over his army. Unable to sleep, his weapons cared for, he left his tent.

"Master?"

"Yes, Elthwyn." Crispan rose from his cot at the sound of the Adept's voice. "Come in."

Wrapped in his cloak, the student entered and stood before the entry flap, shivering a bit from the chill air. "I came to see if you were all right."

Crispan moved the candle a bit closer. "Yes, I'm fine." His voice was low and even.

"Can I be of any help to you now—or tomorrow?"

"No, I think not. You are not ready for Vladur." His voice trailed away, leaving the unmistakable hint that perhaps he was not ready either. "Tomorrow you will take my place with the Emperor. The battle will be between Vladur and me, I presume. You must advise the Emperor as best you can. If need be, you will have to replace me." Elthwyn tried to protest, but Crispan stilled him with a raised hand. "We both know what Vladur has been doing, what he has been studying. We don't know how much his powers have grown. But we are here at the time and place of his choosing. Eliborg would say it was a poor omen." Pain crossed his face as he mentioned one of his fellow Masters. But he quickly recovered and rose. He walked across to Elthwyn and put his hands on his student's shoulders. "Take my copy of *The Magicker's Elementaries* and keep it for me. When you return to your tent, read the marked passage at the beginning."

Elthwyn, clutching the book, left the tent so quickly that he ran right into the Emperor. "Sire!" he exclaimed, drawing back.

"How is he?"

"Composed, I think."

"Tell me, Elthwyn. You know him well. Does he know what will face us—him, tomorrow?"

The Adept shook his head. "I think he does, but if so he has not told me. I believe he has some idea, but how can he be sure?"

Thurka shrugged under his black cloak. "True enough. Get some sleep. Tomorrow will be a long day."

Elthwyn bowed and bid the Emperor good night. Upon returning to his tent he opened the thin, well-worn volume, before he even had doffed his cloak and cowl. Bellapon's name was inscribed on the inside leaf, and then an inscription from him to Crispan. He easily found the passage Crispan had mentioned: "The Magicker must first believe firmly in his mind that what he sets about will work. Only then can he succeed in translating his powers from that which can be to that which is." He read it twice before he went to sleep.

In Crispan's tent the Emperor sat across from the Magician, who was seated on his cot. Thurka poured himself a half cup of wine and drained it in one swallow. Hesitating, he ran his hand over his gray-flecked black beard. Finally, he began. "I have been worried about you—and about tomorrow."

Almost as if he had not heard the Emperor, Crispan's words poured forth. The pain he had carried since Elthwyn's arrival was all too apparent in his eyes and in his words. "I have only just realized how mistaken I have been in all I have done. When I came down out of the Order I was too willing to accept the conditions I found in the World, to listen to you warriors. I feared and hesitated accepting my proper role and I waited for Vladur to reveal himself, hoping he might not. I should have realized that he must be out there, must be with your enemies. Where else could he be? What else could explain Zhyjman's rapid moves, his sudden willingness to accept risks? Instead, I waited. Now, when he is fully prepared, I must face him. I should have gone after him as soon as I left the Order. All could have been saved— the lives at Zifkar and the Gates, and the Order. Instead I tried to preserve my position by not openly seeking him, when all along my position had been compromised by my leaving the Order, even by Vladur's presence in the World himself."

"But surely," said the Emperor, attempting to console the Wizard, "you could not have sought him out. How could you have found him? And what if you had—would he not have killed you then, or had Zhyjman do it?"

Crispan, staring at the ground, shook his head. "You do not understand. This confrontation was fated from the day Vladur was caught in his crimes. He realized it all along. That is why he remained hidden, nurturing his heinous art until he was ready. No, had I sought him earlier I would have found him—he would have let me sooner or later, and I could have rushed his decision. His very pride, which first drove him to necromancy, would have allowed it. He wants this confrontation and has prepared himself for it. He must prove his complete superiority. He realized this long ago. I have been a fool not to see it and to have allowed him so much time. Vladur was our creation, our responsibility. The Order has paid for trying to escape its responsibility as it has tried to isolate itself from the chaos here in the World. We should have realized that this too was foredoomed. Our privileged position blinded us and destroyed us. I am still left with the task, when it is too late for the Order and perhaps for all of you as well."

To this no response was possible, and for a while silence descended. Finally, Thurka Re asked, "Then what shall we do tomorrow?"

"We must be prepared for battle. It will not come to that at first, I believe. I hope it does not come to it at the end. Have the troops form up close behind the ridge.

I do not think they should see what happens, in any event. Other than this we must wait and see."

There seemed to be a new glimmer of hope in Crispan's words and the Emperor snatched at it. "Then you know what he will do?"

"Perhaps. But how can I judge what form his necromancy will take? We must wait and see."

Again, silence. Thurka searched for something more to say, some word of consolation or confidence. Unable to find it, he placed his cup on the table beside him and rose. Crispan followed the Emperor to the tent flap. Stepping into the darkness, Thurka turned and extended his hand. "Sleep. I believe in you, and wish you well for your own sake." His grip was warm and firm. Thurka turned and went into the night.

Crispan returned to his tent and sat on the edge of his cot. His eyes flitted from object to object, table, chair, candle, pack, sword. He felt nothing, he was totally adrift. He was only aware that his mind was racing. He could feel it as it sought something to peacefully concentrate on, someplace to find some rest. As it flew from object to object, from subject to subject, unable to settle, he felt his pulse begin to throb as his mind moved even faster now. All was blurring before him, his thoughts revolved madly, his breath came in short panting gasps. He felt it now on his temples, the heavy pounding. His hands clasped his head and he jumped to his feet. Everything went black, then dull gray. The throbbing died away down his throat, and his vision slowly cleared. His mouth wide open, he took in deep breaths until his body slowly calmed down.

Crispan sat down again, wiping the sweat from his brow. It had matted and soaked his light-brown hair. Was that Vladur, testing him, toying with him? No, he rejected the thought. Having brought him here, the Renegade would be satisfied with nothing less than an open confrontation. Of this Crispan was certain. No, it was his own—what? Fear? Anxiety? Restlessness? Guilt? A last search for a answer? Snuffing out the candle, he let the question go. With great determination and deliberation he lay down on the cot, drawing up the blanket. He forced out audible, regular breaths and let his mind go blank.

XXX

A Battle Unseen

As he rode to the foot of the ridge Crispan tried to remember if he had slept or if he had simply spent the night in some sort of quiet but wakeful rest. He did not feel particularly rested, but neither was he tired.

The camp around him was lively. Soldiers moved about their fires, a luxury on the morning of a battle, warming themselves and preparing hasty meals. Some had already begun assembling on the western edge of the camp. Small clusters of spears could be seen moving among the tents. Soldiers began saddling their mounts and walking them to their assigned places. Flags hung limp on their staffs above all this bustle, for no breeze came to lift them.

The commanders were all gathered now below the crescent ridge. The Emperor Thurka was impressive in his steely armor, bearing his personal symbol, the red boar, across his cuirass. His brother, Prince Belka, towered above the others, his armor decorated in silver and blue. At his side hung his favored weapon, an oversized mace with deadly sharp protrusions. Mikal, refusing his ceremonial armor, wore the suit of brigandine that had carried him across the entire face of the Middle Realm. Zoltan too wore his old familiar armor, his blade especially shiny this morning. Each of the others, the Duke of Larc, the allied Princes and generals, sat on their steady war horses, each resplendent in his decorated panoply. Elthwyn sat in this group as well, fidgeting under the unfamiliar hauberk that Crispan had insisted he wear. Crispan too wore a byrnie under his Master's garb, and carried his helmet on his saddle pommel, but shunned a corselet or other exterior protection. Like the others, he wore his cloak against the unseasonable chill.

"It is odd, very odd," reported Zoltan, "but they are not massed against us. They have increased their scouts and are on alert, but have not drawn up on the plain and make no move to do so. It is as though they do not intend to do battle today. In fact, not all are even at arms yet."

At this, Thurka turned to his Magician. Without showing any emotion, Crispan said, "Keep the army at arms and ready, but behind the ridge. Let us go up on the Bow." He nudged his horse and led the way up the ridge.

The sky was heavy and gray, almost leaden, with no hint of sun as they ranged themselves along the crest. They could barely make out Zhyjman's scouts in his camp far off to their left. All else across the plain and companion ridge was still obscured in the morning mist. Now a light but persistent wind sprang up, blowing across from the northeast. Undisturbed, the thick clouds remained stolidly in place.

It was Elthwyn who first perceived the riders far off on the westernmost tip of the Arrow, the part resembling one barb of a feather. He pointed them out, gasping, "Look!" All leaned forward in their saddles.

"It's Syman!" called Mikal, picking out the solid figure in gray-black armor.

"And Kirion and Zhyjman!" responded Larc, being the only man beside Zoltan in that party to have ever met the Emperor of the North.

"Where?" several of the others cried, unable to tell who was who on the opposite ridge.

"The very lean one in the bright armor, in the middle," Larc said, "that is Zhyjman." All eyes studied the silvery figure, conspicuous in a bright-red cape. "The others must be his lackeys, from Nor and Kyryl."

"But where is Vladur?" Crispan's voice was filled with anguish.

They looked again to the figures on the Arrow. Zhyjman, Kirion, Syman, Nor and Kyryl, each identifiable now as the nearer mist broke up. But no sight of Vladur. Crispan sat in utter disbelief. He turned to Elthwyn on his right. "I saw him, I know it was Vladur!" the Adept cried.

Still they sat, as neither side moved. On the Bow, horses and riders fidgeted openly, but no one spoke. They seemed to sit there forever, waiting.

"Listen!" Crispan heard it first. It was far away but discernible, coming down across the plain. A chorus of deep drums rumbled, growing louder. From somewhere within the mist still hovering north of the Arrow's tip it came. It grew louder now, more insistent. The rumbling became distinct. "Boom-boom-ba-doom! Boom-boom-ba-doom!" Louder still, as each thump came distinct and heavy. They stared into the mist. As though stepping from a rising curtain, a long double line of drummers appeared now, beating their insistent message. "Boom-boom-ba-doom!"

Was it the mist and the distance? The advancing line seemed dull, almost lifeless. Never had any of the Southerners seen so drab a host. The drummers came on again. Behind them, out from the mist, an endless army was appearing. Gathered in meaningless array, cavalry and foot soldiers carelessly mingled, they all moved leadenly, all eerily dull. Elthwyn swallowed hard. The drumming continued.

More troops moved forth out of the mist. Then they suddenly stopped. The drumming ended abruptly. A terrible reeking stench, borne down from out of the host on the wind, assaulted the Southerners. It was an odor of rot and decay, and it made them feel sick. A rider came over the crest of the Arrow and rode to the eastern tip, the other barb of the feather. Crispan stared at him and hissed the name. "Vladur!" The sound went through the others, jolting their attention.

"My scouts found no camp further north!" protested Zoltan.

"Nor could they have," assured Crispan. "Those soldiers were and are dead. Vladur has raised a host of the World's dead warriors."

They all stared again at the gray mass of men. Surely they were not dead. They were there, they were visible. But their movements were so heavy, their forms so drained of vitality.

"Boom-boom-ba-doom!" The dead host was set in motion again. Through each of the warrior Princes' minds ran the same question: How do you kill that which is already dead?

Crispan took his helmet from his pommel and handed it to Elthwyn. "Stay with the Emperor and help him, no matter what." He began to lead his horse down over the crest.

"Crispan!" Thurka protested. "You cannot stop them."

The Magician looked hard at the Emperor. "Can you?"

Crispan flicked at the bay's flanks and guided him down the forward slope. The terrible drumming continued, Vladur's thralls came on. The Magician glanced across at the other ridge. There was another figure there now. The jackal Gorham, he guessed.

He was on the plain now. Except for the ridges before him and behind him it stretched endlessly away on all sides. In front of him the Necromancer's host advanced like a solid gray wall.

"Boom-boom-ba-doom! Boom-boom-ba-doom!" Closer now, probably no more than a short ride at a fast pace. Crispan was well out on the plain now, aware of his lonely position. His own pulse competed with the echo of the drums against his chest. They were coming closer still, and Crispan had no idea how to combat them. The drumming grew louder.

Then they stopped. The only sound across the plain was the low whistle of the increased wind. If it were not for the terrible rank odor it carried to him, Crispan would have welcomed the refreshing coolness as it caressed his face.

He looked up to the ridge, up at Vladur. He could just barely make out his features. The angles seemed sharper than before, Crispan thought, the cheeks more sunken. His musings were halted by the Renegade's sudden movement.

Vladur raised his right arm and snapped his fingers twice. Immediately one of the dead host trotted forward, and Vladur pointed to Crispan. The ghostly warrior lowered his lance. Crispan's horse sensed the horrid nature of the approaching foe and tried to back away, but Crispan tightened his knees around the steed and held it firm. The Wizard understood at once that this was both a display of the Renegade's power and a test of his own courage. Crispan could see the charging warrior clearly now as he bore down on him. He was almost colorless, his features of a grayish hue, meaningless on his lifeless face. The warrior's expression remained absolutely blank as he came on.

Crispan closed his eyes and desperately summoned whatever it was that had first made Bellapon take him to the Order. His whole face tightened as he concentrated all his powers against the lancer pounding towards him. He began to breathe heavily now as he forced himself to bear down even as he could hear the dead horse's hooves nearing him. Then Crispan's eyes flashed open, and as they did the lancer was enveloped in a burst of blue flame. When the flame and its smoke disappeared, an ominous black scorch was all that was left on the ground.

He was sweating freely as he tried to understand what he had summoned. A fireball? A bolt of lightning? Crispan thought not. No, it was something more powerful. He had summoned up all his energies and powers and in one instant made them physically real. He felt terribly drained as he looked across the plain at Vladur's host. His mouth dropped for an instant as he saw yet another gray rider come charging out from the army of the dead. He knew what to do now, but it was more difficult this time. As he forced himself to concentrate, to push even deeper within himself, he could feel his horse slowly shying backwards. He pressed and pressed until his eyes were almost knotted in pain. Already he could hear the impending hoofbeats. Surely he had reached the point of concentration that had succeeded last time. His teeth were clenched, grinding against one another. His body began to shake tensely. Louder the hoofbeats, louder.

Then his eyes sprang open and a sudden blue flash obliterated his foe.

Crispan's mind ached fiercely as he drew his horse back. A few more attacks, one more big rush, and he would be finished. Each effort would drain him of his powers more than the one before. He could imagine Vladur's smiling face as he sat up on the ridge. Vladur must sense his coming triumph. He could prolong and savor his vengeance and victory, and overthrow his enemy when he chose.

When *he* chose! It came to Crispan all at once. Vladur was safe only if *he* held the initiative. He had been discovered only because the great Tehr's spirit had overwhelmed him and caused his powers to fade for a moment. He suddenly recalled the passage in the book Xirvan had sent him, the passage by Feinno of Uindarh which had haunted him so. Perhaps if he could divert Vladur's thoughts, he could find a way.

Crispan continued backing off as these thoughts flashed before him. The deep booming drums started up their rumble again as Vladur sent his entire dread host forward. He would simply advance now until Crispan was overwhelmed or drained himself futilely hurling his lesser powers at the dead warriors.

"Boom-boom-ba-doom!" The noise jarred Crispan to action, and he sent his thoughts racing out over the plain, his mind seeking that of his adversary. But when the challenge went unheeded, Crispan realized why. In controlling his army, Vladur's mind had sunk to a depth where Crispan's would not and could not go. Vladur's attention must be seized, his grip loosened. But how? For an instant he considered conjuring a fireball to hurl at the ridge. Too much time, too much energy. The army kept up their steady advance. No, another way. The host was nearer now, the drums growing louder, causing an echo against Crispan's chest. The awful stench filled his nostrils. Control, control! He narrowed his eyes and shot a glance at the ridge.

Vladur's horse reared up, pawing at the air, neighing madly. Vladur held on desperately and fought his steed down, and in that instant his army came to a sudden halt. It worked! Vladur was distracted. Now Crispan sent his mind out towards Vladur, his thoughts grabbing at the Renegade before he could reconcentrate his powers.

"Very clever, little apprentice, but futile."

"You destroyed the Order!"

"It was old and dying. It did not listen when I offered it new powers."

"Your powers can only destroy—others and yourself!"

"How, Crispan? Two years, two years of exile. Two years of study. I've raised a host, I've conjured Magicians dead for centuries to gain their knowledge."

"No Magician of the Order would help you. Even his spirit would rebel at the idea."

Vladur, up on his ridge, frowned at the truth Crispan had guessed.

"Your power is not complete, Vladur. Can you control your host and your horse at the same time?" Again Crispan's mind attacked the steed, and Vladur fought it down again.

Now Vladur tried to close his mind, to revive his waiting army. But Crispan's thoughts kept at him. Vladur's mind turned, changed, tried to break away. Crispan felt his own thoughts weakening as Vladur struggled to be free. The aching in his head had changed to a dull throb, and now Crispan was covered in sweat. The initiative, he must keep the initiative.

The high screeching noise caught Vladur unawares. His hands rose instinctively to his ears, but the noise was from within, carried on Crispan's thoughts.

"Damn your eyes, boy!" Vladur's thoughts conveyed disgust and contempt as he conjured a fireball before Crispan, resorting to the simple trick Crispan had disdained. Crispan half-turned his horse to shield its eyes and responded with a sudden burst of water.

Vladur was unimpressed and yet somehow defensive. "I'm better than you, Crispan. I taught *you*, remember?"

The hurt sound came through even in his thoughts, and Crispan let the claim go unanswered. He thought hard this time, desperately seeking a new vision with which to assault the Necromancer. His own mind ached, his powers seemed to be at once more substantial than they had ever been before and also very weak at this moment. Somehow he had surpassed those limits of which Omir had spoken, and yet he was aware that he must be fast approaching whatever ultimate limits there were for even the most proficient Master of the Five Arts.

The mere seconds which these thoughts took were too long, for Vladur turned on his antagonist, motioning frantically and almost hurling his hands towards Crispan. The young Wizard reeled in his saddle as if he had been clapped severely above both ears. The pain was sharp and physical, and tears welled in his eyes.

Crispan, through his own pain and exhaustion, could sense that Vladur was tiring as well, but he feared that the Renegade would still outlast him as they flung images, conjuries and physical manifestations of their powers at one another. Vladur's years of practice in exile were probably too much for Crispan to continue the contest on these terms. He had to find another way, a direct combat of powers without conjuries or phantasms.

Then he thought of the Game. What was the Game but a pure contest of power, the stronger combatant drawing power out of the weaker, absorbing these powers and making them his own, flinging them back triumphantly. Could Crispan do it? It would have to be a finely honed assault, for he feared contamination by Vladur's baser arts. Crispan breathed deeply, regathering his strength.

These thoughts had taken but a moment, and Vladur had welcomed the respite as much as Crispan had. The Necromancer now presumed that his young opponent's sudden inactivity indicated his imminent exhaustion, and so the Renegade sent out new assaults to cripple him. But like arrows wide of the mark, these visions went past Crispan without touching him or disturbing him. In desperation Vladur tried again and again, still without effect.

Crispan was risking everything now on a direct confrontation. Carefully husbanding his remaining powers, he had sealed off his mind while elevating his talents to a level far above the base exchange in which he had been caught. He could still sense Vladur's more brutal attacks, but they seemed to be passing away below him while he rose over the plain.

There was a sudden calm about him now as his powers soared, and for a moment the pleasantness of the sensation lulled Crispan, until he remembered that part of his power was being consumed just in maintaining this higher state. His thoughts flung out the time-honored challenge across the plain. "My powers against yours. Your strength shall be mine for I am mighty in the ways of the Five Arts."

Crispan could see Vladur's head cock to one side as the challenge entered his thoughts. The Renegade looked disappointed, even cheated, and for an instant Crispan recalled that in all their years together at the Order Vladur and he had never played the Game against one another. But now, like a tired brawler, Vladur rose to meet this challenge.

Like two sweating wrestlers struggling for a grip, their minds grappled unseen across the plain. Crispan winced as his powers bounced off those of Vladur, unable to catch hold, and then he writhed as the Necromancer assaulted him in turn. This was customary in the Game, the elusive beginning as each Magician warily sought an initial advantage. And then, suddenly, their powers were locked in an awesome mutual grip. Crispan could not tell who had seized whom. Now began the true struggle, the tugging and pulling as each tried to draw out the other's powers, to absorb them and make them his own. How long this battle went on Crispan could not tell. He was oblivious to virtually all sensations save for the terrible pulling that he felt in his own mind, and the tension as he pulled back in turn. At first he felt as though he were being drawn out, and then the grip would relax and he would regain his strength, only to ease up on his own and be subjected to further assaults.

Back and forth it went, an equal contest which seemed to threaten them both with irresolute exhaustion. In that small portion of his mind still free to think Crispan wondered why Vladur had not simply overwhelmed him with his increased powers. Then all at once he realized why. Vladur was holding some of his powers in reserve to control the army of the dead, not daring to risk everything on the Game. For a moment Crispan withdrew his powers into himself, combining those he was already using with that small portion he had kept to himself for the sake of his thoughts. Now all was concentrated into purest power. Crispan's mind was now totally blank, or rather totally absorbed by his powers. All he was aware of was a deep purple glow in his mind, the very color of his Master's amulet. He could feel the grip, the tugging, Vladur's resistance, still strong at first but then weaker, always stubborn. In his mind Crispan pulled and heaved while Vladur desperately pulled back. It was too late now for Vladur to stop. Momentum drew his powers towards Crispan.

Crispan could feel these powers joining his own, and with each breath it became easier to absorb more. Free to think once again, he remembered the danger of absorbing too much of Vladur's strength, of being poisoned by the necromancy. He drew in a little more, and some more still, and then a bit more, trying to gauge his efforts between Vladur's remaining strength and the depths of his corruption. A little more, a little more. He could feel Vladur struggling frantically to get free. A bit more, more —and then Crispan relaxed his grip. Suddenly released, Vladur's remaining powers flew uncontrollably back across the plain.

This usually marked the end of the Game. The Magician who had lost would signal recognition of his defeat, making it unnecessary for the winner to assault him with his now combined strength. After some rest the loser would regain his lost strength, just as the winner would lose those powers he had absorbed. The Game was never played for total subjugation, but rather as a test of strength. But this time it was different. Crispan could not allow Vladur the time to rest and recoup his powers, and he recognized that the Necromancer was not yet finished. Yet he feared assaulting him with all his powers at once.

He wanted Vladur defeated but alive and alert, not some mindless creature unaware of his fate.

Crispan therefore sought out ghastly visions with which to finish the duel against his weakened but still potent foe, visions which bespoke more of his Art than his power. Again he concentrated, and now sent the screaming bats hurtling through space.

Vladur's mind became a dark cave, and the Renegade shook his head as the winged vermin screeched and clawed at his brain. The ferocity of this assault made Vladur's mind reel. He and Crispan both sensed it at the same time. Vladur had almost none of his power left. As the Outcast first sensed this, his mind shuddered. Crispan felt it across the plain. Vladur lost control. His mind panicked and sought refuge. His thoughts scattered in bewilderment at their momentary weakness. His mind cried out for a little rest, a chance to regather his energies.

Crispan was breathing heavily. He too felt drained. But he felt Vladur's weakness and rose to attack it. He took deep breaths and summoned his own weary powers. His thoughts hurled themselves against Vladur's wearying mind. Ghostly visions appeared, giving Vladur no respite. He was drowning in a lake of his own blood; his skin was crawling with maggots. Hot fires supplanted his hair. Again and again Crispan threw out these images, harrying Vladur's thoughts as they sought a moment's relief, just enough time to concentrate again on his army. Vladur felt like a man lost in a labyrinthine cave of his own making. He ran down passages in the dark hoping to elude his enemy. With great effort he threw the younger Magician's thoughts off for an instant.

Vladur was free, free to revive his host. His mind called out to them over the plain. They did not respond. Again he called, and again. Some of the warriors began to stir, but not all. The drums barely responded, giving out a slow and dying rumble. It was not enough. He must control them all. Again he tried, but his thoughts broke over them like waves on the shore. Vladur screamed aloud as his mind recoiled.

Crispan attacked again, throwing his energy against

Vladur. Vladur's mind staggered. His powers were gone, drained out of him. A brilliant white light grew inside his mind, and he was unable to fend it off or shield himself any longer. Crispan concentrated, his teeth gnashing, sweat pouring over him. He bore down and pushed his energy and power far beyond what he would have once thought his limits to be. More, more and more. Vladur flinched, his eyes knotted in pain. The light grew, boiling up in his head. Higher, hotter, bigger, always bigger. His mind yelled in agony. Crispan pushed his own mind farther and farther. Vladur writhed in his saddle as the brilliant light expanded, consuming his brain until he felt that his skull would burst. Larger and larger. He threw his hands up to his head. It still grew, always more intense, always brighter. No more, no more! All went black. Vladur collapsed in his saddle.

In that moment the entire dead host swayed and then vanished as their master collapsed. Crispan managed to stay conscious to see this, and then he too slumped forward in his saddle, completely and utterly drained.

XXXI

Attack

On the Bow the Southerners sat mesmerized by what little they could see of the contest—the weird army, the destruction of the two riders, the fireball. Only Elthwyn among them could sense the titanic struggle of minds that had seethed across the plain. Now, in Vladur's moment of collapse, Elthwyn turned urgently to the Emperor. "Now, my lord, now! Vladur is overthrown! Hurl your army against Zhyjman before he can make ready!"

Thurka Re had to shake himself before he could respond. "Yes, yes. Belka, Churnir! Give the orders at once. Quickly, against Zhyjman's camp!"

His brother turned in his saddle and gave three long blasts on his war trumpet which had hung over his left shoulder. Belka stood in his stirrups and towered over the others, waving his mace to Stova and the waiting cavalry just behind the western tip of the ridge. At the signal they surged out across the plain, moving like the blade of a giant scythe as they came round the ridge.

Elthwyn saw none of this as he raced pell-mell down the north slope of the ridge. He reached the plain at full tilt and rode madly up to Crispan, worried lest the Magician fall prey to the Northerners. "Master! Master!" he cried as he took up Crispan's fallen reins.

Crispan's face was expressionless, his light-brown hair soaked through, clinging in wet strands to his forehead. He sat slumped in his saddle, supported by the high cantle, totally oblivious to all around him. Again Elthwyn called to him, and now, from somewhere far away, Crispan heard him. The blackness before his eyes dissipated, and he could see his Adept's anxious face before him. "Are you all right, Master?"

The Magician nodded several times. How could he explain to anyone what he had seen, how his own efforts had momentarily revealed to him the depths to which Vladur had gone to practice his evil? He let the thought pass and asked, "Where is Vladur?"

"He is overcome. Tell me, how did you do it?" Still the student, Elthwyn was eager to know.

Crispan ignored the question. He looked up to the Arrow just in time to see Gorham reach Vladur over the crest and lead the Necromancer down to Zhyjman's camp. Now Crispan became aware of the tumult to his left. He turned and saw Thurka's legions, a moving mass of spears, pennants, men and horses bearing down on the enemy camp. "We have them, Elthwyn. Zhyjman staked everything on Vladur's army. He is unprepared. No," he said, correcting himself, "Vladur probably insisted on it this way as part of his price. Come, and let us join in the hunt."

Even as he said this he was surrounded by members of the Emperor's bodyguard. "The Emperor's orders," the captain explained. "He said to tell you he would deeply regret losing you now."

The Magician acquiesced, being too exhausted to argue. They slowly made their way towards the scene of battle, moving with deliberation to avoid any chance encounter with the desperate foe. As they rounded the southern tip of the Arrow and could see the battle, Crispan felt a sudden urge to join in the kill, but a voice within him said that he had beaten his opponent that day, that this slaughter was no fight of his.

As Crispan had surmised, Zhyjman's own army was unready to fight when Vladur had collapsed. Assured of his Necromancer's powers, the Emperor of the North had rested his army and intended to watch this more terrible destruction of his foe. No reason to waste live troops when the dead could be raised to fight. And so, the Southerners' attack caught them unprepared. Sweeping over the plain in a great wedge, the Southern army had brushed aside Zhyjman's few scouts and guards and surged into the frantic camp. Northerners, allies and mercenaries alike, were cut down as they emerged half-armed from their tents. Those who sought to hide behind their canvas were surrounded by those on foot who followed in the wake of Stova's rapacious cavalry. In the tents they were left with the easy choice of surrender or slaughter. The lords of the South pressed on with their men, laying about themselves freely with their weapons as all the gloom and defeat of the past evaporated in this heady moment of unexpected victory.

Organized resistance was impossible as the Southerners pushed into the center of the camp in one thrust, while a separate column sealed the camp by riding along its western edge. Bewildered, suddenly desperate, the trapped warriors fought on in small pockets. Their leaders were not with them to give direction, so each fought madly where he stood without orders or hope. Then came the rumor from the edge of the Southern attack. "The Emperor is taken!" Fighting stopped momentarily as both sides waited and the word carried across the field. Which Emperor, they all wondered. Then followed the shouts from the lancers of Thurka Re. "Zhyjman is taken! Kirion and Syman too!" A bellowing roar arose from the Southerners' lips, and as the word spread the Northern soldiers gratefully dropped their weapons.

It was at this moment of jubilation and defeat that Crispan and Elthwyn and their escort began to pick their way through the wreckage of the fallen camp. Tents here and there were burning like untended campfires. Scores of bodies, mostly men in incomplete armor or without shields, lay strewn everywhere. The bodies of Southerners mingled with the Northern dead, for every victory has its price. Thinking again as a warrior rather than a Master of the Five Arts, Crispan was relieved to see that relatively few wore uniforms of the South.

"Crispan, Crispan! We've won!" Mikal's eyes were piercingly bright under his helm. He smiled warmly at the Magician. "Come, everyone is at the center of the camp. They've all been captured—Zhyjman, Syman, everyone!"

"Vladur?" asked Crispan, arching his brow.

"Aye, him and his lackey as well. Come on!"

Crispan froze for a moment at the thought of an encounter with the fallen Renegade. He swallowed very hard and grabbed Elthwyn's arm for a moment, then went on to face the man who had destroyed the Order.

XXXII

Retribution

Thurka's soldiers were already tearing down some tents and carting off bodies to provide a proper clearing before Zhyjman's own grandiose tent. In the short time the battle had taken, there had been much carnage here in particular, as Southern lancers rode down Zhyjman's bodyguard. All the lords of the South were already there when Crispan, Elthwyn and Prince Mikal rode up. As they approached, Crispan could see his friends all standing at the left facing a shorter line of bound men with members of the Emperor Thurka's guards behind them. He checked the line of prisoners twice but could not find Vladur or Gorham. Was Mikal wrong, had they escaped?

He leapt down from his horse as they reached the clearing, his knees momentarily buckling, betraying how truly tired he still was. Thurka rushed up to him and enveloped him in a ferocious hug, which helped the Wizard regain his balance. "You were magnificent!" The Emperor was beaming.

"Where is Vladur?"

"When they found him he was in a stupor, being led by the other one. They're in here." Thurka pointed to Zhyjman's quarters.

"I want to see him now."

Even as Thurka nodded his assent, Crispan strode into the dark tent, thrusting back the flap and planting himself firmly before the two fallen Magicians. They had been sitting on a chaise behind one of Zhyjman's ornately carved tables when he entered, but when they saw him they both rose.

The Necromancer was taller than his former student, and as Elthwyn had said, his features had grown leaner,

285

more hollow during his exile. His gray and black hair was disheveled now, but his pointy beard and sharp moustaches kept their form and accented the increased angularity of his features. Facing his conqueror now, Vladur showed neither defeat nor remorse. His whole bearing bespoke the haughtiness and pride which had brought him to this moment. Gorham, still the lackey, cowered beside him.

Now suddenly face to face with him, and victorious, Crispan did not know what to say. He simply stared at Vladur, seething with anger.

Behind him Thurka and the Southern lords had filed in to witness the confrontation. Sensing his Magician's inability to act, the Emperor forced the matter. "Crispan," he said softly and evenly, "what shall we do with them?"

Without saying a word, Crispan stepped forward and removed the talisman that the Renegade wore. It was as Elthwyn had described it, a round blood-red stone with a hideous white eye in the center. Instead of the five-sided eye of the Order, this charm had a six-sided orb, representing Vladur's additional power as well. Crispan held it at arm's length on its gold chain, looking at it with disgust. Then he placed it on the table, face up. "Belka, your mace, please."

He took the heavy weapon from the tall Prince and lifted it with both hands, bringing it down on the amulet, pulverizing it in one stroke and splintering the table deeply. He moved around the table to Gorham now and took his talisman. It was from the Order. "This must be burned, as is our custom," Crispan said. He turned again to the two captives, and now answered Thurka's question. "They must be punished as he"—he pointed to Vladur —"should have been punished when he was first discovered. They are to be beheaded, tonight. The heads and bodies must be burned separately and the ashes buried far apart. This is our law."

Gorham, aghast at this swift verdict, shouted, "No! No!" Vladur now looked at him with the same contempt that Crispan had made so obvious, and then turned to face the younger man. In a voice that was dry and low he said, "You have learned well." The verdicts made it apparent to Vladur that Crispan had prepared for their confrontation, for he had learned that once a Master had delved into necromancy even his spirit remained dangerous and corrupted. Only this punishment would disable the spirit beyond death.

Without responding, Crispan turned again to the Emperor. "He is still weak and powerless, but this shall not last. As long as he lives he remains a danger. Until the execution he is to be bound, gagged and blindfolded, and kept secluded; Gorham as well."

"As you say, Crispan. I will have it carried out at once," Thurka Re responded.

They moved again into the clearing before the tent. The remaining prisoners had been removed, but Thurka worried over their fate. "Does that punishment apply to Zhyjman as well?"

Crispan shook his head. "No. Zhyjman was an Unknowing One, as we would say in the Order. He did not comprehend what Vladur had done to achieve his success. Although I am sure, had he known, he would have acquiesced, our rules do not allow us to punish him in the same way. He and the others are your concern."

"Then advise me, Crispan. What shall I do with them? Shall I execute them all for the havoc they have wrought?"

"Surely, Father, you cannot blame Syman." It was the former mercenary in Mikal speaking now. "He merely signed a contract with Zhyjman to fight for him. He cannot be executed for that."

Thurka's expression became clouded and pained, but Crispan spoke before he did. "By the same token, can we blame Zhyjman? Was he not seduced by Vladur's promises? Look at his army. We now know why he moved so suddenly and where all his forces were. He moved because Vladur said he was ready. And as we had supposed, he did not have enough armies for Anrehenkar, the Gates and us as well. Zhyjman counted on Vladur's host of dead warriors to overwhelm us. Though they both served

287

one another, who can say which initiated this foul strategy and war?"

"Do you know what they planned beyond this battle?" asked the Emperor.

"I do not think they knew. That is what I would like to ask the Emperor Zhyjman."

The Southern victors sat now behind the long table Zhyjman had used for dining with his generals when on campaign. Ranged before the victors, each flanked by two guards with a third behind, were their other captives. Zhyjman, still in his hauberk of gold and silver but deprived of his silver cuirass and red cape, remained impressive in appearance. He was tall and lithe, and his shiny black hair falling to his shoulders set off his exquisitely curled beard. Still arrogant, he seized the initiative. "Well, Thurka Re, what will you do with me?" He spoke in the sharp accents of the North.

"Less, I suppose, than you would have done to me."

Zhyjman snorted. "Bah! Do you believe that? Do you think you would have ignored the Sorcerer had the opportunity he offered beckoned you?"

Crispan interrupted the two Emperors and turned fully towards Zhyjman. The Magician's eyes were filled with contempt, and he made no effort to hide this. "What do you suppose would have been the future had you won today?"

"Divination is *your* trade, is it not?"

Crispan could not believe that even in defeat Zhyjman continued his posturing. Crispan's voice went ice cold as he addressed the Emperor of the North. "Do you think that a victory over us would have been the end? Do you think that Vladur, having tasted the fullness of his new powers, would have settled for the establishment of some perverse new order? If he could unseat one Emperor, why not a second? Eventually he would have turned on you, or forced you to come after him." Crispan's voice then dropped to a frighteningly low tone. "You may not realize it, but I have saved *you* and *your* Empire today as well."

Zhyjman began to sense that he would personally survive this debacle, and that perception emboldened him.
"Reserve your advice for *your* Master," he said. "Vladur
was right. You are petty fools. Your magic is so important
to you that you can only think of it first. You are so sure
that Vladur was only using me for his own ends."
Zhyjman tried to sound supremely confident, but Crispan
remained unconvinced.

"Even now you refuse to see it. Or worse yet, you see
it and refuse to admit it." Crispan sank back into his seat,
waving his hand at Zhyjman, a gesture which angered the
captive Emperor more than anything that had been said
to him.

Thurka stepped forward again. "Remove them all. I
cannot decide their fates at once. They will remain in
camp here tonight and be conveyed to Kerdineskar in the
morning to await my pleasure."

For the rest of that day Crispan kept busy. First
he made sure that a swift force went north to free
those captives Vladur had taken at the Order. Then he
spent the remainder of the day supervising the collection of
all the possessions of Vladur and Gorham. Books, potions,
vessels, philters and even clothing—he had them all
brought before the clearing and put into one pile. He
could not help but think back to that night at the Order
when the same chore had been done for the same purpose. When all was collected, he and Elthwyn scoured
their tents again, and then he had the structures dismantled and added to the pile as well.

Mikal and Zoltan also thought of the past as they made
their way to the tent where Syman was being kept. The
face, with its familiar stiff gray beard, looked surprised as
they entered. "So you really are the Heir Prince of the
Empire," the mercenary said. "I never quite believed
Zhyjman. It all seemed too incredible. He never could
offer me concrete proof."

Mikal's voice was low, and a bit hurt. "Then why did
you agree to hand me over?"

"I had to. It was part of his contract. If I refused to

accept this term, he threatened to recruit my men away from me. Who would have withstood the promise of the vaults of Anrehenkar? Where would I have been then?"

Mikal and the still-silent Zoltan moved to leave.

"But Mikal!" Syman called. "I told him I could never hand you over while the siege of Aishar lasted. I respected our bargain, did I not? You must take that into account."

To anyone but a mercenary this would have mattered little. But Mikal knew, and understood.

It was evening. Crispan moved across the clearing and entered the gaudily decorated tent. On the freshly scarred table stood a large candle, offering a soft light to the room. He motioned to one of the guards and had him remove the gag and blindfold. Even in the subdued light Vladur winced and then blinked several times.

"Come to gloat, Crispan?" Vladur's voice had an evil edge to it.

"No. I just wanted to know why you had to destroy the Order like that. Was it simply vengeance?"

"What do you think?"

"Then why did you not take it against me alone? I was the one who first exposed you to Omir. I was the one who had come down to fight you. Why did they have to suffer like that?"

Vladur's mouth twisted malignantly. "For all your powers and learning you are still the naive Novice you were when you first entered the Order. It would have come to that eventually. Do you think there could have been any compromise between those plodders and my knowledge? I moved when I did to isolate you, to cut you off, to weaken and hurt you. I had always known *you* were my main threat.

"I was about to take my last examinations as an Adept," he continued, "when Bellapon first brought you to the Order. He told me that night that you had extraordinary powers. I saw you that night in a dream—a dream in which you eclipsed me, my powers." Even after all those years Vladur remembered every detail of that dream. "I dreamt of Bellapon bestowing my Master's talisman on me, shining brightest blue. A shadow came between Bellapon and me, dimming the glow of that talisman. That shadow was you. I never saw you in the dream, but I knew it was you, absolutely certain as I thought of it after awakening.

"I was always considered the best, the most promising, until you came to the Order. But you were just like the others, clinging to the old, limited ways. You all ignored what I offered, the unlimited powers and opportunities. Where," he chortled, "is your precious Order now? Did you save yourselves from me?" Vladur laughed hideously to himself.

There was nothing to say to this final spilling of venomous bile. Crispan ordered the gag and blindfold replaced and left the tent. The soft shades of evening had given way to the deeper dark of night. In the light of torches burning in a score of iron stands he could see Thurka and his attendant lords awaiting him. He noticed that the other captives were there as well, still bound, still under guard. Taking up one of the flaming brands from its tripod, he walked to the pile that had been amassed in the clearing and dropped the torch into it. Flames rose into the night sky, eclipsing the torchlight about the raging pyre. Everyone stood suffused in an orange glow, watching the fire consume its feast ravenously. Shreds of cloth floated free trailing wisps of flame, bottles and philters popped and exploded, their contents going up in sudden multicolored flashes.

Finally the flames spent their initial fury and began to die away. Crispan took a pike and stoked the white-hot ashes in the center of the flames. He took from his robes the amulet that had been Gorham's and consigned it to the flames, where the remains of Vladur's had already been destroyed. He added potions that Elthwyn had brought him from his own tent until the fire's heat grew almost too intense to bear. Crispan continued to stand before the pyre until the talisman gave way with a sudden "Whoosh!" and was reduced at once to ash. Then, with

291

Elthwyn seconding him, Crispan spoke the necessary ancient chants to signify the fall of a Magician.

When it was done, and the last tongues of flame had fallen away, the Wizard signaled to Baron Churnir. From two separate tents Vladur and Gorham were brought before the assembly. Vladur walked stiffly between his guards, still proud and unyielding, free of guilt or remorse. Gorham had to be prodded by his guards as he was almost dragged, whimpering, to the site of his execution. Vladur passed before Crispan but said nothing, satisfied in shooting him one last glare. Gorham's eyes bespoke supplication and mercy, but Crispan hardened his gaze and let him pass.

They were placed on either side of the pile of ashes, and forced to their knees so their heads pointed towards one another. Two guards drew their claymores and placed themselves so that the victims were between them and Crispan.

"You have broken the most sacred rules of the Order," Crispan intoned. "You have betrayed the knowledge and trust that were imparted to you. You have used your powers against the Order and the World. May your names ever be a curse to Men Knowing and Unknowing alike."

The two swords swooped down in quick silver arcs. Blood splattered and flesh rended and the decapitated bodies fell in two heaps.

XXXIII

East to the Order

"You did not sleep, did you?" Elthwyn knew the answer just by looking at the Master's haggard face. "I had hoped all the riding to properly bury the ashes would have wearied you. We must have ridden through most of the night."

Crispan nodded and thought of the remains of one head and one body he had interred, both miles and miles apart in unmarked graves. The other two urns of ashes he had entrusted separately to Zoltan and Mikal, knowing they would see to it that these too were buried far apart. "No, I did not sleep until dawn. I kept seeing Vladur and Gorham kneeling before me. Just as the swords came down upon them they changed—they became Bellapon and Omir. I was powerless to stop the executioners' blades. I feel I have somehow betrayed those two old men."

"Surely not," Elthwyn protested. "You told me Vladur had said he would have attacked the Order sooner or later anyway. How can you blame yourself?"

Stopping in his path towards the main tent, Crispan looked his student directly in the eyes. "When I first was coming to the Order, with Bellapon, he read my future in the stars. Even then he said that it was odd that I had been born so close to the Sword, odd for a Magician. I was too young then to think anything of it, nor did it bother me in all the years that I stayed in the Order. But I think that it was always in the back of my mind once I came down out of the Order. I clung desperately to the Open Eye and tried too hard to avoid the Sword. We were taught to follow our nature in all things, and yet this I refused to do. I imposed naive limits on my actions, limits which may even have conceded too much of an advantage to Vladur, allowing him to pick his time rather than forcing him to show himself. I was too concerned about my image of myself as a Master, too eager to preserve that no matter what. It is ironic, Elthwyn, but I feel I have learned something that could profit the entire Order, and yet there is nothing left of it."

There was a catch in Crispan's voice as he said this. They walked the rest of the way in silence, Crispan unwilling to talk, Elthwyn at a loss for the words that would comfort the Master. Neither of them noticed the diminished ranks in the camp as they made their way to Thurka Re, holding council in Zhyjman's feast tent.

They entered and made their way to the two vacant spaces being held for them near the Emperor. Crispan slumped into his chair and stared at a piece of fruit in a nearby bowl. By his looks Thurka could see that it was no time for pleasantries, so he immediately set about the affairs at hand.

"The prisoners have been sent south to Kerdineskar. Prince Xander of Gar is on his way to Anrehenkar, and Lord Stova is on his way to the Gates. They have with them officers of Zhyjman and Syman to confirm the news of their defeat."

"What about prisoners?" asked Larc, worrying most about the captured mercenaries.

"That depends on what we do with our captives. My son suggests that I hire Syman's men into my own army. I may do this to some extent, but I cannot take them all, nor do I want to. They might prove a dangerous group within my Empire."

"Forgive me, my lord, but you are still avoiding the issue. What about Zhyjman and the others?" The Duke of Larc, emboldened now that he was no longer totally dependent on the Emperor, pressed on. "I say they deserve to die." Finally the question was clearly stated.

"And what would you put in their place?" Crispan's question caught Larc off guard. "Will the Dukedom of Larc now expand and replace the Empire of the North? Do you think that will restore peace and order to the

World?" Crispan turned to the Emperor. "My lord, the Order joined with you to preserve what was left intact from before the Chaos. Destroy the Empire of the North and you will only extend the Chaos. It will seethe across two Empires, it will batter against your frontiers."

The Emperor let go a heavy sigh. "What do you suggest?"

"Enlarge Larc, restore fallen Tharn. Reduce the borders of Zhyjman, Nor and Kyryl. Expand your own realm to make yourself more secure. But do not take more than you can easily hold, and do not wholly remove what remains of order and stability in the North."

"By the Spirits!" Larc was on his feet, red with anger. "Did we fight this war to keep Zhyjman on his throne and his realm virtually intact?"

"I would say," offered Zoltan while staring into his cup, "you fought because you had no choice."

"Enough," interrupted Thurka, cutting off any new bickering. He turned back to Crispan. "What do you have in mind?"

"The Duke is right, m'lord. To restore Zhyjman would not be a solution. You could not trust him to abide by any settlement. And, if you will forgive my saying so, it would be a poor precedent to execute an Emperor. But Zhyjman has a young son. Keep Zhyjman captive in the South and put his son on the throne, with a Regent you can trust behind him. You have little other choice between the restoration of Zhyjman and the dissolution of the Empire of the North than this middle course."

Thurka rubbed his chin, weighing this advice. "Perhaps so. But we must also disarm all the mercenaries. Those I cannot use in the enlarged Empire will be dispersed, settled throughout the Middle Realm. The regular Northern troops will be sent home weaponless."

Mikal, hitherto silent, raised a point everyone had forgotten. "What is to become of Syman and Kirion?" Before his father could answer, the Prince made his own suggestion. "To release Kirion would be a mistake too. He was the Emperor's strategist. But Syman is only guilty of following his profession, nothing more. There is no just or

295

unjust cause to a mercenary, only pay. Exile them both within our realm, separately, as befits their station."

Thurka's reluctance was evident. He again felt the jealousy towards Syman for whatever bond there was between the mercenary and his son. Belka sensed his brother's hesitancy. "It would be a wise move," he said. "At one stroke you deprive the mercenaries of their most vaunted leader and Zhyjman of his ablest general. This, more than reducing his borders and disarming his soldiers, will disable him and help restore peace."

The Emperor drummed the elegantly carved table with his fingers. He scratched at his beard. "Perhaps." He drummed again. "Then it is all settled, at least the broad outlines." He leaned to his right, towards the Magician. "And what is to become of you? What will you do?"

"I do not know," Crispan answered softly. "I am going to go east, to the Order. After that I do not know."

"I would consider it an honor if you would allow me to accompany you. I am sure we all would." All about the table agreed. Larc did so grudgingly, being eager to return to his lands. But like the others he was aware of all he owed to this man.

"Churnir, have an escort of one thousand lancers made ready. That should be sufficient protection with Stova already preceding us to the Gates."

The Prince of Vadul was sent back with the remainder of the army and the prisoners. The High Chamberlain, Gran, was appointed Regent during the absence of the Emperor and his Heir. Only four days after overcoming their enemy the Army of the South broke camp. Even now the soldiers could not quite comprehend their victory. They still did not understand how the Northerners could have been so unprepared. That the Magician Crispan had bewitched them was the common answer. After all, he had saved Zifkar, had he not? And there was still the mystery of those awful drums and that hideous stench. But, like their victory itself, these remained unexplained.

Pennants, standards and gonfalons snapping in the

wind, armor gleaming, they made their way eastward. It was the same track Mikal and Zoltan had followed not so very long ago as they fled from Syman in the early days of spring, and this irony did not escape either of them. They traversed the lush grasslands of summer, already fully grown and almost past their peak, riding freely and easily like the conquerors they were. They followed the path that ran along the Falchions as so many before them had on their way to the Gates.

Crispan tried, almost desperately, to share in their joy. But for him there was little. The dream he had described to Elthwyn still haunted him some nights, and during the day he wondered continually over what he would find within the Great Mountains. He did not even know what had compelled him to go, only that he must.

The plain passed away beneath them and the Falchions came ever closer on their right, and with each passing day he felt more tense about seeing the Order. He dreaded what it would look like in ruins; but he had to go back once more. They rounded the northern shoulder of the mountains and entered the ever-barren Gates, to camp in Stova's vanguard. Here winds already whispering of autumn rode among the crags, hinting at the cold to come.

Crispan had not stood before the east gate since Bellapon had first taken him to the Order. He stared for a long time at the Eye carved into the rock above the niche. "You are useless," he said to it silently. "What you guarded is gone now, and you remain only as a painful reminder of what was." With an escort of less than one hundred to accompany them into the mountains they went on.

They snaked their way north and east. Elthwyn rode among the lords at the head of the column, directing them through the maze of paths. Crispan did not speak at all, huddling ever deeper in his cloak as they rode further into the Great Mountains, where the brief summer was already waning.

As they rode on, the path narrowed and the column lengthened so that they went from four abreast to two. Two outriders headed the column, followed on this day by Elthwyn for guidance and then by Zoltan, who required more room than most. Behind them came Crispan and the Emperor, followed by all the others strung out on the serpentine track.

"Why have we stopped?" called out the Emperor at a sudden halt.

"There is a body blocking the road up ahead, my lord." The outrider pointed to where the road bent away behind an outcrop.

Thurka and Crispan squeezed past the Adept and Zoltan who waited just before the bend. The other outrider had dismounted and stood before the body. The wind whistled low about them, and the outrider's horse pawed the steely ground as it shivered. The body lay face down, its disheveled cloak obscuring it from the knees up. The Emperor and the Wizard came before the inert form. "Turn him over," Thurka ordered, motioning.

The soldier pushed against the body. He had been a big man and had grown terribly stiff. With a grunt the outrider rolled it over.

"No! No!" Crispan yelled as the face was revealed. His own face lost all its color.

"Who is it?" demanded Thurka. Elthwyn, who had wedged his way forward and peered over their shoulders, gasped as he saw the face. "It's Master Nujhir."

"Zoltan, get some soldiers up here. Have him buried at once!" Thurka reached out to steady the visibly shaken Wizard. Crispan felt the churning well up inside him and went into a nearby niche to be sick. While he was gone, Thurka turned to Churnir, who had ridden up with the others. "Send some men up ahead. Elthwyn will explain the way. Any other bodies are to be pulled aside and buried at once. I do not want any more left for him to see."

His orders given, the Emperor sought out the Magician. Crispan was standing at the far end, supporting himself with a hand on either wall. He turned as he heard the footsteps behind him. "Are you all right?" asked Thurka Re. Crispan swallowed hard and nodded. "Are you sure you want to go on? What can you find there?"

"No," Crispan said, swallowing again. "I want to see the Order."

After Nujhir's burial Crispan was seized with a new determination. He was as silent as before, but now it was the silence of man driven on towards a goal, not a man lapsing into lethargy. He urged the others on as much as possible, rousing everyone before dawn so they could ride at first light, driving them relentlessly until they had to stop lest they blunder into a blind passage in the night.

When they reached the Order's outer gate it was already late in the day. The neighboring peaks and tors threw lengthening shadows across the arch. The arch itself still stood intact, but the symbol of the Eye was rent by a hideous crack. One of the two stone gates, the right one, stood a bit ajar. All that remained of the left one was a pile of rubble. As much as he had tried to make himself ready for this moment, Crispan still felt his stomach go tight in a single nasty spasm. He tucked in his chin, aware that everyone watched him. With both hesitation and eagerness he led them to the plateau beyond. Luckily the failing light obscured from view how tightly shut his eyes were as he rode under the sundered gate. When he felt he had cleared it, he opened them again, but refused to look back; he looked only up the road which ran across the plateau.

Thurka was beside him now, his black cape flowing gracefully on the breeze. "Let us camp here for the night."

"But we are almost there," Crispan protested, pointing into the hastening night in the east.

"No, Master," ventured Elthwyn. His concern, mostly for Crispan, was evident on his face. "We might still go wrong in the night. You know the edges of the plateau are scored with deep chasms."

"Crispan," said Thurka, "what is left since Vladur's return will still be there. I know you are eager to see it. But another day now will not matter. We camp here tonight." The word was final, and without rebuttal. Disappointed and overly anxious, Crispan remained in his saddle while the others dismounted and stretched stiff joints as they walked around. Crispan gave out a heavy sigh and then braced himself with a great draught of cold, clear mountain air. "One more night," he kept thinking, "one more night, and then . . ." His thoughts became confused and lost. "And then what?" Again the visions of ruin passed through his mind; and the nagging question, "What is there without the Order?"

For men and beasts alike the plateau was a verdant luxury after the harsh mountains. It was covered in grass not yet yellow and crackling from the cold. It offered abundant fodder for the horses, and for the men soft bedding after nights in the cold, hard mountains. The luxury beckoned them all, and soon very few were left awake.

Only one made no attempt to summon sleep. He remained sitting before the fire, huddled in his cloak and hood, pondering the one question which dominated his thoughts. "What comes after the Order? What is my place?" He was prepared now, he felt, for what he would see on the morrow. He knew there would be nothing left for him there; and he thought of the World beyond the mountains. There was nothing there which attracted him, he knew that. There must be something else. Perhaps there was an answer in the flames. He stared deep into the heart of the fire, summoning his powers to divine an answer, to see where he might go. There was nothing. He tried to bear down, to concentrate, but he could feel that there was little there to summon. He had felt this way ever since the moment he had overcome Vladur. A spark in the flames caught his attention and he involuntarily watched it drift up over the fire. It carried up against the black sky and then snuffed out, and as it did he focused instead on the stars beyond. He watched the stars and picked out the shape of Rosinfar the Dragon, slithering away to the north. It was then, watching the dragon, that he made his decision, and only then did he lay down to sleep.

XXXIV

Over the Northern Horizon

The sun beckoned them across the plateau; the breeze of early morning tussled the greenery at their feet. The road up the slightly inclined plateau was well-defined, but as they rode, gruesome relics lay across their path. The few stray weapons and bits of armor managed to retain their pride even though discarded, but broken vessels and vials, and books now sodden and rotting from the rain lay pathetically all about them.

After the cold and stony discomfort of the mountains the horses reveled in the luxury of the grass. Their heads bobbed rhythmically as they stretched out into longer strides, and more than one rider had to keep a firmer hold on his reins. Crispan, riding in the very front, was driven on as well, albeit for different reasons. He had not breakfasted that morning and he felt somewhat light-headed now. He was aware, too, of the increasing pounding of his heart, of the sudden dryness in his mouth. Horse and rider moved as one across the plateau. Elthwyn, both worried and anxious himself, nudged his spurs into his steed's flanks, eager to be with his Master when they rode into the courtyard of the Order. Rather than be left in their wake, the rest of the party went to their spurs as well.

And then it was in sight. At first just a thin gray line hovering on the horizon, it grew in height and depth as they bore down on it. Soon they could discern the mist of morning still wedged between the wall and the ground. They closed faster now, and the mist no longer obscured the wall's details. The road no longer led to a pair of solid stone gates, but to a gaping black maw instead.

Crispan and Elthwyn reached the ruined portals first.

301

There was no sign of the ornately carved gates that had been there, only blackened rubble. As the others arrived behind the Magicians they too were stunned by the eerie quality of the rubble. They were soldiers who had seen dozens of sacked cities, and yet none could recall having ever seen destruction so viciously thorough.

As he sat on his fidgety horse amidst the ruin, Crispan could see that Vladur had taken great pains to destroy this portal, not just in the physical effort to have it pulled down, but with spells and curses as well. He could sense the very curse which hung now about the site. He did not remember it all, but he could recall the first few words: "Make this a place where stones will not stand . . ." It made him realize once again how deeply the Renegade had come to hate the Order, for the study of curses was but a curiosity that had been barely touched upon in the Order. Their cultivation and use was a hideous aberration.

In the midst of his musings, the Order itself caught his gaze through the dissipating mist. He let out a gasp and his hand involuntarily went up to his mouth. He eye traveled back and forth over the building, seeking to find some feature untouched by the havoc. The front and east wing stood firm, but the dark scars of flame were abundantly evident. Many windows were hollow and blackened. The west wing had suffered far greater damage, and the furthest tower here was but a heap of rubble. Like the mocking mask of a jester, the front was still intact, a cruel facade belying the ruin beyond. Here too was that vicious quality to the destruction, a meanness and thoroughness crying out from every fragmented, scattered stone. Many were deeply scarred with a blackness etched deep within them. Much to everyone's surprise, vagrant wisps and columns of smoke still climbed out of the ruin, defying rain and wind and cold. "Brimstone," thought Crispan. "Only brimstone could do this to stone and still leave heat after so long."

He nudged his horse forward, and the sound of the hooves against the flagstones carried cruelly in the air. Scattered armor, broken vials, torn books lay strewn about the courtyard. It was an apt comment on the type of men who had lived here, and on the type of men who had defiled this place. Curiously, there were no bodies to be seen, and Thurka for one was relieved at this.

Awestruck and hesitant, the party slowly pushed its way across the yard. A passing horse accidentally struck a piece of ruin and neighed sharply over the stone's defiant heat.

Crispan was far ahead, almost halfway across the yard now. In a gliding motion he dismounted and continued his approach on foot. Elthwyn quickly came up to join him, followed by Thurka and the others, but the Magician motioned them back with a wave of his hand without ever turning around to face them. Alone, he must go alone, as if this catastrophe were somehow his creation.

Each step he took was measured, and with each one he sought out some different part of the building to survey in its suffering. "It is only stone," he argued to himself, "it does not mean the end." But another voice rejoined from deeper within him, telling him that this was not true. More than mere stone had been destroyed here.

Now he stood before the doors, left indifferently open to the elements. His efforts to peer inside were rendered futile by the play of shadow and smoke. Elthwyn, the Emperor, Mikal, Belka and Zoltan joined him now, while the others remained near their mounts, unable to comprehend what had really happened here any more than they understood how they had overcome Zhyjman and his cohorts.

Aware of his companions, Crispan stepped across the threshold and into the Great Hall. A shaft of light entered where a window had been and where a gaping hole through wall and roof now stood. Through the contrast of the light against the gloomy interior, one could watch the endlessly whirling dust in its fascinating flight. With the others in his wake, he stepped beyond the beam in his path and went towards the foot of the main stairs.

"The last time I stood here," he said, more to the stairs than to those behind him, "was the morning Mikal and Zoltan took me away. Had I known then—" His words were choked off in his throat.

He wandered about the High Master's chambers down the corridor, on the wall facing the courtyard. Surely Vladur would have been especially vindictive there. Crispan could make out the door through the unfamiliar play of new patterns of light and shadow, but he did not go down the hall. There was something else he would rather see first.

Like an unexpected intruder, Zoltan's voice sprang at him. "Where are you going?"

Looking like one suddenly awakened, Crispan turned at the foot of the stairs. "The east wing still seems to be intact. I want to see my room."

"You cannot," argued Zoltan.

"Why?"

"Those stairs," said the burly warrior, pointing; "they're not safe. Crispan, I have been through enough sieges to know. I can sense when ruins are safe, and my nose is warning me against this place." Sensing the Magician's resolution, Zoltan seized a large piece of fallen masonry before Crispan could move up the stairs. Impervious to the heat through his gloves for an instant, the red beard hoisted the stone high above his head and heaved it hard against the stairway. His great strength carried it near the middle of the stairs, and they gave way immediately under its impact, quickly followed by those steps leading down to where they stood. For a moment the upper stairs hung grotesquely and incongruously from their landing into mid-air. Then they too crashed to the floor. As they all jumped back amidst the billowing clouds of dust and debris, Zoltan turned to the Magician. "You see. And that stone probably weighed a lot less than you do."

Thurka gently led Crispan and the others outside, unwilling to risk their safety any longer. Already Churnir was through the entry, having heard the crash.

Crispan shook his head slowly. "I don't know. I feel cheated, as though Vladur had ultimately won."

The Emperor looked him squarely in the face. "Perhaps not. Perhaps he counted on your coming here and hoped you would die in the ruins. Perhaps this is your final victory over him."

"Perhaps. But there are some things here that I must still do before I go." He turned around and looked across the threshold into the Great Hall. Clasping both hands around his amulet, he silently said the words that would lift any curses Vladur might have laid. Crispan did not know if Vladur had done so, or how efficacious the curses or counterchants would be, but he felt he had to do it. The others watched silently, until he lifted his bowed head. "Elthwyn, take me to Omir's grave."

The Adept led them around past the standing east wing, out to a quiet patch of ground nestled under the edges of the mountains' gentler lower slopes. Oddly, these stones from the ruins which formed the burial mound had lost their warmth, as though in death Omir still fought Vladur's evil. Crispan again bowed his head and clutched the purple talisman with both hands. Out loud he said, "Here is the man to whom you owe your kingdoms." But in his mind he spoke to the dead High Master. "Omir, was it worth all of this? Look what our victory has brought us. Where is the Order now? Did our responsibility run so deep, Omir? Was it worth it? Or perhaps you knew, even as you sent me out, what you were bringing down on us—on yourself. Forgive me, Omir." Then he lapsed into the ancient rites that one Magician says for another when he dies.

It was over, and they were about to turn from the makeshift grave when the ever-present Churnir pointed up to a ledge on the slope. "Look, my lord, there!" Instinctively they all went for their swords. For an anxious moment they stood there until Crispan called out, "By the Spirits! It's Eliborg!" Down from the slope came the elder Master with some two dozen students and servants in tow. Many of the students were the very young ones, the newly arrived Novices.

"Is it really you, Crispan?" cried Eliborg with teary eyes. "Is it you?"

Crispan speechlessly embraced the older man.

"What has happened, tell me what has happened," gasped Eliborg.

"It is over. Vladur is dead and Zhyjman is defeated and a prisoner."

The older Master's deep-brown eyes exploded with joy. "Where? How? Tell me!"

"Wait, wait. First tell me how you came to be here still."

So Eliborg recounted how in the confusion of Vladur's revenge he had managed to slip away, as had some of the others, into the encircling mountains. They hid there separately until long after the Renegade had left, and it was only after some time that they all eventually gathered as they spotted one another venturing among the ruins scavenging for food.

"We lived on what remained in the storehouse and what we could find among the slopes," he continued. "But we dared not venture beyond the mountains for fear that Vladur was victorious already and would seize us. I tell you frankly, Crispan, I do not know what we would have done through the winter. There are some up above who are sick or very weak already. I truly feared it would be the end of us all.

"When we saw you coming today from far off and thought you were Vladur returning, we hid again. But then I saw you over Omir's grave and I watched closely, and—and here we are!"

Crispan just shook his head and smiled, embracing Eliborg again. He then remembered himself and set about making his introductions. Already Churnir and some soldiers were scrambling up the slopes, helping those who were too weak to climb down on their own. "Now you can leave this place with us and come down into the World," Crispan said. "We will leave today, now, as soon as we feed you." As he led Eliborg away toward the waiting horses and men, Crispan felt a welcome moment of solace, which departed all too soon.

They ate on the far side of the courtyard gate, unwilling to allow their small repast to be disturbed by the oppressive ruins. When they had finished with the dried beef and rapidly toughening bread, they found a horse for Eliborg to ride and distributed the students, servants and teachers among the other soldiers. All were mounted securely, and Thurka looked to Crispan, who nodded back. The Emperor motioned out across the plateau. As their horses began to move, Thurka Re saw Crispan begin to rise and half turn in his saddle. He quickly caught him by the arm. "No, Crispan, don't. Remember it as it was, not how it is now."

Back across the plateau they went, and under the once-proud Gate carved into living rock. Down the mountains' labyrinth they came, hastened on by the increasingly bitter cold of autumn. Each day their pace increased as the track widened and grew less tortuous. All were glad to leave this place and reenter the World, all except one. Crispan was still uneasy, although ever since the night he had watched Rosinfar high above the plateau he had known what he would do. Both Elthwyn and Thurka sensed his nervousness and his resolution and did not ask the question uppermost in their minds, fearing his answer.

The track widened and became a path, and the path grew smoother and more regular. And then they each squeezed out of the crevice by the Eye and towards the waiting camp of Thurka Re's host below the silently watching Sentinel. The camp lay before them on the plain between the Gates, a vast mobile city of canvas.

Gauging the sun and the distance, Thurka said, "We can reach it well before dark."

"Wait." Crispan's quiet imperative brought the moment they all now knew was coming, and which they all dreaded. "I am not going with you, my lord."

Half expecting Crispan's decision, Thurka still asked the question. "Why not?"

"I cannot. There is nothing for me out there, and nothing left for me at the Order. I must go elsewhere."

"How can you say there is nothing for you here?" The Emperor was hurt and it showed in his voice. "As you said yourself, there is a new balance to be built in the World, peace to be restored. We must begin quickly.

Surely you will help do that. Is that not what the Order has always hoped to do? And could you not restore the Order here, at Kerdineskar? What about those Vladur took captive—could they not help?"

But Crispan was deaf to the Emperor's pleadings. How could he explain to them all what he now felt in his heart? He realized now more than ever how different he was from all those who had passed through the Order before him. Who else had served as a Master of the Five Arts at so young an age, who else had served in the World as he had? When he had combatted the Renegade he had seen depths of depravity which no Magician should see, and he had survived; this too caused a scar on his heart. And above all, how could he explain to them that the powers first awakened in him by Bellapon had died away, that he feared that now he was a Master of the Five Arts in name only? He could find no words to express these deeply troubling feelings and feared that no one, not even Eliborg or Elthwyn, would really understand.

"No, my lord," he said, "the Order is dead. What there was in that place will never be built again, never be restored. It was not perfect, and its isolation helped lead to its downfall, but its uniqueness can never be recaptured. As for my help, you do not need me now. And you have Eliborg here to aid you."

"Me?" snorted Eliborg. "No, Crispan, I am too old for so great and grave a task."

Crispan turned in another direction. "And there is Elthwyn as well. He is ready, he can help you."

The Adept's fair face blushed. "But Master, surely—" Elthwyn's protest was cut short.

In a thin joke Crispan said, "You told me once that you wanted to be the Magician and adviser to some great lord. Here is such an assignment then, the greatest lord in the Three Realms."

"But I never meant this. You know that." Elthwyn too sounded hurt.

"I know," said Crispan soothingly. His hand reached under his cloak. "Eliborg gave me this. It was Omir's talisman as Master. Now," he said, reaching over Elthwyn's head and placing the chain around his neck, "it is yours. You are a Master of the Five Arts now, and you must advise the Emperor as best you can. And with Eliborg and the others to help you, you can preserve our learning and teach the young ones. There will still be some need for us, but our place now must be here in the World. I was not trained for this, but you can help change the ways of Magicians."

A gentle wind had come up, blowing warmly out of the south, comforting them against the chill radiating from the Great Mountains.

"But where will you go, Crispan?" Mikal's voice also betrayed his concern, and his normally bright-green eyes were clouded. "Conditions in the World are still very much unsettled. There are still bands of mercenaries and brigands roaming across the plains."

"They will not bother one lone rider. And besides"—he smiled towards Zoltan—"I have been taught to care for myself."

Thurka Re brushed back his hood and ran his fingers through his silver-flecked black hair. Having suspected Crispan's departure all along, ever since they reached the remains of the Order, he was now resigned to it. "I would have honored you above all other men. I would have made you a Prince of the Empire. Is there nothing I can do?"

Crispan's gaze became quizzical. "Yes, there is something." Thurka looked expectant, eager. "Find Portar among the army, he who rode with me across the Karsh and to Rennar. He will lead you to an inn I made special note of on my mission to the west. Take the owners of this inn and whatever family they have into your service. The man and wife would make fine stewards of your household; and I would like to see their sons trained in your service."

"Who are these people?" the Emperor asked.

"They are my family."

"Then it is done. But surely there is something more."

"No. Perhaps some day I shall return, and then—"

An embarrassing long silence followed. Belka, flicking

his marvelous white moustaches, broke it gently. "You have a fair wind to travel with, a good omen."

Crispan smiled, shaking his light-brown hair in the breeze. "Thank you, Belka." He grabbed the towering Prince's outstretched hand. He then silently clasped the hands of the others about him, reaching this way and that over his saddle. Thurka's face was etched deeply with resignation; Elthwyn let the tears roll freely now; Mikal and Zoltan removed their helmets as a sign of deference and both felt the unique pain at this leavetaking of their savior and fellow warrior; Eliborg, who understood Crispan's going perhaps better than the rest, sat stiff and upright and clasped Crispan's hand in both of his own. It was all done in silence, for words were inadequate now.

It was time. He led his horse half around. "May the Spirits protect you all."

"And you, Crispan." Thurka spoke for them all, as was his place.

The Magician tugged at the reins and led his horse north, moving at a steady walk. He was tempted to turn about and wave but he remembered the Emperor's advice when they had left the ruined Order. He let the impulse go.

"Tell me," Thurka said to his new Magician, "does he know where he is going?"

Elthwyn, his face streaked with tears, still held Omir's talisman in his hands. "I cannot say. He only knows that he must go."

The lords of the South and their allies sat there, motionless, until the rider, becoming ever more distant as he moved towards the Sentinel, finally disappeared over the northern horizon.

AVON MEANS THE BEST IN FANTASY AND SCIENCE FICTION

URSULA K. LE GUIN

The Lathe of Heaven	38299	1.50
The Dispossessed	38067	1.95

ISAAC ASIMOV

Foundation	38075	1.75
Foundation and Empire	42689	1.95
Second Foundation	38125	1.75
The Foundation Trilogy (Large Format)	26930	4.95

ROGER ZELAZNY

Doorways in the Sand	32086	1.50
Creatures of Light and Darkness	35956	1.50
Lord of Light	33985	1.75
The Doors of His Face The Lamps of His Mouth	38182	1.50
The Guns of Avalon	31112	1.50
Nine Princes in Amber	36756	1.50
Sign of the Unicorn	30973	1.50
The Hand of Oberon	33324	1.50

Include 50¢ per copy for postage and handling,
allow 4-6 weeks for delivery.

Avon Books, Mail Order Dept.
224 W. 57th St., N.Y., N.Y. 10019

SF 1-79